For Howard Morhaim

BOOK ONE

BOOK ONE

1

On the morning the world fell apart, Danny Kelso woke up next to Nora for the last time. The inside of his mouth felt like papier-mâché and he still had the stink of beer in his nostrils. Wiping the crust of sleep from his eyes, he flashed back to the argument the night before, the cruelty of her smile, the angry sex they'd had to make up for it all.

"Shit," he grunted, quietly, so as not to wake her.

Truth was, the sex didn't make up for any of it. Not in the morning. Not now that he was sober. This pattern of fighting followed by sex made him hate himself a little more every day. No matter how often Nora picked a fight, said something that crossed a line, he never got as angry with her as he did with himself.

They'd met in a dive bar in Ginsheim, a block from the Rhine River, him on a stool and her across the counter serving drinks. She liked the uniform, though so close to the army airfield at Wiesbaden there must have been American soldiers in that place every night. Still, he'd noticed the interest in her eyes right off, and the first drink had been on the house—though that, too, might have been standard operating procedure. The rest of the world had learned to hate the

U.S. military over the past seven years, but most of the shops and bars and restaurants in the towns around the base went out of their way to cater to the Americans, happy to take U.S. dollars.

Danny rose and shuffled to the bathroom, pissed and washed his hands, brushed his teeth, and then splashed water in his face. Fully awake, he went back into Nora's bedroom and stood over her, watching her sleep, feeling nothing. No, that was a lie. The hollowness he felt actually had a name—regret. Regret that he knew he wouldn't be coming back. Regret that he'd ever come home with her in the first place, those many months ago.

He glanced about at the mess of her room, the dirty clothes, the sprawl of makeup on the little pink vanity in the corner—the sort that belonged in the bedroom of an eight-year-old girl rather than a twenty-three-year-old woman. Empty lager bottles, half-full bottles of tequila and whiskey, an ashtray overflowing with cigarette butts. There were books, too. Nora might have a host of emotional problems, but she wasn't stupid. If she'd been nothing but a gorgeous airhead with a knowing smile, he never would have stayed with her so long.

Now, though, it was time to go. Last night, she'd finally crossed a line she really couldn't come back from. The words echoed in his brain.

Why don't you go kill a few more babies?

He'd wanted to hit her then. Even raised his hand—something he had never done. Danny served alongside female soldiers and had sparred with them plenty of times in training workouts, but beyond that he'd never hit a woman and didn't intend to start. He hadn't hit Nora. There were things violence could solve—you couldn't be a soldier and not believe that—but this wasn't one of them.

Nora, on the other hand, thought that there wasn't a trouble in the world that couldn't be cured with booze and sex. The time had come for him to stop going along with that philosophy.

He dressed quickly, not wanting to wake her but not overly worried that he would. Nora slept like the dead. The booze kept bad dreams away, she'd always said. More than once he had tried to tell her that it kept good ones away, too. But that was an argument he knew he was never going to win.

In jeans and a faded Five Finger Death Punch T-shirt he'd stolen out of his asshole older brother's bureau when he was sixteen, he sat on the edge of the bed and pulled on his boots. The clock was ticking and he had to head back to base. His shift started at 8 A.M.

Over the past decade the entire globe had fallen into chaos. Heat waves led to droughts which led to food shortages which led to riots. Fuel prices went through the roof, so high that only the privileged seemed to go anywhere these days. Alternative energy sources were available, but the bastards who held the reins were the carbon barons, and they kept the horses headed for the environmental cliff. Rising sea levels. Flooding cities. Calamity after calamity, all punctuated by the usual crap—civil conflicts and international incidents, people rising up to overthrow oppressive rulers, only to replace them with new ones who were just as corrupt.

In most cases, ten years ago when it was all unraveling, nobody had wanted to step in. The United Nations tsk-tsked but could never act, hamstrung by their own Security Council. China and Russia took advantage of the chaos, doing whatever they damn well pleased while the world was busy elsewhere. The only government in the world willing to step into any of those conflicts, to try to bring order to a chaotic globe, belonged to the United States of America. The U.S. Army had spent the past decade doing their damnedest to keep things under control.

And the world hated them for it.

Over the past seven years tensions had only risen. They had a whole planet to patrol, keeping the peace by force, and Sergeant Morello was gravely serious about that responsibility. Danny had to haul ass to get to the base in time. The sarge accepted no excuses.

Nora shifted under the covers, stretching into a sprawl that covered the space where Danny had been sleeping, already adjusting to his absence. Her blond hair half-veiled her face, but he could still see how pretty she was. All the roughness in her vanished while she slept. Without the nose ring and the three thin braids and the Japanese characters tattooed on her neck, she'd have looked as sweet and innocent as a little girl. When he saw her sleeping, he understood that vanity in the corner of her bedroom, a piece of who she'd once been. But you couldn't love someone for who they were while they were sleeping. You had to love them wide-awake, and he didn't. Hadn't. Couldn't.

His brother had once said he was like a shark—he couldn't stay in one place or relationship for long, had to keep swimming just to breathe. So far, the military had been the only exception to that rule, but he had hoped Nora would turn out to be another.

Danny gently pushed the hair away from her face. He thought about kissing her goodbye but did not. It wouldn't have been honest.

He stood and glanced at her one last time, then took out his key ring and slipped off the key to her apartment, placing it on top of her dresser, moving aside the ashtray so that she would be sure to notice it.

When he left, stepping out into a cool late August morning, Danny had no intention of coming back. And that was for the best, because he would never get the chance.

Once upon a time, Wiesbaden Army Airfield had housed only the 66th Military Intelligence Brigade and the 5th Signal Command— the folks who gathered intel and the people who made sure the troops in the field had it. But after the United States started consolidating European bases, it had become HQ for army ops on the continent and home to NATO's Component Command. All operations from Heidelberg and Mannheim had been folded into WAAF, and now dozens of military offices called it home. The Seventh Army had their barracks at Wiesbaden, and they were only a small percentage of the personnel stationed there.

With all that going on, nobody had seemed to notice the army digging in the dirt, hollowing out a massive space underneath the western edge of the base. Of course they *had* noticed, but anyone authorized to get close enough to wonder what was being done there had also received strict orders never to wonder aloud.

They'd built a bunker more secure than the NORAD facility at Cheyenne Mountain, buried underneath two thousand feet of rock. Danny didn't know much about engineering, but he assumed it had been a hell of a task to build something that safe and that deep, especially so close to the Rhine. There had to have been better spots, but somebody obviously figured it made sense to put the Hump at the same facility as Signal Command, with their constant stream of satellite intel. All the fuck-you-up-from-a-distance parts of the U.S. military in Europe living in the same house—one big happy family.

The army called the bunker Humphreys Deep Station One, after Major General A. A. Humphreys, who'd made his bones as a divisional commander of the V Corps at Antietam. What that had to do with Europe, Danny had no idea. Someone who oversaw the naming of things obviously had a soft spot for the Civil War. But soldiers always decided on the real name of the place they lived, and the soldiers stationed in that installation beneath Wiesbaden Army Airfield—the only enlisted men and women with clearance to even speak of its existence—just called it the Hump.

Danny reached the main gate at 0747 hours, later than he'd wanted but not the latest he'd ever been. He showed his ID and managed to get past the guards without any of them giving him a hard time about his car, a ten-year-old Audi e-tron. With all the trouble the United States and the European Union had gone to in order to keep oil flowing, the typical soldier wouldn't have been caught dead in an electric car. Depending on who was at the gate, the guards sometimes challenged him on it, thinking the e-tron was some kind of mute protest of U.S. policy, when the truth was that the crappy little tin can was all he had left of his father, who had bought the thing used when he'd come to live in Germany to be close to Danny. Cancer had taken him just eight months later, a whole twenty-seven days elapsing between diagnosis and death.

He drove onto base, the car sounding like a hair dryer about to burn out, and made his way to the side lot reserved for the Hump. No marking identified it as such, of course. The one metal sign simply read RESTRICTED PARKING; if you didn't have clearance to park there, you wouldn't risk it.

A glance at the dash clock told him it was 0751 hours. On time. Still, he hurried, climbing out and pocketing his keys, slamming the door and hustling along the paved pathway. Several of the oldest buildings had an austere beauty, but the barracks and most of the modern parts of Wiesbaden Army Airfield were utilitarian at best. The giant lump of a building that sat atop Humphreys Deep Station One was the crowning glory of boring architecture. It made federal penitentiaries look like castles constructed of whimsy. The occupants of the offices in the aboveground section of the building were also as boring as possible, paper pushers and budget specialists, people nobody wanted to blow up.

Danny showed his ID again at the door, walked a winding corridor and then showed it twice more—passing through checkpoints requiring rising levels of clearance—until he reached the double doors at the center of the building's sub-basement. There were no guards visible here. Defense systems this close to the Hump were automated and required both palm and retinal scans. The palm scan pricked his flesh, taking a microscopic blood sample, examined his DNA in three or four seconds.

The lock disengaged with several loud thunks and the doors swung inward. He darted inside and the heavy alloy doors moved back into place with a hydraulic hiss, locks clanking. Danny paused a second and took a breath. He wasn't claustrophobic, but it always took him a moment to shake the trapped feeling he got when those doors closed. From this point forward there was no exit and no windows. The place might as well be a tomb, and he was headed for his coffin.

He strode down the short corridor and hit the button for the elevator. The clock on the wall showed 0757 hours. He'd be logged as on time, but barely. Sergeant Morello wouldn't be happy.

A loud beep came from behind him and he turned as the locks began to clatter again, and the doors hissed open to reveal a woman in a wheelchair.

"Kelso, you're late," she said, rolling her chair into the elevator foyer just before the doors reset.

"Good morning to you, too, Corporal Wade," he said.

"Time for breakfast in sunny Damascus," she replied with a scowl.

Danny laughed. "Christ's sake, Kate. Who pissed in your corn-flakes?"

Arching an eyebrow, she allowed herself half a smile. "I just didn't want to get out of bed."

"Really?" Danny said. "Queen of the Tin Men had a little company last night?"

"Yummy company," she said, her gaze going distant. "Oh, those tattoos."

"I didn't know you were into tats."

She shrugged. "Eight hours a day in full-metal-jacket mode, I just want some human contact."

"And you never called me," Danny said. "Corporal, I'm hurt."

A strange look passed over her face and she glanced up at him. "Why, PFC Kelso, you never called me, either."

Something fluttered in his chest. He looked at her, knowing the moment was going on too long and in a blink it would be awkward. With those near-purple eyes and milk chocolate skin, the high cheek-bones and full lips, Kate Wade couldn't be described as anything but beautiful. Even in her uniform and without makeup, she looked lovely. They joked with each other all the time, flirted and played, but they were in the same unit and neither one thought it was a good idea to go further. They'd only spoken of it once, but Danny remembered it clearly. Kate had been married at the time—her ex was a complete prick—and of course Danny had Nora. As of this morning, neither of those things was true, but Kate didn't know that.

"You feeling all right?" she asked.

He smiled and lowered his eyes. "Just thinking about getting a tat-too."

"You wouldn't know what to do with me if you had me," she said. "Besides, I know your type. Spend enough time in port and you can't wait to sail away."

Danny couldn't argue. The memory of leaving a sleeping Nora be-hind was too fresh.

The elevator dinged and opened. Danny stepped in first, knowing

Kate would murder him if he showed her any deference. She wheeled in after him and spun around, so good with the chair that she made it look as if she was in it by choice, a punk street kid on a skateboard or some California girl Rollerblading by the beach. It wasn't a choice, of course, and it wasn't fun, but it was her transport and she had long since mastered it, as she mastered nearly everything.

She had only been in the U.S. Army Remote Infantry Corps for eighteen months, but she'd been regular army before the loss of her legs. Danny had no doubt that Kate would rise quickly through the ranks. One day, she really would be queen of the Tin Men.

"God, I need coffee," she said, as they took the long, swift drop into the depths of the Hump, where the rest of their shift—eighteen hundred men and women—would already be getting prepped.

Danny's stomach rumbled. They were already officially on duty, but they had thirty minutes before they had to be in place—enough time for coffee and a good breakfast, if he ate quickly. The tubes kept them hydrated and filled with nutrients, even pumped serious proteins halfway through the shift, but that was no substitute for a decent meal. At the end of every shift, he was starving.

On an ordinary day, they'd be underground for nine hours or more.

But nothing about today would be ordinary.

Danny hustled down a ramp, regretting the omelet he'd eaten. He'd be tasting the peppers and onions all day. A piece of melon or an orange would have cured the problem but he had run out of time. Lesson learned.

Kate had gone ahead, knowing it might take a few extra minutes before someone would be free to help her into her canister, but he didn't count on her making excuses for him. Morello wouldn't listen even if she did.

At the bottom of the ramp he flashed his ID at the south elevator doors, which slid open to admit him. Humphreys Deep Station One had six subterranean levels that Danny knew about, and it wouldn't have surprised him to learn there were more. Level One consisted of nothing but security gates, an impressive lobby, and conference rooms where the command staff received visitors who didn't have clearance to descend any farther. The staging areas for the Tin Men took up three levels, with research, tech support, staff services, and the mess hall on the bottom two. The whole base was cylindrical, with corridors radiating out from the central Command Core like spokes on a wheel. Danny's destination was at the end of one of those spokes.

He rode the elevator up to Level Three and hurried around the Command Core, crossing to the hallway that would take him to Staging Area 12, which housed the Sixth Battalion of the 1st Remote Infantry Division. Danny's platoon consisted of thirty-six men and women under the command of Lieutenant Khoa Trang, with Sergeant Morello as his second in command. Staging Area 12 looked the same as all the rest, a featureless warehouse of silver canisters that the army liked to call Remote Combat Stations but which appeared to be nothing more than oversized metal coffins. When he'd been in training, Danny had seen at least half a dozen men and women with no history of claustrophobia completely lose their shit after ten minutes inside one, but it had never bothered him. As far as Danny was concerned, the metal coffins were cocoons, and inserting himself into one of them allowed him to emerge as something else—something better—somewhere far away.

Soldiers streamed past him. Several of those coming off the night shift hooted about his lateness and hurled good-natured insults. Outside of his own platoon, there were only a handful of people in the battalion he knew well. When they came out of the canisters, nobody liked to hang around. Unlike traditional soldiers, they weren't forced to live on the base and most preferred to take apartments in the surrounding towns. They needed air and space and time away from guns.

Within platoons, it was different. On duty, they were in one another's heads for eight hours at a time. It was impossible not to get to know the men and women who were covering your ass every day. Of course, some he knew better than others. His platoon had added half a dozen newbies in the past two months; there were a few he hadn't even had a conversation with yet.

His boots thumped the metal steps as he descended from the steel catwalk to the floor of the vast staging area.

"Private Kelso!" a voice rang out. "What the hell are you doing?"

Sergeant Morello stood, arms crossed, in front of a block of canisters. The Remote Combat Stations were arranged in blocks of thirty-six—six by six—and each staging area had three such blocks, one per shift. While only a third of the 1st Remote Infantry Division were normally active during any shift, there were enough canisters for all of the soldiers in the division to be put into the field simultaneously, if a crisis arose. "Sorry, Sarge," Danny said as he ran up, ignoring the amused looks he received from some of the others in his platoon who were already situated inside their metal coffins, sitting up like corpses come back to life and grinning at his plight.

"Every minute you waste is a minute the Cupcakes stay on duty," Sergeant Morello said.

The Cupcakes—Sergeant Morello's nickname for Platoon C. The Babydolls were Platoon B. Lieutenant Trang and Sergeant Morello commanded Platoon A, which the others just called the Assholes. The sergeant wore the badge with pride.

"They're not going to thank you for that, Private," Sergeant Morello went on.

"I know, Sarge."

Morello glared at him, dark eyes set into olive skin, long nose above thick mustache, all combining to give him a very intimidating air, despite his height. Sergeant Morello stood five feet and four inches tall, but even out here, in the flesh-and-blood world, Morello could have broken him into tiny little pieces if he felt like it.

"He knows, he says," Sergeant Morello sniffed, rolling his eyes. Then: "Move your ass, Private Kelso!"

Danny hustled, navigating the narrow spaces between canisters. Several of them were closed already and through the clear polymer lids he could see the faces of his platoon-mates. Hartschorn wore a relaxed expression despite the snugness of the cranial cap and eye-piece that left only his nose and mouth exposed. The guy looked like he was sleeping, even though none of them had been put under yet—thanks to Danny's tardiness. Most of the platoon was having the headgear fitted onto them, sitting up in the canisters, the clear lids standing straight up from the base. Alaina Torres had styled her hair, as always, despite the fact that nobody would be looking at her real self all day. Most of the female soldiers in the USARIC wore their hair in tight ponytails on duty or cut it short. Making it pretty seemed il-logical to Danny, but it wasn't hurting anybody, so even Sergeant Mo-rello never said a word to Torres about it. If you were going to spend eight hours in a metal coffin, you had to be allowed a few indulgences.

As he approached his row, he saw Mavrides and Hawkins playing cards on top of a canister, muttering and stealing glances at Naomi Birnbaum, and he had to bite his tongue. Though she was twenty-four, the tiny Birnbaum would always look young, but with her big brown eyes and long lashes, she would always look beautiful, too. Quiet most of the time, she became wildly animated when talking about music, either performers she loved or the dozen or so instru-ments she herself played.

The thuggish Hawkins had been hitting on Birnbaum since the day he joined the unit, a grinning goon who thought his skills as a soldier made him irresistible. He was a monster in the field, a soldier anyone would want at his side when a mission turned ugly. But in friendly territory, Hawkins was a grade-A cock with wandering hands, a big bastard whose only social skill was intimidation.

Though it seemed backward, Danny had a feeling Birnbaum could destroy Hawkins in a fight. He'd seen her sparring once and had been shocked by her hand-to-hand skills. If Hawkins put a hand on her butt or accidentally brushed against her breasts one more time, Danny figured Naomi might tear him apart.

Then there was the kid talking to Hawkins, the nineteen-year-old computer geek, Zack Mavrides. When Mavrides had joined the pla-toon a few months back, Danny had tried to set an example for him, but the kid had turned out to be a punk. Hawkins had taken

Mavrides under his wing, helping him train, putting himself up as an example of great soldiering, and the kid was young enough to admire Hawkins's gift for efficient violence. He'd learned all he knew about killing from video games, and Hawkins encouraged him to live out his darkest dreams if the right situation arose.

Danny didn't like the way either one of them was looking at Birnbaum right now. As he strode toward his own canister, he watched them, tracking the salacious gaze in the eyes of both men. Danny was torn between telling them off himself or just giving Birnbaum a heads-up so she could take care of them.

"Come on, Kelso!" Sergeant Morello shouted across Staging Area 12. "Hell's not getting any colder!"

The entire unit—those not already lying down—turned his way. Hawkins gave Mavrides a tap on the arm and they started climbing into their canisters. Birnbaum smiled at him and shook her head, hoisting herself up and then vanishing inside the metal cylinder in an instant, the lid starting to descend before she could possibly have strapped herself in. She had it down to a science, even put on her own gear.

A head popped up a few feet away. Private Jim Corcoran needed a shave, but he liked a little stubble to cover up the ugly scar that cut right through his pale, freckled jawline.

"I got Kate squared away," Corcoran said.

Danny came to stand between his canister and Kate's. He glanced inside and saw that she already had her headgear on, ready for deployment. It made him wish he had hurried. Their flirting earlier had gotten him thinking, and all through breakfast he had been toying with the idea of asking her out for a real dinner, just the two of them. She'd scoff, he knew, at the concept of a date. Call it *high school* or something. But he wondered if she might secretly like the idea.

"Thanks for that," Danny said, turning to Corcoran. "Sorry for the holdup."

"Who's going to bitch?" Corcoran said. "The Cupcakes? Screw those guys."

Laughing, Danny climbed into his canister as a tech came running over to help him into his rig. Early twenties, black, lovely in the awkward, never-going-to-realize-I'm-beautiful sort of way that some women had. Aimee Something, her name was, and he thanked her as she held the rig steady while he slid his arms into it. She seemed confident in her work, which would take her far. Techs didn't have to worry about bullets on the way up the ladder.

"Don't worry about Sergeant Morello," Aimee Something said quietly. "You're late, but at least you're here."

Danny lifted the headgear off its hook on the underside of the canister's lid and slipped it on, pressing the green pads into place at his temples and jaws. His pulse thumped in his skull.

"Somebody didn't show up for duty?" he asked.

Aimee Something smiled conspiratorially and glanced around. "North," she said. "He showed up, but with a hell of a hangover. Puked inside his canister and Sergeant Morello nearly made him lie in it for the entire shift. But Morello figured he'd be a liability and told him to hit the infirmary."

Danny frowned. "What happens to his bot?"

"Corresponding soldier on the night shift'll run it over to the embassy before the transition. Probably already done it."

"North. What a dumbass. He'll be written up, for sure," Danny said as he lay down and slid his hands into the silver thin-skin gloves that were linked to the canister's systems.

"No doubt," Aimee Something agreed. "I'm just glad I don't have to clean it up."

He laughed as she examined the readings on the small external touchscreen that allowed techs to view his vitals from the floor. The entire platoon would be monitored from the workstations as well, of course—both by tech supervisors and by auto health programs—but Aimee wasn't about to lock him in without making sure he was properly secured into his rig and his vitals were steady.

"Good to go," she said, and patted the side of the canister.

Danny gave her a thumbs-up and snapped the visor plate of his headgear into place.

"Close lid," he said.

Closing. The electronic reply came from inside his head rather than through his ears, thanks to the comm-pads attached to his temples: a bland, computerized male voice the Tin Men called Uncle, short for Uncle Sam. *Now joining Platoon A of Sixth Battalion, 1st Remote Infantry Division. Be safe, PFC Kelso. Eyes and ears open, mouth closed.*

"Music," Danny said. "The Killers."

He'd been thinking of his father a lot this morning. The Killers had been the old man's favorite band way back in the day, when Ron Kelso was a single father raising two rough boys. Sometimes Danny liked to listen to them while on duty; it felt like his father might be right behind him, guarding his flank.

Caution, PFC Kelso. Music is not prohibited, but R.I. Division studies have shown it to be a potential distraction.

Danny had never seen any harm in having some musical accompaniment. When they were deployed, the music stayed at low volume in the background and went silent anytime his comms unit activated—either with incoming voices or when he himself spoke. The technology boggled his mind so completely that he had stopped asking questions after the first few months with the Remote Infantry Corps. He'd made the mistake of showing some curiosity to an eager tech, who had gone off on a five-minute tangent about how the synthetic ganglia in the robots allowed for one-to-one mapping with their pilots' brains, cutting the lag between thought and action down to the point where the reaction time of the Tin Men was virtually indistinguishable from that of flesh-and-blood people, despite the satellite transmission involved.

Thinking about it hurt his head, so Danny just focused on the mission and let the techs do their jobs.

"Just play it," he said.

With only a moment's delay, the music started up. At the opening chord of "When You Were Young," a needle slid into his thigh. Danny winced but did not cry out. The needle was attached to a tube that fed him fluids and nutrients while he was locked down. Once the lid was closed, he had no choice but to surrender himself. The shift change between Platoon C and Platoon A would be virtually seamless, a rolling deployment transition, soldiers being withdrawn twelve at a time while twelve more were inserted. In the field, the other twenty-four would cover those in the midst of transition; the whole process took no more than eight seconds.

A low, tinny alarm buzzed. Danny breathed deeply of the richly oxygenated air in the canister and felt himself floating, drifting into something not unlike sleep. It felt as if he were sinking into a sea of warm, dark water, an ocean of shadow . . .

Inhaling sharply, Danny opened his eyes to the bright, baking sunlight of the streets of Damascus. He blinked twice, heard the low clicks that went along with blinking, and a silent computer readout sprang to vivid life across his vision. Temperature, time, precise GPS locations for himself and every member of his unit, readout of available weapons and ammunition, and more.

"Those assholes," Kate snapped.

Danny heard her voice in his head, just as he'd heard Uncle's. He glanced around and spotted her a few feet away, standing in the jagged shadow thrown by the ruins of the Khan As'ad Pasha. Even without the markings on her dusty frame, he would have recognized the way she carried herself. He imagined that back when her flesh-and-blood legs had still been in working order, she'd moved in much the same way as she did now, in the robot body assigned to her by the 1st Remote Infantry Division.

Like the rest of them, her frame had an antique sort of bone-white hue that blended well in most old Damascus neighborhoods and could color-shift to black once the sun went down. But Kate and the soldiers from the other two platoons who shared this frame with her had modified it with a pair of devil horns painted on the sides of the metal skull and a small trident pitchfork on the left cheek. Danny's own frame had the number thirteen painted on the forehead, flaunting superstition with his personal number. The soldiers on the other two shifts who shared his frame had appreciated his desire to taunt Lady Luck.

"Which assholes are we talking about exactly?" he asked.

"Cupcakes," Kate said, pointing at his chest. "Look what they did."

Danny glanced down and saw the target on his chest, painted in perfectly concentric circles of red, white, and blue.

"That's not funny," Kate said.

He smiled, knowing that she would recognize the small variation in the expression on his robotic face.

"Well," Danny said slowly, "it's kind of funny."

Before she could reply, Sergeant Morello started barking orders and the platoon gathered in two rows, standing at attention. Lieutenant Trang stood behind Morello. Neither man had any marking on his frame that indicated rank, but anyone watching would have picked up the command structure easily enough. Trang had an infinity symbol on his chest, while Morello's frame was marked only with black stripes under the eyes, the sort football players painted on to cut the sun's glare.

"Platoon C reported zero hostile activity during the past eight hours," the sergeant said. "That might make you lazy assholes feel all cozy and safe, but it ought to make you paranoid as hell. No news is good news, that's what they say, right? I say bullshit. No news means somebody's trying hard to come up with a new way to kill you today. So I want you all extra sharp. You see anything that looks wrong or just feels wrong, you sound off. Got me?"

"Yes, Sergeant!" Platoon A chorused.

He didn't ask them to repeat it.

"Just don't be stupid," Morello said. "Move out!"

Platoon A began to spread out along the broad street in front of the wreckage of what had once been among the most beautiful buildings in the world. The domes of the Khan As'ad Pasha had drawn tourists from around the globe. The shadowed beauty of its interior, the gentle interdependence of its architecture . . . like almost everything else the Syrian people held dear, it had been obliterated in a civil war. Danny had heard the expression "never shit where you eat," and thought it a crude but effective wisdom. The Syrians might hate America now, but they'd been their own worst enemies.

The Tin Men fanned out into the streets and souqs, weapons held at the ready with hydraulic muscles that would never tire. Danny knew that none of them would take Sergeant Morello's warning to heart. Some jihadist prick could nuke Damascus, incinerate their robot frames, and the worst the Tin Men would suffer was psychological trauma. Compared to the old way of soldiering, it was a sweet gig. They could wage war without any casualties on the American side.

They had to stay alert in order to do their jobs properly, to keep the peace and maintain order in a city where they were considered intruders, devils second only to Shaitan. They needed to stay frosty—a single substantial screwup might cause an international incident, and the U.S. Army's remote infantry was controversial enough already— but at the end of the shift, all of them were going to wake up safe and sound in their own bodies, back at the Hump.

Danny hadn't been lying. He did think the target on his chest was a little bit funny. But he hadn't told the entire truth, either. When he'd glanced down and seen that target, he'd shivered—and not only his flesh-and-blood body, back in Germany. His whole robot frame had shuddered just a little.

Snipers and martyrs were always taking shots at the Tin Men, but he had never felt like a target until today.

2

Corporal Kate Wade didn't mind being deployed in Damascus. The anti-American atmosphere could be toxic, but there were a lot of places in the world where that was true. And Damascus was a damn sight better than the edges of the nuclear wasteland left behind after the meltdown of the Narora reactor in northeastern India. So long, Nepal. Nice knowing you.

Even better, she thought, *you could be in Bangladesh.* Her cousin Alonso had been deployed there ever since the food riots a couple of years back. Last time she'd spoken to him he'd told her serving there had gotten worse, that as ugly as it had been to watch people kill one another over food, watching them starve was worse.

Then there was Korea.

Tin Men had been deployed in a dozen locations around the globe where border disputes or religious hatreds had erupted into bloody warfare with no end in sight. In each case, the USARIC had shut down the conflict, forcing both sides into détente. Except in Korea, where the North Koreans and South Koreans continued to try to destroy one another while also expending huge portions of their arsenals attempting to expel the American interlopers.

But the U.S. Army could afford to be patient. They were losing hardware, not humans. As long as they were measuring the cost of keeping the world safe in dollars instead of in lives, the American people wouldn't bitch too loudly. Bringing order to the globe had been just about the only thing that kept the U.S. economy from suffering the same ugliness as the rest of the world. Some of the strands of the web of interdependence that held the global economy together had frayed, a few had broken. Old trade alliances were tenuous, new ones untested. Many nations had turned inward, but the time had long passed when they could rely solely upon themselves for survival.

America, though ... America had robots. Built by American hands. Programmed by American minds. Monitored by American eyes. That meant the United States had enemies that hated her more than ever, and allies who loved—or at least needed—her more as well. The whole thing made Kate uneasy as hell, but she was a good soldier. She followed orders. And at night when she closed her eyes she thanked whatever gods hadn't turned their backs on humanity that the next morning would bring just another boring day running a robot around Damascus.

Not many of the soldiers she knew thought of their country as especially noble or heroic. The Tin Men of Platoon A were not under any illusions about the U.S. government's motives. If they imposed peace on certain regions by force or intimidation, it was to make the world safer and the economy more stable for American interests, not out of any more honorable purpose. But over the years since the en masse deployment of the Tin Men, fewer civilians—fewer children— had been killed by collateral damage or violent oppression, and Kate considered that a win.

Most days, the rest of the world didn't see it that way. Early iterations of Remote Infantry units had been drawn into conflicts with insurgents whose entire purpose had been to goad the prototype Tin Men into killing civilians, and they'd succeeded. At least a dozen small conflicts had broken out for no reason save that the aggressor knew the United States would send Tin Men to intervene and force peace before their enemies could muster a significant retaliation. Somalia's invasion into Kenya had been especially bloody, and now that the USARIC had pulled out of western Africa it seemed likely the Somali dictator would do it all over again, eroding Kenyan resistance to Somali influence one attack at a time.

In truth, though, the growing worldwide resistance to American intervention had not sprung from concerns about casualties or the idea that the Tin Men were being used to shield bad behavior by dictators. The Tin Men had saved countless lives, but the backlash against them had always been centered on the idea of control. The right of self-determination. The idea that national sovereignty and individual voice no longer mattered infected the masses, a terrible poison that stirred first anti-Western sentiment and then outright anarchism. Terrorism and religious jihad had become secondary concerns. They were and always had been fringe elements, capable of doing great damage but with public sentiment against them.

The anarchists were different. Extremists controlled the core anarchist groups, but millions of people tacitly approved of their efforts to disrupt or destroy the robots as a message to the United States that their interference was unwelcome. Kate wished the whole world could see the Tin Men the way she did. They were there to protect and serve on a global scale, often by the invitation of one government or another. Many people did see them that way, she knew, but far too many did not.

Now she scanned the platoon, noting the identifying markings most of the robots had on their shells. She spotted one with a large-breasted blond girl riding a rocket—a reproduction of something that had been painted on the side of a WWII bomber—and strode over.

"Travaglini, you're with me," she said.

The robot dashed off a quick salute. "Yes, ma'am."

At thirty-seven, Ernie Travaglini was by far the oldest member of the platoon, a fourth-generation soldier who had rejoined the military specifically to sign up for the USARIC. Like Kate, he was a corporal, but he had no interest in advancement—only service.

"Can you believe North?" Travaglini said. "Lieutenant's going to fry his ass when this shift is over."

"I knew he was an idiot," Kate said. "I just didn't know how big an idiot. I hope Morello has them leave the puke in his canister for tomorrow."

Kate had always thought Thomas North a clown, but this latest display had pissed her off. Others in the platoon had come on duty hungover, but she'd never seen anyone miss a shift because of it. North had been ordered to the infirmary like some little kid being sent to the principal's office. He ought to have been humiliated, especially with the way Sergeant Morello had dismissed him. Instead, Kate had caught a glimpse of his face as he turned away and seen the smirk forming there. The asshole thought it was funny.

North would pay for his amusement, though. The members of Platoon A would be hesitant to partner up with him on patrol. Nobody would want someone so cavalier about his duties to be watching their back.

"Screw him," Kate said. "We've got work to do."

Around them the platoon began to break off into their assigned pairs and head out, each team with a section of the city to patrol. With the ground speed of the Tin Men, any one of them who came under fire would have to find cover for only a minute or two before they had backup. Kate caught sight of Kelso and Torres heading into an alley to the southwest and Kelso seemed to take notice of her as well. He gave a small nod, half-turned toward her, and she had another glimpse of the target that had been painted on his torso. It gave her the creeps.

"Corporal Wade," Sergeant Morello's voice crackled in her ear. "A moment, please."

Kate frowned as she scanned the street and found him still standing with Lieutenant Trang. Stupid as hell, the two of them together like that. If there were Bot Killers or local snipers around, they could both be taken out in seconds.

"Hang on," she told Travaglini. "Sarge is calling."

Trav nodded and she crossed the square, taking one last look at the alley where Kelso had vanished a moment before. He'd be headed for Al-Buzuriyah Souq, the long market street that would be the heart of his patrol sector today. Kelso was one of the good guys, smarter and kinder than he seemed to believe, but he was hard on himself. Kate was pretty sure the sexual tension she felt between them was not her imagination but for some reason she found it hard to let it go any further. He would flirt and laugh, and he was easy on the eyes, but if the back-and-forth went on too long he would close down like a turtle drawing into its shell—like he didn't believe he deserved the pleasure.

She could have gone to bed with him, but sometimes his mask would slip and she'd catch a hint of pain beneath, confusion and loneliness, and she knew to keep away, that if she ever let things get physical with him it would lead to something more. People in pain were magnetic to each other, and in her experience that never ended well. So she never took Kelso home. Yet somehow, when they were piloting tin cans way out here in Damascus, it was harder to ignore what she had begun to feel. Why was that?

I'm more alive when I'm on duty than when I'm off.

Her therapist would have a field day. All the work they'd done to get her to come to terms with the loss of her legs and she still felt more whole, more like a person, a woman, remotely piloting a robot body while lying in a tube thousands of miles away.

As she approached Morello and Trang she pushed those thoughts off, vowing not to think about Danny Kelso for the rest of the shift.

"What's up, Sarge?" she asked, then nodded to Trang. "Lieutenant."

On commlinks, they could use private channels to talk to one another or open communications to the entire platoon, no matter how far they scattered on patrol, but up close they mostly used external speakers, just as they would while addressing locals.

"You see any faces?" Sergeant Morello asked.

Kate arched a robotic brow, cocked her head to study the lieutenant a moment, and then turned around to scan the square. Only half a dozen members of the platoon were still in view. But no locals.

"None."

"That's what I'm saying," Morello replied.

"Don't jump to conclusions, Sergeant," Trang warned.

"I'm not jumping, sir. I'm making an observation." Sergeant Morello grunted quietly, then focused on Kate again. "Just stay alert, Corporal Wade. We've seen it quiet before, but not like this. I don't like it."

"Yes, sir," Kate replied.

"It's a war, Sergeant," Trang said. "If the insurgents are going to take a run at us today, so be it. We've got techs in the platoon to make repairs, and if anyone's damaged too much for that, we'll gather the parts and bring them in to base."

The faces of robots did not provide a full range of human expression but if one spent enough time around them they became easy enough to read, and Kate could see that Sergeant Morello was barely able to hold his tongue. He didn't like Trang lecturing him about things that even the greenest private knew. The lieutenant should have known better; if something was getting under Morello's skin, it wasn't just the fear of an ambush. When he worried, that meant there was something to be worried about.

Kate had been ambushed dozens of times and there had always been people around. Sometimes they fled just before the shitstorm, giving her some warning, and sometimes they took collateral damage. But Morello was right; she'd never seen Damascus this quiet. Birnbaum and Hartschorn were both techs—technicians who could repair Tin Men in the field—so she wasn't worried about her own safety; she worried about the flesh-and-blood humans around her.

"I'll keep my eyes open," Kate said.

"Maintain an open channel," Sergeant Morello replied.

She snapped off a salute and turned to rejoin Travaglini, who awaited her at the northeast corner of the street. She told him only that the sarge was spooked by the quiet, not that she herself was equally unnerved.

"Aren't we headed toward Damneh Square?" Travaglini asked.

Kate nodded. "Eventually. But we're gonna take the scenic route, up by the Umayyad Mosque first. Don't ask."

Travaglini shrugged. "Suit yourself."

As they headed off into the labyrinth of this strange city, with its collision of the ancient and the modern, she kept looking through windows and at doorways. From time to time she would spot figures moving behind screens or in the cracks between shutters, but nobody came outside. Nobody watched them as they passed, almost as if they were invisible . . . or as if there was something in the streets of Damascus today that they did not want to see. Something more upsetting than American robots patrolling their city.

"Private channel, PFC Daniel Kelso," Kate said.

A click signified that her commlink had been switched over to one-on-one. Even so, she knew her words would not be entirely private. The rest of the platoon wouldn't hear, but all communications were monitored by Uncle. There would be a recording of whatever she said, so she had to watch her choice of words.

"Danny, you read me?"

A tiny burst of static. Weird, electrical buzzing that made her frown. Normally the lines were perfectly clear but today there seemed to be some kind of interference. The thought of it rattled her spine.

"I'm here. What's on your mind?" Kelso replied.

"You seeing any locals out your way? Morello's got me paranoid."

"About what? Hell, I'm glad they painted a target on my chest. I could use a couple of beers and a few hours in some gamers' realm where I don't have to blow anybody's head off."

Kate chuckled. Apparently Kelso was counting on anyone monitoring Uncle's audio back at the Hump to know he was joking. But as she saw it, military brass had a tree stump's sense of humor.

"Seriously," she persisted. "Are you seeing any activity where you are?"

"Am I seeing people on the street? Yes," Kelso said. "I'm in the souq. Obviously I'm seeing people. Am I seeing a *lot* of people? Definitely not. Most of the shops are open but there are no street vendors and only a handful of cars have passed us. A holiday?"

"It's not a holiday," Kate replied, thinking hard and not liking what she was thinking.

Wall-unit air conditioners whirred on the façades of buildings. The smells of cooking wafted out through windows, local spices and minced beef. But where were the taxicabs and the children on their bicycles? Where was the music that sometimes played inside the grubby apartments and shops she and Travaglini were passing even now? The walls were crumbling and marked with graffiti, but Damascus had never felt to her like a ghost town until today.

"You're getting me spooked," Kelso said, his voice crackling in her ear, picking up some kind of interference.

"Listen," she said, "you still tight with the Watermelon Man?"

"On my way there now," Kelso replied.

"All right. Report back to me on this channel."

"Yes, Corporal," he said, all business now.

Kate turned to Travaglini, suddenly all too aware of the gaudy painting on his chassis. "Eyes and ears, Trav."

The bot nodded and they continued their patrol, checking down alleys and watching rooftops and open windows. Patrol was a walk-through, nothing more, just a way for the Tin Men to be a visible presence in the city, to let insurgents know that if they started any shit, the U.S. Army would shut it down fast.

It came as no surprise to Kate that the past seven years had pissed off almost the entire world. There were Remote Infantry units all over now—in Korea and Pakistan and Iran and Venezuela and the Ukraine and a dozen other spots. The Tin Men were mostly utilized for meddling in the business of other nations. They ended civil wars, oversaw fair elections, removed dictators, and by their mere presence they ended regional conflicts. Nobody seemed to notice that Remote Infantry units had not invaded Russia or claimed the Middle Eastern oil fields for the United States or toppled any governments that weren't involved in actively torturing or murdering their citizens. Oppression was being suffocated and the result was a more just and peaceful world, achieved through force and intimidation.

And more people hated the United States and its citizens than ever. Nobody wanted to be forced to behave with a gun to their head.

Little kids in Damascus came in two categories: the ones who wanted to play with them and the ones who would spit and throw rocks as they went by. That was why she loved Kelso's Watermelon

Man. There were friendlies among the local population, people who appreciated the benefits that came from American interference and weren't worried about the audacity of it. She knew a handful of people in Damascus she could trust—*probably* trust, because nothing was for sure—but if anyone would tell them what was going on, it was the Watermelon Man. He had always given Kelso a heads-up if there were insurgents or terrorists or Bot Killers—mercenaries funded by a conglomerate of foreign interests who hunted Remote Infantry units for cash—in the area. Kelso had saved the Watermelon Man's daughter's life, once upon a time, and the man had been indebted to him ever since. He believed in the Americans' mission—that all this imposing of order would lead to peace and justice.

Truth was, the Watermelon Man believed in it more than Kate did.

3

Alexa Day sat in the plush backseat of a gray Mercedes, its tinted windows and struggling air-conditioning shielding her from the worst of the day's heat. Flanked by a pair of formidable security officers, she felt small and alone. When she'd spoken to her friends about this trip they had alternated between being terrified for her and thinking she was walking into some kind of fairy tale. Alexa had rolled her eyes but deep down she had wondered if they might all be a little bit right, if visiting her father in Syria might be dangerous and romantic in equal measure. He was the U.S. ambassador after all, and that had a certain regal air, even if it didn't make her a princess.

Even if she didn't like him very much.

Stop, she told herself. *You promised Mom you'd give him a chance. Give* this *a chance. Keep your promise.* But that was easier said than done. Since the day he had moved out of the family home six years before, Alexa had seen her father only rarely and never for long. His work kept him away much of the time—she knew that—but she had never felt as if he made much of an effort. Now he wanted to make amends by bringing her halfway around the world. He couldn't come to her so she had been persuaded to go to him.

Keep your promise, she thought again.

When her plane had been met by a pair of military vehicles mounted with guns and a sleek Mercedes with blacked-out windows, she'd had a moment of fear followed quickly by bliss. A handful of U.S. Marines—some of them distractingly good-looking and only a couple of years older than her seventeen—were going to be her escorts. It had saddened her when she quickly realized that she wouldn't be traveling in one of the Humvees but would instead ride in the Mercedes with the two brutish guys who were obviously embassy security. Still, she had gazed expectantly at the car. Despite her resentment, she had found herself excited to see her father. The last time had been the day after Thanksgiving—almost a year ago.

Her anticipation had evaporated the moment one of the security men opened the back door of the sedan and revealed that it was empty. Her father had sent these men to fetch her but had not bothered to come himself.

"Mr. Nissim, tell me again why my dad couldn't meet me," she said now, staring at the slim, darkly handsome man behind the wheel of the Mercedes.

Nissim glanced back at her. Like many Middle Eastern men she'd met, he had beautiful eyes with thick lashes that made her jealous. Alexa had watched a lot of Bollywood movies and if Bassel Nissim's embassy job didn't pan out, she thought he had the looks to be a film star.

"Please, call me Baz," he said. "Your father truly regrets being unable to greet you in person, Miss Day. The delay in your flight caused a time conflict with a meeting he had scheduled with the mayor of Damascus. Not to worry, though, he should be no more than an hour or two and I can help you get settled into your room. I think you'll enjoy your stay."

"No worries," she said. "He's got other priorities. Story of my life."

Nissim didn't seem to know how to reply to that, and Alexa was glad to let it drop. As the Mercedes rolled through Damascus with its Marine escort she caught glimpses of buildings and parked cars, but she was surprised that she didn't see more people.

"Is it prayer time or something?" she asked.

"No. Just quiet in the city today," Nissim replied.

"Hunh. Maybe Damascus partied too hard last night."

Nissim laughed softly. "I doubt that."

Alexa focused on him. Maybe twenty-five, no wedding ring, obviously intelligent. She leaned forward and peered out through the windshield, then turned to get a better look out the left side of the car.

"Don't worry," Nissim said. "There's nothing to be afraid of here."

"I'm not afraid," she lied.

In truth, she had been terrified ever since the moment she had first agreed to this visit. Her parents' divorce settlement gave her father four full weeks per year with her but he hadn't made much effort to take advantage of that time. Every year, he extended a perfunctory invitation to have her join him—first in Bahrain, when he'd been ambassador there, and now in Syria. Coming home to spend time with her had apparently always been too much trouble.

It wasn't entirely his fault, she knew. Circumstances had conspired against them. Given her father's line of work, her mother had insisted that the divorce agreement include an exception stating Alexa never had to join him in areas where she might be in danger. Since the divorce, that had been pretty much always. But her sixteenth birthday had triggered a codicil to that agreement, giving her the power to decide whether or not she felt safe joining him wherever he might be working. Her mother had not been fond of the idea of her coming to Syria but Alexa had decided it was time to call her father's bluff. If his invitation had been genuine—if he really wanted her there—she'd find out pretty quickly.

Him not showing up to meet her plane did not bode well.

"Really," Baz Nissim said. "You're okay."

"If there's nothing to be afraid of," she said, "then why do we have an armed escort just to drive from the airport to the embassy?"

Nissim arched an eyebrow and seemed to reassess her. "How old are you again?"

"Seventeen."

"Old enough, then, to know there are always dangers, but that the armed escort and your silent companion back there are the reasons why you needn't fear."

Alexa glanced at the security officer seated to her right, a stocky, square-jawed African-American who'd shaved his head down to the gleaming skin. She couldn't argue Nissim's point. She was probably as safe as she could be—under the circumstances. Syria had been locked in a cycle of violence and rebellion that repeated itself every few years for two decades before the Tin Men had been deployed there to depose an unelected president willing to slaughter every last one of his own people to keep power. Alexa had been listening to her father talk about the situation for as long as she could remember.

She looked out the window again. "You can't really blame them, y'know?"

Nissim studied her. "What do you mean?"

Alexa watched buildings roll by. "We took away their freedom. It's only natural some of 'em are going to hate us."

The security officer shifted awkwardly.

"We gave them freedom," Nissim said. "The Syrian people can be anything they like. Men *and* women. Thanks to us, they get to choose their own paths."

Alexa shot him a dubious look, giving him a small shrug. "Unless they want to fight about which path to take. That's not allowed."

"We brought democracy—"

"Democracy by intimidation," she corrected. "Not quite the same as freedom, is it?"

"You've got a lot of opinions for a seventeen-year-old."

Alexa met his gaze. "Trust me, if you grew up with Arthur Day for a father, you'd understand. If I came to the dinner table without an opinion and the ability to defend it, there was no dessert. That started when I was in the fourth grade. It's one of the reasons my parents aren't married anymore. I never minded it, but it drove my mother crazy."

"I don't expect your teachers appreciated it much, either," Nissim said.

Alexa grinned.

"Well," he said, "you'll be happy to know your father hasn't changed much. He still insists that everyone around him have an opinion. Fortunately for me, he doesn't withhold dessert if I can't back it up."

The car slowed and Alexa looked up to see that they were approaching a building surrounded by a twenty-foot wall, which was itself surrounded by a chain link fence topped with barbed wire. Armed sentries were posted atop the walls. The gates drew back to let the lead car pass through.

"Don't worry," she said, craning her neck to survey their surroundings as the Mercedes glided into the interior courtyard of the embassy compound and came to a stop. "He'll find some way to punish you."

The security officer on her right tensed up. "Mr. Nissim," he said, "the ambassador."

Alexa glanced out the window and saw her father hurrying across the courtyard toward the car. His gray hair needed cutting and he looked thinner than when she'd last seen him many months before. He wore a bright blue tie with a crisp white shirt and gray trousers that looked like half of a suit, as if he'd forgotten the jacket somewhere. He seemed deeply troubled.

Nissim opened his door and climbed out. Alexa wanted to see her father but her security detail did not move. Through the open driver's door, she could hear the men talking.

"Ambassador Day—" Nissim began.

"Baz, listen," her father interrupted. "Did you see anything out of the ordinary? Did anyone approach or follow your car?"

"Not that I noticed."

Only then did Alexa's father rap on the rear passenger window. The security man to her right popped open the door and stepped out. Alexa followed suit, exiting on the left and blinking against the brightness of the sun, lifting her hand to shield her eyes.

"Well, well," her father said as he came around the car to greet her. "Look at you."

"Look at *you*," Alexa replied, making nice, poking her father's belly. "Eat a sandwich once in a while, Ambassador."

He smiled, all of his worry and dignified reserve crumbling as he swept her into his arms.

"Damn it, Lex, it's good to see you!"

"Good to see you, too," she said, grunting as he squeezed her, and she was surprised to realize that she meant it. "Though I'm still rooting for you to be the ambassador to France."

He stepped back, beaming down at her. "Shopping in Paris, I know. I'll work on it."

Alexa went on tiptoe to kiss her father's cheek. He was so tall that she knew she would always feel like a little girl around him, no matter how many years passed. She sort of liked the idea.

Nissim had retrieved Alexa's bag from the trunk. He set it on the ground by her feet.

"You're sure you didn't encounter anything odd?" the ambassador asked again.

"Nothing," Nissim replied.

"The streets are empty," said the previously silent security man.

Alexa's father nodded. "I don't like it."

"You're supposed to be in your meeting with the mayor right now," Nissim said.

"He's not there," the ambassador replied. "There were only a handful of people at his office. The man I spoke to was not his usual receptionist. He told me the mayor's ill and won't be in the office for several days."

Nissim shrugged. "It could be true, rude as it was for them not to call you to cancel."

"It could be," the ambassador said.

The security man glanced uneasily around the courtyard.

"But you think it's something else," Alexa said. She wasn't used to seeing him so intensely focused on something other than writing a speech or reading reports.

Her father glanced at her, his eyes haunted. "I'm sure it's fine. We've got an entire platoon of Tin Men in this city, not to mention a whole lot of U.S. Marines right here in the embassy. If one of these anarchy groups has something in mind, they'll never get past our front door."

The ambassador cast a meaningful glance at Nissim and the security man. His words hadn't been an observation; they'd been an order.

"Yes, sir," said the security man.

Alexa's father lifted up her travel bag and slung the strap across his shoulder, then slid his free arm around her waist and walked her toward the ornate front door of the embassy residence.

"Come on, kid. I'll show you where you'll be sleeping."

She knew he must have someone on staff to do that and it touched her that he wanted to do it himself, but the tension in his arms and the expression in his eyes hadn't gone away completely and his demeanor had her unsettled.

"You said I wouldn't be in any danger here," she said quietly as he led her up the front steps.

He paused with the door halfway open and turned to her. Alexa could smell his scent—same old deodorant, same old Dad—and though the lines in his face had deepened, they hadn't changed much. The steely glint in his eyes was new, though. New to her, at least. She had come to Damascus promising herself that she would try to put away old resentments, only to find a new one. *Don't get me killed,* she thought.

"Take a look out there," he said.

She glanced across the embassy compound. Several cars were parked in the shade of the wall. Armed Marines were posted at various points along its length. Nissim stood talking with her father's security man, out in the open and unafraid. Over the wall she could see the cityscape of Damascus, its towers and domes and blocks of apartments and offices. A plane sliced its white trail across the sky, but otherwise the city was quiet.

"I don't think there's anything we need to worry about, but I'll make you this promise," Arthur Day said, speaking quietly, so only his daughter could hear him. "If trouble comes, I will protect you."

She smiled, on the verge of telling him that, weighing a hundred and sixty pounds and never having fired a gun in his life, he could not do much if the shit hit the fan. Something made her hold her tongue, though, and she wondered if it might be fear—fear that she might be speaking an uneasy truth.

"You can start by feeding me," she said. "I'm starved."

Visibly grateful to move on, her father smiled.

"I can fix that," he said, and led the way deeper into the embassy.

As she swung the door closed, Alexa took one more look out at the city. Heat haze wavered in the air and she saw a blackbird wheeling across the sky, the only thing that moved.

Unnerved, she chuckled softly to herself as she shut the door tightly.

"Welcome to Damascus," she whispered. "Safest place on Earth."

Kate heard Travaglini whisper the words on her commlink.

"Son of a bitch."

They were turning into a narrow street of shops and row houses. Over the tops of the buildings they could see the massive, hulking presence of the Umayyad Mosque. The mosque was the spiritual center of Damascus and also its physical center, dwarfing everything else for blocks around. In the distance, hills rose toward the sky, but here in the city's heart, the Umayyad Mosque was a monolith.

Or it had been. The western half of the mosque had been destroyed during the civil war that had raged here when Kate had been in middle school. It was still in the process of being rebuilt, and for an instant her eyes were drawn to the jagged silhouette of the ongoing construction. When her gaze lowered, she saw the trouble that Travaglini had spotted—a pair of Tin Men dragging a bearded man from the doorway of a market and into the street.

One of the bots shoved the bearded man to the ground and, when he tried to rise, the other struck him in the head, dropping him to his knees. The two robots flanked the bleeding man, who cringed like a dog from his master's wrath. Kate started running and Travaglini fell in beside her, their robot limbs far swifter than even the fastest human.

Kate was no tech—she didn't know how the bots worked—but she loved to run. It felt more natural in this form than when she used the prosthetics her flesh-and-blood body had been fitted with. Most of the time, she preferred the wheelchair. The docs all told her she'd get used to the prosthetics eventually, and she suspected that was true, but this—running with her whole body, her whole self, even if it wasn't really hers—was so much better.

As she hustled toward the two bots, one of them raised a hand as if to strike the man again. A bright yellow smiley face had been painted on the robot's chassis, with pirate-style crossbones beneath it in the same vivid hue.

Hawkins, she thought, *of course.*

"Private Hawkins!" she snapped.

He flinched, twisting to face Kate and Travaglini as they ran up.

"Explain yourself," she demanded.

Kate's external weapon was still holstered at her side but Travaglini had drawn his and held it in both hands, his stance hostile.

"You're out of your sector, Corporal," Hawkins said.

"Answer the question," Travaglini snapped.

Hawkins cocked his head. They were using external speakers, but everything that the Tin Men saw and heard and said was being recorded. Anybody else would be very careful about what they said next, but Hawkins had never seemed all that worried about pissing off the brass.

"We're questioning a civilian about suspicious activities," said the other bot, Hawkins's partner for the day. "Doing our job, or we were until you interrupted."

The bot had a playing card detailed on his forehead—the ace of spades—but Kate didn't need to see the marking to know it would be Mavrides. The two always managed to partner up. If Hawkins had mastered the art of being a prick, Mavrides was his apprentice.

"It's a liquor store," she said, gesturing at the shattered door. The place sold beer and arak and wine. There were a hundred like them in a four-mile radius. "And the sign says it's closed. So what kind of suspicious activity are we talking about here?"

Something shifted inside, a crunch of broken glass, and Kate dropped her hand to her sidearm. She glanced at Travaglini and nodded for him to check it out, even as she returned her attention to Hawkins and Mavrides.

As Travaglini approached the open door, the cringing man who knelt in their midst began to mutter in Arabic, his mouth still bleeding from Hawkins's blows. His eyes were wide with desperation. The onboard translator gave her an approximation of his words—he was pleading for them to leave his girls alone.

Anger rippled through Kate. "Stay cool," she called to Travaglini.

"Look, don't make this more than it is," Hawkins started.

"Yeah? Then maybe you should tell me what it is."

"We already did," Mavrides snapped. "Suspicious fucking activity. We're doing our job, you stupid—"

"Shut it!" Hawkins barked.

Mavrides's head swiveled abruptly to stare at Hawkins, but the kid didn't say another word.

"We were walking by, that's all," Hawkins said. "A shortcut to our sector. City's a ghost town today, like it's holding its breath, waiting for some really bad shit to go down. We see the girls in the shop window, watching us. Then this guy . . ." He gestured to the kneeling man, presumably the shop owner. "He drags them away. I got a glimpse of his face and he didn't look pissed at them, Kate. He looked like he was crapping his pants. Pretty clear he knows something— and if he does, I want to know what it is."

"So you broke in and dragged him into the street?" she asked.

Hawkins and Mavrides didn't answer, maybe to keep the confirmation of their breach of protocol off the record, but they all knew how it had gone down.

"Wade," Travaglini said, coming to the door.

In front of him were a pair of terrified girls, perhaps eight and ten. The second they spotted the shop owner they ran out the door to him and the family embraced. Kate wanted to rip Hawkins and Mavrides to pieces. Hawkins had shot innocents, intimidated locals unnecessarily, and faced disciplinary action multiple times, but he'd never strayed so far across the line that they'd given him his walking papers. This time, though . . .

Kate studied the liquor store owner, listened to him shushing his daughters and telling them all would be well, watched him as he cast frightened glances up and down the street, and she knew: even assholes are right once in a while.

"Shit," she whispered.

The man's gaze locked with hers. He knew he'd made a mistake, knew that she'd realized that it wasn't the Tin Men that terrified him. This guy was afraid of something else entirely.

"Please," he said in English.

Kate surveyed the street, then looked at Travaglini.

"Get them inside," she said.

"Corporal—" Hawkins began.

"Right now!"

"On your feet," Travaglini said to the shop owner. "Take your daughters back into the store, sir. Quickly, please."

He spoke in English, but the bot had an onboard translation system that worked both ways. The words were coming out in Arabic. Kate snatched up her sidearm and put her back against the wall, watching the opposite roof and scanning doorways again. Hawkins and Mavrides followed suit. Twitchy, gun barrel sweeping from side to side, Mavrides seemed all too ready to fire.

Travaglini got the civilians inside and Mavrides followed. Hawkins hesitated a second and then went in, with Kate bringing up the rear. She stayed by the door, brandishing her sidearm.

"What?" Mavrides said. "What'd you see?"

Kate ignored him, turning to the shopkeeper, who had pressed himself against shelves laden with wine bottles, holding his daughters close. The older girl had buried her face in her father's chest, but the younger one glared back at Kate with enormous brown eyes, beautiful and defiant.

"Tell me what you're afraid of and we'll leave you alone," Kate demanded.

The man shook his head, tears springing to his eyes. "I don't know. I swear to you—"

"Bullshit!" Hawkins roared, so loud that the man bumped against the shelves and sent several bottles of wine crashing to the floor, the meaty scent of Lebanese red filling the shop.

"No!" the shopkeeper said, clutching breathlessly at his girls. "I swear it. I heard only that the streets would not be safe for my daughters."

Mavrides pointed his sidearm at the man's left eye and the shopkeeper froze.

"What's the threat?" he snarled. "How are they coming for us?"

"I don't know!" the man wailed. "I don't know!"

Mavrides lowered the weapon, aiming it at the younger daughter.

"Private Mavrides!" Kate snapped. "That's enough!"

His head swiveled toward her. The ace of spades shone starkly white on his gleaming chrome-hued forehead.

"We can't let them—" Mavrides began.

"Stow your weapon, Private," she said.

Travaglini shifted slightly, his stance making it clear he would back her up with bullets if necessary. Kate glanced at Hawkins, whose bot eyes were narrowed with dark contemplation.

"Zack, you're an inch from insubordination," Hawkins warned.

"He's a mile across that line," Travaglini muttered.

Hawkins kept his focus on Mavrides. "This guy doesn't know anything. If he did, he'd have said."

Mavrides hesitated a moment, then took a step back and lowered his gun, but he did not put it away.

"Private channel, Sergeant Morello," Kate said, gesturing for the others to be silent as she opened a commlink. As before, she heard static on the line.

"Morello," the sergeant answered, his voice crackling.

"Sarge, it's Wade. Something's going down. We've got a shopkeeper here who's more spooked than I am. No details, but they were warned to keep their heads down."

"You thinking Bot Killers?" Morello asked.

Kate glanced at Travaglini and the others, at the shopkeeper's daughters, and then at the man himself—at the fear in his eyes.

"I don't know, Sarge," she said. "Maybe something bigger."

Hanif Khan cradled his Dragunov sniper rifle, enjoying the heat that the morning sun had baked into the weapon's stock and barrel, but in his heart he wished for a knife. He had been killing since the age of twelve and had always preferred a blade to a bullet. A knife made murder intimate and real, brought the full weight of the deed's ugliness upon the killer, where Hanif believed it ought to be. Guns were impersonal. You couldn't feel the flesh give way, the scrape of metal on bone, couldn't feel the heat or smell the copper tang of the first spray of blood. Killing had sometimes broken Hanif Khan's heart and other times had given him satisfaction, even a sense of triumph, but it had never felt insignificant to him.

Until the robots.

There could be no murder with the man-shaped drones, the things the American army called Remote Infantry and the Western media called Tin Men and the rest of the world just called robots. They weren't as simple as that, of course. They were life-sized marionettes, really, murderous puppets whose strings were invisible lines of data bounced off satellites and beamed into the complex operating systems of the most sophisticated automatons ever built.

Even the sharpest knife could do little more than scrape the shell of one of the American drone soldiers. The destruction of one required powerful, targeted explosives, but their sensors had a 91 percent success rate at spotting IEDs, and grenades had to be right in their laps to do significant damage. Since the first appearance of the Tin Men, rocket launchers had made the most sense, but their explosives had rarely been powerful enough to do more than temporarily disable the robots. Those old launchers had been good for nothing but keeping the Americans nervous, letting them know that resistance remained.

Today a new breed of rocket launcher would debut, designed specifically for assault on the Tin Men. But just as he preferred a knife to a gun, Hanif Khan had little interest in explosives and technology as a means of killing. Stopping a robot with a rifle was far more difficult, requiring at least two but often three armor-piercing bullets to strike the same square inch of the drone's outer shell. There were only two targets on the drone's carapace weak enough to allow the second or third bullet to pass through, strike the robot's power core, and cause it to explode from within. The upper torso of the robot's external shell consisted of two pieces—the chassis, or back frame, and the chest plate. Three bullets striking the same point on either side—on the seam that connected chassis and chest plate, halfway between armpit and hip—would destroy one of the Tin Men.

Very few people were skilled enough with a rifle to put three bullets in the same square inch of a moving target—even one staggered by the first shot. Hanif Khan had the ability and he had the desire. He had spent years plotting from afar against the arrogance of the Americans, forever haunted by the knowledge that even if he destroyed a thousand robot soldiers it would be nothing more than a nuisance to the enemy, a financial irritation. Broken toys were not casualties, and so destroying Tin Men gave him no satisfaction. The American people were overjoyed that they could fulfill their pompous mission of policing the world without risking the lives of their sons and daughters. They were willing to increase the military's budget as long as the price in blood went down, and a handful of America's allies had begun to share the financial burden of this tyranny in order to reap the benefits of forced world peace.

It would never end, Khan knew. Not if the Americans had a choice in the matter.

Today was about taking that choice away from them.

Once he had been a warlord in his native Afghanistan, the most powerful man in Kunar Province, earning millions of dollars a year by using his private army to aid the American government in its efforts to suppress the Taliban, running secret operations over the border with Pakistan. Until the Pakistani government fell into radical hands and began regular raids into his province, and Khan stopped worrying about whether his attacks on the Pakistanis were done in secret.

The U.S. Remote Infantry were brand new in those days. They had been deployed in Iraq and Libya, but only to safeguard American interests. No one had ever seen them in combat, right up until the day they had been dropped from airplanes, uncrated in warehouses, and unloaded from trucks all along the Af-Pak border—and the American president had announced that no further conflict between the two countries would be permitted. The radical Pakistani government had briefly threatened the use of nuclear weapons before discovering that their nuclear arsenal had been secured by a thousand American robot soldiers.

Hanif Khan had raged at his CIA handlers and U.S. military contacts, all of whom had held the hard line. Their previous relationship meant nothing. From now on, there would be no need for the warlord and his army to do any work on behalf of the Americans. Nothing would be done in secret from this moment on. With thousands of Tin Men in their arsenal and the global cost of war—even the instability caused by the *hint* of war—the Americans had decided that enforcing stability was the only way to keep the global economy from crumbling.

The warlord had put his knife into the heart of the CIA man. He had used his army to test the effectiveness of the robots. Only he and his younger brother, Omed, and half a dozen others had escaped with their lives.

From that day forward, he had a new enemy. Hanif and Omed Khan and the others had spent more than a year fighting a tiny guerilla war against the local platoon of Tin Men. They had captured several of the robots only to find themselves with abandoned technology, vacated by the minds of the men and women who'd piloted them. The first two they imprisoned were destroyed by remote detonation, but Hanif figured out how to prevent that, and soon he and Omed began to learn.

What they were. How they worked. How to destroy them.

In time, they hired themselves out to America's enemies as robot killers. An uneducated regional warlord had become a mercenary whose services were desired by dictators and parliaments in a dozen nations. Several of his men had lost their lives, but he had replaced them with expert killers from around the world. He had Somalis and Bosnians, Russians and Chinese, Egyptians and Germans, a Swede and even an American. Hundreds of Bot Killers working for him in nine robot-occupied hot spots around the globe.

No Pakistanis, though. Fuck those guys. Old enmities died hard.

At the beginning, Khan had spent every day in the field, frustrated and angry, wishing he could bury his blade in American hearts, never satisfied with crippling or even destroying robot soldiers, knowing that their human pilots went home to soft beds and warm lovers when their shifts were over.

Then, nine months ago, Omed had been too slow getting off a roof here in Damascus. The Tin Men had chased him down and tried to take him captive. Omed had attacked, turned one of their weapons against them, and been shot to death by two others in a dirty alley. While the Tin Men stood by, waiting for the local authorities to come and remove the body, a dog had pissed on Omed's corpse.

The bots who had killed Omed and paid no attention to the dog had markings on their shells, as nearly all the Tin Men did. One had red horns painted on its robot skull and the other bore the number thirteen on its forehead. It had been a simple matter for him to interrogate the locals who frequently communicated with the American bots, to find out the names of the soldiers who were piloting the Devil and Thirteen, the ones who killed Omed—Corporal Wade, female, and Private Kelso, male.

Hanif Khan had to kill them, of course. Not just destroy their hardware, but murder Wade and Kelso, the Devil and Thirteen. It was a dilemma that had profoundly troubled him, so much that he had insinuated himself in conversations with his various employers—conversations that both they and he had previously considered above his station. But they feared and needed him, and through persistence he soon learned that he was not the only one who sought a more permanent solution to the Americans' oppression than simply breaking their toys.

This solution had brought him here today, to this rooftop overlooking the souq, with this sun-baked Dragunov in his hands. He had been away from the fight for a time, but he had not forgotten how to shoot. How to kill. Intimately.

Exhaling, he picked up his scope and glanced over the edge of the roof, sighting a pair of bots coming his way through the narrow marketplace streets. One of them had diagonal red stripes across its face and the other a bull's-eye on its abdomen. For a moment, he thought that his luck had gone sour, that the patterns his men had observed had been broken today, but then he noticed the number thirteen on the forehead of the one with the target on its lower torso and he understood. Kelso had new markings.

A target. Its location was inaccurate, but the irony was not lost on Khan.

He withdrew, lying down beneath a black covering that would make it harder for anyone monitoring satellite images to notice him. Drazen—the Bosnian assassin who had become his most trusted lieutenant—had wanted to join him for this surveillance but Khan had insisted on being alone. Drazen and the other Bot Killers in Damascus today had other responsibilities.

A rare smile touched Khan's lips. A trickle of sweat ran down the back of his neck.

His cell phone vibrated in the shirt pocket that held it tight to his chest. A flutter of excitement went through him and he tamped it down. Emotion could get him killed and then he would not live to see the glory of the day.

"Yes," he answered in English, holding the phone to his ear.

They always spoke English—the only tongue they had in common was the language of their enemies. The man on the other end of the call had a thick Chinese accent, but the words were clear enough.

"The countdown has begun."

The Watermelon Man had a daughter named Yalda. Nine years old. Whenever Danny went by the fruit market in Damascus he looked for the dark-eyed girl. Though she had grown old enough to be embarrassed when her father said sweet things about her, Yalda had not yet outgrown the childlike wonder that overcame her every time Danny paid a visit. The little girl would pelt him with olives and smear berries on his chassis or study her reflection in the metal alloy of his chest plate. Sick of hearing others call her beautiful, she was clearly trying to decide for herself if the word was warranted.

Danny never asked the Watermelon Man for anything. He played with Yalda and talked to her father about the weather and the political climate in Syria. The merchant had no hatred for America in his eyes. As long as his daughter was safe, Danny figured the man did not care who provided that safety.

The bomb that had nearly killed her was hidden in a small truck parked in front of a shop that sold varieties of olive oil. Yalda had a soccer ball Danny had given her after a brief argument about the proper name for the sport—she, of course, called it football. She kicked it around the fruit market, maneuvering through the stalls.

The explosion blew Yalda through a fruit stand. If not for the splintered wooden shaft that impaled her side, the nine-year-old would have suffered only superficial burns and ugly bruises. Danny and several other members of the platoon were there in less than thirty seconds, converging on the market from their various patrols in the city. Others remained on guard, wary of further attacks because they so often came in groups.

There had been only one bomb that day. Seven fatalities, and Yalda was not among them. Danny had examined her wound, decided that the ticking clock would do more damage than a bit of bouncing around, and carried her to the nearest surgical team with the inhuman speed that his robot body provided. He had consulted his onboard data systems and determined that it was unlikely any of her organs had been badly damaged and then he had run. PFC Danny Kelso had rolled the dice.

These days, Yalda studied her reflection in Danny's chest plate in order to see how much her burns had healed. She enjoyed showing him how they were fading, and he always told her that scars made you memorable. But Yalda was nearly ten years old, and he saw in her eyes the hint of knowledge, the hue of sadness. Her face would be telling the story of the bomb for the rest of her life.

The Watermelon Man would be forever grateful: she was alive. But she was not allowed to roam so far from her father's shop anymore.

From that day forward, if the Watermelon Man learned of a threat to the Tin Men, he found a way to let Danny know. A quiet word about the weather, a recommendation that certain parts of Damascus were to be avoided for a day or two. Danny tried to tell him to stop—the Watermelon Man was risking his life for soldiers who could be destroyed and then show up days later in a different robot body—but the man could not ignore the debt he felt he owed.

All of which meant that Danny didn't know what to make of the merchant's absence today. When he and Alaina Torres reached the fruit market, at least three quarters of the stalls were empty. Most of the shops were closed up tightly, windows shuttered, only shadows inside. Perhaps a dozen customers browsed the meager offerings in the stalls, old women who frowned disapprovingly as they tested the freshness of melons and pears and cherries. A pair of ancient men with wrinkled-leather faces smoked cigarettes in front of an open butcher shop and watched the Tin Men pass by with an air of indifference perfected over long decades.

"This is fucking spooky," Torres said, external speaker, not bothering to open a channel.

Danny scanned the faces and saw many that were familiar, but none that were friendly. As he and Torres had toured their sector, they had seen even fewer signs of life than were on display in the fruit market.

"It doesn't make sense," Danny said. "If they were going to nuke Damascus or something, these people wouldn't have stayed behind."

"Nobody's nuking Damascus," Torres scoffed. "The only Americans they'd kill would be the embassy folks and the base contingent—a few officers, a lot of grunts, and a dozen suits. It'd be ugly, yeah, but these people aren't going to destroy their own capital for a hit that small. It's not nukes, Kelso. We're missing something."

Danny nodded as he studied closed windows and locked doors. The sensory input system that gave every bot the ability to smell and feel picked up the usual citrus aroma on that narrow street. But beneath its awnings and umbrellas, the partially deserted market also retained the smell of overripe fruit and the faint odor of old piss. Denuded of most of its customers and merchants and the mountains of fruits and vegetables, it was an unsettling sight.

They came to the door of the Watermelon Man's shop and Danny was surprised to find it open. There was an old wooden cart just to the left of the door where the Watermelon Man put his freshest produce each day to attract those who might otherwise keep walking. Today the cart was empty except for a bucket of bruised apples and the stains of days past.

Tucked under the wheels of the cart, put aside as if its owner had meant to come back to it shortly, was the soccer ball Danny had given to Yalda.

"I know what's missing," he said.

Torres looked at him.

"There are no kids," he said. "There are always kids in the market."

Both of them glanced around. Not only were there no children; none of the people in the market that day were under the age of fifty, maybe sixty.

"Not today," Torres said.

Danny shuddered. With his mind riding inside a bot, he had always felt invulnerable. But whatever the hell was going on in Damascus today, it frightened him.

"Sit tight," he said, glancing at Torres. "If you see anything weird, sing out."

With her guarding the door, he entered the shop. A bell jangled overhead, but the sound did not disturb the fat man who sat behind the counter. Danny had seen him before and thought he remembered the Watermelon Man introducing him as a cousin or something, though Danny couldn't remember his name. What he did remember was that the Watermelon Man hated the guy, thought he was a leech and a liar. So why was he looking after the shop, even for a minute?

In the constant heat it was rare to find someone so obese. Given the man's thinning white hair and weathered features, Danny pegged him as maybe mid-sixties. His mouth turned down at the edges.

"What can I do for you?" the fat man asked.

"I'm looking for Ashur," Danny said, using the Watermelon Man's name.

The man behind the counter shifted in his chair. He had enormous sweat stains under his arms and a damp patch at the front of his shirt. The man frowned, deep furrows appearing on his forehead. For a second, Danny wondered if the onboard translator had malfunctioned or if the man was just surprised to hear Arabic coming out of an American robot soldier.

"Not here," the fat man replied in English. If he was trying to prove something, he was failing.

"I can see he's not here. Where is he?"

"Away," the man said in Arabic, having apparently exhausted his English skills.

Danny didn't like it. He walked through the shop, examining the produce. On an ordinary day, the Watermelon Man would have had three times the fruits and vegetables that the fat man had on display. More than that, Danny saw wilted leaves and bruised pears and dimpled cherries. There were watermelons, of course, but far fewer than he had ever seen in the shop.

"I'm going to need more than that," Danny said, letting the threat tint his voice. "Where has he gone, and when will he return?"

As he spoke, Danny moved deeper into the shop. He pulled back a curtain and peered into the back room, which was full of empty wooden crates and not much else. No sign of a struggle, though with Damascus turned into some kind of ghost town he didn't really suspect the fat man of foul play.

"He has taken his daughter and gone to visit his sister in Palmyra."

Danny froze, thinking. He let the curtain drop and turned to study the fat man a moment, then headed for the door. The fat man said nothing, only watched him go.

"What's up?" Torres asked when Danny emerged.

He snapped his gun from its holster, keeping it down at his side, warily scanning the weathered old faces around them.

"We're going," he said.

Torres straightened up, her hand dropping to her own weapon and drawing it, following his example and keeping the gun low.

"You find out what the weirdness is about?" she asked, falling in beside him as he marched out of the fruit market.

The two old men smoking cigarettes took notice of them now, gazes flickering toward the guns before they muttered to each other, their expressions remaining stoic as ever.

"Ashur . . . that's the Watermelon Man . . . he's not here. Neither is his daughter. The guy in charge of the shop right now is someone Ashur fucking hates—he thinks the guy is a total scumbag—and the guy claims Ashur and Yalda have gone off to Palmyra to visit Ashur's sister."

"Why is that so—"

"Ashur did have a sister, but she died in an uprising like ten or twelve years ago. He's got no immediate family left except for Yalda. The thing is, any other day I'd think this bastard had cut Ashur's throat so he could take over the business. But not today."

Torres arrived at a street corner. She put her back against the wall and took a quick glance around, checking to see that no ambush was in the offing.

"Today," Torres said, "you're thinking Ashur got himself and his daughter the fuck out of here."

As they started down the street, weapons out, watching rooftops and alleys, windows and doors, Danny nodded. "We're screwed,

Alaina. I don't know how, but somehow they've figured out a way to fuck us up."

His heart was thousands of miles away, inside his body. Safe underground, in the Hump. But even at that distance Danny felt like he could feel it pounding in his chest, pulse thumping at his temples. He had no throat—no sense of taste, even, in the robot frame—but still he felt it constrict, dry and tight.

"Private channel, Lieutenant Trang and Sergeant Morello," he said, listening to the clicking that switched his commlink into privacy mode. "Sarge, this is Kelso. I've brought the lieutenant into the channel as well. Do you read?"

Static. "Sergeant Morello, do you—"

"—dropped out for a second, but I read you," Morello said, his voice so close it seemed as if the sergeant was standing right beside him.

"The Watermelon Man hit the road. The only way he'd do that is out of fear for his daughter, and the only way he'd do it without warning me is if the danger was imminent."

"Agreed. Reports we're getting from the rest of the platoon say the whole Blue Zone is abandoned, except for the kind of hard-asses and old folks who won't go anywhere. Come on in, Kelso," Morello said. "You and Torres watch your asses."

"Yes, sir," he said, switching over to external voice and turning to Torres. "We're going in."

As he turned back—he and Torres moving around a cracked and broken fountain—Danny caught a glimpse of something moving on a rooftop back the way they'd come. He raised his weapon, sighting along the roofline.

"What is it?" Torres asked.

"Don't know."

"A sniper?"

"Could be. But what's the point? Even if he's good enough to destroy one bot, the rest of us will track his ass down."

The expression on Torres's face was the closest the bots could come to a smile.

"Got that right," she said. "Still, watch the roof."

A bit of static whispered through the comms, followed by the lieutenant's voice. "This is Trang. Return to arrival zone. Use all speed."

Danny and Torres glanced at each other.

"All speed," Danny said.

Torres took off at a run, slicing the air, racing so quickly that no human could have followed. Danny ran in her wake, watching her six, wondering if anyone was watching *his* six . . . someone who wanted to do him harm. Do all of them harm.

Where'd you go, Ashur? he thought.

Whatever it was that had spooked him, the Watermelon Man had left Damascus fast. Last night, probably. Kelso had lied a bit to Torres—at least by omission. It wasn't the sweaty guy manning the Watermelon Man's shop that had convinced him they needed to regroup, or the certainty that Ashur would have warned him if there'd been time.

It had been the soccer ball. No way in hell would Yalda have left it behind. Not by choice.

Danny picked up speed, passing right by Torres. In the midst of all of this tension, he'd been so occupied with trying to figure out what the enemy was planning that he hadn't spared a thought for who else might be in danger.

Now that he had, he found he couldn't think of anything else but Kate.

5

The Grande Bretagne was perhaps the finest hotel in Athens, as renowned for its service and its extensive wine cellars as for the luxury of its appointments. The nighttime views of the Acropolis and the Parthenon, so beautifully lit after dark, were enough to make hotel guests believe there was magic left in the world. Thinking of its butler service and thermal suite, and the unlimited budget provided to all the president's entourage, Felix Wade told himself that he might never leave the Grande Bretagne.

Unfortunately, he was all too aware of the illusory nature of his bliss. Along with the luxury of the hotel came intense security, including armed guards at the entrances, on the roof, and on every floor of the lovely old hotel. Security for a U.S. president traveling abroad had always been a logistical nightmare, but Felix believed the protective measures taken on this trip to be the most extensive ever. President Peter Matheson had not begun the Tin Men program, but he had voted in favor of it while still the junior senator from Massachusetts and he had only furthered the interventionist policies of the previous administration since his election to the Oval Office. Now he'd come to Athens for the G20 summit and all eyes were on him, many of them filled with resentment.

Despite the elegant cigar bar, the incredible politeness of the hotel staff, and the majesty of the sun as it set behind the Acropolis, Felix could not relax enough to enjoy it all. Not with the hotel locked down as if it were the world's most beautiful prison.

He rode the elevator to the fourth floor, happy there was no music to accompany his ride. Something about the hum and clank of the old apparatus comforted him. When the doors slid open, the blond Secret Service woman guarding them glanced at him with her chin high. Her name was Sydney Travers, though everyone from the president on down just called her Syd. Felix found it a strangely casual appellation for a woman whose face was often so expressionless she might as well not have been human. Down the corridor, a pair of Tin Men stood on either side of the double doors to the president's suite. They moved without sound, and their silence did not comfort him at all.

Felix nodded to the Secret Service woman and she replied with a single tilt of her head.

He strode along the corridor, passing rooms he knew to be empty. The president was the only resident of this floor, though he was never unaccompanied by members of his protection unit.

"Good morning, Professor Wade," one of the Tin Men said as Felix approached the double doors. "He's expecting you."

Unlike other Tin Men, these soldiers were not allowed to deface their robot frames with images or symbols. Each of the three robots on the president's protection unit had a small American flag painted over the left breast, but they were otherwise indistinguishable except by their voices. Felix had failed miserably in his attempt to keep track of which soldier was in which frame during which shift, resulting in him being constantly embarrassed until he at last gave up trying.

When the other Tin Man opened the door for him, he could manage nothing more personal than "Thank you."

Felix found President Matheson pacing the living room and muttering quietly to himself. American roots folk music played softly through hidden speakers. Felix had seen this behavior before—

Matheson was trying to memorize the speech he intended to make to the other world leaders at the summit tomorrow—and he knew better than to interrupt. Instead, he leaned against the wall with his hands stuffed in his pockets and tried to remember if he'd heard this particular song before.

"Got it, I think!" President Matheson said happily, his blue eyes bright as always. He went to a sideboard and poured himself a glass of scotch from a crystal decanter. "Want a drink, Felix?"

"I wouldn't say no."

"Want to hear my little monologue?"

"I've heard it."

The president turned to face him, leaning against the sideboard. He sipped his scotch, a strong-jawed Irishman of the sort the United States had stopped electing a long time ago. His hair had begun to gray and thin and the skin at his throat sagged in a slight wattle, but Peter Matheson still maintained the air of a man in charge.

"I've improved it."

"I've no doubt. But unless you've changed your mind—"

President Matheson's eyes iced over. "Let's not start that again. This was your plan and it's a good one."

Felix felt his stomach curdle. The new American economic policy the president intended to deliver to the G20 leaders tomorrow had indeed been Felix's plan. He had conceived it and written it down and presented it to Matheson at a private meeting in the Oval Office as the result of a question the president had posed to him: What would Europe have to do to save its economy from the total meltdown to which it was otherwise surely doomed?

Presuming it a hypothetical, Felix had looked at all the numbers and disregarded such things as political impossibility and the will of the people, and come up with an austerity program like no other. In order to come back from the brink of total economic collapse, the European Union would have to institute unprecedented austerity measures that would dismantle social programs and abandon the poorest and weakest in favor of goals that would help everyone in the long term, if they survived. The austerity measures would pay back some of the debt accumulated by the more irresponsible members of the E.U. and keep their governments afloat. The United States had been weathering the economic storm thanks in large part to the jobs provided by the Tin Men program, but if Europe completely collapsed, America might follow.

Felix's plan included what was essentially a hostile takeover of the International Monetary Fund, and huge punitive measures against governments and corporations that broke the rules established by the World Trade Organization. It had been pure fantasy. Even as he wrote it, he had known that none of the nations involved would agree to the measures he outlined, but he had wanted to give the president an answer that would outline the true depths of the approaching global economic catastrophe.

Trouble was, the president hadn't been posing a hypothetical question.

"I devised the plan," Felix admitted. "But I never imagined that you would present it to them at gunpoint."

President Matheson chuckled and took a sip of scotch. After a minute: "You're full of shit, do you know that?"

"Mr. President—"

"No," he said, raising a hand. "Let's not pretend we don't both know what you're doing. The United States has been making unilateral decisions for the world since we first deployed the robots. We made the United Nations irrelevant. In the interest of safeguarding the future for our people, we took it upon ourselves to defuse the world's hot spots. This is just an extension of that, and for you to pretend that you hadn't so much as contemplated the possibility that I would use the Tin Men to enforce it is disingenuous and insulting."

Felix said nothing. He wanted to refute the argument—he believed in influencing the world with economic rather than military force— but Matheson was the president of the United States and there would be no debate.

Noting his silence, President Matheson set aside his drink and poured one for Felix. When he handed it over, Felix drank half the glass in one burning gulp.

"The time for pulling our punches is in the past, my friend," the president said. "These guys—the whole G20—they're going to sign on to our agenda and then turn around and pretend to their people that we all huddled in a room and came up with this plan together. They're going to do that because they have no choice."

"There must be some other way," Felix said. "Some more ameliorative approach."

President Matheson sighed, moving toward Felix until they were face-to-face, practically nose to nose. "You're my number one global economic advisor, so you tell me: Is there another way? Given the crisis they're in? Given the way austerity measures have met with such a *resounding* welcome in the past? Is there any way in hell the governments we're talking about are going to make the hard decisions necessary to save the continent from free fall without us forcing their hands? Without promising them that any rebellion will be put down by our forces? Without taking over the IMF and compelling the whole world to toe the line where the WTO's rules are concerned? Is there another damn way?"

Felix swallowed hard, meeting the president's gaze, and tipped up his scotch glass for another gulp.

President Matheson nodded. "Exactly."

"It will work for now," Felix said. "I have no doubt. But it won't work forever. No matter how benevolent the motive, we can't subjugate the whole world—financially or otherwise—without consequences."

The president sniffed in disgust. "Felix, we're not subjugating the world, we're freeing it. Freeing them from war and oppression. Freeing up their time so they can figure out how to adapt to the flooding and the food shortages. It's been ugly for a long time, but we're giving them the breathing room to build their own futures."

"They don't see it that way, sir. Someday, perhaps soon, somebody will invent something that makes the Tin Men look like toy soldiers, and there's going to be hell to pay."

President Matheson clinked his glass against Felix's and then raised it in a toast. "Let's hope you're wrong."

The tech Danny Kelso thought of as Aimee Something did, in fact, possess a full name. Twenty-three-year-old Aimee Felicia Bell hailed from Dobbs Ferry, a little town along the Hudson River in Westchester County, New York. The world had moved into the twenty-first century long ago, but one look at Dobbs Ferry's main drag showed how stubbornly it had held on to the twentieth. Pizza parlors and pubs, little boutiques, a comic book shop—and plenty of empty storefronts, of course. Soaped-up windows with FOR LEASE signs prominently displayed: the hallmark of America's main streets these days, and the only sign that Dobbs Ferry even knew the world had moved on.

Dobbs Ferry had bored Aimee. An old story, really. Her parents didn't understand her interest in technology and did not approve of her joining the army to finance her education. They were afraid she would end up dead in a ditch somewhere in the Middle East. And what was she supposed to tell them? That she loved technology because it represented the future she longed for, and that the army was her ticket out? That she loved them and all but, you know, *see ya*. Now she was in Germany, working on mindcasting and VR tech that she understood better than her supervisors, building the future she had dreamed about.

So when Private North sidled up beside her monitoring station, full of blond-haired, blue-eyed swagger and smelling faintly of vomit and whiskey, Aimee Bell did her best to ignore him. They'd had a thing for a while, and she'd thought it a good thing. Then something had happened to North in the field—something ugly that he didn't want to talk about—and he'd changed. The relationship had never been one of candlelit romance, but it turned into torrid sex in maintenance closets. North had vacillated between manic enthusiasm and sullen drunkenness, and for her own sake Aimee had ended it. The one time she had shared her feelings about it with someone else at the Hump, all it had earned her was a shrug. *The shit they see out there,* her friend had said, *you can't expect it not to change them.*

North could be a total ass, but she tried her best not to hold it against him.

Aimee had always had a difficult time with relationships. She had a vague awareness that men found her attractive, but with a few unpleasant exceptions, she had managed to escape the ugliest of their attentions. When she felt interested in a guy, it came in handy to be pretty, but usually once she started talking about hacking or bioengineering or robotics, they veered off fairly quickly. There *was* one guy in Platoon A she had her eye on now, but it sure wasn't Thomas North.

"Morning, Aimee," North said, smiling, hands clasped behind him as if he stood at a sluggish kind of attention. "Been a while since we had some time to ourselves."

"You say that like it's been accidental," she replied.

"Ohhh," North said. "That's how it's gonna be?"

Aimee kept her focus on the grid of viewscreens to the left of her monitoring station. There were more than twenty stations arrayed along the outer curve of the circular chamber, each tracking the movements, video captures, and vital signs of squads of Tin Men currently in the field. Each of the screens on Aimee's grid showed a small square of live imagery from Damascus, and bore the constantly changing vital signs of one member of Platoon A. The Command Core was at the center of the room, an elevated, enclosed platform connected to a raised round catwalk with half a dozen staircases descending to the monitoring chamber's floor. From the Command Core, duty officers oversaw the techs who controlled communications with all members of the battalion currently in the field.

"You can address me as Warrant Officer Bell," Aimee said.

North laughed. There was something so genuine in the sound—a kind of rueful, weary amusement—that she turned to face him. He was studying her with an expression not unlike the one she imagined must be on her own face whenever she tried to puzzle over the mindcasting program used to engage the Remote Infantry soldiers with their robot avatars. Like she was a riddle to be solved.

"Ice cold," North said.

It was possible that she permitted herself just a hint of a smile.

"What's going on?" North asked, gesturing toward the grid of viewscreens. "Looks like they're all on the move. Crisis?"

A sarcastic barb was on the tip of her tongue. After all, if he hadn't shown up hungover and thrown up in his canister, he'd have been in Damascus with them, sharing whatever danger they might be in. But when she glanced at him and saw the worry that furrowed his brow, she found herself softening.

"Something's up," she said. "They're regrouping at the AZ. But if there's a threat, nobody over there has any idea what it is."

North nodded, then glanced up at the Command Core. "What about them? They're listening to the whole thing, tracking satellite images of Damascus right now, I'm sure. Do they have a clue?"

Aimee looked at North, but he barely noticed her now, his focus locked on the Command Core as if he could see through its walls. Something about the way he had asked the question troubled her—a sharp edge to his tone.

"I wouldn't know," she said, the frost returning to her voice. "As you can see, I'm down here watching life signs, not up there with an array of sat-links and Uncle listening to their every word."

"Come on, Aimee. We both know that if you felt like it, you could hack into whatever's going on in the core in three seconds flat."

She shot him a hard look. "If you wanted to be a part of the action today, maybe you shouldn't have—"

North laughed again, but this time all the gentle self-amusement had given way to what she'd always thought of as barroom arrogance. Like he was spoiling for a fight.

"Some people drink for courage," he drawled. "Others drink to forget what a crappy day they've had. But sometimes you gotta drink enough to step out of the world for a while. Sometimes it's either that or check out forever. Trust me, you don't wanna know why I got so shitfaced last night."

He grunted and dropped his gaze. In that moment, looking at the stubble on his chin, his furrowed brow, and the way his shoulders sank with some invisible weight, she wanted a drink herself.

Aimee exhaled, wishing he'd go away. She looked up at the view-screen grid, watching the flickering lights that showed the heartbeats of Platoon A quickening with something that wasn't quite fear. The view through the robots' eyes painted a frantic picture, glimpses of rooftops and alleys as the Tin Men hurried back to the Arrival Zone.

"Looks like it might get ugly there," North said, nodding toward the grid.

Khan left his Dragunov on the roof, wondering if he'd be alive to claim it later. He crashed through the door that led down to the street, risking a call on his phone. A plan had been put in place from the outset to deal with the possibility that the Tin Men might figure out that they were in danger and withdraw, but Khan had never imagined he would need that plan. The Americans were arrogant enough in the flesh, but the robot soldiers had nothing to fear so they never retreated or surrendered.

Has there been some leak? he wondered. *Do they know what's to come?*

It could not be. If they knew, the robots would be scouring the city for enemies, trying to stop it before zero hour.

The only possibility was one that Khan had never fully taken into account: instinct. The abandonment of Damascus had alarmed them, he'd known it would, but he had expected them to redouble their efforts instead of withdrawing. *Would they abandon the robots? Would they leave their techno-avatars empty, hollow shells?*

No, no, he thought as he pounded down the stairs toward the street. *They'd never . . . Especially now, thinking some conspiracy is unfolding, they'd never leave the robots untended.*

Then what?

He reached the street door, opened it, and glanced out, then slipped through and into an alley, faded laundry hanging from clotheslines overheard. Khan bolted to the right, hustling along the alley. He doubted the traditional white hatta he wore on his head made him any less visible on satellite imagery, but it couldn't hurt. As long as he reached his other roost—his Plan B—before anyone laid hands on him, all would be well. A second rifle awaited him there.

They're not withdrawing, he thought. *They're regrouping.*

The robots didn't know what they were up against, so the lieutenant would not want his people spread out across Damascus. He'd want them together, fighting as a unit. That made sense. Khan was glad of the number thirteen that Private Kelso had used to mark his robot shell. It would make it far easier to find him among the other Tin Men. And whoever had painted the target on the robot chassis yesterday—he'd thank them for the gift if he could.

Forcing himself not to exceed a quick walk, he hurried through a maze of alleys, avoiding the main concourse of the souq as much as possible. A pair of old women saw him and turned away. At last Khan crossed the souq and pushed through the door of an antiques shop. Old mirrors showed dusty, warped reflections of him as he hurried past.

Through a side door in the antiques shop, he found a narrow stairwell and ascended the steps at a run. At the top he came to an equally narrow door and paused to fish a set of keys out of his pocket. He slid one into the lock and then left it jutting there while he took out his phone and dialed.

Drazen answered halfway into the first ring. "You've seen them leaving?"

"I'm at the other place now," Khan carefully replied, knowing that every cellular call would be caught by satellite and filtered for words or phrases that the Americans might find troubling. "Be sure everyone makes it to the party."

Khan ended the call. Drazen was a professional; he wouldn't need more instruction than that.

Folded on a shelf by the door was a canvas that had been carefully selected for its gray hue that matched the roof of the building next to the antiques shop. Khan unfolded it and draped it over his head and shoulders like a cloak, unlocked the door, and stepped onto the roof, pushing the door closed behind him—not bothering with the key. He strode steadily across the roof to its edge, then dropped three feet to the roof of the building next door, where his canvas would be a better match. Always, always, the danger of satellite surveillance was a problem. But the time was near—he had just a few minutes, at most—and he could not allow himself to hesitate if he wanted to be sure to destroy Private Kelso—and Corporal Wade as well, if he could manage it.

Khan lay down at the edge of the roof, spreading the canvas around him. Beneath the ledge was a long rectangular bit of strange architecture that did not belong, though it was the same color as the roof. He pulled it up, feeling the texture of the wood he had painted just for this purpose, and dragged out the rifle he had hidden there the night before. Closing the hidden compartment, he laid the rifle on the edge of the roof, only the front of the weapon peeking out from beneath the canvas, and peered through the scope.

More than half the platoon had already returned to the street in front of the ruins of the Khan As'ad Pasha. Their movements were strangely human, a constant nervous energy making them twitch and shift their weight. Only in those brief moments when they were uninhabited—when one soldier extricated himself from the controls back at their German base and the other had not yet taken the reins—did they become inert, as if they were merely strange sculptures instead of an army. As long as there were pilots controlling them through the ether, the robots seemed alive.

Scanning the Tin Men, he frowned. None of their foreheads bore the number thirteen; Kelso was not among them. Corporal Wade was there with her devil's horns. Dissatisfied, he took aim at the vulnerable spot on her upper torso and settled down to wait, his finger on the trigger.

He prayed the call would not come until he had Kelso in his sights.

6

"Chopper!" Kate shouted.

"Wade, don't yell on comms," Naomi Birnbaum snapped. "This your first day?"

Somewhere back in Germany, in the canister where her body was being fed through a tube, Kate figured her cheeks must be blushing. Unless they were under fire, there was no excuse for shouting through a commlink. The rest of the platoon could hear her fine. Not only that, their onboard data displays would show the same thing hers did—a helicopter en route from the Blue Zone base. But knowing it was on the way and actually hearing it approach were two different things.

"Enough of that shit," Sergeant Morello said, moving to the center of the gathered bots. "Corcoran, Prosky, Lahiri, Eliopoulos, I want you in the chopper. Fly a search pattern, rooftops and alleys. Sing out if you see anything."

"And till then?" Hawkins asked, glancing around at the others as if to include them in his question. "We're just gonna sit here in the open and wait to get hit? 'Cause that's what this is, right? The rags have figured out a way to take us out and they're going for it. Hell, maybe they're just gonna nuke the place."

"No one's nuking Damascus, Hawkins," Lieutenant Trang said, his tone full of warning. "That kind of talk does nothing for us."

Kate shifted slightly closer to Trang. Hawkins glared at the lieutenant with his inhuman eyes and Kate knew if their bodies came equipped with laser vision, Trang would have been melted to slag.

A wind kicked up that had nothing to do with the incoming chopper. Road dust swirled around them, little tornadoes of grit that scoured the Tin Men. Kate wondered if Hawkins would push his luck with the lieutenant, but apparently he recognized that he was outnumbered because he didn't say another word. Mavrides had no such wisdom.

"This is bullshit, Lieutenant," Mavrides said. "We oughta corral some of the civilians who are still here and make them talk."

Trang stepped up to him. "And if they know nothing?"

Sergeant Morello used a metal finger to tap Mavrides's robot skull several times, hard enough to echo through comms in all their heads.

"Don't be a dumbass, kid," Morello said. "You're not really here. Nothing to be afraid of."

"I'm not—" Mavrides began to protest.

"Shut up," Hawkins snapped. He could have done it on a private channel, but he said it open comm for them all to hear.

Mavrides didn't say another word. Hawkins and the kid were on edge, amped up. They knew they were in somebody's kill zone and wanted to lash out, break bones, draw blood. Kate understood the urge; she felt it herself. But they were fools if they believed Trang had called them back to the AZ as some kind of retreat. The lieutenant was putting eyes in the air, not relying on satellite imagery. He'd regrouped the platoon in order to be ready to attack in force.

The noise of the chopper grew louder.

"Here we go," Sergeant Morello said. "Corcoran—"

"We're on it, Sarge," Corcoran said, gesturing to the other three who would be boarding the chopper with him.

"And the rest of us, sir?" Birnbaum asked.

"The situation is being analyzed back at the Hump," Lieutenant Trang said. "We await orders."

A crackle of static came over Kate's comm, a private channel being opened.

"Fantastic," Danny Kelso's voice muttered sarcastically in her ear.

Then the chopper came over the top of a row of buildings to the east and Kate looked up into the sun, her vision automatically adjusting to the scorching brightness. The rotors drowned out everything for a second as comms adapted to the noise differential.

"Where the hell are you?" Kate asked, glancing around to look for Danny as the chopper started to descend toward the street.

"A block away," he replied. "We were just taking a closer look at a couple of closed-up shops."

She found his voice in her ear comforting. Searching the square for him, head full of the whap of the chopper's rotors, she caught a glimpse of something out of place. Just a couple of inches of white piping that could have been a lot of things but that her gut told her was not any of them.

This time, she did not shout.

"Gun," she said.

Danny heard that single word in his head, spoken barely above a whisper—thanks to sound modulation, it slipped in amidst the roar of the chopper—and he began to run.

"What're you doing?" Torres called after him.

"It's happening now," Danny said.

Torres raced along thirty feet behind him but Danny didn't wait for her. He bounded into the square and took in the scene: Hartschorn climbing into the chopper after a couple of other bots, the bird already starting to rise. Trang and Morello in the middle of the square with maybe twenty-four other robots standing around, most of them with their weapons out. Mavrides leaned against a lamppost. Hawkins stood watching the chopper take off, maybe thinking he ought to have been on it. But Danny wasn't scanning for Hawkins. He was looking for a bot with devil horns painted at its temples.

Travaglini moved aside, revealing Kate behind him. In Danny's head he could hear Morello and Trang asking for clarification even as Travaglini drew his gun, shouting the same word that Kate had whispered. Side by side now, Kate and Travaglini raised their weapons with inhuman speed and took aim at a rooftop to the west.

The first of the sniper's bullets struck Kate along her side and staggered her to the left. The second bullet hit the same spot and then Danny understood what they were dealing with—what kind of skill. This fucker knew the sweet spot. The seam had been reinforced half a dozen times but the weakness there was a design flaw; it wasn't going to be cured by a patch.

The shooter couldn't kill her, of course. She was a robot. She'd wake up in Germany with a headache. But still he shouted her name and broke into a sprint, shoving a couple new guys out of the way. Inhuman speed, yeah, but not fast enough to beat a bullet.

Travaglini did it for him, grabbed Kate and shielded her, turning his back to the shooter. Then a dozen weapons were trained on the sniper, returning fire, turning the edge of the roof into a shower of rubble but with no sign of the shooter. He was rabbiting.

Danny heard Lieutenant Trang in his head. "Corcoran, do you see him?" Calling out to the bots on the chopper.

"Not yet," Corcoran replied.

They all heard it. The whole platoon listening but not waiting, scanning every damn rooftop, rushing over to investigate every strange outcropping, because where there was one there might well be another.

"Wait," Corcoran said. "I think—"

None of them would ever hear what Private Corcoran said next.

The burst of static made Danny scream, but he had no ears to protect—the sound came from inside his head. He spun around as if to find its source and saw the air ripple like the surface of the lake in front of his grandfather's cabin when the wind would kick up.

All the Tin Men were bent or crouched, trying to escape the screeching that could not be escaped.

Until it simply stopped, leaving only the thump of the chopper's rotors.

Slowing.

Stopping.

Fucking falling.

Danny stood with the other bots and watched the chopper cleave the top story off a decrepit hotel before it struck the ground. He flinched, waiting for the gas tank to go, but the chopper just crumpled. Screams rose into the air, the pilot or one of the other flesh-and-blood members of the flight crew. With a shriek of tearing metal, the door that ought to have been on the starboard side of the helicopter but was now on top shot upward and landed a dozen feet away. Robot hands grasped its frame and Prosky and the others started to climb out like spiders who'd been tipped on their backs for a moment.

Damaged, for sure, but they could be fixed.

The rocket whistled as it passed overhead. It hit the chopper, which exploded with enough force to knock the nearest bots off their feet, blacken their frames. Danny staggered back and caught Torres with his free hand, stayed upright, and found that his weapon was in his hand. He spun, saw Kate was okay, then scouted for the son of a bitch who'd fired the rocket.

He spotted the guy standing on a market roof, out in the open with his launcher as if he didn't have a care in the world. Turned out he only had one—firing off another rocket.

"Open channel," Danny snapped. "Lieutenant, check your six."

Trang stood beside Morello, the two of them talking fast. Hawkins and Mavrides were off in the southeast corner of the square, taking potshots at shadows. Two charred robots were picking themselves up off the ground near the burning wreckage of the helicopter, damaged but in motion. Travaglini and Kate were racing up to the building her shooter had used for a perch, giving chase.

Nobody seemed to have heard him.

"Bot Killers, goddamn it!" Danny screamed. "Open channel! Open fucking channel!"

The rocket hissed as it launched.

Danny saw Birnbaum pounding her skull with the palm of her hand like his grandfather had done to the old TV when Danny was very small.

Sergeant Morello must have heard the rocket screaming through the air. He turned and shoved Trang out of the way. Later, Danny would wonder if Morello regretted it at the last second, if he knew what he was sacrificing.

The rocket hit Morello dead-on. It should have damaged the robot shell, cracked it, blown off limbs at best. Instead, the explosion turned him to shrapnel. Goodbye, Sarge.

This wasn't any ordinary rocket launcher. This was something new.

"No," Danny said. Nobody heard him; nobody was close enough. "No, no, no, no!"

As he ran across the square toward the door Kate and Travaglini had just entered, he could hear the rest of the platoon shouting questions. Lieutenant Trang barked orders as he sprinted past, but Danny couldn't hear them through the commlink.

Alexa Day had been fresh out of the shower, ruminating about the friends she wouldn't see for months, when she'd heard the helicopter taking off. Wrapped in a purple towel, she had rushed to the window of the little bedroom her father had provided and craned her neck to look skyward. The window overlooked a courtyard in the center of the ambassador's residence, complete with gravel pathways and benches half-shaded by sprawling date trees but zero view of the city.

Curious, she had dressed hurriedly in denim shorts, a burgundy Harvard University T-shirt, and black high-tops; run a brush through her hair; and then padded down the hall. She found a corner window that gave her a view of the grounds but also allowed her to see down into the street on the other side of the wall. Once, her father had explained, the ambassador's residence had been the entirety of the embassy, but now it was only one corner of the city block, with a wall around it and a metal fence around that, topped with barbed wire. It had become more military base than embassy. In the courtyard, Marines hurried about on various errands. Several were surrounding a second helicopter and she wondered if it, too, would take flight.

No, she thought. *Stay here, just in case we need you.*

She furrowed her brow, studying the two guards on the wall just below the window. They were in motion, pacing quickly, scanning the horizon and peering down into the road. One of the Marines used the scope on his rifle to examine the windows of a structure across the street, with a sharpness to his movements that created a flutter in her chest.

Breathe, she told herself. *They're probably on high alert twenty-four hours a day.*

She heard a creak behind her and turned to see Baz Nissim coming up the steps. Alexa thought she might have detected a hint of disapproval in his eyes when he caught sight of her bare legs, and a flash of anger went through her. She was prepared to dress modestly when out in public in Damascus, but this was her father's house. Surely she ought to be able to do as she pleased inside these walls.

"Miss Day," Baz said. "If you'll join me in the dining room, a small meal has been prepared."

Alexa thanked him and let him lead her down the stairs and through to the dining room. There were pears and figs and berries, dried meats, bread and cheese, and a bowl of red grapes that had her mouth watering. She made a beeline toward a pitcher of water on the left side of the table, beads of moisture sweating on the glass, but she paused when she saw the single place setting.

"Mr. Nissim?" she said, turning toward him. "My father said he would join me."

He nodded only once, and his expression did not change. "He'll be along."

"Has something come up?" she asked, thinking of all of the times in her life when her father had been absent because something had *come up.* Then she pushed away her childhood resentment—here, of all places, she could forgive him his distractions if they meant keeping the people at the embassy safe.

"The telephone," Baz replied. "Just a quick briefing from the base commander."

Alexa nodded and began to pour herself a glass of water, eyeing the fat, ripe grapes. Her father was the ambassador to Syria; he must have to receive briefings all the time. She had waited this long to spend time with him—what was another few minutes?

Breaking off a small bunch of grapes, she slid into a chair and popped one into her mouth. She'd expected it to be sweet, but the grape had the sour flavor of rot and she turned from Baz to spit it into her hand. *Great,* she thought. *He already disapproves of how I dress—now he's going to think I'm a total pig.*

"I'm sorry," she said, and she felt herself blush as she turned toward him. "Just my luck to pick the one bad grape in the—"

Shouts came from elsewhere in the house and she heard heavy footfalls pounding down the hall toward the dining room. The polite smile Baz had been wearing slipped and he glanced nervously around as a tall, dark-eyed Marine swept into the room with Arthur Day following right behind him.

"Dad, what's going on?" Alexa asked.

Her father held out a hand to her. "Let's go, honey. Right now."

"Ambassador?" Baz said.

"Something's happening," he said. "The power just—"

A boom sounded, muffled by the building around them but still audible. Alexa froze, and in the silence that enveloped them all they could hear was the rattle of distant gunfire followed by another muffled boom. She turned to stare at her father, feeling suddenly very small and very young. Part of her wanted to shout at him—he had promised she would be safe—but another part wanted him to scoop her up in his arms the way he had when she was a little girl.

"Let's go," he said.

Alexa rushed to her father, took his outstretched hand, and began to run. A strange numbness enveloped her, like nothing she had ever felt before. It was as if she existed in a bubble and the rest of the world passed around her, unable to touch her. *Like a fishbowl,* she thought. She knew that fear had taken over, that a little bit of lunacy had crept into her brain, but she did not try to fight it. Lunacy felt safer than reality.

"Where are we going?" she heard herself asking.

Two Marines waited ahead, guarding an open door beyond which a darkened stairwell led downward. Several people—embassy workers, she thought—were moving through the door and down the steps. A Marine passed a flashlight to a heavyset woman in a pantsuit and she moved faster than Alexa would have expected. The bald man who had been Alexa's bodyguard on the drive from the airport ran toward them from the area at the front of the house.

"Ambassador, it's not just the power," he said. "The phones are out. My radio's not working. Robeson says the cars just died in the street, like the engines are fragged."

"Shit," one of the Marines said. "EMP. It's got to be. Whatever's happening, it's big."

Alexa did not like the way their faces all paled at this pronouncement.

"Dad?" she said, her voice far away.

"Just keep moving, honey. We'll be all right."

He went first through the door and started down the stairs, still clutching her hand as he guided her after him.

"Where are we going?" she asked, grabbing a handrail to keep from falling. Something thundered in her ears and she thought it must be more gunfire, more explosions, but then she recognized the rhythm of her own heartbeat.

Don't die, she told herself. *I don't want to die.*

"In a crisis, protocol requires the residence be sealed off from the rest of the embassy. There are only two passages from this building into the rest of the Marine installation, a side exit on the first floor and a basement tunnel. The first floor will have been sealed already— steel doors—but that's okay. Don't be afraid. The tunnel is part of the evacuation we've always planned in case of emergency."

Suddenly she felt angry, and ashamed of her fear. "It's got to be ISIL, right? Who else would go this far?"

Her heart kept pounding as they reached the bottom of the stairs, but she felt more able to breathe. A massive metal door hung open at the far end of the basement and a single Marine stood beside it, ushering and prodding them all into the tunnel beyond.

"It's never as simple as one label," her father said. "It could even just be some local jihadist group. The list of people who'd like the United States out of Syria is a mile long."

Alexa glanced at him, frowning as they entered the tunnel. Voices echoed around them, coming from the employees hurrying ahead and the handful of people bringing up the rear. Somehow she regained her clarity.

"That's not what this is, Dad."

Her father gripped her hand more tightly. "Don't worry, Alexa. I promise, this will all be over—"

"Dad, stop," she said. Blinking, she reached up to swipe at an irritation in her eyes and realized she had been crying. The knowledge made her angrier, which helped. Anger didn't eliminate her fear, but it helped compartmentalize her terror. "You can't hide what this means from me, or protect me from it. I'm not twelve years old. My father is a foreign diplomat. I know enough to know that local jihadists don't set off an electromagnetic pulse. They've burned out every circuit and engine in the city."

In the shuffling darkness, she saw the ambassador blink. "Alexa—"

"Nothing will work until it's replaced," she went on. "Millions of dollars in damages, maybe billions. People don't do that to their own city. It's not jihad. It's anarchy."

Her father looked at her as if he were seeing her—the seventeen-year-old her—for the first time. "You always were wise beyond your years. But no matter how smart you are, I'm your father. I'm still going to try to protect you."

"Fine," she said, "but don't keep me in the dark."

The ambassador nodded.

They hurried along the corridor, following the footfalls ahead and the bobbing flashlight beams. People jostled one another. There were probably emergency lights run by a backup generator, but none of that would work now.

They reached a bottleneck, where people had clustered around to pass through the metal doorway at the end of the hall. Two Marines barked at them. One had an assault rifle pointing at the floor and the other waved a flashlight back and forth as if he was signaling a plane to land. They were grim young men with determined faces and eyes alight with purpose, and immediately she felt a little bit safer.

"You amaze me, you know," her father said when they were on the other side of that door, the residence sealed off from the Marine-base portion of the embassy. They were all shuffling into a large dining hall that would apparently be their holding area for the moment.

Her father edged closer to her. His skin had flushed pink and his eyes darted around as if in search of someone who could give him answers. Alexa could see his anxiousness and confusion. He was the highest-ranking American government official on hand and had grown used to being the decision-maker, but all politics and diplomacy had evaporated with the EMP. Whatever happened now, the decisions would be military.

"I'm serious," he said quietly, bending to speak into her ear so that no one else could hear him. "Why didn't you panic? Everyone around you is panicking—me included—but you're—"

"I'm scared out of my frickin' *mind*," she said, and the admission made her voice quaver, tears welling in her eyes.

"Scared, yes," he said, nodding. "But you've got it under control."

Industrial flashlights had been set at intervals throughout the windowless room and they cast eerie shadows. How they were still working mystified her, but it wasn't like she was an expert on EMPs. Alexa glanced around at the embassy workers and the Marines who were gathered in the cafeteria, wondering what was going on upstairs. They were all terrified, but none of them knew just what it was they were supposed to fear.

"Kids I know," she said, turning toward her father and keeping her voice low, "we grew up thinking the world could blow up anytime."

Alexa wiped her eyes and then took her father's hand again, holding on tightly. "I just never expected it to be so soon."

7

No commlink.

No private channels. No open channels. No Uncle recording everything they said. No satellite uplink back to the Hump. The data in Danny's onboard display still showed ghost numbers scattered across his vision, but they were frozen. Onboard systems were still functional, but external feeds were down.

Gunfire echoed through the square. Another rocket screamed and he turned in time to see it blow apart its targets—two recent additions to Platoon A. Danny spotted the asshole with the launcher and took aim, but before he could even pull the trigger the guy staggered backward, jerking violently as bullets riddled his body. The other Tin Men had taken their vengeance. Another figure appeared on a nearby rooftop with a rocket launcher and bullets tore through him before he'd even fired. He pulled the trigger as he went down and the rocket fired wild, blowing a hole in the face of the Khan As'ad Pasha.

Danny raced toward the building that had been the original sniper's roost. He'd made it to within twenty feet of the door when Kate emerged, devil horns and all, Travaglini behind her. They had gone after the original sniper.

"Did you get him?" Danny asked.

Then he saw Kate's expression: somehow human, full of panic and confusion.

"Comms are cut off," she said.

"Completely," he agreed.

"But how?" she said, her rage tinged with fear.

"Did you see the way the chopper just cut out and fell? Somebody hit us with an EMP. Took out everything in the city. Hard EMP kill means nothing will work now. Anything electronic, anything wired . . . it's all fucked."

He rattled it off fast, trying to put the puzzle together in his head. Did a bunch of Bot Killers with guns and rocket launchers really think they could take a whole platoon of Tin Men? Even without any kind of commlink, they were trained soldiers piloting robot frames that were damned hard to destroy. These new rocket launchers might do a hell of a lot of damage, but the pricks wielding them were still human, still slow.

"Danny," Kate said, robot eyes widening in epiphany.

"We're fully shielded from an EMP," he continued, on a roll. He glanced at Travaglini. "Maybe they didn't know we were shielded. Maybe they figured the Pulse would frag our power cores—which is stupid, right? We're talking nuclear—"

"Danny!" she snapped, and whacked him in the head.

"What the hell?" he said, just about as frayed at the edges as he'd ever been.

Other voices were calling out, shouting for them to form up on the lieutenant, but Danny kept his gaze locked on Kate.

"What?" he said quietly, turning to Travaglini and then back to her again.

"Why are we *still here*?"

He flinched. Took a step back.

"Well . . . the satellites . . ."

"If the satellites were transmitting signals, we'd have communications. That means the satellites are fragged, too, which means this is a hell of a lot bigger than just Damascus."

"No, no, listen," Travaglini said, his voice an unwelcome intrusion into the space between Danny and Kate. "Something's gotta be transmitting or we wouldn't still be here. Bots are just puppets, right? If the EMP fragged whatever satellite was nearest—something in low orbit or whatever—that must've been our comms. But the signal array that lets us pilot the bots must be diverted through another . . ."

Trav glanced down at his hands, frowning as he flexed his fingers. "Anyone getting any lag time?"

Danny studied him. It could be true. Comms might operate through a different system. "So, what, we just have to wait for the planet to spin a bit so a different satellite rotates into orbit and we get comms back?"

"In theory," Travaglini said.

"I don't know," Kate muttered, shaking her head. "Why would the piloting systems and comms be separate?"

Slow horror crept into Danny's metal alloy gut, slid along his circuits, whispered inside his robot brain. The ground shook as another rocket struck the north end of the square. In the back of his mind a terrible suspicion began to take root, but he didn't have time to sort it out now.

"Fuck it," he said. "Let's go kill these assholes and worry about it later."

Kate laid down suppressing fire as they moved out from their sheltered position, but the fight seemed nearly over. No more rocket launchers, just a handful of snipers trying to keep them pinned. Hawkins and Mavrides had formed up around Lieutenant Trang, the three of them firing at a gap in the third-floor wall of a nearby building—a gap that had once been a window. Birnbaum used the smoking wreckage of the chopper for cover and took potshots at two persistent snipers who kept popping up on the roof of a sun-bleached hotel across the square.

Kate lifted her weapon, sighted, and shot one of the hotel-roof snipers. His head snapped back as the bullet punched through his skull and he flailed backward in a tangle of limbs and was lost from sight. The other one turned tail to run. Danny let off a couple of rounds but didn't have Kate's focus. His thoughts were clicking into place and he found it hard to concentrate on anything at all.

"Birnbaum!" he called. "Form on us."

In moments they were all gathering around Lieutenant Trang, and Danny did a head count. Corcoran and half a dozen others were out of commission, including the sarge. Twenty-nine left out of a platoon of thirty-six. And it would be days before they could put new bots in the field.

Twenty-eight, he reminded himself, thinking North picked a very lucky day to have a hangover. Danny intended to knock North on his ass when he made it back to the Hump.

Birnbaum hustled toward them, the stylized bird in flight painted on her robot's chest somehow very dark in the sunshine.

"What's wrong with you assholes?" she said. "Get to cover."

"No point," Private Rawlins said. "Out here we can cover all angles. We see another rocket launcher, motherfucker's dead before he can pull the trigger."

Torres glanced up at a nearby rooftop. "Better be sure of it, 'cause these new rockets are deadly. The way the sarge went out—I don't think it was just the rocket exploding. I think it caused a reaction in his power core."

"I heard a kind of whine, just for a second, right before the rocket hit him," Birnbaum put in. "You could be right."

"Forget that shit, what the hell *happened*?" Mavrides demanded. "The chopper fell out of the damn sky! My uplink's frozen, no comms—"

That started a barrage of questions and commentary. Kate, Trav, Hawkins, and Torres took up positions around the lieutenant, weapons ready as they scanned rooftops and windows.

"We've got to get cover," Birnbaum said.

Rawlins barked laughter. "And then what?"

"We go to ground, wait for the uplink to be reestablished," Hartschorn said.

"An hour or two at most before another satellite comes into range," Travaglini said. "What do we do in the meantime?"

Danny stared at Lieutenant Trang. His robot features looked smooth, as if no human intelligence lurked behind that face. The infinity symbol on his chest had become pitted and scarred, shrapnel from the destruction of Morello's bot. Trang still held his sidearm, but it dangled at his side as if he'd forgotten all about it.

Danny moved up beside him. "Lieutenant, I suggest we fall back to the embassy. Whatever this is, the people there are going to need our help."

Mavrides laughed at him. "Screw those guys. At least they're in their own bodies. I say we—"

"No one gives a shit what you think, kid," Hawkins called, still watching the rooftops, ready for a renewed assault. "You're nineteen. You follow orders."

Mavrides threw up his hands. "We don't have any fucking orders!"

Danny nodded at Hawkins, finding a new respect for the guy. Mavrides was his pal—his sidekick—but under fire, things had changed. Ted Hawkins was an asshole, but he wanted to live.

"Orders, Lieutenant?" Danny asked.

"I . . . I'm awaiting instructions," Trang replied.

"Comms are down," Travaglini said. "We can't just sit here with our thumbs up our asses. Who knows what those fucking Bot Killers are up to now, or what else is going to happen? Half of Damascus didn't skip town just for that little ambush."

"Not another word, Trav," Kate ordered.

The rest of the platoon fell silent, as if she'd been talking to all of them. With Morello dead or at least out of commission, Corporal Kate Wade had just become second in command.

The sun baked them. A plume of black smoke rose from the downed chopper. The air stagnated, barely a breeze to stir it, and in that moment the city seemed not just quiet and deserted, but dead.

"Kelso's right," Kate said. "This wasn't just an attack on us. I don't know what the fallout's gonna be in the long run from this EMP, but it'll have to wait. We head for the embassy, full-court press. Eyes on every window, door, alley, rooftop. You see anyone with a weapon, you light 'em up."

Half the platoon stared at her and the other half at Trang.

Kate turned toward him. "If that's all right with you, Lieutenant."

Trang swiveled his head slowly to look at her, a robot waking from a dream, and then glanced around at the rest of the platoon.

"You heard the corporal," he said, his voice a monotone. "Back to base."

Felix Wade stood on the balcony of his room at the Hotel Grande Bretagne and watched the city of Athens falling apart. Pillars of smoke rose from various spots and screams echoed in the streets. In the sky to the north, a jetliner careened downward in free fall, engines on fire. Felix shuddered, filled with horror more profound than any he had ever imagined. How many people on that plane? Three hundred? And he had seen others falling as well.

The airliner crashed several miles away and the whole city seemed to shake with the impact. Dust bloomed into the air as the plane brought buildings down on top of it.

In the street below, Athenian police, Greek soldiers, and the security teams of twenty different nations were shouting and arguing as they attempted to cordon off the two square blocks where the G20 summit had just been getting under way. From his seventh-floor perch, Felix could see people beyond the barricade, standing around their cars in confusion. Athens had long been a city clogged with automobiles and the smog of their exhaust, but not this morning. Not now. All the cars were at a standstill, leaving their drivers mystified and fearful.

There were no alarms. No growl of running engines. Only human voices raised in anger and terror in the face of catastrophe. They were frightened, Felix knew, because they did not understand what was happening around them. But once they understood, their terror would only deepen.

Felix had spent his life studying international affairs and attempting to help his country navigate the perilous waters of global policy. Ever since his days at the Fletcher School, he had been aware that a nightmare like this could be triggered at any time, but the world community had been able to stave off cataclysm so often that he had come to believe humanity would never allow the worst to happen. Yet here it was.

Someone pounded on the door to his hotel room. Felix took one last look at the city. He had always hoped to pass away quietly in his bed at home with a baseball game on the television, sometime shortly after celebrating his hundredth birthday. Of all the places he had thought he might die, Athens wasn't on the list.

Gunfire erupted somewhere out in the streets, and a volley of shots answered from another direction. The pounding on his door grew more insistent. Felix left the balcony and hurried to answer it.

"Professor Wade," a voice called. "Are you in there?"

He opened the door to find two Secret Service agents in the hall. Other people were out there as well, hustling one way or another, most trying to get their cell phones to work. It amazed him how slow they were to catch on. Nobody's phones would work today.

"Please come with us, Professor," said the taller of the two agents, a slim, dangerous-looking man, so pale he seemed almost made of ivory. He spoke with the cold professionalism his job required, but there could be no hiding his urgency.

"Is there a planned escape route?" Felix asked.

"Professor," said the other agent, broader and shorter, with the look of a Pacific Islander. Stone-faced, just like the ivory man.

Felix stepped into the hall and pulled the door shut. The agents started hustling him down the corridor past other closed doors. He thought he heard someone sobbing behind one.

"What did you take?" the ivory man asked.

"Take?"

"Meds," the islander said. "Something for anxiety, Professor? Or sleeping pills? You seem too calm."

"I haven't taken a blessed thing. I'm in shock. And if you're not in shock, well . . . you ought to be."

The Secret Service agents said nothing. They were trained to say nothing, but it still irritated him. On the other hand, he saw his irritation as a positive sign that his initial shock might be diminishing. Curling up into a fetal ball in the corner of the president's suite would be unproductive.

They took the darkened stairs up one floor and hurried down the hall, Felix thinking nonsensical thoughts, wondering how many presidential suites had ever had actual presidents residing in them. One of the Tin Men stood outside the suite and he rapped three times on the door when he saw them coming. The door swung open and then the two agents hustled Felix inside.

President Matheson had a glass of whiskey in one hand. He glanced up, exhaled loudly, and gave a nod.

"Good," he said. "You're all right."

"Debatable," Felix replied.

Matheson shook his head. "You're alive, and I intend to keep you that way."

Felix gave him a dubious look, still not completely in synch with reality. The world felt like a dreadful dream, but he knew it was not. He took a deep breath. "I'm glad you needed me here this morning," Felix said. "The organizer of the International Financial Architecture panel was irritated when I canceled on him. I felt guilty about it. But if you hadn't asked me to stay for the meeting with Kabinov, I'd be over at the conference center right now and it's got to be chaos—"

"Felix, *stop*." The president stared at him.

"I'm sorry."

"If you can't get your head together—"

"I will. I am. It is." Felix waved his hands. "Please continue."

President Matheson nodded again, knocked back the entire glass of whiskey, and then turned toward the windows, in front of which the other two Tin Men in his personal security detail were standing guard.

"This is happening fast and it's happening now. We have no communications," he said. "Zero."

"EMP," Felix replied. "You wouldn't—"

"I have other policy advisors along on this trip, but none of them are still inside the hotel, and my protectors here . . . well, they're not letting me leave the building just yet. So you're all the counsel I've got. You with me?"

"Yes, Mr. President."

"I don't know how widespread this is yet, but that's a long-term question. The short-term question is, what kind of danger are we in? Until we know differently, we have to assume there's more chaos to come, that every world leader at this summit is a target. There's a damn army's worth of security in the neighborhood, but I'm not taking anything for granted. As soon as we can, we're getting out of here. What's our worst-case scenario?"

Felix glanced at the two agents who'd brought him in, then back at the president. He suddenly felt like he could breathe again; his senses seemed back online. "Worst case is that this is global. We can't be certain—your Tin Men are still functional, so I don't know—"

"We're shielded, Professor," Chapel cut in. "We've been prepped for what an EMP means for us. Protecting the president is our only concern."

Felix nodded. "If this *is* global . . ." He fixed President Matheson with a dark glance. "What we're talking about is total societal breakdown."

Matheson frowned, shaking his head.

"I have a daughter, Mr. President. She lost her legs in combat and I tried to help her build a life for herself. I nearly lost her, after which all I have wished for is that I could keep her safe. When she joined the Remote Infantry Corps, it seemed like the perfect compromise, but it somehow didn't improve our rapport."

Felix cast a glance at the two Tin Men by the windows. "I guess we've never really understood each other, but over the past couple of years . . ." He took a breath and shrugged. "The point is, there's a great deal of tension and resentment there. I need to see her again, you understand? I need to make it right. I can't do that if I can't get back to her. So believe me when I tell you that I know exactly what I'm saying. And what I'm telling you is that if this is global, then the whole world has just lost power and communications and the ability to travel with anything other than their feet or a fucking bicycle."

The president stared at him. "For how long?"

Felix met his gaze firmly, though he wanted very badly to look away. "Until it can all be rebuilt. Every fried circuit is going to stay fried. They can't be repaired, only replaced, and that'll take years."

President Matheson ran his free hand over his face, covered his mouth a moment, and then swore.

"In the meantime—" Felix continued.

"Hospital patients die, refrigerated foods go bad, no new food is shipped," the president interrupted. "We could see civil unrest on a scale we can't imagine. No . . ."

"Worst case, Mr. President," Felix said, "is the twilight of human civilization. You know Yeats. 'Things fall apart; the centre cannot hold.'"

The president closed his eyes and reached up to massage the bridge of his nose. "Jesus Christ."

The tall, pale Secret Service agent cleared his throat. "It may be localized, Mr. President. There's no sign that—"

"It might be, Julian," the president replied. "But go look out the window. It's been fifteen minutes since the power went down. If this is just Athens, or even just Greece, we'd have fighter jets here in twenty-six minutes. So, another eleven minutes and we'll know how local it is. An hour, and we'll know if it's global. But I don't have a good feeling about it, and I get the idea Professor Wade doesn't, either."

Felix glanced away.

"All right, back to the worst case," President Matheson said. He gestured toward the Tin Men. "These guys are still upright. Whatever shielding they have has kept them ticking, so I'm guessing the NORAD base at Cheyenne Mountain is still operational. Maybe a few others—"

One of the Tin Men by the window took a step forward. Felix flinched—sometimes they seemed like statues, or the suits of armor that stood in the dusty corners of old castles. The robot's eyes flashed with intelligence.

"Mr. President, sir," it said, its voice identifying the soldier as male.

"Speak, Chapel. No time for protocol."

"Humphreys Deep Station One, sir. It's entirely secure, and shielded."

"What's this place?" Felix asked.

"Basically Tin Men Central," President Matheson replied. "Under Wiesbaden Airfield in Germany."

The spark of hope that had risen in Felix flared brighter. Could the one safe place for them really be the same place his daughter was stationed?

"Germany," he said, hating the hopeless plea in his voice.

"We need to get you there, Mr. President," Chapel said.

Felix tuned out the conversation that followed. The Secret Service were off and running now that he had confirmed the president's fears. He tried not to imagine the chaos outside, even as he wondered about the nineteen other world leaders who had gathered for the summit. Some of them would already have begun making accusations, pointing fingers, not realizing that blame meant nothing. All that mattered were the consequences.

Katie, he thought.

The last time they'd spoken, he told her that he wanted to be there for her and her response had been succinct: *Why start now?* The words still stung—the truth always did. Now all his regrets came back to haunt him, and his failings as a father were the worst of them.

"All right, Professor," President Matheson said, drawing Felix out of his reverie. "A couple of hours, and we're getting out of here. I'm going to make sure you see that daughter of yours. I want you to help Julian go through the hotel and gather any of our people who weren't over at the convention center when the EMP hit. Bring them up here and Agent Chapel and I will brief everyone on our exit strategy. It's almost half past nine. At eleven-thirty, we're leaving."

Felix had always known there were risks in traveling with the president, but never let himself ponder them too deeply. The temptation to hide under a bed or in a closet was strong, but this crisis wasn't going to vanish while he buried his head.

"All right," he said, turning to Julian. "Lead the way—"

The sky erupted, blowing in the windows and shaking the entire building. Felix cried out and clapped his hands over his ears as tiny glass shards showered across the room. His ears buzzed, the shouts of the Secret Service agents muffled, and he lowered his hands. The curtains blew around the two Tin Men in the room. They had blocked much of the glass and had drawn their sidearms, standing by the windows and sighting on anything moving in the street below.

Julian and the others were yelling about bombs.

"Mr. President!" Felix said, running to grab Matheson's arm. "We've got to get out of here!"

One of the Tin Men—maybe Chapel, maybe not—turned toward him. "We're not going anywhere. That wasn't here at the hotel, it was the conference center. Just stay back from the windows!"

Felix had drifted close enough to them to get a glimpse of the flaming ruin on the next block, but now he backpedaled. His shock had been abating but now it seized him completely, a terrible numbness enveloping him as he forced himself not to think of the faces of friends and colleagues who had just been incinerated inside the conference center.

President Matheson had a hand over his mouth, his eyes wide, as if he might scream. Then he shook himself, visibly gaining control.

"I thought we had shooters on the roof looking out for snipers," the president said.

"We do," Julian said. "And plenty of people and equipment scanning for bombs, but someone got those explosives in."

"So weird," Felix whispered. "Not to hear any alarms."

President Matheson gave him a curious glance. Felix wanted to tell him to listen, that he would realize all the usual city sounds had vanished. No sirens, no car alarms, no engines, no fire alarms . . . just screaming and shouting and the roar of the fire engulfing what remained of the conference center.

"Felix," the president said.

So strange, Felix thought, staring at the Tin Men. He blinked slowly. "The world isn't ending," he said. "It's already over."

The president marched over and grabbed him by the shirtfront.

"Freak out later, Felix. Right now I need you thinking, otherwise you're no damn use to me. You're a good man, but I'm not going to carry you over my shoulder to get you out of here and neither is anybody else, so you'd better wake up."

Felix shook his head to clear it. He took in the room, heard the screams as if for the first time, and held up his hands in surrender.

"I'm all right." He nodded to emphasize it. "I'll do whatever needs doing."

"Mr. President," said the other Tin Man, and for the first time Felix realized that Chapel's partner in the room was a woman. "They're coming."

"What do you mean, *they*, Bingham? Who the hell are *they*?" Matheson barked.

Outside, the shooting began. Chapel and Bingham backed away from the window, using their bodies to shield the president as Julian and the other human Secret Service agents surrounded him and began moving toward the door. Julian called Felix to come with them but he didn't need the encouragement; he was already on the move.

"What are we up against, Chapel?" Matheson snapped.

"At least a hundred, maybe double that, broken into squads, headed for this hotel and the other two," Chapel replied. "We've got sheltered positions and plenty of guns on our side down there and on the roof—as long as the Greek army and the local police don't decide they'd rather be home protecting their families."

Felix flexed the fingers of his right hand. Though he had never been in the military, he knew how to fire a gun. Even so, he'd never wanted one. Until now.

"They're coming for the G20 leaders, Mr. President," Felix said. "They're coming for you."

8

The world felt hyperreal to Kate, everything in sharp focus. She could hear the skitter of pebbles disturbed by the Tin Men's passing, the whir of hydraulics inside her. Fear was taking hold, but her greatest concern wasn't for herself. She was worried about the platoon, worried that Lieutenant Trang was losing it. His bot's eyes were still lit up, but while the others were checking alleys and windows, Trang kept his gaze straight ahead, as if nothing was left of him but the robot he inhabited.

They ran through Al Marjeh Square toward the looming headquarters of the Ministry of the Interior. Businesses and hotels lined the road, nothing at all like the souqs and markets and little shops in the older parts of the city. People were at windows and on balconies. Some had begun to explore the streets, trying to find working cars. Most appeared to be locals, but she could hear voices calling to her platoon—shouting in German and Japanese and French and English. The bot's onboard programs translated them all, but most of the cries were the same, regardless of language. *What happened? Can you help us? Is anyone coming?*

Whatever memo had gone out saying *Get the fuck out of Damascus or at least keep your head down,* the foreigners in the city hadn't received it.

Locals began to shout at them as they ran past the El Tahjh Hotel and then projectiles started flying. Bottles and chunks of masonry landed in the street, but the Tin Men were too fast; not a single object struck its target.

"Sons of bitches," Hawkins said, catching up to Kate on her right. "We oughta go back and let them take another shot. See if they're—"

Mavrides stopped, spun, and shot up the ground in front of several civilians. One of them cried out, crumpling to the ground as a bullet struck the meat of his thigh.

"What the hell?" Danny yelled.

The whole platoon came to a halt, weapons raised as the rest of the civilians began to scream at them, more rocks flying. Several ran to hide behind a taxi they had been trying to start, one of the very few vehicles that had been out on the street this morning.

"That's right!" Mavrides barked. "Have a taste—"

"Mavrides!" Kate snapped. "Don't pull that trigger again!"

The kid turned toward her, the ace of spades painted on his forehead shining in the sun. "Not planning to. Just quelling some agitators."

Kate stared at him. "No more firing unless you're fired upon. That's a direct order."

Mavrides laughed, the sound hollow and metallic. Laughter never sounded natural coming from a robot's mouth, even if it was supposed to be a perfect re-creation of the pilot's voice.

"It's the Stone Age, bitch," Mavrides said. "Orders don't mean much anymore."

Kate stepped up and shot him in the head. The bullet ricocheted off toward the front of a department store, breaking a window, and she instantly regretted it. She'd kill civilians herself if she wasn't careful. The people who'd been screaming at them and hurling bottles thought better of it and retreated to cover, except for two young men who shouted profanities from behind the dead taxi. The cries for help from the hotel had gone silent.

"Got your attention?" she asked. "You shoot another civilian and I'll shove a grenade up your ass and turn you into shrapnel."

Mavrides scoffed.

The lieutenant only stood there, hanging his head. Hot wind blew along the street. Somewhere close by a baby was crying and its angry wail seemed to come from every direction.

"Lieutenant?" Birnbaum ventured.

Trang glanced around, then locked eyes on Mavrides. "Private Mavrides, we may be well and truly screwed," Lieutenant Trang said. "We've only got conjecture so far—"

"What the hell is 'conjecture'?" Mavrides snarled.

"Guessing," Birnbaum replied. "We're fucking guessing."

"The point," Lieutenant Trang said, "is that all is going to be well. You have received a direct order from a superior officer. You do not want to disobey that order. In time, this situation will be resolved. Order will be restored. I promise you that if you don't toe the line now, you will be well and truly fucked later."

Trang stared at Mavrides another few seconds, then turned on his heel and called them to fall in. "Kelso, take point. Corporal Wade, with Sergeant Morello out of commission, I'm naming you acting sergeant," he said. "With me, please."

"Yes, sir," she replied, rushing to catch up, ignoring the strange looks the rest of the platoon gave Trang just as she was ignoring the faces in the windows all around them.

Danny led the way. Travaglini held back, covering their six. Normally Hawkins would have been guarding their flank, but he stayed with Mavrides, the two of them slightly off to the left, talking with each other as the entire platoon began once again to run. Hawkins gave Mavrides a small shove and the younger soldier fell in beside him like a dog coming to heel.

"Sir, I—" Kate began.

"I worry about my wife," Lieutenant Trang said quietly, though loudly enough for Kelso and Janisch and McKelvie and a handful of others to hear. "I wonder what she'll do with my body."

Kate glanced worriedly at him. The guy was coming totally unraveled. "Comms will be up soon, Lieutenant. The second another satellite comes into range, we'll get our orders—"

"The systems at the Hump will keep my body alive," Trang went on, interrupting her. "I guess it could last awhile like that—empty, I mean—but I hope they declare us dead quickly. Otherwise it would be hell for her, with my body there, heart still beating, but just empty."

"Jesus," McKelvie said, catching Trang's panic. "My kids . . ."

"If I'd known," Janisch added, "there's no way I would've—"

"Stop," Kate snapped. As they hustled along Al Jalaa, in sight of the Egyptian embassy, the two of them glared at her. That hyperreality persisted, as if all Kate's senses had been amplified, and she caught every detail of their expressions as she glared back. "You'll see them again. Just focus on right now. We protect the embassy and we wait for comms to be restored."

Kate glanced at Trang but he chose not to reply. Running, enjoying the way her robot legs moved beneath her and the agility and speed of her body, she told herself that he was wrong. It was something she needed to believe.

Someone grunted and swore as pottery shattered. Kate spun in time to see the remains of a potted plant spilling to the street, dirt raining down from Rawlins's head.

"Son of a bitch!" Rawlins said, backing up, gun pointed upward.

They formed a rough circle, backs toward one another, and scanned the rooftops and upper windows. Anyone could have thrown the pot—a grandmother, a kid, any Syrian who thought the Americans had outstayed their welcome—and Kate figured that would be most of them. Plenty of locals had seemed relieved when the Tin Men had been deployed to put an end to the civil strife tearing the city and the country apart, but she knew the longer they had stayed, the more it must have felt like an occupation instead of a helping hand. And now . . .

She narrowed her eyes, heard the zippy little sound it made when the transparent sun-filters that passed for eyelids came down, and her vision telescoped, giving her a close-up of the roof of a small apartment building. Had she seen something move there, or was it just the flap of the bleached white laundry on the clothesline?

"They blame us," Danny said, turning to face the others.

Kate stared at him, ignoring the useless Trang. He hadn't even raised the barrel of his weapon.

"You're saying they think *we* set off the EMP?" McKelvie asked.

One of the others—new tin, a private Kate had barely spoken to—gave a mirthless laugh. "If you were them, wouldn't you think Americans did this? Or our allies?"

Hartschorn started walking again, slowly at first. "Can you be sure we didn't?"

Something moved on the apartment-house roof. Torres spun and fired, putting two bullets through a flapping bedsheet.

They all hesitated, scanning the roofs for enemies.

"Move out," Kate snapped, not waiting for Trang.

As they picked up speed, Kate saw the occasional frightened face at a window, saw a mangy yellow cat slip behind a dead moped, and all she wanted was to get to the embassy as swiftly as possible. If anyone wanted to take shots at them—potted plants or shoulder rockets—she didn't give a damn.

"You're doing fine," Danny said, easing up beside her. "*You* hold it together, and *we'll* hold it together."

At his words, the hyperreality subsided a little. She knew it then: as long as she had Danny, she could get through this. She didn't know why he suddenly seemed so important to her—their flirtations didn't explain the bond—but she knew that she needed him.

More gunfire erupted somewhere in the city. At first, none of them paid it much attention—in a city with so many guns, with chaos unfolding, it was surely only the beginning—but then there came several more quick volleys.

"Sarge," Hawkins said, quickly approaching her. "That's coming from the northeast. I think it's—"

"The embassy," Danny finished.

Two small explosions punctured the morning sky.

"This is it," Kate called, hating the tinny buzz of her own voice. "Go, go, go!"

Nobody looked to Trang for orders. The lieutenant had folded his tent and they all knew it. Hawkins, of all people, had called her Sarge, since Trang had made her acting sergeant. But Trang ran by her side, weapon ready, and they all moved ahead.

Danny took point, the city a blur as he raced to the end of the street and peered around the corner. He'd expected some kind of organized assault, but the men gathered outside the embassy were not Syrian army, nor were they any sort of revolutionary force. He gauged the crowd of insurgents at more than two hundred, bearded men ranging from seventeen to seventy. Some wore keffiyeh scarves but most did not. They shook guns in the air, shouting for the murder of the ambassador, and then breaking into a chant: "USA *out*! USA *out*!"

He had seen this kind of gathering before and knew there would be jihadists in the crowd, calling for holy war against the Americans. But the past decade had exposed a shift in terrorist violence. Jihadists were dangerous, but anarchists were worse. The modern anarchist movement had begun with Internet hackers wreaking havoc and exposing government secrets, but the movement had spread and deepened and grown more violent—especially in response to the Tin Men. Still, most of the protestors were likely to be ordinary locals, pissed off and afraid. They were panicked, and Danny couldn't really blame them.

Windows in the ambassador's residence had been shattered and part of one wall had been blown out and blackened—the explosions they'd heard, probably grenades. The ambassador and his staff would have evacuated into the main part of the base compound at the first sign of trouble, but he saw figures moving about inside the ambassador's residence. It had been breached.

Men clung to the white wrought-iron fence around the embassy wall. Sentries fired warning shots from guard towers, but some of the people began to climb toward the barbed wire at the top. A beast of a man on the ground passed a pair of bolt cutters up to a smaller man already on the fence, who handed them off to a skinny young guy who had made it nearly to the top. He lifted the bolt cutters and a sentry opened fire. The skinny guy jerked as the bullets struck him and then he tumbled backward into the crowd, bolt cutters falling among them.

Danny glanced over his shoulder at the rest of the platoon. They had spread out into two squads, one on either side of the street. They could have split up, come into the intersection from two different angles, caught the crowd in a crossfire, but when the Tin Men went into a demonstration like this, the object was to draw fire and then disperse the anarchists. To make themselves targets.

He nodded at Kate and Trang. The lieutenant raised a hand and gestured for them to move out. As one, the Tin Men rushed into the intersection. Kate slid over to lead the second squad, leaving the first to Trang, but Danny knew to stay with the lieutenant.

"Do not fire unless there is an imminent threat!" Trang ordered.

Standard protocol, but the violence had already begun on the fence around the embassy. It was too late for protocol.

Only a second or two passed before the crowd saw the Tin Men coming. Shouts broke up the chanting and people turned. Those with guns took aim at the robots. One of the Marines on the wall cheered and threw his fist in the air and was shot in the throat by a protestor. The bullet spun him into a pirouette and he spilled off the wall, tumbling across the fence and into the crowd.

Hawkins and Mavrides were the first of the Tin Men to open fire. Onboard targeting systems let them pick their shots with perfect accuracy and one by one the men carrying rifles began to go down.

A bullet dinged off Danny's left temple, knocking his head to the side. He took aim, his sighting computer automatically sensing his intent, and his targeting system found the shooter, a burly man with a thick beard and a keffiyeh on his head. Running into the intersection with the rest of his squad, Danny sighted and fired without breaking step and the bullet hit the bearish man dead center.

The Tin Men formed a semicircle and marched across the intersection, closing the distance between themselves and the crowd, creating a dragnet. Mavrides shot two more, and the crowd began to break. Groups of three and four peeled off and fled. Only the ones who had no interest in surviving would stand and face a platoon of Tin Men. The sentries on the embassy wall shot two more climbers, who toppled from the fence into the dwindling crowd.

Kate dropped back a few feet and crossed toward Danny and Lieutenant Trang.

"Don't surround them," she called, now at the center of the semicircle. "Just drive them away."

Danny signaled in the affirmative but glanced at Trang to see if he'd countermand the order. The lieutenant barely seemed to have heard it. Abruptly, the gunfire and shouting in front of the embassy was drowned out by the scream of a rocket. Danny turned in time to see the rocket streak toward Janisch. A tiny sliver of a second passed between impact and blast—*chain reaction,* he thought, before the explosion threw him across the pavement with a clatter. His audio sensors muffled the blast, but he felt an impact against his back—a piece of Janisch's carapace that had struck him. Had Danny been flesh and blood, it would have killed him.

Bot Killers, he thought. *Sons of bitches.*

He leaped to his feet as more specialized rockets streaked down from the roofs of nearby buildings. Hartschorn dodged and one hit the pavement, the blast hurling him through the air. Kasturi took a rocket to the face that blew her head off and cracked her chest plate open—no core explosion, but destroyed just the same. Jones opened fire, strafing the roof of a furniture store, and a rocket struck him in the back and sent shrapnel slicing through half a dozen civilians who had resisted being herded. Now, at last, they ran.

In seconds, all hell had broken loose. The anarchists were fleeing, but they had gotten what they wanted.

"Bastards," Kate snarled. "They knew we'd head to base. Fuckin' planned this. Two ambushes, you've gotta be—"

Bullets pinged off Danny's shoulder and skull. He tracked the angle and spun, targeting system sighting on the shooter, who knelt on the corner of an office building's roof. Another crouched beside him, raising a rocket launcher. For half a second, he thought himself the target, but then he heard Kate behind him, shouting at the rest of the platoon to get inside the buildings, to take the fight to the Bot Killers, and he knew the bastard was aiming for her.

Danny took him out with one shot, and Hawkins killed the sniper who'd been taking potshots.

A bullet knocked Danny backward, the gunshot lost amidst the cacophony of explosions and other gunfire. He frowned, weapon extended, targeting system scanning the rooftop in search of the shooter. A second bullet hit him and he heard a tiny sound that made him think of glass cracking.

A bot tackled him to the ground. He thought it was Kate until he saw the smiley face and crossbones and realized Hawkins had just saved his life. The shooter had hit the sweet spot along the seam on Danny's carapace, twice. *Has to be the same one who shot at Kate,* he thought. *Couldn't be two of them that good.*

"Where's the shooter?" Danny barked. "I scanned the roof."

Hawkins rose to a crouch, shoulder turned toward the unseen sniper. Mavrides and Rawlins had retreated behind a white box truck twenty yards back the way they'd come, but Kate stood exposed in the street.

"There!" she called, pointing at the office building. "Third-floor window."

Danny turned to scan it and another bullet struck him, only inches away from the sweet spot. That cracking-glass sound came again, but the shot had been off. Danny saw him now, nothing more than the top of his dark-haired head and the barrel of his rifle jutting from the open window, but he'd marked him. The sniper had not finished the job, and Danny had no intention of giving him another chance.

"I've got him," he called.

The gunfire continued in the intersection. Another rocket exploded—maybe killing another member of the platoon, maybe not—and he knew the Bot Killers were on the run again, scurrying like rats, possibly retreating to launch a third ambush on the platoon later.

Not this guy, Danny thought.

He left the others behind, running full-out toward the façade of the office building. The Bot Killers knew what they were up against—they knew they were risking their lives and by his count at least ten of them had paid that price—but this guy had an agenda. He could have used a rocket launcher, but instead he'd chosen a rifle, as if his skill was more important to him than certainty. Or just to show he was *that* certain of his talents. And he could have gone after any of them, but he had targeted Danny and Kate.

Yeah, no question. Asshole had an agenda. Danny didn't care what it was—he just wanted to kill the guy with his own rifle—but the world was falling apart and these bastards had been waiting for their cue, which meant they had known it was coming. Whatever information they had, Danny intended to get it.

Full tilt, once they got going, Remote Infantry units could do seventy-five miles per hour on foot. Danny didn't have the room to get up to that speed, but he hit the front of the office building at what he figured was thirty miles per hour or better. With a leap, he crashed through a massive section of plate glass and broken shards of it showered around him as he landed on the carpet inside.

He hadn't had time for the door.

9

Hanif Khan tossed his rifle aside as he ran from the room, heart thundering in his chest. He had destroyed Tin Men with a rifle in the past, put three bullets into the weak spot in their armor and ruptured their power cores. It had been a matter of pride, and now he cursed himself for it. Today he had managed to blow two carefully arranged opportunities to take out both Thirteen and the Devil.

Now he ran.

Khan and Drazen, his second, had planned the first and second assaults thinking that between the two ambushes they would be able to destroy most if not all of the platoon stationed in Damascus, but from the moment he had learned the truth about the robots—and what the EMP would do to them—Khan's only real goal had been to kill Kelso and Wade. Now he felt ashamed. His brother, Omed, had died at their hands, but Thirteen and the Devil still lived. Killing them remained his only goal.

Live, he thought. *Live to give them each the third bullet.*

He dashed from the room and into the corridor, footsteps too loud. Kelso had breached the building. Khan could hear him crashing about downstairs. With the sensors built into the Tin Men, Kelso would be hearing Khan's every step, tracking him. Sweat ran down the back of his neck and beaded on his forehead as he burst through the stairwell door and started upward.

Khan swore as he rounded the landing that led to the roof. Gunther and Arun had been up there, likely dead by now. He had known that many of his people would die today, and it had not troubled him. Some were anarchists and some terrorists and some merely mercenaries, but they all knew the risk.

He had been shocked when his employers had revealed their plans to him, but he had covered it well. If he had objected they would have killed him. And what did he care, really? What did the end of modern civilization mean to him?

Khan heard Kelso crash into the stairwell far below, heard the clatter of the robot as he raced up the stairs so much faster than any human could have moved. He had left the door propped open with a cinder block. As he hurtled out into the sunshine of the roof he shoved the block aside and the heavy door clanged shut. The sky blazed a vivid, cloudless blue and a hot breeze seared his skin. An idyllic day, full of bullets and bloodshed.

Crouched low, Khan darted across the broad roof, toward the housing for the building's rear stairwell. That door also stood propped open. Would Kelso listen to the pounding of his boots and try to anticipate him and cut him off when he descended, or would he fear that Khan had another route off the roof to a neighboring building?

He reached the rear door and shoved the cinder block away with the heel of his boot. From behind him came the crump of twisting metal and a grinding shriek as the door in the other housing—which he'd closed only moments before—tore from its hinges. Khan spun to see the robot emerge onto the roof, saw the target painted on Kelso's abdomen, the number thirteen on his forehead, and a fresh wave of hatred flooded his heart. He thought of the dull look in Omed's eyes and the way the Tin Men had just stood around while a dog pissed on his corpse.

Khan wanted to stay. To kill. But his hands were flesh and bone and he was unarmed . . . for the moment.

"Who the hell are you?" the robot shouted in its artificial voice.

Khan slammed the door hard enough to shake its entire housing. He descended the steps two at a time and then leaped to the first landing, knowing Kelso would be right behind him. As he turned, getting his bearings, a robot fist punched through the metal door, reaching for the knob on the inside.

A long, thin wire ran from the base of the door down the stairwell, over the railing, down to the entrance to the third-floor hallway. Dangling from the wire was a black box with a red plastic button on it. Khan hurled himself down from the turn in the stairwell to the third-floor landing, grabbed the black box, and pressed the button.

The explosion blew him through the propped-open third-floor hallway door and into the opposite wall. The impact knocked the air out of him as plaster rained from the ceiling and dust blew down the stairs. His eardrums throbbed and his vision went foggy for a second, but then he wheezed in a painful breath and crawled to his feet. He had lined the roof access door with explosives, but he couldn't afford to be complacent. Even if he'd blown Kelso apart, Kate Wade and the surviving members of their platoon were still out on the street.

He wished he could be sure Kelso was dead, but he couldn't afford to check.

Don't worry, he thought. *If he's alive, you'll know it.*

Staggering at first, he made his way down the corridor, passing office doors and frosted glass partitions that had been cracked or shattered by the explosion. The sound of his own breathing too loud inside his head, he ran to the bank of elevators. Glass crunched under his boots. The elevators were frozen, but he forced open the doors of the one on the left. He had disabled it earlier that morning, before the EMP, so that when the power went out it remained on the basement level. Now he tore off his keffiyeh and reached into the yawning shaft to wrap the black and white fabric around the elevator cable.

The clank of robot footsteps came from down the hall.

Khan glanced that way and caught a glimpse of Kelso. His carapace had been slightly charred and he was missing his left hand, the one he had punched through the door, but otherwise he was unharmed.

"Should've planted the charges on the outside," Kelso said, stalking toward the elevator bank. "You blew the door right at me, saved my ass."

Khan had never seen hatred in the eyes of a robot before; in that moment, it looked almost human. He jumped into the elevator shaft, hands gripping the cloth-wrapped cable, and began to slide. The roof hatch on the elevator was below.

Through the hatch, out the jammed-open elevator doors, and into the building's basement, then out through a rear loading bay, and then the sewers. He had planned his escape route for days—every step—never truly believing he would be able to use it.

Kelso did not bother with the cable. The robot leaped into the elevator shaft and plummeted downward, letting out a cry of anger. As he fell he grabbed hold of Khan with his remaining hand. Khan lost his grip, his keffiyeh fluttering above him as he flailed in the robot's grasp, and they hit the roof of the elevator together. Kelso broke the fall, but the impact sent spikes of pain through Khan. His chest burned as he drew a breath. He rolled off the robot and felt grinding in his rib cage. Something had cracked inside him.

The robot shot out a hand and grabbed him by the throat. Khan grunted and tried to beat at its arm. Kelso shoved him down through the open hatch on top of the elevator and Khan pinwheeled his arms as he fell. When he hit the ground, the pain of his cracked ribs stabbed so sharply that he hissed in a breath and then cried out, unashamed. Pain was pain, he would not deny it.

Kelso dropped beside him, crouched over him like a spider. The robot grabbed his throat, propping himself up on the metal alloy stump of his left hand.

"You are going to die," Kelso said.

Khan said nothing. Yet as Kelso squeezed his throat, cutting off his air, still he fought. He might have expected to die, but that was not the same as being willing. As the pure need for air burned in his chest and his eyes bulged and his brain felt as if it was swelling, pushing against the inside of his skull, Khan beat at the robot's arms and face. Its eyes glowed. *Power,* he thought. Technology and energy drove this thing; they were the most effective of all weapons. They were the tools of domination.

As the blackness flooded in at the edges of his vision and all the strength fled his limbs, Khan at last understood the philosophy of the anarchists. Take away all modern contrivances and what remained— first and foremost—was equality.

Robots, he thought, with all the venom his fading mind could muster.

And then . . .

Omed.

The darkness swallowed him.

Aimee Bell stood at her monitoring station and stared at the dozens of screens, large and small, arrayed before her. They should have been full of washed-out buildings and dusty streets, everything from high-class hotels to riotously colorful marketplaces. Instead, every screen showed pure blue. A low hum emitted from the monitors, which glitched now and again, a little fritz of static that made it clear they were still open for a signal.

No signal seemed forthcoming.

She barely noticed the rustle of clothing and heavy footfalls that should have signaled another soldier's arrival.

"Bell."

Startled, Aimee flinched and then turned to find Security Officer Ken Wheeler standing six feet away. Buzz-cut, blond, blue-eyed, and built like a freight train, Kenny Wheeler had always looked to her like a superhero out of costume.

Numb, she stared at him.

Wheeler cocked his head and frowned oddly at her. "Chief Schuler wants you at Command Core immediately."

The words did not make sense to her. "You left your post."

Wheeler frowned. "What?"

"You left—"

"No, Bell, I heard what you said. All comms are down. We're on backup power and all external instruments are apparently fried. Until all of this shit gets repaired, I don't have a post and neither do you. The chief warrant officer has asked you to report to Command Core. Are you—"

"Yes," she said quietly, glancing at the glitchy blue screens at her station—the screens where she ought to have seen the members of Platoon A, Sixth Battalion in action. "Yeah, I'm coming."

Wheeler turned on his heel and started off, boots squeaking on the industrial rubberized floor. Aimee followed, glancing around as if she were Alice, freshly awakened in Wonderland. So many blue screens, all doing that same glitchy frizz. Warrant officers and other techs were at computer monitors, harvesting information through self-diagnostics. Up on the catwalk that radiated outward toward the Staging Areas where the entire morning shift—nearly a thousand soldiers—lay inside their Remote Combat Stations like coma patients, inert.

A shudder went through her. She didn't want to think about the soldiers, especially those from Platoon A. That morning, Ernie Travaglini had been wearing a T-shirt trumpeting a band called Bewilderbeast. Not the kind of music she'd have listened to in a million years, but Trav apparently liked them and it hadn't occurred to her to ask why. Maybe she would learn to appreciate the music through someone else's perspective. Even if all she'd accomplished was to get to know Trav better . . .

It made her want to weep to think of how many questions she would never get to ask, how many people she would never get to know better.

The whole control center buzzed with activity, people rebooting systems and shutting down alarms. Lights flickered, a little fritz just like the glitch on the viewscreens. Cold, clipped voices filled the heavy air of Humphreys Deep Station One, nobody truly frantic just yet. At least not outwardly.

She knew that would change. Frantic-ville was just around the corner. The duty officers and the CO weren't panicked yet because they didn't understand the technology enough to really be freaking out. But they would.

Wheeler hurried to the Command Core and Aimee kept pace,

feeling his urgency. There were hundreds of soldiers on duty in the Hump right now—including dozens of warrant officers—what did Chief Schuler want with her?

As they hustled up the slatted metal steps, Aimee felt like she couldn't breathe. Her best friend, Sarah, had just given birth to a daughter—her first child—and Aimee had agreed to be the godmother. Her brother was in college in New York. The instant the system had crashed and they'd lost comms, she had put up a little wall inside her mind, trying her best not to think of the people she loved and what might be happening to them. Her first duty was to her post and that meant following orders.

A soldier opened the door for them and stood back while Aimee and Wheeler entered the Command Core. If the control room was like a spider's web of information, then this chamber had to be the spider, an octagonal room on a raised platform with windows that looked out over the entire operation. To her left, she could see her own abandoned monitoring station, fifty yards away.

Small flickering blue screens lined the lower half of the chamber, interrupted only by three computer monitoring stations that seemed to be spilling data so fast they blurred. A pair of officers and three techs were examining the computers. An image popped up on one of them but before she could feel even a dash of hope, Aimee realized what she saw was a recording of activity inside the control room before the shutdown.

A circular conference table occupied the center of the room and half a dozen officers sat around it. Aimee recognized only three of them, but she noted the rank of each one. The Hump's commanding officer was Colonel Dafna Koines, but the colonel had been off base this morning. Chief Warrant Officer Schuler sat beside Captain Annette Cameron, but it seemed to Aimee that Major Eli Zander was the acting CO, unless and until Colonel Koines returned.

Great, Aimee thought.

Major Zander had never so much as glanced at her, but irritation seemed to flow in his wake whenever he entered a room. Just past fifty, judging by the whispers she'd heard on his birthday last month, the puffy-faced, flinty-eyed major had the features of a man who loved whiskey more than he loved himself, a 1940s film star gone partway to seed. Still, whatever his private issues, Eli Zander brought nothing but stone cold professionalism to his duties.

"Warrant Officer Bell, sir," Wheeler announced.

"I can see that," Major Zander said.

Aimee stood at attention. Those working at the computer stations ignored her arrival, but the men and women at the table ceased all conversation and turned to study her as if she were a dubious suitor, come to take one of their sons or daughters to the prom.

"Bell," Major Zander said, as if getting a taste for the name.

"Yes, sir."

Major Zander's eyes were steel gray, full of clouds just before a rain. "You understand what's happened here, Bell?"

"EMP, sir."

The major nodded, then tilted his head to indicate the techs and officers working at the computer stations. "We've got no communication with the outside world, Warrant Officer Bell. The Hump is shielded well enough that all of our backup systems are intact. We're self-sustaining. Could be everything's all right topside except for the effects of the EMP, but—"

"You don't think it's nuclear, sir?" Aimee interrupted. The explosion of a nuclear warhead would emit an electromagnetic pulse.

Major Zander knitted his brow. He clearly did not like to be interrupted.

"We haven't detected any radiation spike, but who's to say what's working properly and what isn't?"

Aimee exhaled in relief. "We're shielded from radiation, sir, but even if external sensors are fragged, the sensors just inside the doors would pick up a slight rise in radiation. If you haven't seen anything like—"

"Bell," Major Zander said sharply.

She stood even straighter. "Sir."

"Let me tell you what we *do* have," he said. "We've got the audio and video from every camera feed from every robot in the field.

We've got the data readings from all of our instruments at the Hump and topside at the airfield, everything leading up to and including the moment of the Pulse. These folks are sifting that data to see if we can't figure out how big a deal this is, who did it, and why. I want you to help them."

Aimee frowned. "Yes, sir, but, if I may . . ."

"I don't seem able to stop you."

"Why me, sir?"

One of the officers at the table wore an expression that suggested she had been wondering the same thing.

Major Zander frowned. "Chief Schuler told me that you were by far the most talented and most creative tech at the Hump."

Aimee blinked in surprise. "Oh."

The major glanced at Chief Schuler. "So far, I haven't seen anything to persuade me that his faith is well placed," he said, then turned back to stare at Aimee. "Why don't you set about convincing me?"

"Sir, yes sir."

Khan lay in a gray mist. He could hear voices around him but felt nothing, not even the weight of his own flesh. It seemed almost as if he were floating, as if his spirit had left the cage of his body behind and drifted now, merely a phantom.

The voices spoke in English. Some of them had the tinny artificiality of robot voices. *I'll haunt them,* he thought. *They will never be rid of me.*

"His eyes are open," one of the voices said. A human voice. American.

"They've been like that for half an hour," a robot replied.

Khan remembered that voice. *Danny Kelso.*

A groan escaped his lips and he took a deep, shuddering breath as he swam up from the depths of consciousness and broke the surface. The weight of his body returned and with it came the pain, as if it had been dropped down on him from above. His jaw tightened and he hissed air through his teeth.

His ribs. Something definitely fractured in there.

But he was alive and he could breathe. If he'd punctured a lung he'd likely have died already.

How long was I out? he wondered.

His eyes opened not to a world of gray mist but to a cell of gray walls. Danny Kelso sat there, robot face serene. Much of the char had been washed from his carapace but it pleased Khan to see the delicate mechanisms jutting from the stump where his left hand had been.

There were two other robots in the room—one with devil horns and the other with an infinity symbol on his forehead—and Khan knew them both. Kate Wade and her lieutenant ... what was his name? Trang. Along with them were two U.S. soldiers obviously posted as guards and an officer with captain's bars on his uniform.

"Nah, look at him," Wade said. "He's awake."

They all turned to stare at him. Khan just returned the glare. So they had him? What would it earn them? Nothing. He could not turn the power back on. Anything he told them would not aid them in their efforts to survive the chaos that must already be spreading. The only things left in this world that Khan could do were to kill his enemies or be killed by them.

He wondered how many of his own people had survived. And how long it would be before they launched another attack. If Drazen had survived, it would be soon. The mercenaries might abandon the fight, but the rest of the Bot Killers each had their own reasons for wanting to kill Tin Men.

Kelso and Wade had made him their prisoner, but all they had really managed to do was to bring Death under their own roof.

Hanif Khan smiled through his pain.

Aimee stood in the Command Core, back against the computer array, and stared at the officers gathered around the circular conference table. Out beyond the windows, the control room remained a beehive of activity, as techs attempted to get some of the external sensors functioning without actually going outside. They had succeeded in getting signals from some of the topside cameras because they worked like telescopes, with all of the electrical parts underground and shielded, but even those were frozen in place, giving only a sliver image of the outside world.

Important work, she knew. But any answers they might hope for would be coming out of the Command Core.

With Major Zander, Chief Schuler, and the others all staring at her, her memory flashed back to the fourth grade, when Joey Hoffman had wet his pants during the spelling bee.

Great, she thought. *Now I have to pee.*

"All right, Warrant Officer Bell," Chief Schuler said. "Tell them what you've got."

"We've pinpointed a massive energy fluctuation just before the EMP . . ."

Major Zander shot Schuler a dubious glance, as if to say, *This is the smartest tech you've got?*

"Of course, that's to be expected," Aimee hurried on. "But we're not just talking about a surge. Prior to the Pulse, our instruments recorded a significant weakening in nineteen specific satellite signals—call it a drag—for a duration of three-point-seven seconds leading up to the surge."

Her heart thudded in her chest. She wet her lips and shifted her weight, trying to remain at perfect attention. Aimee had grown up with a theater-geek brother but had never been able to get over her own stage fright.

"You're nervous, Warrant Officer Bell," one of the other officers said.

"Yes, ma'am."

"What do you have to be nervous about?"

Aimee stared at the window opposite her position, not truly seeing anything. "I don't like being the center of attention, ma'am. I don't even sing in the shower."

Captain Cameron leaned back in her chair, one finger tapping anxiously at the edge of the table. "So this *drag,* as you call it . . . how is that anything? All comms signals experience high-traffic slow-downs. And not just comms. Video freezes all the time, same way it did when I was in high school."

"Yes, ma'am." Aimee gave Cameron a nod. "We took that into consideration. This far exceeded any typical lag. The only way I can read it is as a drain on the satellites themselves—and the surge we recorded originated with those same nineteen."

The only change in Major Zander's expression was a slight narrowing of his eyes. Their gray hue seemed to turn darker.

"You think the EMP came from those satellites," the major said.

"Yes, sir. That is, I *know* it did."

Captain Cameron ceased drumming her fingers on the table. One of the other officers swore. Kenny Wheeler and the rest of the soldiers and techs in the room just stared at her.

Chief Schuler massaged the bridge of his nose, maybe fighting a headache. *Worst headache of his life,* Aimee thought. *Never going away.*

"What can you tell us about them, Warrant Officer Bell?" the major asked, and she felt pretty sure there was a bit of a *good job, kid* in there. Which she needed. She wanted to cry or beat the hell out of someone or both, just to settle her nerves.

"All nineteen satellites were built within the past eight years," she said. "All of them were constructed and launched by the Monteforte Corporation."

Captain Cameron scoffed.

Major Zander shot her an appraising look. "Yes?"

Cameron shook her head. "Sorry, Major. There's no way the Monteforte people are behind this. They're in business, and if this is as bad as we think it is, their business has been destroyed along with everything else."

Stung, Aimee lifted her chin, trying to maintain some dignity without looking too pissed off. "Ma'am, the data doesn't lie."

"You're saying—" Captain Cameron began.

"She's not saying the corporation, Captain," Major Zander interrupted. "The board of directors doesn't build those satellites. Hundreds of people are part of the process of manufacturing those satellites and putting them in orbit and they all have access."

"So now we know," said the lieutenant beside Cameron, a lanky black man with high cheekbones and a shaved head. "How does that help us?"

Major Zander stared at the smooth surface of the table. "It doesn't."

Cameron flinched. "You're saying we just sit here?"

"You want to try your luck outside?" the major said quietly. "As soon as people realize the machines aren't coming back online any-time soon . . ."

Major Zander didn't finish the statement. They could all imagine the fallout.

"Anything else, Bell?" Chief Schuler asked, almost hopeful. She could read his eyes. *Tell us there's a way to reboot. Give us some hope.*

"No, sir."

CHRISTOPHER GOLDEN

10

The officer in charge of the U.S. Marine Corps detachment stationed at the embassy in Damascus was a square-jawed captain named Bartleby Finch. He'd started to go gray as a young man and now the contrast with his dark skin made him appear much older than he actually was. The illusion of age went well with his general demeanor, which was so cantankerous on the best of days that it seemed only slightly crankier on this, the very worst of days.

"Where do we stand?" Finch asked in his Texas drawl.

Danny looked at him, wondering how the guy stayed so calm. He told himself it was all a front, that inside, Finch was running around in circles, screaming, just like the rest of them.

He flexed the fingers of his new hand, trying it out. Birnbaum had taken it off the robot that North usually piloted, which stood in a corner inside the muster room by the barracks. Of the two techs, Birnbaum seemed the more skilled, and Danny had watched in fascination as she had taken out her tool kit and grafted the hand on for him. It seemed somehow ghoulish.

"We've doubled the sentries on the wall and supplemented them with some of the Tin Men," said Finch's second, Lieutenant Winslow. "Though after the job the RIC did in dispersing them, further attack seems unlikely."

"Unless the populace riots," Captain Finch said thoughtfully.

No one had a response for that. They had gathered in Finch's office—Trang, Kate, Finch, Winslow, and Danny, whom Kate had dragged along with Trang's grudging assent. They all stood except for Finch himself.

"Casualties?" Finch asked.

"Three of ours," Winslow replied. "Seven embassy staff."

"Five of mine," Lieutenant Trang said.

"Six," Kate corrected. "They found Jablonsky's head."

Trang gave a curt nod. "Six. With the losses we'd already incurred, the platoon is down to twenty-two, myself included."

Finch just took it all in. "The ambassador?"

"Wounded," Winslow said. "He'll be all right. Just a little glass shrapnel from a Molotov. Stitches in his face and arm, some aspirin. He'd have come himself but he wasn't ready to leave his daughter's side."

For a moment, the curtain over Finch's eyes rose to reveal an ocean of sadness, but the emotion vanished so quickly that Danny wondered if he'd imagined it.

"I'd forgotten the girl was here," Finch said. "She's injured?"

"Just shaken," Winslow replied.

Finch nodded, stroking his chin. "Recommendations?"

"We wait," Trang said. "Whatever this is, it can't last forever. We have our people protected, food enough to sustain them. The army will find a way to reestablish communications. Until then, we wait for orders."

Danny shot a look at the back of Trang's head, then glanced at Kate. The guy had been shaken up, but Danny thought he had gotten his shit together. Apparently not.

Finch seemed unsure. "And if no one comes?"

"Someone will come," Trang announced.

Finch did not seem convinced. It eased Danny's mind to know that at least one of the officers had not lost his mind.

"The prisoners?" Finch asked.

"We got what we could from the German before he died," Winslow replied. He nodded at Trang. "The lieutenant recommended one of his men, Private Hawkins, to assist in the questioning and Hawkins turned out to be very persuasive. The intel from this anarchist, Ingo, will prove invaluable—"

"But he's dead, isn't he?" Finch asked.

Danny blinked. "Wait, what? His injuries weren't that severe."

They all stared at him and he realized he had spoken out of turn.

"They were worse than they looked," Lieutenant Winslow replied. "And Private Hawkins didn't hesitate to take advantage of that. The prisoner expired. But now we know their numbers and we know their location. We know they have at least two vehicles—"

"Working vehicles?" Finch asked.

"Yes, sir. This has been in the planning stages a long time. None of these Bot Killers are local and all of them intend to return to their own homes if they survive the chaos. They have Humvee-TSVs whose engines and starters were removed and encased in heavy shielding. By now they'll have reinstalled those parts."

Danny thought about that. The Bot Killers had Humvee Troop Support Vehicles. He wondered what else they had shielded from the Pulse.

"Will they bug out, or come for their leader?" Trang asked.

"The million dollar question," Winslow replied.

"How do we know the other prisoner is their leader?" Finch asked.

"By the smile on his face," Kate muttered.

"Sergeant?" Finch asked.

"Sorry, sir. His cockiness is . . . unsettling," Kate explained. "Whoever he is, I get the feeling he knows a lot more about all this than we do. He's not just some Bot Killer."

"All right, then," Finch said, eyes narrowing. "Good information. Now that you've got it, let's use it against him. Sergeant Wade, you take lead on the interrogation. Without Hawkins. If this man is the leader, I don't want him *expiring* as well. But by all means you should feel free to *break* him."

Danny smiled. The son of a bitch had targeted him and Kate and they still didn't know why. The idea of breaking the man appealed to him very much.

Aimee's security pass unlocked the door to 12, where she found a pair of support specialists babysitting the bodies of Platoon A. The canisters gave off rhythmic beeps, and status lights flickered on their control panels. Other than that, the room had a heavy silence that made her want to hold her breath as she began to weave among the canisters.

Someone else was in the room, had dragged a chair from somewhere and planted himself down among the Remote Combat Units. North glanced up at her approach and exhaled, shaking his head.

"Don't try to tell me I've gotta move," he said.

"You're good where you are."

"Damn right," he said.

Aimee went from unit to unit, checking vitals. A couple of soldiers inside the canisters looked pale to her; their vitals were low, but within normal parameters. She stole glances at North, the guilt etched into his features making her feel as if she ought to say something. Then again, she didn't want to alleviate his guilt; North had let down his platoon.

"You going to tell me?" North asked.

Aimee froze, one hand on the smooth lid of Sergeant Morello's canister. She glanced back at him.

"Tell you what?"

North snorted, as if he might still be drunk and spoiling for a fight. She knew he was sober, but the latter part . . . she wasn't sure.

"Why aren't they awake? If an EMP fried everything—"

"Nineteen EMPs," she corrected.

His eyes flared. "Jesus," he said, massaging his temples. "Okay, nineteen EMPs. If comms are down and everything's fried, they should be regaining consciousness. But the Staging Area's got a skeleton crew and everyone else is in the control room trying to get something back online."

She had to look away from the accusation in his eyes.

"The only thing I can think of—and this doesn't make any sense at all, Aimee—is that nobody's in here trying to wake them up because every one of you *knows* that they're not going to wake up. I mean, otherwise this place would be flooded with techs and med staff, right?"

North got up from his chair, its legs scraping the floor, and approached her. He stood eighteen inches away, close enough to breathe the same air. A small scar ran from just beneath his left nostril to his lip, thin and white, a souvenir from childhood. Once she'd thought it sexy. His eyes were a bright blue, lacking the fear she'd seen in Kenny Wheeler's gaze. North didn't look afraid; he looked angry, a little bit crazy.

"Tell me what everyone else here already seems to know," he demanded.

"God, I *hate* this," she sighed, reaching up to tuck a lock of her short hair behind her ear.

"What do you hate?"

Aimee only hesitated for a moment. She had always hated the secrecy of her job and now secrets seemed meaningless. What difference would it make if she told the truth?

"If things ever go back to normal, you've got to swear—"

North slammed a palm down on top of Morello's canister. "Damn it!"

The two support specialists glanced worriedly at them. Aimee held up a hand to let them know she had things under control, though she was far from certain of that.

"Maybe you want to sit back down," she suggested.

To her surprise, North did. He sat waiting for her to speak like some errant schoolboy wondering how many detentions he would receive. He had always seemed arrogant and irritable to her—which had been sexy before it became infuriating—but for the first time she found herself thinking of him as sad.

This was his platoon. Someone owed this man the truth.

"The Tin Men have never been virtual reality soldiers," she said. "They aren't really Remote Infantry at all."

North scowled. "What are you—"

"It's called mindcasting. Transmitting consciousness like electrical signals from a human brain to a synthetic one. The robots have biological ganglia that map one-to-one with human brains. Actually, every bot has three brains, each with individualized software that imprints with and then mimics the neural pathways of its—"

His stare stopped her. The panic in his eyes made her think he might scream.

"Don't fuck with me," he said, his voice cold but more than a little on the verge.

Aimee's throat went dry. "Tom, I'm not. I swear. This is all classified. Need to know. They never thought you needed to know—"

"Needed to know? They've been . . ." He glanced at the canisters all around them and began to shake his head. "No."

"They're not dead," she assured him. "They're not waking up because they're not in their bodies at all. For all intents and purposes, right now they *are* the robots. With the shielding on the Tin Men and the atomic power source in every bot, they're still operational."

North spun around, growing more frantic. He went to Kate Wade's canister and looked down through the small viewing window at her face, most of it covered by the headgear all the soldiers wore inside the Remote Combat Units.

"What if they're attacked?" he asked. He ran his hands through his hair. "Christ, what if the robots are destroyed? What happens to their minds?"

Aimee took a deep breath. She lifted her hand to push her hair back again and saw that her fingers were trembling.

"There's nothing we can do," she admitted, hating herself in that moment. None of this had been her doing or her fault, but in that moment she felt the weight of the secret she had been charged with keeping. "They're on their own."

North's eyes widened and he whipped around, staring at the walls as if he could see through them. "Nineteen satellites."

"Yes."

He barely seemed to hear her. "It's not just my platoon. It's . . . Jesus, it's all of them."

Aimee didn't reply, but she knew her silence was confirmation enough. North ran a hand along the smooth lid of Wade's canister, then turned and slammed his fist into Travaglini's.

"Fuck!" He leaned on top of Travaglini's canister and buried his face in his hands. "I'm so sorry," he said quietly. "I should be with you."

North apologized again, then again. Aimee had a feeling he would be apologizing in his heart forever. She wanted to comfort him, but knew there was nothing she could say. For the moment, deep underground, he was alive and safe and whole—but those were the very facts that were tearing him apart inside.

She left him there, moving from canister to canister, checking vitals and telling herself that there was still hope for the men and women of Platoon A.

A pair of MPs unlocked the metal door that led into the brig. One of them stayed behind while the other accompanied Danny, Kate, and Winslow to the only occupied cell. The anarchist lay on the single cot with his arms behind his head, staring at the ceiling. His upper torso had been tightly wrapped to keep his cracked ribs from moving around much; if he punctured a lung, they'd get no answers.

Danny knocked his metal knuckles against the bars. "Wake up, fuckface."

Bruised and bloodied, the anarchist did not spare them so much as a glance. "I'm not sleeping."

"We're so glad," Kate said.

As the MP unlocked the cell, the bearded man propped himself up to get a look at them. Danny kept his hand at his side, fingers twitching near the handle of his gun. A strange sensation passed through him; for a moment, he felt almost human, as if that twitch had been in his real fingers.

The anarchist's curious expression blossomed into something that looked to Danny like real pleasure.

"Private Kelso," the man said in his clipped accent. *Afghani*, Danny thought. "Corporal Wade. I'm glad they've sent you. Stay close, please. If the opportunity arises, I still intend to kill you."

"*Sergeant* Wade," Danny said, stepping in beside Kate, the two of them creating a kind of wall between the man and his freedom.

The MP stayed in the hall. Winslow moved inside the cell but stayed silent, just observing.

"A battlefield promotion," the man said, sitting up on the edge of the cot, grim intellect gleaming in his eyes. "Congratulations, Kate."

The intimacy of her first name set Danny off. He stepped forward, cocked his hand back to strike, but Kate grabbed his wrist.

The bastard's grin widened. "If we kill a few more robots, you'll be lieutenant by nightfall."

Kate grabbed him by the throat, too fast for him to react, and hurled him against the wall. His head thumped concrete and he fell to the cot in a sprawl of limbs, sliding onto the floor, grunting at the pain in his ribs. The devil horns on Kate's head glinted in the false light of the cell.

"Damn it!" Winslow snapped, pushing up past Danny. "This guy's our best chance for real answers and you just—"

Danny gave Winslow a light shove, just hard enough to get his attention. He said nothing, letting the stare of robot eyes say everything to silence the lieutenant.

"He'll live," Kate said, though Danny wasn't so sure. The bastard had hit his head pretty hard. "If he doesn't wake up in the next ten seconds, you can piss on him to bring him around."

"Or set him on fire," Danny said.

The anarchist groaned. When he lolled his head to one side and blinked away his disorientation, Danny saw the murder in his eyes.

"You know a lot about us," Danny said. "Now it's our turn to get to know you."

The man climbed back onto the cot and sat on the edge. He grabbed the sides of his head as if he feared it might fall apart, then searched his scalp for damage. When his fingers came away bloody, he gave a humorless laugh.

"What would you like to know?" he asked, glancing up at them. "I have no reason not to answer your questions. The trigger has been pulled. The apocalypse is here."

Kate slapped the anarchist hard, metal fingers raising red welts.

This time, Winslow said nothing, but Danny saw the guy fidgeting. He wanted to step in, afraid that Kate would kill the bastard or give him brain damage or something. Out in the corridor, the MP watched without any reaction at all. If Danny read his body language correctly, the MP wanted Kate to hit the son of a bitch again.

"You're going to answer my questions," Kate instructed.

The anarchist spit blood onto the floor. He did not seem afraid of pain or death, just curious. "I said as much before you hit me."

"Oh, *that*?" Kate said. "That was just to stop you smiling."

"But if the smile comes back," Danny added, "we can make it so you're incapable."

The smile did not return. The anarchist stared at them, then wiped the blood from his mouth. He might not be afraid of pain, but he didn't seem inclined to ask for more.

"Shall I start with my name?" the man asked. When he spoke, Danny could see blood on his teeth from the blow Kate had given him.

"We know your name," Danny told him. "Hanif Khan. Your man Ingo shared a lot before he died."

The stillness that came over Khan's face with that revelation pleased Danny very much. He hadn't expected that.

"Your questions, then?" the anarchist said.

"You know who set off the EMP?"

Khan shook his head. "I know the name of the man who gave me my instructions, and I knew the EMP would happen. Not how it was done or who was behind it. As I said, what I know will not help you. My men were only one squad of what you call Bot Killers. There are many more. Everywhere on the planet where American robots are deployed, right now there is a group of anarchists or a jihadist sect risking their lives to destroy those robots."

"Why?" Danny asked.

At this, Khan's smile returned, but it was wistful. Actually amused.

"Out of hatred, Private Kelso. And a desire to finish the job that the EMP began . . . the end of Western influence in the Middle East. The end of American influence in the world." The beaten, bloody man gave a small shrug. "The end of *America*."

"This is worldwide," Kate said.

"Oh, Ingo didn't tell you that?" Khan mused.

"He didn't need to confirm it," Danny quietly replied. "If there were any satellites still in operation, one of them would have come in range of our comms by now."

Danny and Kate had been hiding from the truth until that moment. Even the dimmest bulbs in Platoon A had to have realized that enough time had passed for another satellite to orbit into range, but they hadn't faced it until Danny said it aloud. Kate shot him a dark look. She was not happy to have the illusion shattered.

"Who could organize something like that?" she said. "Who *would*?"

The anarchist scowled. "Those who have spent their lives hating the corrupt, whorish American culture and the past seven years watching the Americans take control of the world—"

"We freed people!" Kate snarled.

Danny put a hand on her arm, quieting her, but he shared her fury. America had gotten tired of waiting for the global bullshit to end and found itself with the tools to do something about it. With the Tin Men, the United States had forced dictators to stop killing, disrupted civil wars, freed up food supplies and medicines . . . hell, they'd saved a thousand times more lives than they had taken. But he knew that, to many, no good they accomplished would ever be justification enough, and a part of him understood.

"You forced your will upon the world," Khan said quietly, his voice the hiss of a cobra. "Forced your culture and your democracy and your beliefs—"

"Your people are the jihadists," Danny replied.

"Some," Khan agreed. "At least *I* admit it. Powerful religious sects, yes, but they aren't your only enemies here. Government factions and militant groups and ordinary people are desperate to throw off the Western yoke. With the robots, your government made themselves the effective rulers of Earth, and there are many willing to risk anything to see that come to an end."

Kate picked him up again, slammed him into the wall, and held him there, feet dangling off the ground. One of his shoes fell off and thumped to the floor.

"Follow protocol, Kate!" Danny barked.

She twisted to glare at him, still holding Khan against the wall. The little pitchfork painted on her cheek looked like a scar. For half a second, Danny forgot that this *wasn't* Kate, that Kate had purple eyes and smooth brown skin and had lost her legs. He wanted to comfort her but doubted they could give each other any solace while inside these bodies.

"Fuck protocol," she said, but she let Khan drop to the floor. He staggered a bit before he leaned against the wall. Kate stared at Danny. "We keep him alive while we decide our next move, just in case we need him. And then we—"

"We'll need him," Danny said, studying Khan.

"Yeah?" Kate asked. "Why's that?"

"We know where his people here in Damascus are, but what about all the others he mentioned?" Danny said. "He's not just some hired gun. You can see that. Whatever this operation is, he knows more than he's telling. If that intel can save lives down the line and we kill him now . . ."

Kate gave a slow nod.

She slammed a fist into the wall, stared at Winslow and the MP out in the corridor, and then turned toward the anarchist. The only lead they had to whoever had planned all of this, and whatever else they might have in store.

"These people you're working for," she said, "they just sent the whole world back to the Stone Age, and you're okay with that?"

Khan took a shaky breath and righted himself, pushing off from the wall to stand upright. He had just taken part in the ruination of modern civilization, had contributed to the deaths of who-knew-how-many, and he was proud of himself.

"My people lived in caves in the mountains of Afghanistan," he said. "Some live in deserts and others in slums. Most of them exist in something like the Stone Age already. Their lives will hardly change. Humanity will return to tribes and small nation-states. Warfare will be local. Savage conquerors will be confined to their own landmasses and the reach of their ground forces. Tell me, why should any of that trouble me?"

A hard rap came on the metal bars of the cell.

"Hey," Winslow said. "Let's go. I need to report to the captain."

Danny and Kate exchanged a glance and she nodded. She exited first and Danny followed, backing out of the cell. Hanif Khan watched them depart, beginning to hunch a little from the pain of the physical punishment he'd taken at the time of his capture and during this visit.

"You didn't ask the most important question," he said, attempting to comb the blood-matted parts of his beard with his fingers.

Danny froze. "Why you targeted the two of us, you mean?"

Khan's eyes darkened. They were a shark's eyes then. Black and dead, full of hunger and disdain.

"Not the question I had in mind," Khan replied. "No, I'm just surprised you haven't asked me why you're still here, you Tin Men. The so-called *Remote* Infantry. Still inside your robots."

"We didn't ask because we know the answer," Danny said. "We *know*."

Kate shot him a haunted look and Danny glanced away. He couldn't look at her right now, not when Khan had just confirmed the worst fears that had been niggling at the back of his mind.

Khan spit on the floor again, this time more in commentary than to rid his mouth of blood. "You thought another satellite would pass by, that your minds would transmit then."

"We hoped, yes," Kate admitted.

"And now you're trapped inside those shells forever and you don't have the first clue how it's possible," Khan said, voice full of mocking sympathy. "But that isn't what would bother me the most, if I were you. No, what would really trouble me was that your superiors kept you in the dark all this time, that you had no idea what was really being done to you . . .

"But your enemies knew all along."

11

Danny and Kate gathered most of the survivors of Platoon A into the shadow of the ambassador's residence. Tin Men had cleared the building but for security purposes it was still off-limits—the ambassador and his staff would be bunking with their military neighbors until further notice.

"Where's the lieutenant?" McKelvie asked, fear in his voice.

"Meeting with Finch," Kate replied.

The rest of them were quiet. Danny glanced up at the wall and saw one of the sentries watching them instead of the street. He tried to imagine this picture from the sentry's point of view—a bunch of armed killer robots gathered in a quiet corner of the courtyard, conspiring among themselves.

Only we aren't conspiring, Danny thought. *We're just like the rest of you—we're freaking the fuck out.*

Kate had just finished relating their conversation with Hanif Khan to the rest of them—including what they thought had really happened to the Tin Men during the Pulse.

"No offense, Sergeant," Hawkins sneered, "but that shit is impossible."

"Look," Travaglini said, "I'm no god of biomechanics—"

"We're still here, Hawkins," Danny interrupted.

"Kelso—" Hawkins began.

"No, listen!" Danny snapped, scanning the gathered members of his platoon. Kate and Torres. Trav and Hawkins. Birnbaum, Hartschorn, Lahiri, Prosky, McKelvie. Mavrides, who was quiet for once.

"The EMP fragged *all* transmissions," Danny said. "I'm talking global. Deep down, I think we all knew it. Believing our piloting relay was on a separate satellite? That comms would come back if we waited long enough? That's a fairy tale."

"We're *shielded*," Prosky whined, as if that was the answer to everything.

Kate held up a hand. "Yes, our hardware has shielding that would protect onboard ops and power cores from a pulse like that, but if we were really piloting the bots remotely, we wouldn't still be here." She looked around, meeting the eyes of each soldier. "You understand what I'm saying? Our minds are in the bots."

"That's impossible," Hawkins sneered. "You can't transmit a human mind via fucking satellite."

"You sure about that?" Danny asked.

"It might be possible," Hartschorn said. "There've been experiments with synthetic brain modification—like adding data storage. If science can do that, it means your consciousness can spread from organic to synthetic neurological materials. From there to transmission . . . it's not out of the question."

He and Birnbaum were both techs, but Hartschorn was their resident science geek. They all glared at him, hating him for not telling them it couldn't be true.

"No way," Hawkins said. "I'm lying in my big fucking can back in Germany, waiting for some tech to pop the top and unplug me. So EMPs blew the shit out of everything, so what? There are so many satellites in distant orbit . . . you're telling me whatever this EMP was, it fried every damn one of them?"

"Near enough," Danny replied.

"Your body," Kate said.

Hawkins stared at her, looking more hurt than angry. He didn't want to know. "What?"

"Your body is lying in that can, Hawkins," Kate said. "Your mind is here. Somehow it's always been here. Not just this time—every time."

"Uncle Sam lied," Danny said. "It wasn't our mental impulses they were routing through those satellites, it was us. Our minds."

"That's just . . ." Hawkins started again, but faltered.

"Oh, no," Birnbaum said quietly. "The sarge. Kasturi and Jones. Corcoran."

"Eliopoulos," Torres said. "He invited me to his wedding."

"Oh, no," Birnbaum said again. She put her hands over her curved metal abdomen and her legs went out from under her, just as if she were human. She slid to the ground and sat there among them. Hawkins knelt beside her, put a hand on her shoulder, and for a few seconds they all just listened.

None of them had ever heard a robot weep before. There were no tears, of course. The Tin Men were incapable of shedding tears. But Birnbaum's soft moan of sorrow was enough to break all of their absent hearts.

"If you're right," Torres said, "if comms are down and their minds were trapped when the bots were destroyed, what happens now? Their bodies are still there, back at the Hump. That place is massively shielded. Hell, *our* bodies are still there. So is that it for those guys? Just . . . brain dead, back in Germany?"

For the first time, Danny looked at Travaglini's rocket-riding blonde and Hawkins's smiley with crossbones and they weren't amusing anymore. So many of the Remote Infantry Corps had grown up on video games and looked at deployment as just leveling up. Danny had never been quite that cavalier, but now, more than ever, it wasn't a game. This time there would be no bonus lives.

"That's what made the Bot Killers so determined," Danny said. "They knew this time they were killing us for real."

Ever since he had first signed on for the Remote Infantry Corps— the first time he'd slid into a canister in Germany and opened his eyes to peer out from inside a robot shell—Danny had been having a recurring dream in which he was a ghost in the midst of a war. He often felt that way while piloting his robot: uprooted, as if he had truly left the physical world behind. And now it seemed that he had.

I'm a ghost, he thought numbly.

"Damn it, the sarge," Hawkins groaned.

Mavrides said nothing, studying them.

"My mom and my little sister live in Vermont," McKelvie said. "They're probably okay, don't you think? I mean . . . once people really understand what's happened it's going to be a shitstorm, but places like that will be okay, right? It's not like Chicago or something."

"I'm from Chicago," Prosky said. "Got an ex-wife there. My little boy, Amos . . . he's nine."

A cold silence settled in. They'd been so focused on themselves that they hadn't taken a moment to really envision how the rest of the world might be reacting to the fragged engines, the burnt-out circuitry. Panic would war with hope at first. People would want to think that everything would be okay, that someone would be along to fix it all. Local governments would organize their citizens and attempt to brave the worst of it, pull together. Danny didn't know about the rest of the world, but in America the populaces of major cities would attempt to live up to the myths they had created about themselves.

Some would recognize the truth more quickly, do the math and figure out how long it would take for everything—hell, *anything*—to get fixed, and know that the chances of a major city holding itself together that long were practically nil. The looting would start, the shooting. The world had too many damn guns. People would want to circle the wagons, gather their loved ones and as much food as they could find, and then they would do whatever they had to in order to protect themselves.

TVs were dead. Phones. No more movies. No Internet.

Jesus, Danny thought. *No Internet.* All the data that had been stored there, all the books and journals—the knowledge—that had never made it onto paper . . . all that was gone forever, as if the Library of Alexandria had spanned the world, and these fucking anarchists Hanif Khan worked for had just burned the whole thing down.

Some places might make it work—places where there were still farms, or where people were hardy and could adapt—but soon enough those areas would come under attack by others who wanted what they had. It would get ugly almost everywhere; the big cities would be the worst. Prosky's son, Amos, had a life expectancy measured in months unless his mother was smart and saw it coming, got the hell out of Chicago.

The others began to talk about their loved ones, the people they feared for. All except Danny, who had no one, and Mavrides, who remained sullenly silent. Danny's father was dead, his older brother was a prick, and he hadn't seen his mother since she'd taken off with her dealer when he was ten years old. He had friends, of course, but oddly he thought of Nora, so soft and warm and alive in bed with him that morning. He thought of her little-girl vanity and the fights they'd had and how good her sheets always smelled, full of her perfume and her sweat and the sex they'd had in the softness of that bed. In the time they had been together, he had never once felt as if they were truly bonded, as if they had a future. Sharks had to keep swimming, keep moving, or they would die.

Of all of them, Danny thought he was the best suited to live through this chaos, because there was no one alive he loved enough to distract him from the hard work of surviving.

He looked at Kate and found her looking back. Suddenly memories of Nora blurred and were replaced by images of Kate in the flesh, her lovely skin and the intelligence and mischief in her eyes. He wanted to keep Kate alive, too, and not just because she was a member of his platoon.

The urge worried him. That sort of thing could get him killed.

Torres swore under her breath. "All that shit Lieutenant Trang was saying, about his wife pulling the plug on his body. He knew it right away."

Mavrides let out a short bark of a laugh. "Trang was falling the fuck apart, and you were all just holding your dicks. Stay on mission.

Run back to base. Pledge allegiance to the fucking flag, right?" He laughed again, a terrible sound, the giggle of a child pulling the wings off a fly. "Sayonara to that shit."

Danny stared at him, at the damn death card on his forehead, and realized that Trang hadn't been the only one who had figured it all out right away. Mavrides had essentially said as much when he'd shot that civilian in the leg, but the rest of them had still been living the fairy tale, waiting for another satellite to come in range.

"So what do we do now?" Hawkins asked.

"I'll tell you what we do," Torres said. "Our duty. The USA gave me everything I have. I signed on to serve my country because I believe in it, and I'm going to keep doing that."

"What country?" Hartschorn said. "Seriously. How much of the great old USA is still going to be standing in a year? Look, I had cancer as a kid. I never figured I'd live this long, but I did. My body's alive in that goddamn canister, and I intend to get back to Germany. If there's still power at the Hump, they've gotta have a way to get us into our bodies again. After that, I'll fight for the people I love, but not for my country—"

"Not for the government that did *this* to us," Lahiri said, his voice quietly powerful. "The government that *fucked* us like this."

Hawkins had been crouched beside Birnbaum. Danny had no idea what was going on in Naomi's head and was amazed that she had accepted any kindness from a guy who had infuriated her with his piggish come-ons for months, but now they seemed to have a bond.

"What about you, Kate?" Hawkins asked, his voice a low mechanical growl. "You're acting sergeant now. What's your take?"

"Her take?" Rawlins said. "Trang's the lieutenant. I'm more interested in—"

"Shut the fuck up," Hawkins snapped, and Rawlins knew better than to argue.

"Well?" Danny said, glancing at Kate.

Kate took a moment, then gave a single grim nod.

"My take is we shag our asses back to Germany," she said. "When we hit the Hump, I'm gonna have a few questions for the brass."

Torres rapped on Danny's arm and he glanced over to see Lieutenant Winslow approaching. The remnants of Platoon A turned toward Winslow, the conversation halted.

The lieutenant was still flesh and blood. He was not one of them.

"Sergeant Wade," Winslow said, "Captain Finch wants you and Private Kelso in the conference room in ten minutes."

Kate nodded. "We'll be right along."

Winslow frowned, scanned the gathered Tin Men, then gave a nod before retreating. He had sensed the tension among them, that was obvious, but what could he say? They were not his to command.

Danny had begun to think they weren't anyone's to command. Not anymore.

Kate turned to the others. "Turn this over in your heads all you want," she said. "But do not discuss it where you might be overheard. When we visit this topic again it's going to be with Lieutenant Trang. Sit tight. Don't do anything stupid.

"Hawkins," she said. "In the lieutenant's and my absence, you're in charge. Keep it together. Keep *them* together."

Mavrides scoffed.

Hawkins ignored him. "You got it, Sarge."

Danny still didn't trust Hawkins—he'd have put Torres in charge—but he knew Kate well enough to understand. Mavrides was a mad dog, and Hawkins was the only one she trusted to keep him on a leash.

Alexa Day needed caffeine. Which seemed counterintuitive, considering that her hands kept trembling—normally the kind of thing that indicated *too much* caffeine. But the craving for a Coca-Cola had come upon her and now it was all she could think about.

She glanced back into the corridor. Marines and civilian embassy personnel buzzed around, trying to figure out what they were supposed to do next. Nobody was keeping watch over her. The sentries were out on the wall, waiting for another attack, and her father had gone to Captain Finch's quarters to borrow a clean shirt. The bloodstains on the one he'd been wearing would never come out.

Alexa hurried around the conference table toward the back of the room and pretended that the tremor in her hands hadn't just gotten worse. She thought of the fresh black stitches that ran like a zipper across her father's left cheek and temple and the smaller set on his arm. Arthur Day had always been handsome. These scars wouldn't erase his handsomeness, but from now on his features would be different. Grimmer.

Exhaling heavily, she pulled open the door at the rear of the conference room. There was a single small window in the room and she was grateful for it—otherwise the kitchen would have been pitch black. She wondered how many candles there were at the embassy and then decided she didn't want to think about nightfall.

Baz Nissim had told her there would be soda and snacks in the kitchen and he hadn't been wrong. She tugged a bag of pretzels from a cabinet and then opened the quickly warming fridge to find assorted flavored waters and sodas.

Alexa fetched a can of Coke from the dark, dead fridge, the can still retaining some of the cold from when the appliance had been working. Closing the refrigerator door, she popped the can and lifted it to her lips. The first sip became a deep gulp and she found herself drinking greedily, draining half the can in no time.

Her lips began to tremble the way her hands had done only moments before. Tears welled in her eyes and she set the can on the counter. Her father had tried to console her, told her that her mother would be all right, but Alexa had felt herself flushing with emotion and been unable to reply. At seventeen, she was old enough to know there was nothing she could do to protect her mother and nothing her mom could do to protect her.

Live, she thought.

The word had been echoing through her mind all morning. If Alexa had been able to talk to her, she knew that would have been her mother's advice. *Live. Survive. Make it home.* She kept sending those same thoughts out into the universe, hoping that God or whatever power might be listening would carry the message to her mother. *Live. Survive. Wait for me.*

She stared at the Coke can, but she no longer had any desire to drink the soda. The taste of it did remind her of home, of her mother, and she needed to toughen up. To make it out of this godforsaken war zone, she would have to dry her tears and stiffen her spine and make her own decisions.

Pouring the Coke into the sink, she paused at the sound of someone entering the conference room. Heavy steps, the low hum of machinery—a sound that had mostly vanished from the base—and she knew the people who'd just come in were robots. Tin Men. Not people at all.

Alexa left the can on the counter and reached for the door, intending to announce herself, but then the robots started talking and she hesitated.

"Mavrides is losing it," one of them said. A female.

"He'll pull it together," replied the other. A male.

Of course robots were neither male nor female, but the soldiers piloting them were. She wondered how close to their actual voices these electronic simulations were.

The voices had gone quiet. Standing just behind the kitchen door, Alexa cocked her head, listening to the silence for a moment before a rush of panic went through her. Had she made a sound? Had she given herself away? They would think she had been eavesdropping. She *had* been, but not in any sneaky way. It had just kind of happened—but Alexa knew they'd never believe it.

"What about you?" the female said, her voice gentle.

"Me?" the male replied.

"How's your morale?"

Alexa quietly exhaled. They had no idea she was listening.

The male robot gave a low, cynical laugh. "My morale is shit, Kate. But I'm not going to let that get in the way of the mission—whatever we decide the mission ought to be. I'm all right."

The robots fell quiet again. Alexa knew they could normally communicate through internal channels, so others could not overhear, and she wondered if that was what they were doing. The kitchen door was open an inch or so and she decided to take the risk of being overheard. She adjusted her position, pressed her eye to the gap, and shifted until she had a view of the two robots.

At first, what she saw confused her. One of them—the number

thirteen painted on its forehead—held a hand against the face of the other, almost cupping its cheek.

"You're not alone, Danny," said the female, Kate. "None of us is."

Alexa blinked, a smile spreading across her face. She'd kept thinking of them as robots, but of course that had been foolish of her. They were people. Soldiers. Men and women who were just as frightened as she was.

Danny turned away. "We're all alone."

Kate stared at him, expression unreadable. "Is that how you want it?"

"Want's got nothing to do with it. That's just how it is."

Alexa couldn't breathe. What was going on between these two?

The door to the conference room opened abruptly and Alexa stepped back an inch or so. The robots came to attention as Captain Finch and Lieutenant Winslow entered the room, followed by Alexa's father. The ambassador wore a clean shirt and he looked more alert than he had fifteen minutes ago when Finch had taken him off in search of one. The skin around the stitches on his face had turned an angry red and she wondered how much the wound hurt.

A third robot entered the room and the first two snapped off a crisp salute.

A pair of soldiers began to enter, but Captain Finch held up a hand and instructed them to wait in the hall. Whatever this meeting was, it was for command staff only. Alexa felt her face flush and her pulse began to race. Eavesdropping on Danny and Kate had been bad enough, but that had been sort of an accident. Spying on this meeting was a terrible idea; her father would be furious if he discovered her. She tried to make herself move, but if she revealed her presence, Danny and Kate would know they had been overheard.

Don't be stupid, she thought. *Just go—*

"Sergeant Wade," Finch said. "I'd like your thoughts about our prisoner."

"A moment, Captain," said the third robot, who had the infinity symbol painted on his chest.

"Lieutenant Trang?" Finch replied. So infinity bot was a lieutenant.

Trang ignored Finch, staring at Danny and Kate. Robots had facial expressions, but Alexa had always thought of them as fairly limited because so much emotion came through human eyes. Even so, Trang's irritation was evident.

"Sergeant Wade is here to make a report," Trang said. "There's no reason for Private Kelso to be here as well. Whatever decisions are made at command level should remain private until we are prepared to disclose them."

The moment of tension that followed made Alexa hold her breath. Hostility filled the room like some kind of poison gas.

Kate turned to Finch. "Captain, Private Kelso and I questioned the prisoner together. I thought his perspective might be valuable."

"You have a lot of thoughts today," Lieutenant Trang said.

Finch held up a hand. "Enough, Lieutenant. Day's ugly enough without whatever issues you may have within your platoon." He turned his attention back to Kate. "The prisoner, Sergeant. What've we got?"

Kate nodded, ignoring Trang now. "Hanif Khan. Afghani. Had definite foreknowledge of today's events, but not who or how. The why is the same as every anarchist group encountered over the past twenty years has had, just taken to the furthest extreme."

"They think we're the bad guys," Finch said.

"Maybe we *are*," the ambassador replied.

Alexa flinched, hating the exhaustion in her father's voice and stung by his words.

"Ambassador?" Captain Finch said.

Alexa shifted to get a better look at her father. He had taken a seat at the conference table—something the others hadn't bothered to do—and he looked gray and weary. The stitches gave him an air of wisdom, but it was an ugly sort of wisdom. A bleak, hopeless sort. Alexa thought it was no wonder he hadn't been very good at comforting her.

"I'm not saying the world deserved this," the ambassador said. "But we were kind of asking for it, don't you think?"

"I certainly don't think—" Finch began angrily.

"What do you call someone strong who pushes around people who are weaker, Captain? A bully. No matter our rationale—some of which was sound, some selfish—we were bullies. Well, the weaker kid just changed the fucking rules, and the schoolyard's never going to be the same."

Alexa's mouth opened. Her father never swore.

"That line of thinking isn't exactly helpful, Mr. Ambassador," Lieutenant Winslow said.

The ambassador stood up. "You guys need to get your heads out of your asses. Decisions have to be made about the immediate concerns of the people inside these walls. My daughter is here, for Christ's sake! She's got to be my first priority."

"With all due respect, Ambassador Day," Trang said, "your first priority should be your post."

Alexa watched her father scowl.

"This is what I'm talking about," he said. "*Pay attention.* Folks are going to be turning on each other pretty damn soon. There are plenty of weapons and ammunition inside our walls. We might be weeks or even months away from some upstart warlord deciding to try to take them, but it's going to happen."

"In which case," Winslow said, "what about nukes?"

"Shielded," Danny replied. "At least, I'm pretty sure all of those facilities are shielded. They'd still have power. And the defenses at those places . . . nobody's going to get in there."

"In the United States," Kate said. "I just hope the rest of the world's arsenals are as well guarded."

"What if somebody launches?" Danny asked.

In the adjacent room, Alexa hugged herself, icy fingers clutching her heart.

"Not going to happen," Captain Finch said. "Without satellite guidance the missiles could not be relied upon to find their targets. And without communication relays, who would give the order? The president's not going to be in any position to do it unless he sends the order by smoke signal."

Kate straightened up.

Alexa tried to read the strange expression on her face—was that fear or confusion?—but hadn't been around enough robots to make sense of it.

"What is it, Kate?" Danny asked.

"Sergeant Wade?" Finch said. "Something you want to—"

"Sorry, Captain," Kate said, her voice sounding more robotic somehow. Hollow. "I'm going to need a minute."

As Trang began to harangue her about protocol and chain of command, she threw open the door and vanished into the corridor. Danny didn't hesitate or ask permission, just rushed out behind her. Alexa remembered the moment of tenderness she had witnessed between them and quietly prayed they would be all right.

Lieutenant Trang directed his tirade toward Captain Finch as Winslow shut the door behind the departed robots. Through the gap between the kitchen door and its frame, Alexa watched her father return to his seat. He leaned back in the chair and stared at the ceiling as if he expected answers to come down from Heaven.

None were forthcoming.

Danny knew where Kate was headed as soon as she hit the stairs. He followed her down the darkened stairwell and into the waiting area outside the brig. Oil lamps and candles threw long, shuddery shadows upon the walls and it occurred to Danny that they wouldn't last very long. Plan B for a power outage was to use the generators, but they were just as fried as everything else. How much oil could they have stocked up for those lamps?

"Kate," he said as he caught up to her, just outside the brig.

The two MPs gazed at them curiously as Kate reached for the door handle and Danny tapped her shoulder.

"Wait a second," he said.

She rounded on him, inhuman eyes blazing brightly. "You don't understand!"

"No," he said, "I don't. Clue me in?"

She was still for a moment. Then, with a glance at the MPs, she took his arm and walked him back toward the bottom of the steps, where they could speak with a modicum of privacy.

"Today's August thirtieth," she said.

Danny shrugged. "And?"

"It's the first day of the G20 summit in Athens," she said. When she spoke again her voice seemed quieter, smaller somehow. "I thought my dad was home, Danny. Not safe—nobody's safe, if this is global— but home where he'd have friends around him. Instead . . ."

It took a second for her words to click. Then he remembered. "Your dad's in Athens."

Kate nodded. "And I don't think that's the worst of it."

She spun away from him and strode straight toward the brig. One of the MPs—a thin Asian man—opened the door for her. The soldier looked up at her, this seven-foot robot with devil horns and a pitch-fork painted on its cheek, and Danny could see he was intimidated. A healthy response to encountering Kate, Danny thought.

Queen of the Tin Men, they often joked. But it was no joke.

"Sorry, Sergeant," the MP said. "I can't let you through without Lieutenant Winslow or Captain Finch. I wouldn't have opened the door if the intercom was still working."

Kate shoved him aside effortlessly. The MP snapped at her and started to draw his weapon. Danny grabbed his wrist as, inside the small cubicle that passed for a guardhouse, the other MP did the same.

"Don't," Danny said, lifting his arm straight up, forcing him to aim his weapon at the ceiling. "You're not going to hurt us, pal. More likely you'll kill your partner with a ricochet. She just wants to talk to the prisoner. You guys can listen in, report whatever you hear if you're worried about what she might say."

"We have our orders," the MP said.

Danny glanced at the man. "I'm not sure orders mean much any-more."

The MPs exchanged a glance through the cubicle glass and then the one Danny had grabbed gave a nod. Danny felt the guy's arm go slack and released him. Moments later, all three of them were catch-ing up to Kate, who had arrived at the door to Hanif Khan's cell.

The anarchist had moved the mattress of his little cot onto the floor. He lay there staring at the ceiling, not acknowledging their arrival.

"I want to ask you something," Kate said, anger boiling in her voice.

"More questions?" Khan said wearily.

"About timing," Kate replied. "The G20 summit—"

"Yes."

Danny stiffened. He moved nearer to Kate so that he could get a better view of Khan through the bars. The asshole just lay there, still not bothering to look at them.

"What do you mean, 'yes'?" Kate demanded.

"To your question," Khan replied. "You want to know if part of the plan was to assassinate the world leaders gathered in Athens. The answer is yes."

"Son of a bitch," one of the MPs said, exhaling the words in a rasp.

Danny studied the anarchist. Maybe he truly had no idea who had masterminded all this chaos, but he knew more about the plan than he'd admitted and now he was taking pleasure in their dawning horror.

"There's more," Danny said, certain of it.

Khan sat up with a jaunty grin. "Of course there is. Someone who goes to this extent to obliterate the global power structure will make sure they've taken away the ability of that hierarchy to reestablish itself."

Where the hell did this guy go to school? Danny wondered. He didn't talk like some desert warrior.

"You going to tell us?" Kate asked. "Or you want to keep playing games?"

Khan managed to look insulted. "I think I've been very forthcoming. I'm happy to tell you because there is nothing you can do to prevent any of it from happening. The knowledge will increase your suffering, and that pleases me."

"Go on, then," Danny said. "Increase our suffering."

"There are strike teams in Athens, yes," Hanif Khan said. "And, as you know, strike teams everywhere there are Tin Men deployed. But it's not enough to destroy the Tin Men if you leave alive the possibility that they will ever be utilized again. It isn't enough to destroy the hardware. You must destroy the software, too."

Danny stared at him, a chill racing up his spine. Robot frame or not, he could still feel horror.

"They'll destroy our bodies," he said numbly.

Khan did not smile.

"One way or another," the anarchist said, "this day will see you dead."

12

Aimee tried not to let herself think too far ahead. Major Zander had instituted something called Phoenix Protocols, and she didn't like the sound of that at all. According to legend, the phoenix rose from the ashes of its own demise. Maybe calling their plan of action Phoenix Protocols had been intended to inspire hope for the future, but to Aimee it was just confirmation that as far as Major Zander and the other officers sitting up in the Command Core were concerned, they were all fucked.

Soldiers hustled back and forth along the catwalks. Some of them were standing guard but the rest were engaged in the one part of the Phoenix Protocols that actually seemed to make sense—inventory. Food and medical supplies were being cataloged and Major Zander had issued an order that rationing would begin immediately. Chief Schuler and his staff were organizing shifts and sleeping accommodations.

Everyone had started thinking long term, and Aimee couldn't wrap her head around that yet. Her thoughts kept going back to her friend Julissa, who lived in New Orleans with her wife and son.

They'd arranged to vid-chat tonight after Aimee's shift and she knew they would've talked about nothing much important. Julissa had been slogging her way through law school, so that and her son were pretty much all she ever talked about.

"Damn it," Aimee whispered, burying her face in her hands.

The main screen of her monitoring station glowed a soft blue. She sighed and turned her attention back to the task she'd been given, to the list on that screen. Thirty-one locations of bases she was reasonably certain were shielded from EMP attacks. Some were American, but there were other nations represented on that list, from Britain to South Africa to China. The list had been broken down into five subsets and those smaller lists assigned to five techs. Aimee stared at the full list, but only the first six locations were her responsibility.

She put on her headpiece and tapped the fourth name on her list. A small map appeared on-screen and a light began to blink over Vancouver, British Columbia. The line crackled and she straightened up in her chair. No buzz to indicate an attempted connection, but that crackle surely meant an open line, didn't it? The Phoenix Protocols included a continuous effort to make contact, to attempt to establish a network. Whoever had loaded nineteen Monteforte Corporation satellites with EMPs had certainly intended to wipe out any possibility of contact, but the first communication satellite had been launched in 1962, and there was no way to know for sure what was still floating around up there.

Tech changed so quickly that the last few generations of satellites had been low-orbit products, meant to be multitudinous and disposable, with enough fuel cells to stay at the edges of the atmosphere for four or five years before burning up. Most of the older, still-active satellites would have been taken out by the Pulse—military geosynchronous tech included—but it was possible that some of the aging, abandoned geosynch satellites had been out of range of the EMPs, perhaps in a more distant orbit.

"This is Wiesbaden Army Airfield hailing Barker's Victoria Cross," she said. "Wiesbaden hailing Barker's Victoria Cross. Please respond."

Pause. Holding her breath. Listening to the crackling.

"Please respond."

Aimee stared at the blinking light over Vancouver on her screen map and a terrible old joke swam up into her thoughts. Dark and ugly, but she had laughed the first time she'd heard it.

Knock, knock.

Who's there?

No one. You're going to die alone.

Here she was knocking, but if she had indeed found an open channel, a satellite relay, it seemed nobody was home.

"This is Wiesbaden Army Airfield hailing Barker's Victoria Cross," she said again, wondering if someone was on the line, listening. Barker's Victoria Cross was a secret installation north of Vancouver, an underground research facility sponsored jointly by the Canadian government and the British. She pictured someone just like her, a young soldier with strict instructions, unable to answer a hail to an installation that wasn't supposed to even exist.

Aimee held her breath a moment, glanced around, and lowered her voice. "This is *Humphreys Deep Station One* hailing Barker's Victoria Cross. Can anyone read me?"

The crackle on the line grew worse and for a second or two she thought for sure someone would answer, but still there was nothing. Maybe nobody was there after all.

Hope could keep a person going. She knew that. But right then hope felt like poison.

Her finger hovered over the screen, ready to tap the fifth location on her list.

"Bell!" a voice called.

The suddenness of it made her jump in her seat and then she swore under her breath. For half a second she'd allowed herself to imagine the voice had been coming through her headset.

She spun her chair around. Steve Mendelsohn beckoned to her from two stations away, but it wasn't Mendelsohn's waving that had her attention, it was the monitors on the screens in front of his station. On the largest one, soldiers used metal dollies to hustle crates of supplies across the parking lot of Wiesbaden Army Airfield. On one of the other screens, several officers stood in conversation, grave expressions on their faces. On a third . . .

Aimee had barely realized she was in motion and then she was beside Mendelsohn and the two other techs who had rushed over at his summons. She stared at the third screen, upon which troops were busy pushing cars and trucks with dead engines across green grass, lining them up as a barricade against the airfield's inner fence. *Cover,* she thought, *in case of attack.*

"Is this now?" she asked. "This is live?"

Mendelsohn nodded. "Live."

"How the hell did you get them working?" one of the others asked. Half a dozen of them had been at it for over an hour, trying to get images from the external cameras.

"I didn't," Mendelsohn said, gesturing at his computer. "I rebooted the whole system about twenty times before I remembered we had five of them off-line for repair. What you're seeing are the three I was able to repair quickly—"

"You went topside?" one of the techs—Lazlo, she thought—said.

Aimee stared at the guy. "The Hump is fully shielded. That includes the systems that operate the cameras. The EMP fried the mechanism that made the damn things rotate. That has to be what burned them out."

"Has to be," Mendelsohn agreed. He gestured to the images on his monitors, to the soldiers rushing about in crisis mode. "We're not going to get any movement from these cameras either, but the fact they were shut down during the EMP saved them any further damage. What you see is what you get, but at least it's something."

"Damn right it is," she said. "We can't open the doors yet, but at some point—"

Boots came running. Aimee turned to see Chief Schuler and half a dozen soldiers racing toward them from the Command Core. Mendelsohn had reported the working cameras and they were coming to see for themselves.

"Steve," she said, and he turned to her. "Well done."

Mendelsohn nodded. *Small victories,* Aimee thought. They might not fix anything, but they were a happy distraction.

"Warrant Officer Mendelsohn," Chief Schuler began.

He never completed his thought. Lazlo cursed loudly and grabbed Aimee's arm, spun her back around to face the cameras. Others swore and shouted and they all crowded around Mendelsohn's station to stare at the monitors. The cameras revealed many more soldiers now, most of them taking cover where they could. They shouldered their weapons and fired in a strange, silent pantomime. Atop a Jeep that had been shoved over in front of the fence, one soldier jerked three times and then fell backward. The airfield was under attack, but down in the Hump all they could do was watch the battle begin.

Aimee felt a shroud of sorrow enfold her. Nausea roiled in her gut. Part of her wished that Mendelsohn had never fixed the cameras.

"Go, go, go!" a Secret Service agent shouted.

A hand took Felix's arm to hustle him forward and he shook it off. Running down an inside stairwell in near darkness without letting panic defeat him—without puking or screaming or crying—was hard enough without anyone shoving him.

"Don't try to help me!" he said, shaking free.

He had no idea who had grabbed him, but they didn't try it again. Here in the stairwell, with only the emergency torchlight that shone from the chests of the three Tin Men who guarded the president, the gunfire and madness outside the hotel seemed muffled and distant but there were shots that were closer, inside. *Nearby.* Those were the ones that worried him the most. Seconds ago, the building had shaken with a thump that could only have been an explosion somewhere in the hotel's corridors, and that was most definitely a problem. Anarchists on staff, he figured, or working for one of the foreign dignitaries on-site.

How many? he thought now. How many people inside the hotel wanted the president of the United States dead?

One of the Tin Men—Chapel—was coming down behind Felix. The shaft of light that shone from his chest bounced as he descended the stairs and, in that light, Felix could see the backs of the heads of those racing downward in front of him. A handful of Secret Service agents, four aides, and the president, with the other two Tin Men in front of him. As they rounded a landing, Felix stared at the back of the president's head and hated him. Absolutely hated him. Peter Matheson had neither conceived of the Tin Men nor given the order for their initial deployment, but he had made them into his bullwhip, his punishment for flouting American demands.

Did it matter that his intentions had been good?

Felix could barely hear the thunder of human and robot feet upon the stairs, thanks to the terrified pounding of his heart—so today? now? It did not matter at all.

Someone bumped him from behind, one of the other agents, and Felix stumbled. He reached out to grab the railing and his hand missed and for an instant he felt free of all gravity, as if he might float away. That same hand caught him again and tugged him back. The Secret Service agent was doing his job, keeping the president safe. Right now that meant keeping them all safe, but only as long as the needs of the group didn't compromise Matheson's safety.

Still, he was grateful.

"One more flight," said one of the Tin Men at the front—Bingham, the female—and he wondered why they hadn't been Tin Soldiers instead of Tin Men and knew it was because Tin Men made people think of *The Wizard of Oz* and people liked *The Wizard of Oz*.

Stop, he thought. *Be still.*

His mind felt slippery. Terror had pushed him to the edge of a kind of panic he had never experienced. He breathed and forced his thoughts to be still and kept moving. The aides were ahead of him on the stairs. They were the only other people in the group who hadn't taken an oath to die in order to keep the president alive. He knew two of them by name—Maggie and Jun—and he hoped they lived to see home again. Bingham and the other robot stopped at the bottom of the steps and they all halted while she put her hand on the door. Felix could hear nothing but his own breathing now—even his heart had been silenced—and then Bingham opened the door and stepped out, leaned back in, and beckoned to them . . . and then they were running again, moving through a service corridor. There were offices and bulletin boards with notes and notices tacked all over them.

Again he thought of Kate. Chapel had suggested they head for Humphreys Deep Station One. It was the nearest truly secure location for the president that he knew would have been shielded from the EMP. Felix's heart had leaped with the hope that they would arrive to find Kate alive and well, and perhaps they would. But Germany was far away and his daughter was a soldier—she would be fighting. Even if Felix got there alive it wasn't likely she would be there waiting, and how likely was it that he would get there alive in the first place? He was just an advisor. The Secret Service agents had not made a vow to take a bullet for *him*.

President Matheson glanced back, his eyes hard.

"Come on, Felix. Don't fall behind," he said.

So Felix kept up. If he had any chance of living until tomorrow it was by staying as close as possible to a man the world wanted to kill. He recognized the irony.

Abruptly, he saw daylight.

They streamed out a door at the back of the hotel—some kind of service entrance—into a short alley lined with Dumpsters and half a dozen corpses. Garbage debris littered the pavement, some of it stained with blood, and Felix saw a rat on top of a dead man, nose inside a bullet hole. The rat ignored them as they ran by and Felix felt his capacity for horror reach a kind of threshold. Not the limit—he was sure there would be more horrors to come—but for the moment he went numb, seeing it all as if he were a passenger inside his own body. In a way, he was. The president was the driver now, and the Secret Service the vehicle to get them out of immediate danger.

Only immediate danger, though. There might not be such a thing as entirely out of danger anymore. If there ever had been.

Gunshots cracked overhead, echoing off the alley walls. The Secret Service agent who'd saved him on the stairs staggered back and fell, legs going out from under him, blood jetting from the hole in his neck.

Two snipers on the roof of the building adjacent to the hotel. The president's Tin Men killed them before the rest of the Secret Service agents even had time to aim.

Then they were at the end of the alley. Bingham held up a hand to halt them as she looked out into what had been a fairly busy back street before the G20 security barricades had been put up. Bingham didn't beckon them forward, though, and Felix had gotten close enough to the president and his security to see why.

The police and military guarding the barricades had broken into clusters, not holding any firm line. Gunfire came from all directions, shattering the windows of official vehicles and pinging off concrete slabs that had been used to block the streets for the duration of the G20. U.N. troops sheltered behind several of those blocks, returning fire. Athenian cops had taken cover inside a restaurant across the street, all of its windows shattered. As Felix stared, two of them stepped out, back to back, and fired off several rounds at enemies that those in the alley could not see. One of the cops took a round through his skull and went down but the other somehow made it back inside.

There were two men in the street who seemed out of place.

Directly across from the mouth of the alley was a white armored car with U.N. markings—a troop carrier. The men who sat inside the open back of the carrier were not soldiers, though both had guns. They had discarded their jackets but the two men had been wearing suits and still had their ties on.

All around the rear of the troop carrier were other men in suits. Dead men in tailored gray and black, lying in the sun.

Chapel pushed past Felix and even the president, past Maggie and Jun as if they weren't there, and joined Bingham.

"Ambush, Mr. President," Chapel said, that deep voice so clear amidst the sounds of combat.

Felix frowned. Who the hell had been ambushed?

"Go get them," President Matheson said.

Chapel did as he was told, taking the third bot with him and leaving Bingham to guard the president. The two robots—*Marquez*, Felix thought, *that was the other one's name*—raced across the street. They took fire, a handful of shots that did nothing but leave scuff marks, and then Chapel and Marquez were at the troop carrier and the two men who had been pinned down suddenly had an escort. *Now or never,* Felix thought, and they must have realized it as well, for they leaped from the carrier and raced back toward the mouth of the alley.

Felix stared at the two men.

"Holy shit," he said.

One of the ambush survivors was thirty, blue-eyed, and square-jawed. He wore a red tie.

The other one was the Russian president, Kazimir Rostov.

"Go to Route B," Chapel ordered, and the Secret Service men began to hurry them all back through the alley toward the hotel.

They had more than one exit strategy, of course, and Felix hoped this one would lead to a clearer path. He found himself next to Rostov and his lone surviving bodyguard, but then Rostov—fifty-one, face like a tombstone, strong and hard-edged—dropped back to run beside Matheson. The two men had always put on their most courteous faces for the public, but they hated each other, it was well known. Now Rostov had put his life in the hands of the American president because he had no choice.

"I blame you," Rostov said in his gravelly voice, not trying to keep his voice down as they reached the doorway and pushed back inside the hotel. "For all of this."

Felix cringed as they ran through the service corridor of the hotel, footfalls echoing off the walls. Didn't Rostov know this wasn't the time or the place? Didn't he realize they were all just trying to get out alive?

But Matheson did not deny the accusation. As Felix glanced back, the American president shot the Russian a withering glance.

"Not my fault alone," he said.

They turned corners, two Tin Men in front and one in back like before, and in moments Felix wrinkled his nose at the smell of grease and burnt meat, and then they were pounding through the hotel's kitchen.

Five men waited there for them—men who had spent their whole lives dreaming of murdering presidents.

• • •

Kate and Danny hustled through the embassy corridors, heading back to the conference room, their heavy footfalls making the walls tremble. Kate had adjusted to spending eight hours a day five days a week in a robot body, adjusted to the size and weight of it and rejoiced in the ability to walk—to run—again. She had become so familiar with her bot that sometimes she forgot about the grave air of consequence that followed in their wake. They were intimidating as hell, and right now she felt the power of that. Yet in the aftermath of the morning—and in anticipation of the dark unknown future—she also felt fragile and alone. When anything might happen, all things seemed fragile.

They heard the voices before they rounded the corner and Kate recognized two of them right off—Ted Hawkins and Lieutenant Trang. That didn't bode well, but when they actually turned the corner the reality was worse. Half the remaining members of Platoon A were strung along the corridor while Hawkins and Trang faced off, with Captain Finch and Lieutenant Winslow looking on.

"You!" Trang boomed when he saw Kate and Danny approaching. He thrust out a shaking finger. Light coming into the hall from the conference room slashed a bright stripe across his chassis. "This is your doing, *Corporal* Wade."

"Sergeant, remember?" Kate said. "We need to talk, Lieutenant."

"Damn right we—"

Kate shot a look at Finch. "We all need to talk."

As she and Danny came to a halt, Trang poked her chest, the sound echoing along the hall.

"Not another word, *Corporal*. When I say we need to talk, I mean that I need to talk and you need to listen. Privates Hawkins and Mavrides tell me that you've given the order that Platoon A is to return on foot to Germany—"

"That's not the plan anymore," Kate replied.

Thump went that finger against her chest.

"I never gave such an order and you have no authority to do so!" Trang barked.

"Maybe she should," Danny said.

Trang's head swiveled. "Don't start, Kelso. You're a private. You're not even in this conversation."

Hartschorn rapped on the wall to get their attention, startling them all. Everyone turned to look at him, even Captain Finch.

"All due respect, Lieutenant, I think we're *all* in this conversation."

"You stormed out of a meeting with your platoon leader and this base's commanding officer," Trang said, focusing on Kate again. "Then I hear this. Let me make this perfectly clear, Corporal. Platoon A will be sitting tight, making camp, and protecting the American civilians right here until help arrives."

"Are you fucking kidding me?" Hawkins roared. "Help is not coming!"

"Private Hawkins!" Captain Finch barked. "That will be enough."

Torres and Birnbaum had stood together—the two women seemingly in accord—but now Torres took a step toward Trang.

"Sir, yes sir," she said.

"Alaina . . ." Birnbaum said softly, but Torres didn't look at her.

Kate stared at her. Torres had wanted action, but now because Trang had given the order she was going to toe the line. Kate supposed she shouldn't be surprised—Torres had made it clear that her country came first, and to her that meant following orders.

"Don't do this," Birnbaum said to Torres. Their friendship was volatile, and Kate had the idea that the two women had once been more than friends. Now Birnbaum had a husband and a kid back in Germany and she was having a problem with Torres's idea of patriotism.

Hawkins turned to Kate. "Do something, Wade."

"There's nothing she can do," Lieutenant Winslow said.

No one paid any attention to that—Winslow wasn't one of them, so to hell with what he thought.

Kate glanced at Danny, who gave a single nod. He was with her.

"Do you understand me, Corporal Wade?" Trang demanded, awaiting a salute, some sign of obedience.

She jammed a finger into his chest, metal ringing loudly. "It's time for you to listen, Khoa—"

Trang reared back. She wondered if it was the poke or his first name that had shocked him more.

"You have been falling apart since this began," she said. "Your leadership is unreliable, Lieutenant. You are not thinking clearly and should relinquish your duties."

"How dare you?"

Kate spun, took a step, and stood face-to-face with Captain Finch. Him, she saluted. "Captain, there are things you don't know, sir."

"You're way, way out of line, soldier," Finch drawled, but he could not hide his interest.

"During our meeting, I had a terrible thought," she went on.

"Look at me, Corporal," Trang said. "Look at me right now or I swear to God when this is over—"

"Lieutenant Trang," Finch said curtly. "I want to hear what Wade has to say. When your platoon is on the embassy grounds, I have operational control. I will decide what happens next."

Mavrides laughed. "Burn."

"Private Kelso and I went back to the brig to confirm my suspicion with Hanif Khan," Kate said. "The timing of this attack was not coincidental. Right now, the G20 summit in Athens is under attack. The president is there, sir."

"Not just *our* president, either," Danny added.

Of course it wasn't just presidents Wade was worried about, but she didn't want them to think saving her father's life was her only agenda. That would stay between her and Danny.

Finch blanched and his face fell. "You want to take your platoon to Athens, is that it?"

"No," Trang said, voice quavering. "No, damn it, we stay here. We wait for orders. Help will come."

His voice had turned shrill, an edge of madness to it. His metal alloy hands moved as if he had no idea what to do with them. The lieutenant had been unraveling all day, but now his fear seemed about to break him.

"Wait a minute," Mavrides said. "You want to march back to Germany, okay, but—"

"The *president* is under attack, Mavrides," Danny said.

"Which means he'll be dead by the time we get there," Mavrides replied. "And what is he president *of* now, anyway? He gonna hold the United States together by Pony Express? There's no authority anymore, Kelso. Nobody's in *charge*."

Hawkins bashed Mavrides with the heel of his hand. "Shut it, kid. You sound like a fuckin' anarchist." He turned to Kate. "I don't agree with Zack, but the president has Tin Men as part of his Secret Service detail. He doesn't need us."

"Sergeant Wade—" Finch began.

Kate shot him a dark look. "Pardon me a second, Captain."

Ignoring Trang, who had taken to staring at his feet, she turned to Mavrides and Hawkins and the rest of them gathered there in the corridor.

"Protecting the president is the same thing as protecting the homeland. I've got people I love back in the States. I can't do anything to help them from so far away, but we can do *this*. At home, right now, hell is breaking loose. But in that hell there will be people fighting to keep it all together, to keep the nation intact." She stared at Hawkins. "Our part of that fight is in Athens, at least for now."

Kate saw movement in the conference room behind Finch and only then did she see that Ambassador Day had been there all along, overhearing the conversation. He noticed that she'd seen him and gave a small nod, though whether in greeting or approval she could not tell.

"Permission to speak, Captain?" Danny said.

Winslow shook his head. "Oh, look, someone's asking permission. Isn't that cute?"

"Go ahead, Kelso," Finch replied.

"There are elements here we haven't dealt with," Danny said. "The civilians at the embassy are in danger, as are your troops. Ideally, we'd get the hell out of Damascus and take every American with us, but we can't travel to Athens with all of these people. Lieutenant Trang believes he should stay and some of the platoon may agree with him. Maybe that's the solution, sir. We'd need Hanif Khan with us for whatever we can learn from him about the G20 attack and for potential trade value down the line, but I suggest that we break into two squads, one to stay and one to go to Athens."

All eyes turned to Trang. His head still hung and it wasn't clear whether he was even listening.

"Lieutenant?" Finch prodded.

Trang raised his head but he would not meet the gaze of anyone but Finch. "As you say, Captain, you have OPCON."

"I'm asking for your thoughts, Lieutenant Trang."

"Do I have your word that when order is restored you will faithfully recount all that has transpired here?" Trang asked.

Finch stiffened. "Of course, but order may be a long time coming."

Trang turned to Kate. "Go, then. I'll see you at your court-martial."

Kate nodded, then scanned the rest of them. "Who's with me?"

Birnbaum and Danny were in immediately, followed by Hartschorn and Hawkins. Lahiri, Prosky, and McKelvie took another moment, but raised their hands.

"I'll stay with the lieutenant," Rawlins said.

Guzzo and Reilly backed him up. Travaglini refused to commit either way. Kate stared at him, surprised until she remembered: a fourth-generation soldier with a bloodline of genuine war heroes. Finch might have OPCON, but Trang was Trav's CO.

"After Athens we go back to the Hump? To our bodies?" Mavrides asked.

Kate nodded.

"I'm in," Mavrides replied.

Yippee, she nearly said.

Birnbaum turned to stare at Torres. "Alaina?"

A robot's face could be only so expressive, but the storm raging inside Torres was obvious to anyone who cared to look. Torres got on well with Danny but she had never liked Kate much. This would only have made it worse. She had a deep respect for the promises she had made to her country and for the chain of command that went along with it. Now she had to decide between protocol and a suicide mission to save the president, knowing Peter Matheson might be dead before they ever got to Greece. But she had to see that Trang had suffered some kind of breakdown.

Torres turned to Kate. "I'm in."

"So are we," a girlish voice piped up.

They all turned to see a teenage girl pushing past the ambassador inside the conference room. Finch and Winslow turned to stare at her, even as Ambassador Day grabbed her shoulder.

"Alexa . . ." the ambassador began.

The girl's eyes were red and her face was streaked with drying tears. She might have been crying before but now she looked bold and determined. Kate figured her for sixteen or so, but whatever her age the kid had grit.

"If you're getting out of here," Alexa said, tucking her hair behind her ears, "me and my dad are coming with you."

Kate stared at her—this girl who'd been eavesdropping on the goings-on in the conference room for who knew how long—and wished she could say yes.

"Not a chance."

"Alexa," the ambassador said, studying his daughter with sad eyes before he drew her back from the open doorway. Then it was his turn to stand between Finch and Winslow and stare down the Tin Men in the hall. "Whatever happens to me, I can't allow my daughter to stay here. By yourselves, you could go on foot, but if you're going to bring Khan you'll need some kind of transport. If you're taking him, you can take Alexa."

Kate felt time rushing past her. "Fine, but we've gotta move fast."

Hawkins raised his hand. "I got you, Sarge." He smiled. "Thanks to our Bot Killer friend Ingo, we know there are at least a couple of working Humvee-TSVs we oughta be able to lay our hands on."

Mavrides laughed. "We might have to kill some anarchist fuckheads, though."

Kate nodded. At last there was something upon which they could all agree.

13

The Bot Killer base was one of a dozen identical warehouses that lined either side of a narrow street branching off from Al Katheeb Lane in the northeastern part of the city. Trang had stayed at the embassy with a complement of Tin Men to help guard the walls while Kate took a dozen with her to see if Ingo's too-good-to-be-true story about Humvee Troop Support Vehicles with shielded engines checked out.

They broke into three teams, one each for the front and back entrances, one for the rooftops. In broad daylight, their stealth tech left something to be desired. While in the dark it was effective, in direct sunlight it worked well only if the bot stood completely still. Research to improve the tech had been ongoing, but now it would never be completed. Danny didn't worry about that, though. Most of the time, the Tin Men wanted to be seen. The intimidation factor was useful in combat . . . as was the ability to kick the shit out of the enemy.

What the bots lacked in stealth they made up for with speed. They weren't Special Forces, they were infantry: grunts in shining armor. When they went after a nest of Bot Killers, they kicked in every door and blew the shit out of everything that got in the way. No stealth required.

The noon hour had come and gone but the sun still bleached the city, ripples of heat rising from the pavement. Danny led Birnbaum and Travaglini across the roof of the building that abutted the western wall of the Bot Killers' nest. Danny had the feeling Birnbaum was starting to fall apart and he hoped a mission would help shock her out of it. So weird that she had chosen Hawkins to be her rock during all this.

They kept low to the ground, moving swiftly and as silently as possible. Danny signaled and Trav and Birnbaum fanned out to his right, all three of them racing toward the low wall that ran around the perimeter of the adjacent building's roof. One of the Bot Killers paced along the near side of the opposite roof.

Danny knelt, took aim, and put a silenced bullet through the man's skull. Arms flailed and he spun backward to sprawl on the roof. On the far side of the roof a second guard's patrol of the perimeter brought him out from behind a massive air vent.

"Got him," Birnbaum said, and she fired twice, both kill shots.

Twelve seconds.

They took a running start and leaped across the alley. Danny landed three feet from the guard he'd killed, rolled, and came up with his weapon ready.

Seven seconds.

They searched the roof for other guards, ducking behind massive ducts and air-con units and a hulking, rusty water tank from some old-fashioned sprinkler system. They signaled one another with the all clear.

Two seconds.

Trav took the eastern roof access. Danny kept Birnbaum with him. The last second ticked down, Danny gave the signal, and he and Trav kicked in both doors at once. Fuck stealth.

He and Birnbaum crashed into the stairwell and raced downward, gunfire erupting below. The teams led by Kate and Hawkins had smashed their way in and the shit had started to fly.

Danny and Birnbaum took a corner and emerged on a metal walk-way suspended sixty feet above the floor of the warehouse. Trav came out onto a parallel walkway fifty yards away, but the real action unfolded beneath them. Danny absorbed it in a single glance—metal shipping containers stacked three and four high around the inner edges of the warehouse floor as if to suggest that the building was full, when instead they protected a large clearing at the core of the place that had been turned into a camp for the Bot Killers. Cots and bedrolls, food and water—and most important, two enormous black Humvee-TSVs and a whole array of mechanics' tools and equipment. The TSVs were sleek armored trucks with three rows of seating, plus a long storage bed in the rear.

A dozen Bot Killers scrambled for their weapons. Some already had them in hand and were returning fire as best they could, but Kate's team and Hawkins's team had them in a pincer. With robots coming through the alleys between stacks of metal containers, their only chance at survival was to run. Some of them did. Danny tracked a guy in a black keffiyeh who fled between two army green containers; he sighted and took the shot.

Trav went over the railing first. Danny saw him drop to the top of a shipping container with a clang and then Birnbaum jumped. Danny came right behind her, slamming down onto a container and then dropping forty feet to land in a crouch between the Humvees.

Two Humvees, Danny thought. But it had been clear from above that there had been six vehicles here. Six vehicles parked, six vehicles worked on, six vehicles that had left spots of oil and fluid on the concrete floor. Four of them were gone and if the story about keeping the engines shielded was true . . . they'd been driven out of here after the EMP. That explained why there were fewer Bot Killers than he'd expected.

Four other TSVs, he thought. How many damn Bot Killers were there in Damascus? They didn't even know for sure this was the only warehouse.

A bearded blond guy in a T-shirt and fatigues raced around one TSV and dove between them, thinking he was taking cover. He looked up from the rough concrete and spotted Danny just before the bullet took him.

Shouts of triumph erupted in the warehouse. Danny stepped over the dead German. Three of the Bot Killers had thrown down their weapons and were kneeling on the floor, surrounded by Tin Men.

"Kelso!" Kate called, weapon still trained on the surviving Bot Killers, as if these three scruffy, weaponless anarchists had any fight left in them. "Secure the vehicles."

"You got it, Sarge," he said. A quick glance and he spotted McKelvie. "Mac, take the second one."

The rest of the squad was still celebrating, happy to have any kind of win in the shadow of the day's horrors.

Danny circled the nearest TSV while McKelvie went around to the other one. Danny opened the rear door on the driver's side and looked inside. The upholstery had suffered some wear but the Humvee had been cleaned out recently. Something niggled at the back of his mind and wormed its way under his skin. The smell of fresh motor oil wafted off the Humvees and there seemed no doubt they had been recently tuned up. These two vehicles were precisely what the platoon needed if they were going to take anyone with them to the coast—perfect, really, and maybe that was what bothered him.

Good luck hides its price tag, his father had told him a thousand times, so he couldn't help but wonder what this stroke of ridiculous good luck would cost them. *And again: Where are the other four vehicles?*

He opened the driver's door, reached in, and popped the hood, then walked around to the front end and hauled it up to expose the engine.

"Hey, Kelso," McKelvie called. "The keys are in it."

If Danny had still had a heart, the sound of McKelvie trying the Humvee's ignition would have broken it. Danny's hands worked quicker than his mouth, fingers darting down to pull wires even as he shouted "Down, down, down!"

McKelvie's Humvee exploded in a ball of flame and shrapnel. The hood blew off and blazing engine parts crashed into walls as Danny crouched beside the other vehicle, praying the blast wouldn't cause a chain reaction. Most of the second TSV's windows blew in and it rocked up onto its left wheels for an eye blink, but it didn't explode.

Bots were shouting fury as the first vehicle burned. Kate roared orders and Danny looked up to see Birnbaum peeling herself off the ground, tossing aside a fiery bit of melting metal and plastic. Two of the Bot Killers who'd been on their knees in the middle of the warehouse floor were dead. One had taken a gasket or something to the chest and lay bleeding on his side on the concrete with smoke coming out of his wound. The third stood up and began to scream while Kate snapped at Mavrides to lower his weapon and the bloodthirsty punk shouted about booby traps. *No shit, dumbass,* Danny thought. *What was your first clue?*

He didn't think about McKelvie because McKelvie was done.

Danny moved around to look at the intact vehicle's engine again, the thing wired with so much Semtex Six that it had been impossible to hide it. Opening the hood before starting it up had saved him— saved some of the others, too, because this one had shielded them from the worst of the explosion.

A shot rang out. Danny whipped around and saw the last Bot Killer with his head snapped back, a hole in his skull, dead as he toppled to the floor.

"Fucking Mavrides!" someone barked.

But Danny looked at Mavrides and even with those robot features he could see the kid was as shocked as anyone. He hadn't pulled the trigger . . . and the angle was all wrong. Danny looked up at the same time Kate and Trav and a few others did and they saw the sniper up on the suspended walkway.

The sniper didn't bother trying to kill them, just stood there while the Tin Men shot him full of holes. He hung over the railing, blood falling in a crimson rain to spatter on the concrete sixty feet below. Danny stared at the dead man and all he could think was *How?* He and Trav and Birnbaum had cleared the roof and the stairwells coming down and that could only mean one thing—this guy had shown up after them, come across from another rooftop just the way they'd done it.

By himself? Just to finish off the survivors?

"Kate, we've gotta get out of here!" he called. "It's not just the trucks!"

Slamming the Humvee's hood, he raced around and jumped inside. Broken glass crunched on the seat beneath him as he started it up. The engine roared to life and he counted to two and then smiled because he hadn't exploded. He might not be able to disarm Mavrides just yet, but he'd disarmed the Semtex Six under the hood.

Trav appeared beside the window. "What's the story?"

Danny jammed the Humvee-TSV into gear and gave it gas, pulling away from the burning wreckage of its twin.

"Get in!" he snapped at Trav.

Kate trusted him enough that she hadn't thought to question his instincts. She barked orders and they started to withdraw, moving quickly through the openings between stacks of shipping containers. Trav climbed into the Humvee and Danny drove after the squad, watching the containers, wondering how much Semtex Six the bastards had been able to get their hands on. The soldiers hustled between containers and Danny could see past them now to the hangar-style doors they'd left open.

Couldn't be the containers. They'd never have sent someone in to silence the survivors if they'd rigged the whole warehouse. That left only one option.

"Speed!" he shouted out the window. "Make speed!"

Kate turned as she reached the splash of sunlight from outside. He saw her devil horns though he couldn't make out the little pitchfork from this distance. She had her weapon ready as she called to the rest of the squad . . . and then they were gone, zipping out the door so fast that they seemed to have vanished.

Lahiri was last to leave. The first rocket landed right behind him, the blast blowing him forward into the street.

"Stop!" Trav shouted.

Danny hung a left past the last of the containers, flooring the gas pedal as the Humvee roared along just inside the warehouse wall. As they left the entrance behind, rockets obliterated the doors and another punched through the wall of the warehouse twenty feet above them, blowing metal shrapnel inside. Explosions sounded in the street and gunfire cracked the air, but it was muffled inside the Humvee as Danny and Trav raced between the row of containers and the wall.

"What do you say, Trav? Mostly corrugated metal, right? The steel beams would be a problem, but otherwise it's not so bad."

"What are you thinking, Kelso?" Trav demanded.

Danny had spent months training to pilot a bot, learning to adjust to the additional weight and power of the Tin Men so he didn't accidentally destroy anything. He didn't worry about damaging the Humvee, just floored it with all he had. They approached the far wall of the warehouse at fifty mph and gaining. Trav shouted at him as he aimed between two of the wall's vertical beams, and Danny wondered if the wide TSV could fit between them.

They'd make it through the wall. He was banking on it. If not, they'd have to leave the Humvee behind, and then Ambassador Day and his daughter and Hanif Khan were not going to make it to Athens.

"We'll get there!" he told Trav. "One way or another—"

"Kelso, the fucking explosives!" Trav shouted.

Danny hit the brake, whipped the wheel hard left, and the Humvee rocked up on two wheels as he skidded around the containers in the corner of the warehouse. The rearview mirror on Trav's side smashed off and the Humvee scraped the wall as Danny held on to the steering wheel. Then they were rocketing through the open space just inside the west side of the warehouse.

"Holy shit," Trav said.

"Idiot!" Danny snapped, angry with himself. If he'd driven head-on into the wall with all that Semtex Six under the hood—

The Humvee's headlights picked out a door straight ahead. Closed, but some sort of delivery door, and not the one the squad had used to come through the back.

"Trav, do you see it?" he barked.

Already in motion, Trav scrambled out the window and onto the hood, leaped to the concrete and raced alongside, quickly outpacing the Humvee. Danny tapped the brakes as Trav reached the door, tore off the lock, and hauled it open. As the door rattled back on its tracks, Danny floored the accelerator and started counting in his head. How many seconds before one of the Bot Killers spotted the open door and swung a rocket launcher around to take aim?

The TSV roared out into the back alley and Danny cranked the wheel to the left, rolling the dice that they'd expect him to turn toward the embassy instead. The tires skidded and the Humvee sideswiped a Dumpster and knocked over a crowd of garbage cans. A rocket struck the warehouse only feet from their exit and the wall blew inward with a shriek of metal and a roar of flame.

Something struck the Humvee from behind and the vehicle bounced and juddered on its shocks. Thunder slammed over his head and Danny glanced around to see a dusty metal leg hanging over the edge of the Humvee's roof . . . and he smiled.

Trav scrambled to keep purchase on top of the Humvee as Danny swerved around a second Dumpster, half a second before a rocket hit it and blew it apart. A third rocket struck the side of another warehouse twenty feet ahead of them and Danny steered the Humvee through a curtain of smoke and flame and into an intersection.

"Hang on, Trav," he said.

Trav cried out as Danny took a hard right. Robot fingers came down to grip the frame of the broken passenger window and Danny heard Trav scrambling on the roof. He righted the Humvee and jammed his foot down on the pedal again, and an instant later they were roaring down a wide street.

In his rearview mirror, Danny spotted a pair of Bot Killers running out into the intersection behind them. They leveled Steyr assault rifles and started firing, bullets spraying the buildings and the stalled vehicles. One or two hit the TSV, but nothing vital on it.

Danny found himself laughing out loud, and a second later, Trav joined in.

Whatever his body was made of, it felt good to be alive.

Aimee sat at her monitoring station and tried to block out everything but her search for a satellite signal. It seemed useless. Aboveground, men and women were dying. The feed from the cameras Mendelsohn had been able to get working had been rerouted inside the Command Core. Too many people had been standing around gawking at it and Major Zander had put a stop to that. Access to the Command Core was restricted; only those with access could see what transpired aboveground.

Aimee glanced over at Mendelsohn's monitoring station. As much as it pissed her off not to be able to keep tabs on the battle outside, she could only imagine how furious Mendelsohn had been when he received the order. He had abandoned his station—gone off to get something to eat—but that had been nearly an hour ago and he had not returned.

"Barker's Victoria Cross, this is Wiesbaden Army Airfield," she said, once again trying to raise the underground base in Vancouver. She had sought others, but she had kept coming back to this one because it seemed to have such potential. And yet—the same quiet hiss of an open line. Nobody answered, but she couldn't help feeling that someone might. It was that hiss, like a promise.

"Do you read?" she asked. Sinking down over her station, Aimee hung her head. "For Christ's sake, does *anybody* read me?"

The odds of the Pulse having knocked out every single satellite in orbit were infinitesimal. The bad news was that there were only a handful of places in the world that were likely to still have the capacity to broadcast to antique satellites. The good news was that those places would have people searching for signals the same way she was. Aimee believed that in time they would make contact, but wasn't sure what there was to gain by it. What was she going to say if she got an answer? *Hi there, we're fucked. Oh, you're fucked, too? Okay, well, see ya.*

Klaxons sounded, a terrible alarm that instilled immediate terror. She spun to see a pair of sentries rushing along a catwalk. Chief Schuler appeared from the entrance of the Command Core and waved an all clear, trying to inspire calm and confidence, but Aimee didn't buy it.

She glanced at her station. With the apocalyptic blare of that horn she wouldn't be able to hear a damn thing even if a chorus of angels tried to talk to her over that line, so there was no point in sitting still. After a moment's deliberation she set off toward the steps and almost collided with Ken Wheeler. The security officer was rushing to respond to the alarms himself. Aimee didn't ask permission to tag along and he didn't try to dissuade her. Soon they were racing along the catwalk and she realized that she was returning yet again to Staging Area 12.

An icy nugget of dread formed in her gut and it only grew when she followed Wheeler into Staging Area 12 and saw the fifteen or so people scattered about the room. The medics were bent over a pair of open canisters, transparent lids jutting straight upward. Sentries were reporting to an officer who looked as furious as the sentries seemed crestfallen. Several techs raced through the six-by-six aisles of canisters, checking readouts and peering through lids.

"I've got another one over here!" a tall, redheaded female tech called, her words nearly drowned out by the alarms.

The officer roared at the sentries to kill the alarm. Aimee stood by the railing at the top of the stairs as Wheeler hurried down to offer assistance. She felt paralyzed by the scene before her. Others passed, jostling her, but she barely moved as the full weight of what she was seeing settled upon her.

Platoon A. These were *her* soldiers. She looked after them, monitored their vitals as well as their activity in the field. Major Zander had ordered her to focus on searching for a satellite signal and she had done that, turning her attention away from the men and women in their canisters in Staging Area 12. They hadn't needed her attention; they weren't going anywhere.

But apparently they *had* needed someone.

"Shit," she whispered, as the alarms went silent at last. Her footfalls rang on the metal steps as she hurried down to the staging area floor. She raced toward the nearest tech, a parchment-pale guy named Powers. "What happened? Are any of them . . . ?"

Powers took a second to place her and she saw the glint of recognition when he realized that she was assigned to Staging Area 12. He didn't ask her why she hadn't been paying attention or why so many other techs had responded more quickly to the alarm. Later, Aimee would feel grateful for that.

"Oxygen deprivation," he said, and no two words had ever made less sense or made her feel so sick.

"No, no. The systems were all online and functioning. I was here not much more than an hour ago," she said. "It all checked out. The EMP didn't even interrupt—"

"It wasn't the EMP," Powers said. "Someone shut down life support to the first two rows. With everyone on inventory, the area was clear for at least thirty minutes. A sentry came through and saw red lights blinking."

Aimee glanced around, trying to figure out whose canisters were on either side of her. Corcoran and Hawkins, and their lights glowed green, so they were safe. She hadn't been on the job long enough to get to know every member of the platoon—there wasn't enough one-on-one conversation for her to have matched all the names with the faces yet—but she'd been getting better.

"Two rows," she said. "Twelve casualties."

"Four."

Aimee went numb. "Four *rows*?"

"Nah, nah. Two rows, four casualties. When we can get 'em all back, could be some of the others have some brain damage, but the sentry got the system back online fast enough to save most of their lives."

Four, Aimee thought. *Okay, four.* They were dead—four soldiers with people out there worrying about them, people who loved them—but somehow four seemed better than twelve.

"Who'd we lose?" she asked.

"Sergeant Morello, for one," Powers said, shaking his head. "I knew that guy. A hard-ass, but the kind I was proud to serve with. Other names were Rawlins and Kasturi. I don't know the fourth one."

Morello she knew. And Kasturi—funny, amiable woman. She couldn't dredge up a face to match Rawlins's name and she didn't want to.

"Thanks," she said, patting Powers on the arm.

She turned and headed through the maze of canisters toward where a tech had called out that he'd found another one. Aimee assumed that was the fourth one, the name Powers couldn't remember. As she made her way toward the tall redhead, she passed between the two rows that had been affected by the shutdown, the hum of working machinery providing cold comfort.

Shutdown? Bullshit, it's pure sabotage.

The faces visible through the canister lids were half-covered by the headpieces the Tin Men wore, so their features were hard to make out. The display screens at the foot of each unit, however, clearly identified each of the soldiers from Platoon A whose life support had been temporarily off-line, and she counted them down in her head as she walked by. Torres. Janisch. Guzzo. Mavrides. Prosky.

Not Travaglini, Aimee thought. His canister was in the next row. It made her feel very small and very cruel to be so focused on one soldier—a guy who had never seemed to notice her schoolgirl crush—but she couldn't help the relief she felt.

Eliopoulos. McKelvie. Wade.

"This your platoon?" the redhead asked.

Aimee nodded. Not that she served in that platoon—the two techs understood each other—but that they were her charges.

"Who's that last one? The one you just found?"

The redhead glanced back at the canister she'd left behind. "Private Hartschorn, it says. E. Hartschorn. Poor bastard. No body to come home to. I wonder what happens to him now."

Aimee swallowed hard. Hartschorn. He'd always had a smile for her, a kind of lopsided grin that went well with the scruffy bristle of his hair and made him look like somebody's kid brother. Only now somebody's kid brother was dead.

"That's always the question, isn't it?" Aimee said. "What happens to us now?"

Her eyes burned as she turned away. Others had arrived while she had moved among the canisters and she saw Major Zander speaking to the officer who had been with the sentries when Aimee had arrived. The major's features were stony, as if his face were shrouded in shadows that had no source.

The major wouldn't blame her, not when she had been following his orders. He would be too busy worrying about them all surviving inside the Hump and the battle raging outside, and trying to figure out who had just killed four members of Platoon A. There would be questions, but he would want her to keep searching for contact. His priorities were clear. The only person who would condemn her for these deaths was herself.

Sabotage, she thought again as she walked back to the stairs. She climbed the steps to the catwalk and almost bumped into Private North.

"Oh, hey," she said.

His eyes were full of such pain that she forgot her own. North's survivor's guilt had been bad enough already, and now this?

"Who the hell would do it?" he asked her.

So he knew. One of the sentries had probably laid it out for him.

"I'm sorry?" she said.

"Who did we lose?"

Aimee briefed him; she didn't see any reason not to level with the guy. Her patience with any sort of bullshit or dissembling had gone extinct.

"You asked who would do it," Aimee said, leaning against the railing as she gazed into North's blue eyes. "Don't you think the real question is why? Nobody snapped and did this. We're all under pressure, but this wasn't somebody going nuts and spraying bullets everywhere. This had purpose. It took patience and timing."

North paled. "Someone working with the anarchists? An inside man?"

"Or woman."

"Someone who knew exactly what to do," North said, those blue eyes narrowing. "Maybe a tech."

He'd wanted to say *maybe one of you*—she could see it in his expression—and she was glad he hadn't.

"Maybe," she said, glancing over her shoulder, her eyes tracking

Powers and then the redhead, wondering. North definitely had a point.

"We've got to talk to the major," North said.

Aimee studied the grief and fury in his face and recognized it as a mirror to her own. He was bereft, and she felt the loss.

"You think Major Zander hasn't thought of all this?" she asked.

North gripped the railing and gazed out across Staging Area 12. She felt sure he was focused on the canisters whose lights were glowing red.

"Let's make sure he has," North said. "And then let's you and me have a little chat and see if we come up with any theories about which motherfucker I'm going to have to kill."

14

In the hotel kitchen, Chapel and the president's other Tin Men made short work of the killers who'd been lying in wait. Secret Service agents clustered around President Matheson as bullets flew, ricocheting off oven hoods and shattering chinaware. Felix found himself between two of the aides, Maggie and Jun, and he made sure to keep pace with them because the only people behind him were the Russian president and his bodyguard, and they were dangerous variables.

A Secret Service agent cried out in pain as a bullet punched through his chest. Maggie faltered as blood spattered her, and she dropped to her knees behind a metal table, afraid to continue. Jun kept running but Felix crouched beside her.

"Maggie, *please.*"

Up ahead, Matheson and his protectors had kept going. The assassins were all dead, or at least down and dying.

"If we're left behind," he said, "we're as good as dead."

Rostov shoved Felix out of the way, grabbed Maggie's arm, and hauled her to her feet. His iron eyes were alight with rage.

"Then we must not be left behind," the Russian president said.

Rostov hurried Maggie along. Felix glanced once at the Secret Service man who lay on the floor just a few feet away, dying from a sucking chest wound, and knew he didn't want that to be him. Rostov's bodyguard passed by and Felix knew he was out of time. He careened across the rest of the kitchen, hurrying through a short hallway to a heavy metal door that hung open.

Outside in the sunshine the air thundered with gunfire. Felix pursued the others across a narrow access road to the concrete shadows of a three-story parking garage. As he scrambled over a low cement wall, the bot he knew as Marquez came back for him.

"Move it, Professor," Marquez said.

Breathing hard, Felix only nodded. *I'm moving it,* he thought. *Trust me, soldier. I am moving it as fast as I can.*

Bullets chinked off the outside of the parking garage just as he ran into the shade of its upper floors, blowing concrete divots across the floor and at cars. Marquez didn't even bother returning fire—they were out of range now.

Up ahead, Chapel and Brigham led the way to a central stairwell and they all raced down single file. Then they were rushing along a sublevel of the parking garage, the Tin Men's guide lights illuminating their path, and Felix realized they were underground. He breathed, happy that the anarchists outside could not shoot through the concrete at them. But he knew there might also be enemies waiting down here.

"You!" Rostov growled, pushing past Syd, still carrying a gun in his hand. "We're not under fire now, Matheson. You're going to answer for—"

Syd grabbed Rostov by the wrist and spun him around, disarmed him, and slammed him to the concrete floor, his face inches from an oil smear. Rostov's bodyguard began to shout in Russian and leveled his weapon at the Secret Service agent on top of his president. Marquez shoved Felix out of the way and took aim. The four remaining Secret Service agents pointed their guns at the bodyguard, each with a two-handed clutch, not intending to miss.

Chapel and Bingham shielded the president even as they aimed at the bodyguard, but President Matheson pushed between them. Felix thought Matheson would tell them to lower their weapons, but he did not do that.

Instead, Matheson pointed at the bodyguard. "If he even exhales, drop him."

"Mr. President," Felix said warily.

Matheson dropped to one knee beside Rostov, who was face-first on the concrete, held there by Syd, a slender but powerful woman with shoulder-length blond hair, the only Secret Service agent not wearing a tie.

"What do you know, Kazimir?" Matheson asked. "You're so sure it's my fault . . . *America's* fault . . . but you're too damn sure. If we're going to survive, it will have to be together. So tell me what you know."

Matheson tapped Syd's shoulder. "Sydney? Let President Rostov up, please." He glanced around, then pointed at the bodyguard. "But my instructions still stand regarding *that* guy."

Rostov stared at him, granite face etched with contempt. After a second or two, he gestured to his bodyguard and the man lowered his weapon. Syd took a step farther back from Rostov and lowered her own weapon. She knelt to pick up Rostov's gun but did not return it.

"Perhaps you are not solely to blame," Rostov said, raising his chin. "Several years ago, we heard whispers through back channels of a small, anonymous anarchist group who claimed to have a plan to free the world of American influence. There was some talk even then of chaos and one mention of what they called the Pulse."

Maggie took Jun's hand.

"You did nothing." President Matheson stared, eyes narrowed with fury.

"What could he have done?" Felix said, and all eyes turned to him. He continued nervously. "Mr. President, do you have any idea how many threats against the United States are overheard by the Russian intelligence services in a single year? Hundreds, at least. In the past decade, that number has to have gone up exponentially, year after year, as resentment built."

Matheson hesitated. Breathed in and breathed out. "I'll bear the weight of my part in the precipitation of all this. That's going to haunt me for the rest of my life."

Chapel stepped up beside him. "All due respect, sir, that won't be long if we don't move our asses."

Matheson and Rostov stared at each other for another second or two. *Practical men,* Felix thought. The two presidents understood each other better than perhaps anyone else in the world could have. Matheson reached out and Syd handed him the Russian president's gun, which he then returned to Rostov.

"Hold our fight for another day?" Matheson asked.

Rostov nodded. "If we are alive in the morning, we can decide if we still want to kill each other."

The Tin Men heading for Athens needed speed. The Pulse had struck just before 0900 hours and they had not hit the road out of Damascus until after 1300 hours. And what had the world leaders in Athens been doing in that four and a half hours? Danny figured many of them had been busy dying.

Danny drove the Humvee-TSV along a narrow, rutted highway, kept his hands tight on the steering wheel, and did his damnedest to keep his mouth shut about what they might find waiting for them in Athens. To Kate, Peter Matheson wasn't just the president, he was her father's best chance at survival.

Any overland route to Athens would take forever, even if they weren't in the midst of a slow-motion apocalypse. The immediate catastrophes caused by the EMP were just the beginning. The fallout would be so much worse, and the longer they took to reach their destination the more of that chaos they would have to travel through, which meant a sea journey across the Mediterranean from Haifa to the west coast of Greece, as close to Athens as they could get.

First things first, Danny thought. *The road.*

Before the Pulse, there would have been no debate about what route to take from Damascus to Haifa. South on Highway 15 toward

Daraa, then west through Irbid and all the way into Israel until the road curved northward again. A hundred and sixty miles, give or take, maybe three hours at the speed limit. But the Pulse had canceled anything remotely resembling a speed limit and they didn't have three hours.

They took Highway 7 to the southwest. Danny and Kate up front. Prosky, Trav, and Hartschorn on the roof. Hawkins, Mavrides, Birnbaum, Torres, and Lahiri in back with Ambassador Day, his daughter, and the fucking anarchist. Hanif Khan had been eager to talk earlier, to gloat, but from the second he realized they were going to jam him into the back of the TSV and haul ass in an attempt to save the president's life, he'd been dead quiet. Danny liked that.

Ten robot soldiers, a middle-aged diplomat and his seventeen-year-old daughter, and a killer who'd helped engineer the end of civilization, all cooped up in an oversized black troop-sized Humvee. It sounded like the beginning of an odd joke, but Danny wasn't laughing.

Inside the city perimeter of Damascus, the broken-down cars and trucks were a problem. Several times Prosky and Hartschorn had to run ahead and shove vehicles off the road. People heard the engine and hurried into the street or to their windows. Some cheered and others shot at them. Children raced beside the Humvee for a block before they were left behind. Old women wept and reached yearning hands toward the Humvee, searching not so much for aid as answers. That was how Danny saw it, at least.

And what were the answers, anyway? Did they matter? To him, the only answer that meant anything was, *It's over, folks. You're on your own. Rebuild the best you can and protect your stuff because someone will try to take it away.*

"Next time, do better," Danny said quietly as he drove, just to hear his own voice.

"What's that?" Kate asked.

He didn't repeat himself. He didn't need her to remind him there might not be a next time.

"You sure this trimaran is going to be there?" she asked.

The TSV approached a tractor-trailer that had died in the road. At the sound of their engine, the driver emerged, hanging halfway out the truck's open door and waving to them in a frenzied combination of panic and relief. He thought he'd been rescued, and Danny refused to look at the trucker's face as he accelerated around the vehicle, leaving the man baking in the desert. He had made it five hours, waiting for help to arrive. How long before he realized it was not coming?

"We talked about this," Danny said. "Of all the ports we might target, Haifa's most likely to have a hydroptere, maybe more than one. With the wealth that's migrated to that city in the last fifteen years, it's our best shot."

Kate glanced out the window. From this angle, she looked like any other robot, but he could see just a fragment of the pitchfork on her cheek.

"What if there isn't one?" she asked. "The people who own those boats . . . you really think they wouldn't already have taken off in them?"

Danny narrowed his eyes against the sun glaring through the windshield. "Kate, you've got to stop—"

"I mean, sure, some of those guys are probably dead," she went on. "Maybe they're rich assholes who don't live anywhere near the harbor. Could be it hasn't occurred to them yet or maybe they're afraid of just sailing off into the sunset without knowing what's waiting for them wherever they make port. They've gotta be confused just like everyone else."

Danny reached out for her hand, knowing that one of the others might get a glimpse between the seats but not caring. He took her hand, felt her fingers wrap around his, and squeezed.

"We'll take the fastest boat we can find," he said. "It's the best we can do."

Kate let go of his hand. She shot him a sidelong glance. "If I'm alone out here, Kelso, it's important I remember that."

Danny couldn't argue with her. To do so would have implied a promise he could not bring himself to make. He felt himself splintering inside. Why hadn't he ever felt this connection with her before?

They'd shared friendship, yes, and attraction, but now he felt as if they were becoming tethered, and it troubled him deeply. He would back her up in combat, but could he give her any more than that?

"You should promise," she whispered. "Do that much for me, at least. Tell me we're going to get there."

"You don't want bullshit, Sergeant," he said sternly. "Bullshit isn't going to help you do your job. It's not going to help us reach the president."

Or your father, he thought.

Much of the city had been deserted, but in places where the warnings had not come soon enough, people gathered beneath awnings and fanned themselves on balconies. Smoke rose in twisting spires in the distance where fires had begun without anyone to put them out. When they passed within a block of the wreckage of a passenger jet, Danny slowed for a moment to gape at the plane's mangled nose cone, which had come to rest on the steps of a school. The rest of the fuselage had broken up and destroyed much of the next two blocks, and two apartment buildings were still on fire. A woman sat on the curb outside a corner shop, her face buried in her hands. One of the plane's engines lay inside the shop as if its walls were a nest, the engine an egg.

The world unraveled, and the Tin Men kept rolling.

"Hey, Kelso," Lahiri called up to them. "What's the deal with this boat you're hoping to find?"

"It's a sailing hydrofoil," Birnbaum answered for him. "A trimaran big enough for all of us, but so fast it'll do fifty knots on the open sea. Maybe a little less, given our weight."

"Aw, the rich girl knows sailboats," Mavrides said.

"Looks that way," Hawkins agreed. "Thank God for that."

Danny knew how to sail as well. Had, in fact, been on a hydroptere before, back in high school, but not because he was rich. His father had been a working sailor, part of the crew of a steel gaff schooner owned by the CEO of a nu-energy corporation, which was one of the old-school oil companies retrofitted to look as if they gave a shit about the environment. Danny's father had taught him how to sail from childhood and made him promise he would have his own ship one day, and never crew someone else's.

If they were lucky, today he would break that promise.

Haifa had thrived since the Tin Men had forced relative peace on the region. During that same period, the hydroptere had become a status symbol for rich assholes and a gift to adventurers with a genuine interest in mastering the seas.

They could make the journey from Haifa to Athens in just about any sailing ship large enough to hold them—Danny and Birnbaum could see to that—but minutes might matter, and a hydroptere would save *hours*.

With the city behind them and miles blazing past, they came upon fewer vehicles. Danny weaved in and out and spoke a silent apology to each pilgrim they passed on the road and every voice that cried out from those dead cars and trucks. This route would cut fifty or sixty miles off the trip, but better yet, out here in what Mavrides called the Great Big Nothing there were simply fewer people.

He tried not to think about how many of them were going to die.

"Hey," Kate said, too softly for the others to hear over the growl of the engine.

Danny glanced at her. "What's up?"

"You really believe you're alone in the world?" she said, studying him. "I mean *really* believe it?"

He looked back and forth between her and the road, slid the Humvee around a pristine silver BMW, and then turned to Kate again.

"I think it's safer like that."

Kate glanced away, the hesitation full of such vulnerability that he could almost see her human face.

"I had the idea we were looking out for each other," she said quietly.

Danny watched the road, hands still tight on the wheel. When he looked back at her, the terrain to the west had turned into rough stone hills, orange and red like some alien landscape. They were as far from whatever they called home as they would ever be. He had no idea how to even define "home" anymore. Was this it, right here with Kate?

"You going to tell me I've been imagining this thing?" she went on. "'Cause you seemed to like the idea until today."

How many times had he imagined what it would be like to take her to bed? *Or let her take you to bed,* he thought. *This is Kate we're talking about.*

Now here they were. But even if he allowed himself to stop swimming, just for a second, to see if he could handle all these things he never allowed himself to feel . . . what would be the point? Trapped inside the tin, what was the use of tenderness?

"I liked the idea, yeah," he confessed. Danny glanced at her, wondering how much his robot eyes revealed. "But look at us, Kate. There's no point in having this conversation while we're like this."

She glanced away.

"The irony's fucking brutal, isn't it?" he asked quietly.

"What is?" she asked, trying to draw him out, make him spell it out for her.

"Never mind."

Danny glanced over his shoulder. The others were still talking, speculating, arguing. None of them were paying attention to the front seat, as if he and Kate were the parents and the rest of them the squabbling children. All but Khan, who remained silent. Danny glanced in the rearview trying to get a glimpse of the anarchist, but instead he saw the girl, Alexa Day, watching his eyes in the mirror.

"I get it," Kate said. "The irony."

"You said you didn't," Danny replied quietly.

Kate stared straight out through the windshield. "It's not the same for me."

"Why isn't it?"

"Your end goal is to get back to the Hump," Kate said. "Get back to your body, just like the rest of them. And I want to make sure that happens for you. It's important to me that you make it back there."

Danny steered around a dusty white delivery van, but saw no sign of whoever had been driving it this morning.

He glanced at Kate, not sure he'd understood. "You saying you don't want to get back to the Hump? You got some plan to martyr yourself along the way?"

"Nothing like that," Kate replied, then turned to meet his gaze, unflinching. "I just don't give a shit if I ever get my body back. The bot might get scratched or charred, but barring some seriously bad luck I could live a thousand years. Hell, maybe forever."

"Kate—"

"And there's the other thing, y'know?" she said, glancing out the window again. "Like this, I have legs. I can run."

Danny stared a moment longer, then turned his attention back to the road. Three motorcycles had been dumped on the hardscrabble shoulder of the highway, their owners nowhere to be seen.

Kate's hand touched his, a brief moment. A metal caress. Then she withdrew her touch, not wanting to draw attention from the rear of the vehicle.

She prefers the robot, he thought.

And the Tin Men rolled on.

BOOK TWO

15

Alexa felt as if she couldn't breathe. The bots weren't troubled by the heat, but in the back with her father and the anarchist and half a dozen Tin Men, the temperature just kept rising. Hot wind blew through the shattered windows but did nothing to cool her. The vehicle bumped through a pothole and swayed as they moved around another car that had died on the highway.

She shifted in her seat, careful not to jostle her father too much. The ambassador's injuries weren't life-threatening, but he'd been given some heavy painkillers and was sleeping off and on.

"He looks almost peaceful," a low, accented voice said, just behind her. "In the midst of all this, that's quite a feat."

Alexa stiffened. Her father was sleeping but Hanif Khan was not. She glanced out the broken window and watched the brown hills for a while before she realized that she could see the anarchist's reflection in the gleaming metal door frame. If he'd had a knife he could have cut her throat or stabbed her through the seat.

"You're lucky they didn't just shoot you," she said quietly, heart pounding. With all the other dangers she had faced today and then the exodus from Damascus, she'd barely thought about Khan.

"Shoot me for what? Fighting back?" he replied softly, his voice somehow both rough and silky at the same time. "If you had lived my life, girl, you would—"

Khan's head slammed hard against the TSV's interior. The anarchist hissed and spun to stare hatefully at the robot beside him. Alexa turned halfway round in her seat. The soldier had a smiley face with pirate-flag crossbones beneath it on his forehead. *Hawkins,* she remembered.

"Don't talk to the girl," Hawkins said. "Don't even look at her."

How can he not look at me when you put him right behind me? Alexa thought.

"Words aren't going to hurt me," she said instead. "What can he do? He's a prisoner."

Khan smiled. "You think that means I've lost? There are no victors here."

Hawkins smashed his head against the metal again. A hand touched Alexa's shoulder and she turned to see that her father was awake.

"That's enough," the ambassador said. He glared over the seat at Hawkins. "I know you're looking out for my daughter, but she doesn't need anyone to bleed for her."

"You defending this piece of crap?" Hawkins asked, his robotic features attempting a sneer. "After what this guy did—"

"Coming up to Al Quneitra," Kate called back to the rest of them.

Bending to peer through the windshield, Alexa saw that they were moving along a street of faded two- and three-story residences. People were camped on top of the dusty, useless cars in the road, and they rose to watch the vehicle roll past, anger and suspicion and confusion on their faces.

The Humvee sped up and Alexa was glad. She didn't want to look.

Minutes blurred past and sometime later the Humvee jerked as it slowed to a halt on the side of the road. Alexa looked up to see that they were well clear of the town and had stopped in the middle of nowhere.

"What are we doing?" she asked.

Kate popped open her door. "Robots don't have to pee, but we figured those among us with bladders might want a quick break."

Hanif Khan groaned with relief. Alexa hadn't even been thinking about needing to go, but now that Kate had mentioned it she realized she had to. They all piled out of the TSV except for Trav, who remained behind the wheel, and Torres marched Khan off toward a stand of trees to relieve himself.

Alexa glanced up the grassy slope to her right, saw an outcropping of rocks surrounded by thick bushes, and made a beeline for cover.

"Hold on," her father called. "You should have someone with you."

"I think I can manage!"

Even with the sweat that had beaded on her skin, she was thrilled to be out of the Humvee. The sun felt good and a breeze rustled the bushes around her as she slid her pants down. When she had finished and rearranged her clothes, she leaned against the rocks for a minute, enjoying the solitude. Staring out across the land, she saw no sign of civilization save for a handful of distant farm buildings. For that brief time it was possible to imagine that nothing at all had changed, that it was the same old world it had been the day before.

On her way back to the Humvee she came upon Danny and Hawkins talking quietly. She slowed down, hesitant to interrupt what seemed like a serious conversation, and she overheard enough to realize that Hawkins was just finishing some kind of message to his mother. *A goodbye*, Alexa thought. *In case.*

She frowned, wondering where the camera might be, and then it occurred to her that Danny was functioning as the camera, somehow recording the farewell message with the eyes and ears of the robot he inhabited.

"Your turn," Hawkins said.

"Nah, I'm good," Danny replied.

Neither had noticed Alexa yet and she stood there, awkwardly frozen. What was she supposed to say now?

Hawkins grunted his disapproval. "Come on, Kelso. You telling me if things go tits up, there's nobody you're gonna want to know that you were thinking of them at the end?"

"Sorry to disappoint."

"Bullshit," Hawkins said. "What about Kate?"

Danny held up a hand. "I don't know what you think—"

Hawkins shook his head. "All right, Kelso. It ain't my business. All I know is, if I didn't have anyone worth living for, I'd top myself right now. Be done with it."

Alexa tried to take a step, hoping to circle around them, but in the quiet that had fallen between the two soldiers the crunch of her foot-fall seemed inordinately loud. Danny and Hawkins both glanced at her.

"Sorry," she said sheepishly. "Just going back to the Humvee."

Hawkins nodded. "Me, too, kid. Thanks for your help, Kelso."

Alexa strode to the vehicle, Hawkins at her side. He said nothing about the conversation she had just overheard and she was glad. She'd felt awkward enough without having to acknowledge it. At one point she glanced over her shoulder and saw that Danny hadn't moved. He stood still, staring into the sky.

They found several of the Tin Men gathered behind the vehicle in conversation with her father. Behind the wheel, Trav started the engine and it rumbled to noisy life.

Alexa sat on the roadside, propped herself up on her arms with her legs out straight, and listened to his voice.

"Many of them will see us as the enemy, passing through these towns," the ambassador was saying. "You've got to find a way to let them know that you're no different from them. It won't be easy, but, look, you're all someone's child. Some of you have kids of your own. We all hoped for a future better than the past. We have that in common."

"But they *do* see us as the enemy," Birnbaum said.

Alexa watched her father shake his head like a tired schoolteacher who wasn't getting through to his students. She'd seen that expression on his face so many times.

"There are no enemies now," he continued, the pain in his voice almost mesmerizing in its depth. "Every country is going to have to turn its attention inward. We all just want to go home, to be with the people we love and help them rebuild."

He paused for a breath. Alexa couldn't hear it over the rumble of the Humvee-TSV's engine but she saw his chest rise and fall. She frowned, thinking that it sounded as if the Humvee's engine had an echo.

Confused, she started to glance around, and so missed the sight of the bullet punching into her father's back and exiting his chest. She whipped her head around in time to see the spurt of blood that spattered two of the Tin Men. Her father fell forward, crashing into Prosky's arms. Birnbaum and Lahiri turned in the direction from which the shot had come and opened fire.

Around the front of the TSV, Kate shoved Hanif Khan to the ground.

Alexa realized she was screaming. She saw them all gathering around the vehicle and taking aim, and she heard the echo of the Humvee's engine growing louder, and now she understood it.

A second black TSV had rolled up to idle two hundred yards behind them.

The Bot Killers had followed their trail. They wanted their boss.

Kate snapped off orders but her squad didn't need to be told what to do. Hawkins grabbed Alexa and shoved her farther back, pushing her to the ground so that she was nearly forced under the vehicle. Bullets plinked against robot bodies and off the rear of their TSV.

Alexa kept screaming and tried to rise.

"Stay down, kid!" Birnbaum called, kneeling beside her and trying to hold her as Alexa batted at the robot.

In some calm place deep in her brain, she knew what she had seen: her father falling to the ground. The rest of her could only scream and cry and buck against the weight of the robot trying to cover her.

See? that calm shard of herself thought. *What do you want to see?*

Alexa planted her feet and shoved Birnbaum away. Birnbaum shouted at her as she rose, but Alexa ran toward where she saw her father lying in the road, his arms and legs at odd angles, blood pooling around him.

Daddy, she thought, grief clawing at her heart.

An image crashed into her mind of her bedroom at home, her closet doors yawning wide as they always seemed to be, clothes and shoes spilling out. Before she'd left to come here she had cleaned that closet. In the back, in a box, she had found a pair of glittery purple sneakers that her dad had bought her when she was six years old. He'd bought them not because she'd begged but because, he said, he'd seen the way her eyes lit up when she saw them in the store window.

Cleaning out that closet, she had thrown away the sneakers. Then she had gotten on a plane and flown halfway around the planet to visit her father, and the world had fallen apart.

Alexa stood over her father's bloody corpse and stared at the sad, surprised look on his face and she wailed in anguish, hating herself for having thrown away those glittery purple shoes.

Bullets kicked up chunks of road and dirt around her. Birnbaum ran over, took up a protective position between Alexa and the anarchists, and started shooting.

"Hit the deck, kid!" Birnbaum snapped.

Alexa fell to her knees in the street, picked up her dead father's hand and held it.

"I hate you," she whispered.

She was speaking to him. She was speaking to herself.

"Your people want you back so badly," Kate shouted into Hanif Khan's ear, "they'd better be careful where they shoot."

As if to underline her words, the gunfire from up the road ceased, its dying echoes swallowed as the Tin Men continued to fire. Kate started forward, pushing Khan ahead of her as the rest of the squad fell in beside her. Windows shattered in the anarchists' Humvee. The bastards had spread out, taking cover behind trees and in a gulley beside the road. One of them stepped out a second too long and Kate shot him through the throat. Another died, but not by her bullet.

Hanif Khan glanced back at her. "They didn't come for me. They came to finish the job they were given."

The words repeated in her head just as she saw the two men emerge from behind the anarchists' Humvee with rocket launchers on their shoulders. The other Bot Killers started firing at the same instant, a spray of bullets for distraction.

"Scatter!" Kate shouted, and she bolted to the left, dragging Khan to the ground with her.

As the Bot-Killer rockets streaked along the dusty road, she saw Mavrides haul Hawkins to the ground. One of the rockets hit a stand of trees where Danny had taken cover, blowing splintered wood and leaves apart and knocking him backward. The second hit the ground right between Hartschorn and Prosky.

The explosion tore them apart, blasting smoking pieces of robot all over the road.

Alexa lay on her back on the ground. Her ears were ringing from the explosions and her cheek felt damp. One hand fluttered up to touch the wetness there. She held her fingers in front of her eyes and saw red. Her blood, from a piece of shrapnel that would have taken her eye if it had struck two inches higher.

With a groan she rolled onto her side on the hot road and found herself staring at her father's corpse not six feet away. His eyes were open. A lone fly buzzed around his face with great interest and then began to investigate the exit wound on his chest. A fresh wave of grief rushed up through her and new tears sprang to her eyes even as the sounds around her returned.

Gunfire.

She forced herself up to her knees, checking herself for injuries. She turned and saw Birnbaum fifteen feet to the north, down on one knee, firing at the Bot Killers in the distance, not worried about the other members of her platoon who were in the crossfire, knowing her bullets could do nothing to them.

Alexa pressed her eyes closed. She heard boots striking pavement and then hands grabbed hold of her. Her eyes flew open and she struggled even before she saw the grim features of Hanif Khan. She tried to fight him but he batted her hands away, shouted something at her, and threw her over his shoulder in a fireman's carry. Alexa screamed and beat at his back as he ran with her.

Seconds later he put her down, none too gently, in front of their

Humvee TSV, the only real protection they had. His hands were still cuffed, but in front of him now instead of behind.

She shoved him away. "Don't touch me, you fucking—"

Hanif Khan shoved her against the TSV's grill and pinned her there with his cuffed hands, his arms like iron bars.

"You'll be killed, you idiot!" he barked.

Before Alexa could reply, they heard the scream of another rocket. Both of them turned just in time to see it strike the pavement ten feet from Birnbaum. The road erupted with the explosion, hurling the robot backward so that she hit the ground and rolled until she was parallel to Alexa's father's body.

When Birnbaum rose, Alexa saw that the robot's legs had been painted red. She had slid through the pool of Arthur Day's blood.

Whatever fear or anger had been holding Alexa up gave way and she sank to her knees. Numb, she stared from the safety of the alley at her father's body.

Khan crouched beside her. Alexa realized for the first time that he had probably saved her life. All she could do was wonder why.

"Don't worry for your father, girl," he said, his voice a deep, rasping growl. "For him, the fight is over. Worry instead for yourself."

Kate killed two of the rocket-launcher men herself. The other ran for the open door of the Bot Killers' TSV and went down in a barrage of gunfire. Their TSV's tires kicked up dirt as it roared off, headed back the way it had come. Several other men rushed the vehicle and leaped in through open or shattered windows.

"Trav, you and Torres check to see if Hartschorn and Prosky are still functioning!" Kate called as she moved to the center of the road and the rest of the squad started to form around her. "Hawkins," she said, focusing on the familiar smiley-and-crossbones. "Take Mavrides and Lahiri and go kill those motherfuckers."

On foot, the three Tin Men caught up to the Bot Killers in no time. The bastards shot uselessly at them from the retreating TSV until Hawkins—she assumed it was Hawkins—reached in while running alongside and dragged the driver from behind the wheel. Kate turned away then. Whether Hawkins, Mavrides, and Lahiri wanted it quick or took their time, she was fine with it. The Bot Killers were getting what they had coming.

Her foot kicked something hard and she looked down to see that it was the blackened head of a robot, its eyes dark and dead. She had no idea if it was Prosky or Hartschorn, but now—reduced to this—it didn't seem to matter.

It wasn't supposed to be like this, she thought. *The whole point of drones was to* prevent *this.*

Only then did she notice that she had lost track of Hanif Khan.

Danny clambered to his feet, head ringing from the explosion of the rocket that had nearly done him in. If not for those trees, he'd be scrap metal now. He started toward the Humvee, feeling useless and pissed off, then saw Khan crouched behind the vehicle with Alexa Day. With the last gunshots resonating in his head, he strode toward them. Birnbaum knelt over the ambassador's corpse in the middle of the street but Danny walked right by her. The rest of the squad was back along the road a ways, dealing with their attackers, but Danny's interest was in Khan.

The anarchist's brown eyes tracked him as he approached, but Khan did not try to flee. He had managed to slip the chain on the cuffs beneath his feet so that he would have his hands in front, but he did nothing to protect himself as Danny stomped up and grabbed him by the shirtfront.

"There were other TSVs," Danny said. "That means the motherfuckers my squad just killed are not the only ones out there. So I'm asking . . . how many men did you have with you this morning? How many more of them might be in pursuit?"

Sweat glistened on Khan's expressionless face.

"Many," the anarchist said. "Very many."

Alexa Day backed away from them both. Danny shook Khan again.

"Why are they doing this?" he demanded. "You didn't strike me as jihadists."

"We are not."

"Then why? People don't sacrifice themselves like that unless it's for faith!"

Now Khan sneered, upper lip curling back in revulsion. "Faith," he said, "or revenge. Every one of the men working with me lost someone they loved—not combatants, you understand, but innocents—to your kind. They know you are all vulnerable now and they are not going to stop until you are dead. Or they are."

Danny hated him, but as he studied the man's eyes he understood that Hanif Khan's hatred was greater than his own.

"What about you?" he asked. "Who did you lose?"

"Not an innocent," Khan admitted. "But it doesn't matter. If not for you, he would still be alive."

Alexa Day made a small sound, one Danny feared was born of sympathy. He wanted to remind the girl that her father lay dead forty feet away . . . but when he looked at her he saw her staring at Khan with such hatred that he realized he didn't need to say a word.

Danny grabbed Khan by the back of the neck and shoved him, stumbling, around the side of the Humvee. There were so many retorts struggling to make it to his lips, but he spoke none of them. He held on to the belief that the Tin Men had done more good in the world than harm—he had to believe that—but he couldn't argue with Khan's hate. Only with his actions.

He hauled open a door and shoved Khan into the back of the Humvee. "From now on, *I'm* your keeper."

16

The bullet struck the president on the left side of the head. Felix was standing beside him when it happened, and a little spray of blood spattered onto his shirt. President Matheson pirouetted and began to stumble out into the street, fully exposed to the gunfire that ripped pavement and plinked dead cars and shot out the windows of shops.

Felix took a step after him. Maggie snatched his shirt collar and dragged him back into the doorway where they'd been hiding.

"Don't be stupid!" she said angrily, blood seeping from a forehead scrape she'd gotten from a fall.

"It's the . . ." Felix began, but stopped himself.

The trio of Tin Men were already out on the street, flanking Matheson, hustling him back toward the open doorway. Blood streamed down the left side of his face but he was alive. Felix stared, trying to make sense of it, and as the robots pushed Matheson into the doorway he saw the furrow along the man's skull and realized the bullet had only grazed him. The skin had been torn open and the blood flowed, but his brains were still inside his head.

"What now?" Felix asked, turning to Syd, the ranking Secret Service agent left alive.

Syd gave an angry look. "Same as the last hour. Stay alive."

There were fourteen of them now—President Matheson, three Tin Men, four staffers, three flesh-and-blood Secret Service agents, President Rostov and his bodyguard, and Felix. Of all of them, Felix felt the most expendable, and that feeling haunted him. It crawled underneath his skin like tiny metal ants, able to magnetically attract bullets. Yet he'd been expecting death ever since they'd left the hotel and somehow he still lived. For Kate, he kept moving. Nobody had handed him a gun yet, but he felt sure it would come to that. What he would do with one he had no idea.

The ground shook from an explosion not far off and Felix gritted his teeth. There had been so many that he ought to have been used to it by now. Instead, it frightened him more deeply every time. One of the Secret Service agents snapped at the aides to stay back. Rostov's bodyguard said nothing, only ducked his head out into the street then pulled back in, expression grimmer than ever.

Rostov stood staring at the three Tin Men clustered around the president. For a second, his gaze flickered toward Felix and something passed between them—perhaps a mutual acknowledgment that if Matheson died, the protection they'd received so far would evaporate. *At least you have your bodyguard,* Felix thought. The ugly, granite-faced Russian seemed to have no problem with the idea of dying for his president. Felix didn't want to die for anyone.

Especially not in a dress boutique full of colorfully clad mannequins.

"Come on!" Jun cried out. "We can't just stay *here*!"

Syd turned to face him, blond hair bedraggled with sweat. "The president is down, kid. Nobody—"

"Scratch that," a deep voice said, and they all turned to see Chapel, the leader of the president's Tin Men detachment, stepping away from the others. "The president is *up*."

Matheson had stitches in the side of his scalp. The blood had stopped flowing but still smeared his temple and cheek. He glanced around, clearly disoriented, but then Bingham—the female among the bots—took his arm and guided him to Felix.

The robot stared into his eyes. "Minor concussion. Maybe worse. Stay with him and we'll try this again."

Felix nodded and then they were all in motion. Chapel and Bingham went to the open doorway and the gunfire aimed at them started up again. The rest of them stayed back. Felix felt the president's grip on his arm tighten and he turned to see a dazed, frantic light in Matheson's eyes.

"They don't know it's us, Felix," Matheson said. "Rostov and me. If they did, this whole building would already be down. You hear all of those other explosions, the rest of the gunfire? Right now they're hunting everyone from the conference, trying to make sure we're dead. But that's going to be over soon and then they'll be more thorough. This is our one chance."

"I'm with you, Peter," Felix said, hoping he sounded comforting, worried now about the extent of this concussion.

Matheson cupped a hand on the back of Felix's neck and drew him close. Eye to eye, it was plain that the man still had his wits about him, though he seemed in pain.

"I'm sorry," the president said.

The three Tin Men stepped out into the street and opened fire, Bingham and Marquez in one direction and Chapel in the other. They shouted for the others to go, and Felix's legs were in motion before he could command them to stop. Syd and the other Secret Service agents surrounded him and Matheson, with Rostov and his bodyguard just behind, followed by three of the aides. The fourth aide, a pale and lanky man Felix couldn't have named, remained in the recessed doorway and only shook his head in refusal as the rest of them departed. Nobody shouted at him to follow or tried to get back to force him. He had made his choice.

Felix's final glimpse of that aide, ghostly as he slipped back into the shadows of the shop, would remain with him until his last breath.

Maggie began to shout over the gunfire. Jun held her hand and they ducked down low as they ran. Felix had President Matheson's arm and they hid behind the Tin Men as they raced diagonally across the street toward the darkened entrance of a Metro station whose cavernous mouth offered the promise of quiet and refuge.

Bullets strafed one of the Secret Service agents just as he came abreast of Rostov, his presence saving the life of the Russian president in an irony that made Felix want to weep. Rostov's bodyguard took a bullet to the shoulder but instead of slowing him it sped him up. He grabbed Rostov's arm and rushed him forward, hurling the two of them into the open Metro stairwell. Felix and Matheson followed a moment later with the others on their heels. Last inside were Bingham and Chapel, who turned to shout at Marquez that they were clear—they were safe.

A rocket struck ten feet from Marquez, blowing him back along the road. The explosion brought concrete dust raining down on their heads in the Metro stairwell and blew in windows across the street. Felix held his breath as he watched Marquez rise to his feet, turn, and begin to return fire.

The second rocket hit him dead center, blew apart his carapace, and ignited his power core, which went up with a muffled crump of metal and enough force that it knocked Maggie and Jun off their feet. The president stumbled but Felix kept him from falling as they all began shuffling down the stairs into the darkness, nearly tripping over several terrified people who had taken shelter there.

"Bingham, take point!" Chapel ordered.

As she moved ahead of them, her chest plate blossomed with illumination so bright that the people sheltered on the stairs threw up their hands to shield their eyes. The guide light turned the stairs into a dusty gloom that made Felix think of a shipwreck deep on the ocean floor. They began to descend into that eerie void with the echo of Marquez's death still ringing in their ears.

Eleven left, Felix thought.

The president tumbled on the stairs, squeezing his eyes shut and opening them several times in a row as if trying to clear his vision. Chapel hustled along behind them, his own guide light coming to brilliant life in the darkness.

Felix glanced back up at the square of rapidly diminishing sunlight they'd left behind and felt the concrete closing in around him. He'd thought the Metro station would provide them a quiet refuge, but now he reminded himself that the same could be said of a tomb.

They reached the station lobby and hurried over the turnstiles, down another flight of stairs. Syd stopped at the edge of the platform. Rostov and his bodyguard didn't even slow. They clambered down and dropped to the subway tracks, then turned to stare at Chapel. No one acknowledged that Matheson's injury had called his leadership into question, but they all recognized it.

"We must make it to Piraeus, get to open ocean," Rostov said. "The only way we get out of here is on something with sails."

"So which way?" Syd asked.

Bingham jumped down to the tracks and turned left. "Port of Piraeus is this way."

"You sure?" Chapel asked.

Bingham glanced at him and Felix saw that in the depths of the subterranean darkness, their eyes were bright.

"All right," Chapel said, pointing. "That way."

The Tin Men helped Matheson down to the tracks as Felix sat on the platform and slid himself off, taking care not to twist an ankle. He didn't want to be left behind like the ghost in the dress shop doorway.

Finding himself once more partnered with Matheson, Felix held his arm and helped him stumble quickly along the tracks, but his thoughts were plagued by something the man had said—something that had rung false even then.

"You have Tin Men with you, Mr. President," Felix whispered to him, eardrums still thrumming from the hellish noises they'd endured. "You don't think they knew who they were shooting at?"

Matheson looked at him, features bathed in the light that came from Chapel's chest as the robot guarded their flank.

"Felix," Matheson said.

"Professor Wade is right," Chapel said. "The word will have gone out. If they have communications of any kind, they've got to be limited, but the shooters up there were trying to keep us pinned down, waiting for backup. Once it gets here they'll be after us."

Rostov had stopped ahead of them. "Don't despair," he said. "An hour ago, most of you thought you would not live another hour. Let's see how we've fared an hour from now."

As they all set off into the darkness with Bingham's guide light leading the way, Maggie fell into step beside Felix and tapped him on the arm.

"Hey," she whispered. "How screwed are we when the Russian president is our resident optimist?"

Aimee and North stood in a corridor near the Command Core with Major Zander. He had an office somewhere nearby but didn't seem inclined to invite them for tea.

"What happened to chain of command?" Zander asked, fixing Aimee with a hard glare. They had drawn him out of a meeting for a quiet word and he was impatient.

"Yes, sir, it's only that—"

"Sabotage trumps chain of command," North said.

Aimee shot North a look. First he'd wanted her to do the talking, but now—what? He wanted the glory? When had he *ever* been gung ho about anything other than a drink or a great set of tits?

"You're talking about Staging Area 12?" Major Zander asked, eyes narrowed. "Those deaths weren't an accident?"

"I don't believe so, sir," Aimee replied.

Major Zander normally kept a fairly icy façade in place, but for just a moment it broke. Anger and frustration brought color to his cheeks and he glanced at the ground for a brief moment.

"Son of a bitch," he whispered, just loud enough for them to hear.

North let out a huff of breath. "We'll get the bastard, sir. You give the word and I'll put a gun to every head if I have to. Whatever it takes to figure out who's behind it."

The ice returned to Major Zander's eyes. "I don't condone that cowboy shit, Private. You could've been more help in the field today with your platoon instead of leaving your bot to gather dust because you soiled your canister. I'm sure they could've used you. Can I assume you were assigned a task?"

Aimee saw North's jaw working as he tried to contain his reaction—embarrassment or anger, maybe both—but then he nodded.

"Inventory, sir."

"Then get back to it. We have an entire security team to handle this. I'm going to put them on it. They may want to speak with you, but otherwise you are not to discuss your suspicions with anyone else. We have enough goddamn problems down here."

With a short nod toward Aimee, Major Zander turned and strode back toward the Hub. Aimee didn't even have to look at North to know he was fuming; she could practically feel the anger emanating from him.

"I don't expect him to kiss my ring," North muttered, "but Jesus."

"Pretty sure he's got other things on his mind," she said.

"He's still a dick."

Aimee shrugged. "But he's right. We've all got jobs to do and mine isn't to play Nancy Drew. I'm supposed to be at my station, trying to find an open channel."

North shot her a dark look. "What's stopping you?"

She held up her hands. "Okay. I guess we all have a right to be assholes today, but you go be one somewhere else."

With a scowl, North turned on his heel and started along the corridor, heading away from the Hub.

"Aren't you supposed to be doing inventory?" Aimee asked. "You're not going to get to the kitchen or the storerooms that way."

North paused, his back to her, but he had his head cocked slightly so she could just make out his profile. She didn't like what she saw there. Whatever had happened in the field to change him, North had developed a dark streak, a twisted knot of fear and self-loathing that seemed to run deep.

"Need to clear my head," he said, and then off he went, without looking back.

"I'll say," she muttered to herself.

But as she walked away, the image of his profile lingered in her mind and she found her thoughts following a path that made a chill grip her spine. Just how dark was North's dark streak, really? It would have embarrassed her to admit how little she actually knew a guy with whom she'd had sex several dozen times.

Don't be stupid. You know him well enough. You saw him grieving.

Still, the look on his face began to haunt her, and he had ignored Major Zander's order to return to inventory. Even the most disgruntled soldier did not disobey a direct order without a better reason than a need to clear his head.

Her skin felt flushed as she hurried along the catwalk, moving as quickly as she could without breaking into a run. Several soldiers cast odd glances her way as she passed but by the time she reached the stairs that led down toward her station there were very few people around.

Quieting the panic in her heart, she rushed to her station. Focused on their own tasks and worries, her fellow tech-monkeys paid little attention to her. Aimee sat down, ignoring her headset and the job she was supposed to be returning to—the quiet crackle of what might have been an open channel to Vancouver would have to wait. Instead, she tapped at her keyboard, plugged in her access code, and started to scan the live surveillance video of the corridor where she and North had parted ways. That particular spoke led to the Staging Areas for the Eighth Battalion and the expansion currently under construction for the Thirteenth.

Shifting from camera to camera, she was able to search the corridor but saw no sign of North. Who did he know in the Eighth Battalion?

"Where the hell are you?" she whispered.

A commotion began to stir several stations away and she glanced over to see people gathered in front of a screen, watching the battle that continued aboveground. Either Major Zander had changed his stance on confining the video feed to the Core or someone was breaking the rules. From the troubled expressions on the pale faces of her colleagues, she knew the attack had not been repelled, but the tension in them also told her that the fight had not been decided yet. People were dying up there, both allies and enemies, and the knowledge fueled her purpose. People had died down below as well, and if there were enemies here, she wanted them exposed.

Surfing through camera feeds from the Eighth Battalion's staging areas, she saw no sign of North, but he could have been in the bathroom or something.

She kept coming back to that look on his face, that grim profile. As much as it had been full of fear and frustration, there had been purpose in it, too. Purpose and pain and something else as well—regret. Perhaps even guilt.

Someone cheered over at the other station, people not doing their jobs but instead focusing on the topside battle. She glanced at her headset—they weren't the only ones ignoring their duties, but she couldn't shake the fear that had taken hold of her. Paranoia? Perhaps, but so be it. If there was ever a day to be paranoid, this was it.

She scanned the corridor again. The one other place he could be was in one of the unfinished Staging Areas for the Thirteenth Battalion, and there were no slumbering soldiers there, nobody he could hurt . . . if he had been the saboteur. What harm could he do?

Aimee felt sick. *No way. He has no access. He's a Tin Man, not a tech.*

Still, she switched over to view the unfinished Staging Areas. All work had stopped this morning when the shit had hit the fan and so the place was truly empty, the lights dimmed. All three of those sprawling rooms looked the same, full of the tech that would serve as the foundation for the new canisters that would be brought in, but each with several monitoring stations already in place.

In Staging Area 32, one of the monitors glowed blue in the otherwise shadowy room and a figure sat before it, tapping away at the keyboard. Aimee zoomed in on the live feed to confirm what she already knew.

North.

How the hell had he even accessed the station? He'd have needed an authorization code and, from there, at least a fundamental knowledge of how to navigate through the Hump's operational systems. The USARIC didn't train their soldiers for that. And what was he up to?

"Okay," she whispered. "You want to play?"

She had seen the anguish in him when he realized that his platoon had been cut off, that their minds were trapped inside their bots, and his pain when he'd discovered that four of them had died after that sabotage had clearly been real as well.

But did that mean he hadn't been the one responsible?

There weren't a lot of things Aimee Bell was good at. She'd tried sports and musical instruments and dance and theater as a little girl and sucked at all of them. She couldn't really even tell a story or a joke without fumbling along and blowing the punchline. Her flirting skills were painful. But this? Making a computer do her bidding? She was a virtuoso.

Her fingers worked the keyboard. With a final tap, she summoned an image to her top screen—live video showing North's face, hard at work. Every monitoring station had a camera for face-to-face communication, but they could be made to work in more than one direction if you knew the right codes. She slipped on her headphones and listened to him cursing quietly to himself, staring at the pained expression on his face. North looked frightened and loaded with regret, so pale she thought he might throw up.

"I'm going to Hell," she heard him whisper. And on-screen, she saw a twisted, frantic smile part his lips. "Fuck, I'm already there."

Working fast—speed had to be everything right now—she hacked his station. It was the sort of thing she had been doing since the age of twelve and it would've scared the shit out of her bosses. If her superiors ever had any idea how easy it was for Aimee and people like her to manipulate their systems, they'd never have hired them. Historically, governments and armies did not like to place their trust in people who were so obviously smarter than they were.

Her lower screen showed every one of North's keystrokes. Aimee frowned as she studied the unfamiliar options on display, but it took her only a moment to understand what North had been doing instead of trying to clear his head. The Hump had been on lockdown since the Pulse. Now, with the airfield under attack by what the CO had estimated to be as many as six hundred heavily armed anarchists, the son of a bitch was trying to cancel the Phoenix Protocols so he could release the door locks and make the elevators function again.

She held her breath, staring at the screen, then lifted her gaze to study the desperation etched in North's face. However many anarchists were out there, he intended to let them in.

Not a fucking chance.

The stale underground air seemed to fuzz with static. She ignored North's desperate eyes on her top screen and focused on the bottom. Wings of panic spread and fluttered in her chest but she forced her hands to remain steady as she typed in codes that broke a dozen rules. She'd already hacked the monitoring station North had commandeered, and it wasn't difficult to take it one step further.

With a final click of the mouse, she took over his station, slaving its functions to her own.

She glanced at the upper screen, taking grim satisfaction in the bafflement on North's face. Frowning, he glared at his workstation and kept typing and trying the mouse. The screen he had been looking at would be frozen. When he attempted to start the process over again or reboot his workstation . . .

North slid back from the station and threw his hands in the air. She couldn't hear him swearing but she could read the words on his lips and knew what he had just seen. His screen had gone dark.

"Bastard," Aimee whispered, dropping her gaze to her lower screen.

It took her thirteen seconds to abort the complicated process North had begun. Even as she did so, her thoughts whirled. However North had gotten into the system, he'd had access codes—some kind of authorization. As fast as it occurred to her, Aimee quickly reset the administrative passwords for the Hump's defensive and surveillance systems. With every keystroke, she felt the weight of her actions closing in around her. She'd done the only thing she could think of to safeguard the base. She'd have to face the consequences later.

"Choudhry! Parker!" she called, barely looking up. "Get over here!"

Heart pounding, she stared at the lower screen and forced herself to calm down. Had she done everything possible to keep him from trying again? *Breathe,* she told herself. *Think.*

Her fingers rested on the keypad and she stared at them for a second or two as a terrible question occurred to her. What if he hadn't had a real authorization code at all? What if he'd found a backdoor in the system?

North? she thought. *Even if there is a backdoor, how could he have found it?*

She glanced to her right, over at the distant workstation where people had gathered to watch the battle raging topside, making her question her doubts. Whoever the anarchists were out there—the people killing Americans practically over her head—North had been working with them.

She swore loudly and started typing again, blinking, thinking too fast. If the system had a backdoor, she had to find it and close it or at least alter it enough that nobody else would be able to use it, not North and not the killers assaulting the airfield right now.

"Choudhry!" she shouted, with another quick glance.

This time, Warrant Officer Arun Choudhry seemed to hear her, even turned her way, but something caught Aimee's eye and she pulled her attention away from him. She ceased breathing a moment as she gazed at the upper screen, which showed the workstation North had commandeered. The chair he'd been sitting in was empty.

Aimee felt as if some kind of bubble had formed around her. Caught up in the shock of North's treason, frantic to stop him, she'd ignored everyone else. Parker and Choudhry and the rest were focused on the enemy attacking from outside while she had been fighting the one within.

"Goddamn it, Choudhry!" she screamed, hating the edge of panic in her voice.

Thoughts in chaos, she snatched up the headset from her station, tapped a key to open an internal line, and stared at the empty chair on her upper screen. How long since he'd been gone? Where would he hide?

"Command Core. Corporal Collins."

Aimee tapped the side of her headset. "Collins, this is Warrant Officer Aimee Bell. I need Major Zander immediately."

Something shifted beside her and she glanced up to see that an irritated Choudhry had at last torn himself away from the combat spectators down the row. He looked pissed, but must have seen the sincerity of her panic because his expression softened and he mouthed a question: *What's going on?*

"In case you didn't know, Bell," Collins said, *"we're a little busy up—"*

"We've got an enemy inside, Corporal. Put him on."

"I think Command Core would know if there'd been a breach."

"I'm not talking about—"

"Look, he's in the middle of something. It'll take you two minutes to walk over here. You want his attention, you're more likely to get it face-to-face."

She whipped off her headset and threw it at the workstation. Rising, she turned to look at the surprise on Choudhry's face. His rich brown eyes were narrowed.

"What?" he asked.

"We've got a traitor down here. Private Tom North."

"North?" Choudhry echoed dubiously.

She pointed to her station, already moving away. "Start tracking back the surveillance on Staging Area 13 and you'll find it. And watch that screen! You see anything weird, report it to Command Core."

"You were just on with them and they weren't listening," he said as she raced away.

At the metal stairs, she turned to call back over her shoulder. "They're going to *have* to listen."

A hundred thoughts filled her mind as she ran along the catwalk. Faces turned to watch her go, brows knitted in concern. If enough time passed, some of the people down here were going to unravel, no matter how well trained. She wondered if they thought it had already happened to her.

Fifty feet from the Command Core, she spotted Chief Schuler standing in front of the doors with Kenny Wheeler and a security officer she didn't recognize. When Schuler spotted her approaching, his back stiffened and his eyes went cold. She'd always had the impression he didn't like her very much, but there was something different about this. A tiny alarm began to jangle in her head.

"That's close enough, Bell," Chief Schuler said.

Aimee froze ten steps away from them, reading his tone and the body language from the security officer. Kenny Wheeler's facial expression told the rest of the story.

"I know the identity of our saboteur, sir," she said.

"Yes," Schuler said. "So do we."

The doors to the Command Core slid open and Major Zander stepped out with North right behind him. North looked at her with a mixture of pity and disgust that made her scream inside.

"Corporal," Major Zander said to the security officer, "put Warrant Officer Bell in a hole so dark that mushrooms will grow out of her goddamn eyes."

Felix heard the first cries from the darkness a full two minutes before Chapel's guide light illuminated three figures sitting on the subway tracks. All three were adults, which meant that the plaintive cry could not have come from them. That had been a baby, no question in his mind.

The people on the tracks stirred excitedly, muttering to one another as they shifted and sat up. They shielded their eyes from the sudden glare even as they tried to see past it, to identify the shadowed faces of the new arrivals.

"Oh, thank God," one of them said in Greek. The man shot to his feet, cocking his head and trying to see into the shadows around Chapel. He squinted against the brightness of the robot's light. "Who are you? Are others coming?"

An old woman who'd been sitting beside him glanced up with terror in her eyes. "What's happened?" she asked, also in Greek. "They kept telling me someone would come but no one was coming, and so I told them something terrible must have happened for the police and the train people to leave us down here like this."

"Even the flashlights—" the man began.

He cut himself off mid-sentence, his words ceasing because he had realized that he was not talking to another man—at least not the way he saw it.

"Sir, please step aside," Chapel said.

Felix frowned. He had never liked the translation program used in the Tin Men. Their voices were inhuman enough when speaking English, but at least then the voices were patterned after their own. Run through the auto-translate program that allowed the soldiers to respond in whatever language they had last been addressed, their voices sounded oppressively technological.

"Tin Men," the old woman said, this in English. She spat on the subway tracks.

"What are you doing here?" the man said, also shifting to English. "Have you come to help? Did your government send you?"

In the darkness, Felix knew he and the others must be indistinct, faceless shapes to these people, and he thought it best to keep it that way—at least for the two presidents.

"Step—" Chapel started.

"We'll do what we can," Felix said, moving into the light, drawing the track-sitters' attention.

"We don't have time to—" Syd began, stepping out of darkness.

By then voices had begun to rise farther along the tracks. Others had seen Chapel's guide light and were calling out, some stumbling toward what they believed to be their rescue. *Syd's right,* Felix thought. *We don't have time for this.* But they had little choice. The tunnels were their path to survival and they had known from the outset that they would encounter stranded passengers.

"Chapel . . ." Syd said, his name some combination of question and warning, like *Whatever you're going to do, make it smart and make it now.*

"Sir, let's gather the other passengers so I don't have to repeat my-self," Chapel said. "I can light the way for you to lead me to them."

The Greek squinted, trying to make out the rest of them in the darkness, perhaps taking a head count. But he had been down in the dark underground for hours, so he did not question the offer of help.

The old woman rose with aid from another man, and then ambled along behind Chapel. Maggie and Jun passed by Felix and President Matheson and that was good—human camouflage for the two presidents. Bingham brought up the rear, making sure to angle her guide light so that the two presidents remained in shadow.

As they neared the stalled subway train, Chapel's light picked out dozens of others camped around the rear of the dead metal tube. People glanced up hopefully when bathed in that light, and many of them started talking, grateful that the dark had been pushed back even a little. A quartet of children cheered.

"Everyone please stay calm," Chapel said. "We're going to do a head count and examine the train and will have instructions for you in just a few minutes."

Felix felt sick. He caught the ghosts of faces in that subterranean purgatory, and it was not the anger or desperation or even the suspicion that made his stomach roil with self-loathing and doubt—it was the hope he saw. The deception made him want to stop, to help, to speak the truth, but he knew that he would be jeopardizing the president if he did any of those things—not to mention imperiling his own chances of seeing Kate again.

Maggie came up beside him and whispered his name. Felix shushed her. In the glow from Bingham's chest plate, he glanced over at Jun and saw grim acceptance. As they began to make their way around the train, asking passengers to move aside, they all knew precisely what they were doing. Chapel began to count aloud, even stopped to speak to a woman with a broken leg and a man who held his squalling infant in his arms.

Felix had always been a bit claustrophobic and he had worried from the moment they had descended into the Metro station that this would be too much for him. So far he had surprised himself. Despite the oppressive Athenian heat aboveground, a cool breeze moved through the tunnels, which were high and wide enough that he never felt like the earth was caving in on him. The air was thick and moist and in many places it smelled of urine and worse, but it moved enough that he never felt as if it might choke him.

Not until now.

He slid past people, brushing arms and backs and shoulders in the narrow space between train and wall. Blinking, trying to control his fidgeting heart, he avoided the faces of the passengers. He began to focus on the idea of fresh air and freedom.

Matheson and Rostov kept to the shadows. Syd and Kirkham, the other surviving Secret Service agent, closed ranks with the two presidents and with Rostov's bodyguard. The bodyguard had been shot in the shoulder as they escaped down into the underground. At some point he'd torn up his lightweight gray suit jacket to bandage the shoulder; he had lost enough blood that he had grown pale, but he did not seem any weaker.

As they reached each new cluster of people gathered alongside the train, Chapel blinded the passengers for a moment with his light, got them blinking, and they all kept moving. Bingham counted heads aloud as she walked, another distraction, and in that way they passed four of the five subway cars.

Felix saw the recognition on the young woman's face before she had even spoken. A college student, he thought, gauging by her age and clothing. She stared at him, mouth hanging wide, and she whispered a Greek word that he had always loved. *Archimalakas*. It meant "chief of assholes," as in the worst asshole in the world.

"Oh, you bastards, what are you doing?" she said in English.

He could not make the argument that they had come to help. He could not tell that lie to her face when he had seen the recognition in her eyes. The presidents of the United States and Russia were ten feet away, but this college kid had just recognized Peter Matheson's chief global economic advisor in a near-pitch-black subway tunnel.

"Please, don't—" Felix began.

The girl shoved him out of the way, cursing as she shouldered past. She scanned the others with him, dismissed Jun and Maggie in an instant and focused on the two human Secret Service agents and the men behind them.

"Fuck," the college girl said, her accent noticeable even in that one word. "What are you *doing* down here?"

The edge in her tone made it plain she understood already. Maybe she didn't have the whole answer, but their presence told her enough that she reached up with a shaking hand and her breath hitched in her throat. In the reflected glow of Chapel's guide light, her eyes filled with tears.

"What's happened?" she pleaded in Greek, glancing upward as if she could have seen through thousands of tons of concrete and earth and stone. "What's happened up there?"

The man they'd first encountered tried to comfort her but she spun on him. "Are you an idiot? Don't you see who this is?"

Chapel pointed his weapon upward and fired twice, the gunshots so much louder in the echoing cavern of the tunnel. People screamed and pushed themselves against the wall or the train or dropped to the ground in a cowering crouch.

"Move aside! Move aside now!" Chapel roared, first in Greek and then in English.

Syd shouted to Matheson to move and then they were all hustling through the terrified passengers. People were shoved and knocked aside. A young boy began to scream.

Felix fell into step with Matheson and Rostov and the rest of them, trying to stay ahead of Bingham. Felix felt a deep well of guilt, wanted to cry out his regret to the passengers, but he was also grateful. The gunshots had cleared the people from his path, had driven away the suffocating press of human flesh around him.

"What now?" he asked Syd as they reached the front of the train.

He bumped into Chapel and the robot soldier shoved him out of the way. Felix staggered into some of the passengers who had been camped in the darkness at the front of the train. His fingers touched cloth and skin, the soft, giving flab of someone's arm.

No, Felix thought. *No, don't leave me.*

"I'm sorry," he said to the doughy woman beside him, whose features were only partly visible here on the periphery of Chapel's light.

"All of you, keep back and pay close attention, because I'm only going to say this once!" Chapel announced.

Felix watched the others gather around him—Maggie and Jun, Syd and Agent Kirkham, Rostov and his bodyguard, Matheson and Bingham and Chapel. It felt as if they had moved away from him, as if they had stepped through some wardrobe into a Narnia called survival and left him behind.

"You can't leave these people here!" Felix said.

Somehow his voice quieted a dozen others. Many of the people in the shadows held their tongues, shifting to look at him. Taking a deep breath, Felix recovered his bearings. The presidents and the Tin Men and the others had moved beyond the stranded passengers now, west of the broken-down subway train.

"Ladies and gentlemen, we did not come here to help you," Chapel began, as the people along either side of the dead train cars began to fill in those tight spaces.

"Peter, don't let him do it!" Felix said.

In the shadows, President Matheson said nothing. The college girl who had identified him began to shout his name, pushing past a few others and demanding answers about what had happened to the world today.

"We did not come here to help you!" Chapel said again, and he glared at Felix with those robot eyes, his tone brooking no argument. "Catastrophe has struck. Your whole city is in crisis. Maybe the world. We have hard decisions to make and no time to see to the needs of so many people while we're making those decisions."

"Goddamn it, Chapel!" Felix growled, hands curling into fists.

"But we can't just leave you here," Chapel continued.

Felix exhaled, fists opening.

President Matheson stepped out of the shadows. Bathed in the illumination provided by Chapel's guide light, he gestured for Rostov to do the same. When people saw the two presidents together, Felix thought that at least some of them would curse the two men, but no one did.

"We're continuing on immediately," President Matheson told the crowd, and Chapel repeated the words in Greek. "The only lights we have are from the robot soldiers who are with us. I am sorry we can't provide more for you or make the journey safer, but anyone who wants to follow us, please gather your things and leave with us now.

We will guide you as far as the next station, where you will be able to reach the surface. From there, you will be on your own."

Matheson surprised Felix. Even if the immediate major effects of his concussion were wearing off, he had to still be disoriented. He had to be holding himself together through sheer force of will.

When Chapel finished translating, people began talking anxiously as they gathered whatever they had with them. Felix saw a man half-shrouded in darkness slip his laptop case onto his shoulder, then look down at it for a moment before discarding it completely. Trapped underground, these people could only have suspected what had happened, but this man knew that his laptop had become so much slag.

"Felix!"

He turned to see the president staring at him.

"You coming?" Matheson asked.

Felix exhaled and slipped away from the passengers. Rostov and his bodyguard were talking quietly as Felix passed them and the bodyguard gave him a disdainful glance.

"Screw," Felix muttered to them.

Then he was beside the president, with Chapel, Syd, and Kirkham closing in around them. President Matheson looked him over warily.

"You seem a bit shaken up, my friend, but we've got to move. You going to be able to keep up?"

Felix tried to read the president's tone. Was that genuine concern or some sort of warning?

"I guess we'll all have to," Felix said. He glanced at the shadowed crowd. "One thing worries me, though. When we reach a station and these people actually get outside, they're going to tell anyone who'll listen that they saw you down here. You and Rostov. Chances are pretty good that the anarchists will figure it out. If they're not already tracking us down here, they will be."

Matheson stared at him. He winced and massaged his left temple as he sagged for a moment, then only shook his head as if he had been trying to send a message Felix had not received.

Rostov had been eavesdropping. Now he sneered, half his face lit by Bingham's guide light and the other half cast in deep blue shadow.

"You just insisted they not be left behind, Professor," Rostov said. "You can't have it both ways."

"I thought you'd have left them," Felix said.

Rostov shook his head. "I am a practical man." He pointed to his bodyguard. "Grigori, though . . . he would have been very happy if we had chosen to simplify matters by shooting them all."

The bodyguard—Grigori—smirked at Felix and then broke into a grin that revealed a chipped front tooth and stretched the white scars on his face. Then they all began to march onward. Careful not to stumble on the tracks, Felix cast a sidelong glance at Grigori and then at Rostov. The Russian president had just made a joke.

Felix swallowed, his chest tightening. He *thought* it was a joke.

Somewhere on the road to Haifa, Danny began to daydream. Sitting in the passenger seat of the Humvee-TSV, he stared out the window and his mind began to drift. He ought to have been working hard to stay alert. There were more Bot Killers out there—at least two more TSVs, he figured—and Hanif Khan had made it clear they would keep after the remnants of Platoon A until they had destroyed every robot they could find. It made him wonder about Trang and the others they'd left behind in Damascus, but he couldn't think about those guys now. The Bot Killers would have to get through the embassy walls and the Marines guarding those walls before they could even take a shot.

No, he had to focus on his squad—Kate's squad, really, since she was leading them. The Bot Killers might not be pursuing them solely to rescue Khan but it seemed clear they weren't going to risk the life of their chief unnecessarily. If they could destroy the squad and keep Khan alive, they would do it . . . otherwise they would have blown the Humvee apart with rockets or an IED on the road.

On the road? Only if they can get ahead of us.

Unless they're already ahead of us.

Danny sat in the passenger seat and stared out his shattered window at the sun-baked hills. He felt trapped, he felt like he was sweating, but of course that was impossible. The Tin Men weren't knights in armor. They had nothing but thoughts and data inside them.

Bullshit. Everything I am is inside this thing.

Tattoos didn't matter. Scars didn't matter. This was the naked substance of him. He had never been harder to kill, but he had never been more afraid.

God, he thought, *I'm so tired.*

He flinched—a small tic in the function of the robot he inhabited. What was he thinking? Tin Men could not sweat and they definitely could not get tired.

And yet he *was.* He stared out the window, pushing away the groan of the engine and the voices of Torres and Birnbaum, the only people still talking inside the Humvee.

There hadn't been a lot of talk since Ambassador Day had been killed. The man's body had been wrapped up tightly in blankets taken from some villager's clothesline and they had brought the ambassador with them at the request of his daughter. How long, Danny wondered, before the corpse would *really* begin to smell? They would reach Haifa soon, and then if all went well they would be at sea and the breeze would take some of the stink away, but at some point that seventeen-year-old girl was going to have to fight to keep from throwing up because of the smell of her father's corpse, and that was the sort of thing that Danny didn't ever want to see.

Alexa had lost her father. Danny had lost his father, too, but he still remembered when he had reached out to a friend's wife after she'd lost her mother, to say that he understood.

"It's not a fucking club," his friend's wife had said. "Your grief doesn't make my grief any easier, so keep it to yourself."

Later, he'd wished that he had told her off. Later still, he'd been grateful that he had been too shocked to even consider doing such a thing, because the friend's wife had been right. Danny couldn't remember her name—his friend, Brossi, had been married twice since then—and the woman had been exhausting, but she had been right.

His grief wasn't going to make Alexa Day's grief any easier, so while she wept in the seat right behind his, he kept silent. When she drifted off to sleep, he wished he could tuck a blanket over her. Stupid, in the middle of Syria, but the urge was there. He couldn't take away her grief, but somebody had to look after her.

The tiredness settled more deeply inside him. If he could have breathed, could have felt a real heart beating inside of him, he knew he would have felt more alert. Instead he began to think about the original Tin Man, rusting in the woods alongside the Yellow Brick Road.

"Oil can," he whispered, and laughed softly to himself. The laugh troubled him. He felt detached from it, as if it had issued from someone else's lips.

Out across the brown scrubland, a lone man stood watching them pass. Danny frowned and stared at the distant figure. Against the rise of the hill behind him, the man seemed very small, but as they rounded a turn in the road Danny realized that they were going to drive within fifty yards of him. He almost opened his mouth to warn the others, thinking it might be one of the anarchists with a roadside bomb. Something stopped him from bringing it up, a strange familiarity, as if he knew the distant man by his silhouette alone, by his long, thin arms and the sad stoop of his shoulders.

Mesmerized, Danny stared at the man as the Humvee-TSV drew nearer. Then they were passing by and he stared at the tall, angular man with his librarian spectacles, and Danny felt paralyzed.

The man smiled and raised a hand in a laconic wave.

Danny lifted his own hand to return the wave and a violent shudder went through him. The twitch made him blink several times. When he focused on that brown scrubland again, he saw that the man was gone.

Impossible, he thought. His father had been dead nearly a decade, and yet . . .

"You all right?" Kate asked from her seat behind the driver.

Danny glanced at her and gave another soft laugh. "Are you?"

She studied him a bit more closely, but didn't inquire any further. Danny glanced out at the scrubland again but there was nothing.

What the hell was that? he thought—but then realized he knew.

The robots might be indefatigable but the human mind was not. If this was the result of his mind being overtaxed, what would happen when they were unable to end their shift, to cycle out of the bots? The Tin Men would need to find some way to rest, to shut down. Questions swam into his head, fears about the long-term effects. *Hallucinations, for one*—that was pretty clear. With time, would their minds go on the fritz? Danny wondered how long they had before their memories or cognitive functions would begin to deteriorate.

Leaning his head against the frame of his broken window, he tried to let his thoughts drift the way he did when he put his head on his pillow at night. He didn't fall asleep, but it calmed him enough that twenty minutes later, as they rolled into Haifa, he felt more alert and the world around him no longer seemed quite so surreal. When he thought of his father, of the vision of the man he'd seen on the side of the road, he felt haunted.

Ping.

Danny blinked and sat up. Had any of the others heard that or was it just inside his head? They drove around a van that had died in the road and he saw there were many other cars ahead. Weaving among them would be a challenge. He spotted people sitting on balconies and old men in folding chairs in front of residential buildings as if they were standing guard.

Ping.

All the Tin Men in the Humvee shifted. Mavrides banged on the roof and hung his head down to look through Danny's window.

"Did you guys—" Mavrides began.

"Yes," Danny said quickly, glancing around to study the faces of the other robots. "Just seconds ago it happened again. You all felt it?"

Torres and Birnbaum agreed that they had.

"What the hell is it?" Kate asked.

Ping.

Danny closed his eyes, trying to see and feel the echo of the noise.

"I don't hear anything," Alexa Day said.

He looked at her and then at Khan, whose eyes were slitted like a snake's as he studied them all with keen interest.

"It's not audible," Danny said. "It's . . . internal. A signal."

"It's directional, too," Kate replied. "Can't you feel it? Due west, I'd say."

"And maybe slightly north," Lahiri said.

Danny nodded. That felt right to him. He turned to glance back at Kate again and paused, staring at Travaglini, who had been driving. Behind the wheel, Trav wore the curious smile of someone who had just received a surprise gift and was trying to figure out what it was before he unwrapped it.

"What's with the dreamy look?" Danny asked. "You know something we don't?"

Trav glanced at him. "Don't they teach you kids anything these days?"

Ping.

Kate punched the back of his seat. "If you know what this is, old man, you'd better spit it out."

Trav slowed the TSV at an intersection where a tractor-trailer partially blocked the right turn. As he maneuvered around the dead truck, Israeli men and women began to emerge from buildings to stare, drawn by the sound of a working engine. Down a narrow alley, Danny saw a group of people cooking at a gas grill and wondered how long before all the uncured meat in Haifa went bad.

"It's us," Trav said.

"What do you mean, us?" Danny demanded.

"Well, not *us* us. Not our platoon. What you're hearing is a Remote Infantry retrieval beacon."

"Holy shit," Torres said. "I forgot all about the beacons."

Ping.

Danny stared at Trav. "I don't even know what you two are talking about. Whatever emergency comms we have were burned out by the EMP. And I don't remember anything about a beacon."

"I remember now," Kate said. "In training, they said the beacons were outmoded. Improvements in satellite systems made tracking damaged or stolen bots much simpler—"

"Exactly," Trav said. "But the bots still have a retrieval beacon.

We've lost all satellite-based comms but the beacons are radio transmissions and the transmitters are shielded. We're picking up—"

Ping.

"—the signal. I don't know how many Tin Men were stationed in Haifa, but at least one of them was smart enough to trigger his beacon. They need help."

Birnbaum scoffed. "We all need help."

"Go," Kate said, ignoring her. "Maybe they need our help and maybe they're just using the beacon to let friendly forces know they're still alive. Either way, we can use all the reinforcements we can get. Head toward the signal, Trav."

"Already on it."

As Trav drove northwest, Danny glanced back at Hanif Khan. The anarchist sat quietly, his gaze distant and impassive. He had already indicated that there were squads of Bot Killers pretty much everywhere the Tin Men had been deployed. It made Danny wonder if the son of a bitch was smiling inside. If the beacon turned out to be a distress call, it was a sure bet that Bot Killers were causing that distress. It could be that they were driving into even more trouble than they'd already escaped.

But Tin Men were in trouble. His brothers and sisters in the USARIC, whose bodies were lying in canisters back at the Hump. That meant the president would have to wait. Kate's father would have to wait. Returning to their own flesh would have to wait.

Ping.

"Trav," Danny said. "Drive faster."

Aimee stared at North, hate filling her belly as Major Zander's words echoed in her head.

She spun on the major. "You think this is *me*? That I sabotaged those Remote Combat Stations? *Killed* those people?"

The unfamiliar security officer took a step toward her, hand hovering over his sidearm. "Come with me, please," he said.

Taking a step back, Aimee pointed at North. "This is *him*. The hangover from this morning was bullshit, a way to keep him from being stuck in his bot with the rest of his platoon. All of his fucking grief is theater—"

Kenny Wheeler sniffed. "That's what he said you'd say."

"Of course it's what I'd say! It's the truth. And it's not just what he did to his platoon or sabotaging those canisters. North made a big show of wanting to help and then he ran off to Staging Area 13 and tried to shut down the defensive grid and open the doors. Whoever's out there, he's been working with them from the beginning—"

"That's enough!" Major Zander snapped.

His voice echoed off the sterile walls. Other soldiers along the catwalk froze and turned to watch from yards away. Aimee held her breath and in those few seconds, when they all seemed paralyzed, fear began to replace the fury that had been burning in her gut.

"How can you . . . ?" she started. But there was no way to sum it up.

Major Zander held up a hand and the security officer backed off. Zander stepped toward her, searching her face with a dark curiosity.

"My people just tracked back the access code used to shut down those canisters in Staging Area 12. Your code, Bell."

Her mouth opened. "Sir, I . . . Why would anyone be that stupid? That's my platoon. I'm supposed to look after them—"

North grunted. "You looked after them, all right."

His eyes were bright with a predatory glint.

Aimee felt a reflexive savagery blossom in her own heart. A slow smile grew on her face and she shook her head. How could North think this would work? The only thing she could imagine was that he was trying to buy time. If he managed to divert suspicion to her for even a few minutes, maybe he thought he could try again. All he needed to do for his betrayal to be complete was to get the doors open and the elevators working. Then it wouldn't matter who knew about his treachery.

"This is stupid," she said, exhaling before she stood at attention in front of Major Zander. "Sir, the video feed from Staging Area 13 will show I'm telling the truth. Warrant Officer Choudhry should have that feed ready for viewing immediately. Sounds to me as if you're also going to find my access code was used to start the process of bringing us out of lockdown. I caught North on camera doing just that, hacked into the system, and stopped him. Blocked him out. That's what brought him running to you."

Major Zander cocked his head as if he'd grown hard of hearing. "You hacked the system?"

She straightened even further. "Yes, sir. And I'll accept whatever consequences that brings. It was the only way—"

"Major, this is . . ." North sputtered. "Nobody can hack this system. It was designed by the Pentagon."

"That's not a persuasive argument, Private," Zander said. His body language shifted slightly, but enough to let Aimee know that the major didn't trust North anymore. That he didn't know who to trust.

"I'm not even a tech," North said. "I wouldn't know where to begin."

"Corporal," Major Zander said, "I want both of them brought to the stockade for questioning. If either of them attempts to resist that order, you are authorized to shoot."

Wheeler called along the catwalk to two others, who rushed over at his summons. Aimee no longer smiled, but she felt a strange calm enfold her. She would be happy to spend a couple of hours in the stockade if it meant the truth coming to light.

The glint in North's eyes turned desperate, but she wondered if anyone else could see it.

"Major, wait," North said. "We don't know what other harm she's done. I can—"

The corporal unholstered his weapon and held it at his side, aimed loosely at the floor.

"Time to go, Private North," Wheeler said, and then glanced at Aimee. "You, too."

Aimee stared at North, held her chin high. It was that, or try to kill him with her bare hands, and that wouldn't help anything. North would get what was coming to him.

"Let's go," one of the other security officers said.

Aimee nodded and began to walk.

"Gladly," she said, and then back at Major Zander: "Don't be long. He might not be the only one."

18

Alexa sat baking in the sun that streamed through the Humvee's broken windows. Her father's body lay in the back of the vehicle, wrapped up tightly, just his feet visible at one end and some of his hair at the other. She knew that he was gone, and yet somehow his corpse had a dreadful presence, a weight that she had never felt from anyone still living.

For a short time after his death she had stopped listening to the conversations around her. Slowly she came to realize that listening might be the only thing keeping her from joining her father in the back of the TSV. Or perhaps not even there—if she died, she thought the Tin Men might just dig them both a grave and leave them behind the way they left behind the shattered pieces of the robots who'd been destroyed. Alexa had wanted to ask them about that, to remind them that while their bodies might be back at the Hump, their minds were here inside these robots. Did that mean the ruined bots ought to be brought home, or even buried in roadside graves out of respect?

She didn't know the answers—she might be only a year or two younger than some of these soldiers had been when they'd enlisted, but she felt like a child in their presence. The last thing she'd do would be to question their dedication to their fellow soldiers.

Instead she kept her mouth shut and studied them. Learned their names and their demeanors. Tried to figure out which of them would be most likely to save her life, and which would be most likely to get her killed. Danny and Kate seemed her best bet if she was looking for someone to keep her safe, so it troubled Alexa when Trav pulled the Humvee-TSV in front of a concrete and glass tower and killed the engine, only to have Danny and Kate be the first to exit the vehicle.

Danny glanced through his open door, robot eyes pinning her in her seat.

"Stay put," he said.

"Where are we?" she asked.

Birnbaum had started to climb out of the vehicle as well. "Bank Yahav, it says."

Then the Tin Men were talking among themselves and she was forgotten. They all exited the TSV except for Trav—who stayed behind the wheel—and Torres, whose task it was to guard Hanif Khan. Alexa could feel the weight of Khan's gaze upon the back of her head. When he spoke, his voice seemed to slink into her thoughts and cloud her mind, and his eyes could have the same effect. Someone was going to kill Khan eventually; all she hoped was that it would be sooner rather than later.

"Ask yourself this," he whispered. "You see me as the villain, but where are the heroes?"

Alexa heard his grunt and the slap of a blow and glanced back to see that Torres had just elbowed Khan in the jaw. The anarchist's eyes were lit with a fury he normally kept hidden and he spit a gob of blood onto the floor before shooting a murderous glance at Torres.

"Right now, Private Torres is my hero," Alexa said.

She slid over to the broken window facing the bank. The main building had a rounded façade and a V-shaped fan of glass windows, but the entrance was through an ugly little two-story structure that jutted from the front. Once there had no doubt been a beehive of activity inside that building, but now it was as dead as the abandoned cars on the road.

". . . we sure the signal is coming from inside?" Danny asked.

Kate drew her weapon. "I can feel it. So can the rest of you."

"And we're sure it's not some kind of trap?" Birnbaum asked.

"Khan's assholes are behind us," Kate said. "Whatever happened here might have been an ambush, but it wasn't our ambush."

"Still could be a trap," Danny said.

"Yeah, it could," Kate replied. She turned and surveyed the rest of her squad. "Hawkins, Mavrides, and Lahiri, stay with the transport. Birnbaum and Kelso are with me. How's everyone for ammunition?"

"Getting low," Mavrides said.

"Me, too," Birnbaum echoed.

"All right," Kate said. "When we're done here, everyone reload. There are two cases of shells in the back of the TSV. Top off, just in case we have to leave them behind."

Alexa leaned into the front seat and tapped Trav on the shoulder. "Weird question, I know. But I've never seen one of you guys reload. What's up with that?"

Trav glanced in the rearview mirror. "Half the weight of the bot is ammunition. We start the day with thousands of rounds. Every time I holster my sidearm, the autoloader refills it from internal magazines."

"You're screwing with me," Alexa muttered.

"Nope."

She sat back against her seat, thinking about that. Thousands of rounds without having to reload. "Wow."

The Humvee tilted as Mavrides jumped down from the roof. Hawkins stayed on top of the vehicle, keeping watch as Mavrides and Lahiri took up posts at either end of the transport with their weapons drawn.

Alexa watched Danny, Kate, and Birnbaum enter the bank through the shattered front door, crunching broken glass underfoot as they moved inside and vanished into the shadows there. She had to fight the urge to go in after them. Anything could happen in there.

Anything could happen out here, she reminded herself. But then again there were five Tin Men in and around the TSV, so she comforted herself with those odds. Five Tin Men guarding a homicidal anarchist and a seventeen-year-old American girl. Arthur Day's status as ambassador didn't seem to matter much anymore. Now he was just the dead father of a grieving girl.

"Company," Hawkins said from the roof.

Alexa whipped around and stared out the unbroken window: a woman had emerged from a building across the street. Several other people followed her, all glancing around warily. A thirtyish man whose yarmulke and prayer shawl made her think he was a rabbi came walking around a corner farther along the street. Half a dozen others followed him, including two in the uniforms of local police.

"That's close enough, folks," Lahiri said, moving toward the civilians and pausing about five feet from the Humvee-TSV. "Keep your distance."

"We want answers!" one of the cops shouted.

The rabbi held up a hand to hush him but kept walking. Despite Lahiri's warning, the others took their cue from the rabbi and continued to advance.

"More coming from the south," Hawkins announced from his perch.

"My friend is correct," the rabbi said, walking slowly toward the vehicle with his hands raised at his sides, palms upward to show he held no weapon. "We have questions and we believe that you people can answer them."

"People?" a woman scoffed.

Alexa took hold of the door latch. Torres reached up from the seat behind her and clamped a hand on her shoulder, locking her into place.

"Stay where you are, kid. We're not here to fix anything," Torres said.

"Nothing we could fix," Trav warned from the driver's seat.

Alexa watched as more people appeared. Those who had seen the Humvee pass by or heard its rumble must have told others and now a crowd had begun to form. She studied the faces of the Israelis in the street, expressions full of sadness and confusion and fear, and she wanted to speak to them. The Tin Men were human inside—their minds, at least—but in the eyes of the rabbi and the worried features of an old woman who seemed alone even in the crowd, Alexa saw something more familiar. These people would feel her grief. They would understand.

"Keep your distance!" Lahiri said again.

"What's happened?" the rabbi demanded. "Your vehicle is the only one we've seen that's running. Are others on the way? Is help coming?"

For several seconds, the Tin Men made no reply. Alexa cringed at those few seconds of silence.

"I'm sure help will come," Hawkins said. "But I can't tell you when. This trouble is widespread. Look after one another."

"Bullshit!" the second police officer said. His face reddened and somehow underlined his obvious youth. Alexa thought he couldn't have been more than twenty-one. "Tell us what you know!"

"We're not your enemy!" Lahiri shouted at them.

"Maybe not," the rabbi called back, "but are you our friends?"

"Trav," Torres said from the backseat. "Look at Mavrides."

Alexa shifted around to get a decent view of Mavrides, who was still in front of the Humvee. He had begun to pace. The robot's facial expression was flat, impossible to read, but he kept twitching his head and now Alexa could hear his voice, muttering low to himself.

"What's he saying?" she asked.

"I can't make it out," Trav replied.

Behind Alexa, Hanif Khan laughed.

The crowd began to close in, more of them shouting questions at Hawkins and Lahiri, who had been the ones to reply. Alexa slid down in her seat, feeling vulnerable, suddenly afraid of the people who only moments ago she had thought would understand her.

"Give us the vehicle!" a man shouted.

The first cop echoed him and then a dozen voices more, turning it into a chant. Desperation drove them. Alexa knew they were just afraid, the same as she, but their need frightened her.

Mavrides started to scream. "Back off, motherfuckers! Stand back or I swear to God—"

Almost as one, the crowd reared away from him. Mavrides waved his weapon and the crowd shrank back farther. But then Alexa saw the rabbi's blue eyes harden and his chin rise in righteous defiance, and he stepped forward.

"You can swear to God all you like, soldier," the rabbi said. "But He would tell you to help us—"

Mavrides shot him twice in the chest.

The crowd screamed and separated, some hurling themselves to the ground and others retreating. A handful knelt by the rabbi, trying to help.

"What about *now*?" Mavrides howled. "Is He listening now?"

Kate led the way into the bank. At first glance, it seemed deserted. Beyond the front doors there was no visible damage, though a stack of deposit slips had been scattered onto the floor. A row of teller windows ran the length of the counter on the right, and at the rear of the bank on the same side she could see the massive vault door hanging open.

With a gesture, she sent Birnbaum to check the desks for anyone who might be hiding there.

Ping.

All three of them froze. Kate stared at the open vault door. She glanced at Danny, wishing they still had the ability to communicate through private channels. Maybe this was some kind of ambush after all. An image swam into her head of a robot torso—no head, no limbs—lying on the floor just inside the vault, transmitting whatever radio signal gave off that—

Ping.

—because the beacon was coming from inside the vault.

Birnbaum clanked around behind the desks—Tin Men weren't much for stealth in a place like this—then gave a thumbs-up: all clear.

Kate gestured forward and all three of them advanced toward the vault. She pointed to the teller windows and Danny started in that direction.

Ping.

"Screw it," she said, and then raised her voice. "This is Sergeant Kate Wade. Sixth Battalion, USARIC. We are receiving your distress signal. If you do not show yourselves immediately we will assume you are hostile."

Something clanked behind the teller windows. Danny and Birnbaum leveled their weapons, taking aim in that direction, but Kate kept her gaze fixed on the open door to the vault.

"Oh, Zuzu, you idiot," said a voice from under the counter, and then a figure rose up behind a teller window. A robot, hands raised, Batman symbol painted on his chest. "Sergeant Wade, I'm Lieutenant Tom Randall. Fourth Battalion."

"Are you alone, Lieutenant?" Kate asked.

Another robot rose, farther along the line of teller windows, this one emblazoned with a stylized eagle carrying lightning bolts in its talons.

"Wish I were," Lieutenant Randall said. "This is Private Mimi Nguyen."

"The ping's coming from the vault," Birnbaum said.

Danny kept Randall and Nguyen covered, but Kate and Birnbaum were more interested in the vault now.

"Come out, you assholes," Lieutenant Randall called.

"Who are you calling assholes?" a female voice replied from inside the vault, and then two other Tin Men stepped out into the bank. One of them had no markings save for a double X on his forehead, while the other had colorful flowers painted on her chest plate.

"You must be Zuzu," Kate said.

"Shit, I don't even know what that means," the bot said, in a deep, very male voice.

Kate stared at him, then glanced at the bot with the double X on its head, realizing that this was the female who had spoken.

"Tanya Broaddus," she said, then slapped Zuzu on the back of the head. "You had it right, though. This is Zuzu. He's never seen the movie."

"Fucksake, *what* movie?" Zuzu asked, exasperated.

Kate understood then. Every platoon shared robots with two others. Whoever had Zuzu's bot for one of the other shifts had arranged for the flowers to be painted on its chest and it was clear that he wasn't happy about it.

"*It's a Wonderful Life*," Danny said.

"Zuzu's petals," Birnbaum said. "Come on, *everyone's* seen that movie."

Kate held up a hand. "Enough." She turned to Randall. "You didn't seem happy to see us, Lieutenant. Which is weird, considering you sent out that distress signal."

"Zuzu did that," Randall replied, still behind the counter, watching her through the teller window. "Did it on his own initiative, for which I'd kill him if we hadn't already lost six good soldiers. I'd forgotten all about it until you walked in."

"There were only ten of you?" Danny asked.

"Ten," Randall confirmed. "We were deployed here as a deterrent to terror attacks on the port."

"But you're not at the port," Kate said, unable to keep the disapproval out of her voice.

Randall gave her a hard look. "We were ambushed this morning. Tried to fight them off but they had these new rockets—cause some kind of chain reaction in a bot's core if they score a direct hit. Blew our guys to Hell. Drove us back here about four hours ago and we've been sitting tight ever since. I've checked outside every half hour and they're still out there, waiting for us to make a move. They're keeping us pinned here for now."

"We just walked in," Danny said. "There are no Bot Killers out there."

"I'm sorry to say there are," Broaddus said. "We're surrounded. And now you are, too."

Kate hung her head. Of course the Bot Killers had let them walk right in. Why wouldn't they? Just more flies for their web. Right now they probably had rockets aimed at the TSV. She glanced up at Danny.

"We're on a clock here, Lieutenant," Kate said. "In more ways than one. The thing that's ticking most immediately is that there are more Bot Killers on the way. They've been trailing us since we left Damascus. We killed a lot of theirs and they killed some of ours. We don't know how many of them there are, but we're not waiting to find out."

"Sergeant?" Randall said, and in his tone was a reminder that he outranked her.

"Sir," Kate replied, "the G20 summit began today. The president may already be dead, but if not, he is likely trapped in Athens. We intend to commandeer a sailing vessel and make all speed for Greece. I don't know how many Bot Killers have you surrounded, but my squad is getting out of here before the others arrive."

"Holy shit," Randall muttered. Then he shook his head. "I'm sorry, Sergeant Wade, but half of you will get your asses blown off if you go out there without a plan."

"All due respect, Lieutenant, but you've been here four hours and apparently still don't have a plan. I've got more people out front. As for half of us getting our asses blown off . . . I guess the other half can still make their way to Athens and try to protect their commander-in-chief."

Randall glared at her.

"Damn," Zuzu whispered.

From outside, there came the sound of gunshots.

"We're going," Kate said. "If you're lucky, we'll take down most of the Bot Killers for you, clear you a path."

Lieutenant Randall actually laughed. "Now you're just rubbing my nose in it. All right, fuck it." He turned to his three surviving Tin Men. "Let's go!"

Alexa moved without thinking, pushing open the Humvee's door. Some people stayed on the ground while others rushed screaming for cover, running in a crouch and hoping they didn't get a bullet in the back for their troubles.

"What the hell was that?" Lahiri shouted. He kept his weapon trained on the civilians, aiming at the two cops who had accompanied the rabbi.

A grim young woman was one of several people who knelt around the rabbi, trying to staunch the bleeding with the dying man's own prayer shawl. Alexa found herself standing only a few feet from Mavrides, staring at the blood that had begun to pool on the pavement around the rabbi. The young woman's skirt had been a summery yellow, but now she knelt in blood and the yellow fabric had begun to soak crimson.

It was the prayer shawl that bothered Alexa. The man had come in peace seeking answers, seeking help, and now his prayer shawl, this sacred cloth, was being pressed to his chest in a desperate attempt to stop his bleeding.

"Alexa!" a voice shouted behind her. She glanced back and saw Torres halfway out of the Humvee. "Get back in here!"

"Mavrides, stand down!" Lahiri barked, still aiming at the two cops.

The TSV shifted and Alexa looked up to see Hawkins still on the vehicle's roof. Like Lahiri, he aimed his weapon at the crowd, but his gaze was locked on Mavrides. His smiley face with crossbones gleamed in the sunlight and seemed almost to mock the dying rabbi.

"Do something!" she screamed at Hawkins.

Mavrides had been standing still as stone, watching the efforts to save the rabbi. Now her voice shook him out of his reverie and he spun to stare at her.

"I *did* do something!" he shouted.

Alexa felt tears welling in her eyes. "I wasn't talking to you! You're as bad as the ones who killed my father!"

Rage boiled up inside her. She hurled herself at him, shoved him with both hands, but the robot didn't move an inch.

"Fucking asshole!" she screamed.

Mavrides struck her with the back of his hand. The blow rattled her brain and she crashed backward into the Humvee. The scent of blood filled her nostrils and she knew it was her own blood.

"Zack!" Hawkins barked furiously from atop the vehicle. "You raise a hand to that kid again—"

Torres and Travaglini were shouting from inside the Humvee-TSV, but they had their orders and weren't moving. Alexa stared at Mavrides, but then shifted her gaze to look beyond him. He had turned his back on the crowd for a few seconds but they were already in motion. The two policemen rushed at Mavrides and several others joined them.

"No!" Lahiri screamed. "Keep back! You're only going to make things worse!"

Mavrides turned just as the two cops reached him. He threw back an elbow that caved in the skull of one, then grabbed the other by the hair and shot him through the left eye.

The screams of the crowd tore at the sky. The grim young woman trying to keep the rabbi alive rose from her crouch, his bloody prayer shawl clutched in her hands, and Alexa knew the man of God had died.

It all turned to chaos then. The others who had rushed at Mavrides jerked backward, trying to get clear of the bloodthirsty soldier, but more people shoved forward, rushing at him. Lahiri fired two shots into the air and Hawkins jumped down from the roof. Alexa stared in horror at the sight of them lining up beside Mavrides as if they approved of what he'd done.

"Get back!" Hawkins boomed, taking a step toward the crowd.

The crowd seemed to take a deep breath, wanting justice but weighing the cost. Encouraged, Mavrides raised his weapon and took aim at a hard-looking woman at the front of the crowd. Hawkins spun and shoved him into the Humvee. A teenage girl might not be able to budge one of the Tin Men, but they could certainly move one another.

"Stay there and don't move!" Hawkins roared at him.

Mavrides glared. "You had my back! You always said you had my goddamn back!"

"That's when you were a soldier," Hawkins replied.

"Murderer," Alexa whispered, staring at Mavrides. Grief had lit a fire inside her, and it felt good to let it burn.

Mavrides turned his gun on her, aimed right between her eyes.

Alexa held her breath, crying silent tears as she realized she was about to join her father. Then Hawkins stepped between her and Mavrides, tore the gun from his grasp, and slammed him against the TSV again.

"You're more trouble than you're worth," Hawkins growled. He held his own gun against Mavrides's robot eye.

"What are you doing, Hawkins?" Lahiri demanded.

Hawkins never had a chance to answer. Shouts rose above the noise of the people in the street. Alexa stood and peered through the broken TSV windows and saw Kate and Danny rushing out of the shattered bank doors with other Tin Men in tow. Birnbaum had been the only robot to enter the bank with them but now there were four more.

"Alexa!" Torres shouted from the Humvee. "Get your ass in here!"

Hawkins yanked open the door and shoved her in. Torres hauled her across the seat. In the rear of the vehicle, Hanif Khan crouched, a thin smile on his face, amused by the conflict and bloodshed.

"Drive, Trav!" Kate yelled, waving them away. "Get out of here! Meet us at the harbor!"

Trav didn't wait for an explanation. The engine roared to life and he dropped the Humvee-TSV into gear and hit the gas. Alexa scrambled around in the seat to look out the rear window, over the wrapped corpse of her father. Khan had twisted around as well, his expression troubled.

Gunfire erupted all along the street, hitting Tin Men and civilians alike. Bullets struck the Humvee-TSV and Torres shouted for Alexa to get her head down. She obeyed, but a moment later she heard the scream of multiple rockets and she lifted her head up for one last glance.

She saw the rocket hit Lahiri, saw him explode in flaming shrapnel. Other rockets struck the street, killing and maiming the people in the crowd, who ran screaming and died without a word. A rocket hit a second robot, but she couldn't see who it was. *Please not Danny or Kate,* she thought. Then: *Please not Hawkins.*

Trav skidded the Humvee around a corner and Alexa could see no more of the melee in front of the bank. She did hear the guns and the shriek of more rockets, though, and the thunder of further explosions.

She looked around the inside of the TSV and felt her chances at survival shrinking. Trav and Torres were the only protection she had left. The other two flesh-and-blood people inside the vehicle were a dead man and a man she wished dead.

Stop, she chided herself, staring past Khan at the thatch of her father's hair. *Stop wishing people dead.*

Alexa had seen enough death to last her a lifetime. But she feared it was only beginning.

"Take 'em out!" Danny shouted, ignoring the bullets that ricocheted off his carapace. "No more running!"

Fifteen feet away, Kate stood on the patch of pavement the Humvee-TSV had occupied thirty seconds before. She shot him a grim look, but he only glanced at her for a second. A head popped up on a rooftop and Danny put a bullet through it, telling himself that civilians wouldn't be that stupid. The people on the street were running for cover. The only faces coming into view on rooftops and in broken office windows were those of the Bot Killers who'd pinned down Lieutenant Randall and his squad.

Danny heard the whistle of a rocket and spun to see the man who'd fired it crouched inside a broken window in the bank's office tower. He darted to the left, made it eight steps before the rocket hit the spot he'd left behind, then threw himself forward. He hit the ground and rolled, then rose and shot the rocket-man, who crumpled and fell out the broken window, rocket launcher tumbling beside him.

"Move!" Lieutenant Randall shouted. "Don't make yourself a target!"

Danny saw Randall and Zuzu heading back into the bank building, where other enemies had appeared in upper-floor windows. Nguyen had already been destroyed, parts of her bot scattered in the street with whatever was left of Lahiri.

"There!" Hawkins shouted even as he shot a rocket-man perched on the edge of a four-story boutique hotel off to the right.

The rocket launched as the bullet struck the man. It fired wild, screaming over their heads and striking a stalled Mercedes. As the

Mercedes exploded, its gas tank rupturing into a cloud of flames, Danny saw Birnbaum and Broaddus heading into the building next to the bank. Across the street, Kate and Mavrides were rushing into an older office building. He scanned the rooftops again, then saw Hawkins rushing toward the little hotel, bullets raining down on him from the Bot Killers on the roof and in the windows—a lot of them.

Danny spared one last glance for Kate. He had caught a glimpse of Mavrides pointing his gun at Alexa Day and Hawkins standing in the way. Whatever ugliness had gone down while he was inside the bank, Mavrides had taken it too far and Danny didn't like leaving Kate on her own with the little prick.

Queen of the Tin Men, remember? he thought. *Kate Wade can take care of herself.*

He dashed across the street after Hawkins, crashed through one of the elegant front windows of the little boutique hotel, and hit the stairs only a dozen feet after Hawkins himself. Danny felt a dreadful chill spreading through him, as if his bot's circuits were ice, and he understood that this same chill had been settling inside him all day. His entire life he'd been a shark, swimming to live, but now the water was freezing solid around him, claustrophobia setting in.

No more running, he thought.

First the Tin Men would destroy Haifa's Bot Killers, and then they would make sure any of the bastards who had followed them from Damascus joined the others in their graves.

19

Alexa huddled on the floor of the Humvee, right behind the driver's seat. She wished she could sink down inside the metal, become a part of it, imbue herself into the steel the same way that the Tin Men inhabited their robots. She wanted to be bulletproof, to wrap herself in metal and feel nothing.

No, she thought. *You saw Danny and Kate. They feel.*

Even Mavrides felt something, she realized. Felt enough to drive him right over the edge. Alexa could never forgive him, but on some level she understood. Desperation, sorrow, helplessness—these things bred madness.

She tried to push away the things she had seen, tried to focus on what would happen next, but there was one image that she could not erase—Lahiri and Hawkins standing side by side with Mavrides against the crowd, even after all that Mavrides had done.

They take care of their own, she told herself. *Hawkins wanted to deal with Mavrides himself.*

The logic felt genuine. Still, she could not forgive them.

Her eyes were itchy and dry and she pressed the heels of her palms against them. The Humvee rumbled over a curb and she swayed as it went around a corner. Torres and Travaglini kept silent, focused on finding the harbor and watching for any sign of further attack. Alexa began to think about the harbor, about the boats they hoped to find there. The end of this journey would bring her home to her mother and Alexa told herself that she could endure anything as long as she made it home. Whatever the world had in store for her now, she would be all right as long as she didn't have to face it alone.

A frown creased her brow. Despite the breeze blasting through the broken windows, despite the scent of the sea, she caught the trace of a different odor inside the TSV. Once upon a time their house had lost power while she and her mother had been away for a few days. This smell reminded her of the stench that had wafted out of the refrigerator upon their return. Not as strong, but growing worse.

She tried to tell herself this new smell came from the sea, that it was the stink of low tide. But she knew that wasn't it.

"Now you see the world as I see it," Hanif Khan said.

Alexa flinched and looked up to see him watching her through the gap between the second row of seats.

"Who says I didn't already?" she sneered.

Trav hit the brakes. "We're here."

Alexa climbed up onto the seat as the Humvee slid to a halt. She popped the door and climbed out, breathing deeply of the salt air. Seagulls cawed overhead as she stared out across the harbor, watching the boats bobbing on the water. The ravages of the past two decades of sea-level rise were immediately evident. Some buildings that had once been elegant hotels and restaurants at the seaside had been partly submerged, others torn down. Whatever the harbor had looked like two decades before, most of it seemed to have been removed, a new harborside district created and new docks and piers built to adjust to the changing tides.

A fresh coat of paint to mask the rotting face of the world.

Running up the stairs in the little hotel, Danny had to remind himself that Haifa was not Damascus. Whatever whispered suggestions the population of Damascus had received about evacuating, the people of Haifa hadn't gotten the memo. There had been plenty of civilians in the street and he'd seen faces through windows. Some of the hotel guests would be hunkered down in their rooms.

"Watch your shots," he said as he hustled up the steps after Hawkins. "No more civilians."

Hawkins reached the third-floor landing and spun to face him, weapon aimed at the ceiling.

"We didn't kill those people," Hawkins said. "Mavrides did."

"He's one of ours," Danny replied.

Hawkins looked disgusted. "He's not mine, Kelso. You want to claim the kid, go ahead. Yeah, I took him under my wing, but that doesn't mean shit to me now. I'm a soldier first and last."

Danny shrugged by way of explanation. "I had you pegged wrong."

"You think I fucking care how you 'pegged' me?"

Hawkins yanked open the door to the third floor and moved into the carpeted corridor. Danny followed and in a second they were back to back, weapons aimed in opposite directions. Three rooms along, a door opened and a man poked his head out. Danny might have mistaken the man, bearded and olive-skinned, for a Bot Killer if not for the way his eyes widened with terror.

"Back inside," Danny whispered. "Keep your head down."

The man nodded and retreated, slamming his door.

"This way," Hawkins said. "I saw two of them in a room up here."

Danny followed him as Hawkins counted doors, trying to figure out which room the Bot Killers had been in.

"I'm more worried about the roof," Danny said.

"I'm worried about anyone pointing a rocket at me," Hawkins said quietly as he stopped in front of a door, gestured for Danny to stand aside, and kicked the door in. Wood splintered and the frame shattered.

Hawkins darted away from the open door. Danny heard the scream of the rocket and then it streaked from inside the room and across the corridor to strike the opposite door. The explosion blew Danny and Hawkins into the wall and Danny dropped to the carpet, grateful that his audio receptors automatically adjusted for volume. He turned to see Hawkins already on his feet.

"I've got this," Hawkins said as he ducked into the room.

Automatic-weapons fire greeted him, but it lasted only seconds before Hawkins managed to take out both Bot Killers in the room. Danny turned to look at the wreckage of the hotel room across the corridor, where a woman knelt by her bloodied husband, trying to scream her horror but unable to find her voice. She turned to look at him and he wondered why they hadn't just made a dash for the harbor. Maybe *no more running* had been a terrible idea.

"The roof," Hawkins said as he came back into the hallway.

"Let's finish this," Danny said.

He took the lead, running ahead of Hawkins to the emergency exit. The sign on the stairwell door said ROOF ACCESS: AUTHORIZED PERSONNEL ONLY. Danny pushed through it and took the steps two at a time. His footfalls echoed around him and he thought again of his father, the image of his old man by the side of the road. He wondered if the whispers he heard were his subconscious telling him that he was closer now to his father than he had ever been. Closer to the land of the dead than the land of the living.

He had spent most of his adult life convinced that he was alone in the world—that *alone* was the only way he could survive. It troubled him to think of anyone, even ghosts, observing him as he went through his life. It hurt him to think that his decisions might matter to someone. Maybe that was what it really meant to be haunted.

With Hawkins behind him, Danny reached the top, where a steel door bore the same ROOF ACCESS sign he'd seen a floor below. He dropped his shoulder and hurled himself against the door, which tore off its hinges with a shriek of metal. Sunlight splashed into the stairwell as Danny lunged and dropped into a roll. A pair of rockets screamed a duet across the rooftop. The Bot Killers had known they were coming and laid in wait.

Rockets struck the doorway and exploded, blowing apart the entire exit structure. Danny had a second to think of Hawkins, but then he was up and taking aim. There were four Bot Killers on the roof. He ignored the bullets and focused on the two rocket-men who were already reloading, hoping to take another crack at him. Danny shot one in the chest and the other in the pelvis and leg. Rocket launchers clattered to the roof and Danny turned to the two who were armed only with guns.

"Die!" one of them said, his accent Turkish or Kurdish. "This is not your world anymore."

Danny shot him first in the left shoulder and then the right and the man cried out and collapsed to the roof. With medical attention, he would live, but it would be a while before he could effectively wield a gun.

The other looked German or Scandinavian. He stopped shooting, only stood and glared at Danny, waiting for his death without a glimmer of fear in his eyes.

"Go ahead," the blond man said. "Kill what you don't understand."

Danny froze, staring at him as the Turk moaned and writhed in pain.

"You're American."

The guy sneered at him. "I was born there, but I surrendered my citizenship. I couldn't live with being part of a system that kept the entire world oppressed."

Danny strode toward him. The blond backed up toward the edge of the roof.

"You little puke," Danny said. "We protected the world from anarchy—"

"Anarchy is exactly what the world needs!" the man spat. "Self-determination."

Danny holstered his weapon. "Well, you got what you wanted, then. I guess you win."

He grabbed the guy by the throat and crotch, lifted him up and hurled him off the roof. The man screamed on the way down. Danny stood at the edge of the roof and watched him hit the ground, watched him die. He hated himself for such brutality, but he hated the traitor more.

"Hey!" someone shouted.

Danny spun and saw Hawkins clambering out of the smoking ruin that had been the stairwell door, his carapace scorched and blackened far worse than before.

"Next time, maybe tell me what you've got in mind so I can duck?" Hawkins said.

Danny gave him a nod. "Sorry about that. Got carried away. Glad you were able to get out of the way."

Hawkins waved off the apology. "Jumped down a flight of stairs."

Danny turned to scan the street below, spotted Zuzu and Randall. Broaddus stood silhouetted in one of the bank tower's shattered windows across the street. Kate and Mavrides came out of the office block a couple of buildings over. The gunfire had ceased, but all of the Tin Men were watching rooftops and windows, hesitant to call this a victory until they knew there were no more Bot Killers, no more rockets.

Hawkins came to stand beside him. "Kelso."

Something in his tone made Danny turn. Hawkins wasn't scanning the street below or the rooftops; he wasn't looking at the Tin Men down on the road. Danny bent forward to peer southward, and he saw what had grabbed Hawkins's attention.

Four blocks away, two black Humvee-TSVs were coming around a corner.

Hanif Khan's men had followed them all the way from Damascus. The sounds of battle had drawn Khan's Bot Killers in. Danny felt that dreadful ice spreading further within him as he watched those Humvees advance.

The fight wasn't over, but it was about to be.

As Kate and Mavrides emerged from the office building, she heard voices shouting above and ahead of them. She glanced up and saw Danny and Hawkins standing on the edge of a hotel roof four stories off the ground. They were pointing, alarmed by something.

"What's up with them?" Mavrides asked, his voice full of that familiar tough guy swagger.

Other Tin Men had begun to move toward them, returning to the street after pursuing and eliminating the Bot Killers who had ambushed Lieutenant Randall's squad. Kate narrowed her eyes and stared at Danny and Hawkins, then glanced along the road past dead cars and an abandoned delivery truck.

When she saw the first Humvee-TSV come around the corner, four blocks away, she swore quietly.

"Son of a bitch," Mavrides said.

Kate glanced at the others. She saw Randall and Zuzu and Birnbaum.

"Let's finish this!" she called. "Move over the rooftops or through the side streets. Don't leave any of them standing!"

Birnbaum started back into the bank building, obeying her orders, but Randall hesitated and Zuzu did the same, taking his cue from his commanding officer. Lieutenant Randall outranked her.

"This way," Kate said to Mavrides, and started toward the little hotel.

"I don't think so, Sarge, but you have fun," Mavrides sneered. "See you at the harbor, if you make it."

Kate stared after Mavrides as the kid turned tail and ran westward, keeping in the shadows of the buildings. She almost gave chase, but the shriek of a rocket forced her to turn toward Randall just in time to see the rocket hit the ground beside him. It tore him open, spilling coolant and bullets from blown magazines and blasting shrapnel that struck both Kate and Zuzu. The secondary explosion of Randall's power core blew Zuzu off his feet and he rolled hard up against the outer wall of the bank.

Kate rose. "Zuzu, go!" she cried. "Inside. Use the buildings. Right through the damn walls if you have to."

Zuzu might not have had much of a sense of humor about the flowers painted on his chassis, but he was no fool. Randall had just been taken off the chessboard. That made Kate the ranking officer, and he didn't even hesitate as he crashed through the bank entrance.

When Kate heard the next rocket, she barely had time to turn toward the sound.

Danny and Hawkins ran along the little hotel's roof, weapons out, intent on killing the Bot Killers in the TSVs. When the rocket took out Randall, Danny stopped and turned to see Kate standing in the road, shouting something at Zuzu . . . and a second rocket streaking toward her.

He roared her name, took two strides, and hurled himself off the hotel's roof. As he plummeted four stories he saw Kate spin toward the rocket and try to dart out of its path. The rocket struck her left shoulder and exploded. Her body pinwheeled through the air.

Danny hit the ground in a crouch, the impact buckling the sidewalk beneath him. Something cracked in his right leg. Kate's bot lay in a scorched, blackened sprawl. He screamed and ran toward her, hobbled slightly by a new limp.

"Kate!" he shouted, but she wasn't moving.

He stood over her, staring. He had joined the army hoping that he had finally found the purpose he'd sought, that a guy who always felt alone might be able to help protect those who were lucky enough to have someone else to live for. His girlfriends—even Nora, who had lasted the longest—had never been able to make him feel necessary. Desired, yes, but not *alive*.

Danny felt as if the rocket had struck him instead of Kate. He stared down at the blackened carapace and the thin cables jutting from the shoulder socket, the jagged metal where the arm had been blown off, and he hated the robot—hated what he had become—and yet he hated the human part of himself as well, for giving a damn.

Gunfire erupted down the street. He turned to see one of the Tin Men crash out of a third-floor apartment window and slam down on top of the lead Humvee. Across the street, Hawkins jumped down to street level and opened fire on the two vehicles. A rocket shot toward him but it had been hastily aimed and went far wide, striking one of the structures along that side street.

Other Tin Men busted through windows. With Mavrides rabbiting and Kate gone, that left only five, Danny included. Khan's lunatic minions had gotten too close this time. They weren't going to quit until they had completed their mission. Well, neither would the Tin Men, and their mission priority had just changed.

"Kelso," came the weak rasp of a voice behind him.

Danny spun, squinting against the low sun, and stared at Kate's scorched remains. Except that they weren't her remains at all. Her charred face had turned toward him and with the sun behind her he could see the glint of light in her eyes.

"Don't just stand there," she said quietly. "Go finish them."

For a second he couldn't take his eyes off her.

"Stay right there," he said.

She raised her remaining hand in half a shrug: *Where would I go?*

Danny smiled. "That's a good look for you."

Gunfire ripped through the air back along the street. Two more explosions shook the ground in quick succession.

All she said was, "Go."

Danny went. The harbor awaited them, and a whole world of trouble beyond that. He didn't want any of it following behind.

20

Alexa climbed out of the car, staring at the blue-green Mediterranean waters glistening in the afternoon sun. Despite all she had endured and all she feared might await them across the sea, she allowed herself to be calmed. They had seen the working port of Haifa just to the south, but only merchant vessels and fishing boats were docked there. Trav had driven north for a mile before he pulled over and now here they were, parked at a marina where the wealthy and the ambitious had docked their boats in the world of yesterday.

Her father's body still lay in the rear of the TSV, but while Torres muscled Hanif Khan from the back of the vehicle and Trav climbed out of the driver's seat, Alexa turned away from them all. The weight of his death lay upon her shoulders, a heavy yoke, but she would not let grief destroy her. Her mother would be counting on her, and there were others as well.

"Most everyone cleared out, I guess," Trav said, coming up beside her.

Alexa scanned the marina. Half the slips were empty.

"Anyone who could have," she agreed. "Everything with a sail must've been pushed out by hand."

Down along the dock an old woman sat on the wooden boards, leaning against a piling. She had three children around her, one boy of about thirteen, the other two girls, perhaps five, twins. The boy wore jeans and a lemon-yellow T-shirt, the girls tank tops and shorts and mismatched bows in their hair, one red and the other purple. All three dark-haired children stared out at the water, as if salvation might sail in at any moment.

The old woman did not look toward the sea. Instead, she stared at the Humvee that had drawn up at the dock and the robots who had climbed out. She did not speak or beckon in any way, made no effort to ask for help. Neither Alexa nor Trav mentioned the old woman and the kids, as if they were ghosts each of them was afraid the other could not see.

"Is this just us getting lucky?" Alexa asked.

A massive trimaran bobbed out in the bay beyond the marina, where the darker water hinted at greater depth. Alexa had seen a hydroptere before but she had never sailed on one. The speed frightened her, yet it was a gift to them now. Her mother would have said they needed the wings of angels. Alexa wondered if the Pulse had killed the last of the angels when it shut out the lights of the world . . . or if instead, perhaps, it had woken them up. Time would tell.

"I don't think it's luck," Trav told her. "It's a complicated vessel. I'd figure there were three or four of them anchored out there, along with half a dozen larger sailing ships. But the hydroptere requires at least someone on board to know what the hell they're doing. My vision is better than yours, but if you look closely, you'll see there are people on that boat."

Alexa flinched. "What?" She walked a dozen feet onto the dock, staring at the hydroptere, and confirmed what Trav had said. Two figures—no, three—moving about on the span of the trimaran, one on the aft of the central float and two others on the right wing.

Heart racing, she spun and stared at Travaglini. "What if you're wrong? What if they know exactly what they're doing?"

"They would've left here by now," he said. "But just in case, we ought to get out there. Bring it in."

Alexa strode back to him. "Do you know how to sail it?"

Trav tapped the painting on his chest of the World War II–era blonde riding a rocket. "I'm an old-fashioned guy, kid. I'm walking around inside modern tech, but I don't understand any of it. Birnbaum, though? In college she was on the sailing team. Grew up in Newport, where sailing is all rich people care about."

"She's rich?"

"Filthy. And I'm sure she's crewed a hydroptere before. Captained, no, but we're damn lucky to have her."

Alexa glanced past him. Torres stood at the back of the Humvee, weapon in hand. Khan sat cross-legged on the ground nearby as if he hadn't a care in the world. Both of them were watching the road to the south, waiting for the others to catch up.

"In that case, I wish Birnbaum had come with us instead of staying with them," Alexa said. "Just in case. Is that horrible to say?"

"If it is, we're both horrible, 'cause I was thinking the same thing." Trav looked out at the Mediterranean.

Alexa caught a glimpse of profound sorrow on his face, and it hurt her heart so deeply, she wished whoever had created the Tin Men had not made the robots' faces so expressive.

"Torres," Trav said. "I'm going to see if I can find a rowboat or a kayak or something. I figure they're all gone, but I'll look."

He turned to head down the dock. Alexa glanced past him at the gray-haired old woman and the three kids she figured were the woman's grandchildren. An afternoon breeze had kicked up, growing stronger as the sun slid lower in the sky. The twin girls' hair blew across their faces and the one with the purple bow grabbed it as if fearful the wind would steal it away. The old woman wrapped her arms around herself, steadfast in her refusal to look out to sea as the children did, perhaps afraid that she would not see whatever it was they were so eagerly awaiting.

"Trav!" Torres shouted.

Alexa automatically looked southward. A robot had appeared at the turn of the seaside drive, a quarter mile away. She watched that curve in the road thinking that others would follow, but none were in evidence.

Trav stalked up the dock to stand beside Alexa.

"Which one?" she asked, remembering that his vision was much more powerful than hers.

"Mavrides." He spoke the name as if he didn't like the flavor of it in his mouth.

Alexa walked toward the Humvee but thought better of it and moved off to her right, not wanting to be close to Hanif Khan. Not wanting to see her father's body any more than she had to.

Trav moved close to Torres and Khan as Mavrides raced up to them.

"Did you find the boat we need?" Mavrides asked, frowning as he glanced out at the marina and the bay beyond. In the late afternoon sun, the ace of spades on his forehead looked almost faded.

"We found one, yeah," Trav replied. "Where are the others?"

Mavrides shook his head. "Not coming. It's just me."

Alexa felt the world crumbling beneath her.

"What?" Torres snapped. She took a step toward Mavrides. "I don't believe you."

"You think I'd lie about this?" Mavrides said. "I get you don't like me. But seriously, Hawkins was . . . I don't have a lot of people in my life to look up to, but I looked up to him. The guy's dead. And Birnbaum—"

Torres sagged on her feet, grief cutting her deep. Her robot eyes searched the curve of the street from which Mavrides had appeared and she gave her head a single shake before covering her eyes with her left hand, weapon dangling forgotten in her right.

"Look, I'm sorry," Mavrides said.

Torres pointed her gun at him. "Don't mention her again. You aren't worthy of speaking her name."

Mavrides threw his hands up. "Fine, okay? *Fuck you.*"

Trav took a step toward him, one hand up to silence him. "Tell it to me from the beginning. What did you actually see? Can you be absolutely sure they've all been destroyed? A dozen Bot Killers isn't enough to take down a squad of Tin Men unless they've got a nuke, and I didn't see a mushroom cloud."

Mavrides stared at him. "It wasn't just the guys who'd trapped the bots in that bank. Right after you drove off we saw the first TSV. The fuckers from Damascus caught up with us and there were a hell of a lot more than we thought. We were pinned down, Trav. They had so many rockets and the ones around the bank, they'd set some IEDs. We didn't have a chance."

Torres stepped nearer to him. "But *you're* here. *You* made it. Sole survivor, Mavrides. How does that work?"

"Look, we don't have time for this. I don't think they saw which way I went, but you can bet they'll figure out the waterfront in a heartbeat and it'll take them minutes to find us. We've got to reach that ship and get out of here!"

The argument continued, voices growing more hostile, but Alexa had stopped listening. In the midst of it, she caught herself glancing at Hanif Khan. His dark eyes were on Mavrides but Alexa saw the change in his expression when Mavrides started talking about the Bot Killers from Damascus—Khan's own men. The ghost of a smile had flitted across Khan's face but then his brow had knitted with confusion, as if Mavrides's words did not make sense.

"Oh, my God," Alexa whispered.

Robots had better hearing than humans. All three of the Tin Men turned to stare at her.

Shaking, Alexa started toward Mavrides. Grief and horror made a volatile mix within her and she felt like she might explode.

"You're lying," she said, marching up to him. "I don't know why, but you're—"

It came to her then. She halted a foot in front of him.

"You ran," she said.

Trav loomed behind her. "Alexa, explain."

She half-turned toward Trav and Torres, pointing at the seated Khan.

"If you'd seen his face when this guy was talking about the Bot Killers, you'd know he was full of shit." She turned to the anarchist, who managed to keep his face blank. "You'd suck at poker."

Anger fueled her, pushing away sorrow. She turned back to Mavrides. "I hate you, but I didn't think you were a coward."

Mavrides lashed out and Alexa flinched, but he didn't hit her. His arm wrapped around her neck and he dragged her close, squeezing too tight and cutting off her air. As Trav shouted and drew his weapon, Alexa twisted herself around just in time to see Mavrides shove the barrel of his gun into Torres's face and shoot her through the eye.

Torres cried out and spun away, falling to one knee and clutching her face.

Khan started scrambling toward the Humvee.

Mavrides shot him in the shoulder. Shot him from behind.

Trav roared at him. Alexa could barely make out the words over the chaos of her thoughts. She tried to scream, tried to twist free, but Mavrides had her. Her face flushed with heat as she tried to breathe. Mavrides dragged her backward and she moved her feet to keep up with him, afraid that if she let him just *take* her he would break her neck.

Frantic, she looked around for Torres, who leaned against the Humvee, one hand still over her gun-shot eye. Without her, they would never be able to sail the hydroptere. They might never leave Israel.

"Let the girl go, Mavrides!" Trav yelled. "Let her go or I'll rip out your fucking core myself!"

"Here's what's going to happen," Mavrides said. "We're going out to that ship. The three of us and the girl. Khan gets another bullet, this one in the head."

Hanif Khan lay groaning on the ground, blood soaking into the shoulder of his shirt. The hatred and pain in his eyes gave him the savage countenance of a wounded beast. He grabbed the top of the Humvee's tire and tried to rise.

Mavrides went on. "Find something to row us out there. My gun's on the girl the whole time—"

Torres stumbled over beside Trav, slightly hunched, gray smoke rising from the hole where her right eye had been.

"The girl has a name," Torres said, a tinny buzz to her voice. "It's Alexa. And you're choking her to death."

Alexa gasped as Mavrides loosened his hold on her, dragging air into her burning lungs.

"The girl gets a bullet in the head if I'm interrupted again."

Alexa squeezed her eyes closed. In the darkness inside her mind, she felt almost as if she could see her father in the back of the TSV. She imagined being wrapped up with him, tufts of her hair sticking out the way his did. Weariness enveloped her and she sank back against Mavrides, thinking of the gentle smile on her father's face whenever she'd come into her parents' room in the middle of the night, frightened by a nightmare. He had always walked her back to bed and stroked her hair awhile to make the bad dreams go away. Nurturing had generally been her mother's job, but the middle of the night was for some reason her father's province. His voice had always soothed her when she was a little girl, afraid of the dark.

Perhaps death would not be so terrible. Perhaps he would be there to talk to her and stroke her hair as she tried to forget her fears.

I'm sorry, Mom, she thought.

"Fuck Athens," Mavrides said. "President's on his own."

"It won't work—" Torres said.

Alexa opened her eyes, daylight making her catch her breath. Shaking, she shushed Torres, but none of them seemed to hear her.

Mavrides jammed the gun hard against her temple. "I told you—"

"It won't work!" Torres shouted, grotesque with her gaping, ruined eye. "There aren't enough of us! Birnbaum told me it takes a minimum of five to crew the hydroptere, and Khan's not in any condition."

Alexa felt Mavrides freeze, felt him hesitate.

"Bullshit!" he barked. "You're just saying—"

Mavrides froze again. Footsteps coming fast behind them. Mavrides started to yell and Alexa could feel the gun push harder at her skull and then he pulled it away, spun her around, and took aim at the tin man hurtling toward them. Alexa recognized the target on Danny Kelso's chest.

Danny shouted as he smashed the gun out of Mavrides's hand and kept going, reaching over Alexa's head to grab Mavrides by the throat, peeling the lunatic off her. Mavrides caught her by the arm and dragged her along as Danny took him down. The three of them hit the ground with a clack of metal and bone. Her skull struck wood but Mavrides lost his grip and momentum kept her rolling.

Alexa tumbled off the sea wall, flailing at the air until she hit the water below.

Panicked, she clawed at it, but she didn't know which way was up.

Danny clamped his hands on the sides of Mavrides's head and slammed it hard onto the wooden pier. Mavrides tried to push him off and Danny pummeled him with four blows in quick succession: left, right, left, right.

"Trav, get the girl!" Danny snapped.

Travaglini was already ahead of him. His feet made the boards of the pier thunder as he pounded toward the edge and leaped into the water. The weight of his bot took him under and the water made a gulp and then flowed in to fill the place where he'd entered, as if the sea had claimed him.

Mavrides raised his hands again, but Danny batted them away and then shoved off him, stood up, and drew his weapon. Only as he took aim at Mavrides did he glance around and see that the others had caught up with him. Hawkins covered Khan, prodding him with a foot to make sure he was alive—or maybe for the satisfaction of hearing the wounded man scream. Birnbaum stood by Torres, investigating the ragged hole where her eye used to be. Zuzu and Broaddus held their weapons, knees bent, as they moved to either side of Danny, covering Mavrides, who groaned and tried to rise.

"Stay down, shit-for-brains!" Zuzu snapped.

Broaddus fired once, deliberately shooting Mavrides in the forehead.

"What the fuck was that?" Mavrides said, rubbing the small new dent in his bot. He glared at Broaddus. "Who the hell are you?"

Mavrides tried to rise and Danny kicked him in the head, dumping him onto the pier again.

Wooden boards creaked as another bot approached along the pier. His aim steady, Danny glanced back to see Kate approaching. Much of her chassis had been charred black, even warped in some places by the heat of the rocket explosion that had caught her, and she carried her left arm in her right. It dangled downward, almost scraping the pier.

Mavrides saw Kate and laughed. "Damn, woman, you look a mess."

It was then that Danny felt something give inside him, another little piece of whatever armor he wore around his heart breaking away. He turned and kicked Mavrides again and found himself doing it a third time and a fourth time.

Mavrides grabbed Danny's foot mid-kick and shoved him backward. Danny staggered as Mavrides launched to his feet, driving a fist into his jaw. Danny shook it off and took aim again. He'd let his mind wander . . . kept kicking without even realizing he was doing it. Just how much of a robot had he become?

"Zack, goddamn it, not another step!" Hawkins roared, drawing his own gun.

Mavrides froze, staring as Hawkins came toward him, joining Broaddus and Danny and Zuzu. Guns surrounded Mavrides. The kid had no weapon, but he was one of the Tin Men—they could do plenty of damage with just their hands.

"All of them," Hanif Khan said, voice tremulous with hate. "You killed all of them. Even Drazen."

As most of the Tin Men turned toward Khan, Mavrides kept his eyes on Hawkins. Something ugly lived beneath the younger soldier's metal skin, lingered behind his eyes, but now that ugliness had turned petulant. He stared at Hawkins with the gaze of a spoiled child whose mother has finally learned to say no.

"Man, you were different before," Mavrides whined. "You didn't take shit from anyone. Half the platoon out for a beer and us on the outside. You never said a nice word about any of them but now here you are, kissing their asses. That EMP must've taken more than your comms away. It took your balls."

A choking sound came from behind Mavrides. Danny glanced

past him just as Alexa Day dragged herself up onto the pier, soaking wet and coughing up seawater. Her hair hung in a sodden curtain that covered her face as she knelt there, more vulnerable than ever. Danny thought Mavrides would go for her again, but then Trav came up out of the sea behind her, hands clanking as he gripped the old wooden boards and hoisted himself onto the pier. Mavrides didn't dare.

"What's your plan, anyway?" Hawkins said. "You abandon the squad, shoot Torres . . . you had to have a plan."

Mavrides stood alone. Trav put a hand on Alexa Day's shoulder and guided the girl away from him, moving back toward the TSV, where Torres stood by while Birnbaum tried to doctor Hanif Khan's gunshot wound.

"He told us you were all dead," Torres said. "Figured he could get us to leave with him, just take the hydroptere and get back to the Hump, to hell with POTUS. I just finished telling him Birnbaum said you need five to sail the bitch."

Mavrides took two steps toward Hawkins, who lifted his weapon higher, aiming at the kid's eye.

"You were my friend," Mavrides said.

Hawkins kept his weapon in place. "I *was*. Tried to teach you how to be a goddamn soldier. Maybe my way of soldierin' ain't everybody's, but it's the only one I know. I got some thorns on me—I get that. But killing civvies just cuz you feel like it? Betraying your platoon? We ain't friends, kid."

Mavrides hung his head. Danny thought sadness had claimed him, that he'd surrendered. Then a sound built in Mavrides's chest, something between a battle roar and a scream of pain, and he hurtled toward Hawkins, who tried to defend himself, only to find he was not the kid's target. Mavrides knocked his gun hand aside and kept going.

Zuzu fired, hit Mavrides once and the Humvee twice.

"Watch out for the kid!" Broaddus barked.

Danny tried to get a bead but Hawkins was in his way. Mavrides went for Kate, raked her severed arm from her good hand, and then jammed his fingers into the hollow of the wound. He dug and twisted, tried to tear something loose—with a doglike snarl, doing whatever he could to hurt her. Torres lunged for them, got hold of Kate, and tried to drive a wedge between them.

All thought left Danny. He shoved past Hawkins and jammed his gun against Mavrides's temple, then pulled the trigger twice. The bot's head jerked to the side but he turned and grinned.

"I've got hold of something in here," he said, hand sunk into that wound where Kate's arm had been.

Kate clutched his throat, but Tin Men didn't breathe. She couldn't choke him. Instead she grasped Mavrides's wrist to keep him from pulling and turned to Danny.

Hawkins pushed Danny aside.

Mavrides looked at him, forlorn.

"Zack," Hawkins said. "Some things you can't come back from."

With his left hand he grabbed the back of Mavrides's neck even as he stepped closer to the kid. Hawkins pressed his gun to the sweet spot on the seam between Mavrides's chassis and chest plate, and fired twice. The kid's eyes went wide and he started to argue, to try to twist free.

Danny dove to the ground, dragging Kate behind him.

Hawkins hugged Mavrides close. If he said anything to him in that last moment, Danny couldn't hear the words. Hawkins pulled the trigger a third time, but there was no whine of ricochet or clang of the round stopping dead. The bullet punched through with a crack and then Hawkins dropped his gun.

He lifted the kid off the ground, took four staggering steps, and threw him from the pier. Mavrides hadn't even hit the water when his power core exploded, knocking Hawkins off his feet. Hawkins cracked the wooden planks beneath him when he fell.

For a second, Danny held Kate against him. The burnt smell that clung to her filled his senses.

"I think we're clear, lover boy," she whispered to him.

Danny rose to his knees, reached out and picked up her scorched, severed arm, then handed it to her. "A few inches to the right and that rocket downtown would've done you in. Don't joke, okay?"

They rose together. Danny had one hand on the small of her back as he turned to face the others. Trav had Alexa safe behind the Humvee. Birnbaum and Torres stood by Khan as if they were guarding him, but the bullet wound in his shoulder had kept the anarchist from trying to flee; he'd gone pale from blood loss. Zuzu and Broaddus stayed back, aware they were not a part of this squad.

Hawkins stood at the edge of the pier. The wooden pilings had caught fire from the explosion and the flames had begun to spread.

Kate shuffled slowly toward him, the burnt wreckage of a one-armed robot.

"You're a good man, Hawkins," she said.

"That what I am?"

"A good soldier, then."

Hawkins nodded once.

Danny walked over to where Birnbaum and Torres were watching Khan.

"Her eye going to be all right?" he asked, nodding at Torres.

Birnbaum gave him a look that told him how stupid the question had been. "Other than the fact that it's gone? Nothing I can do for her, Kelso. If I had a spare I might be able to wire it in, but we left all our spare parts littering the street downtown."

Torres gave him a nod. "I'll be okay. Thanks."

Movement on the dock caught Danny's attention. He glanced over and saw an old woman with three children, an older boy and two little girls, coming off the dock and staring anxiously at the fire spreading along the pier. He realized they had been out there the whole time, among the slips and dead-engine boats, and he had never seen them.

"Ma'am, are you all right?" he called.

The Tin Men all turned to look at her but she ushered the kids away, shaking her head as tears ran down her face. He wondered if they had frightened her into crying or if she had left someone behind out there on the dock, or at sea. Whatever it was, she couldn't wait to get those children as far from the fire and from the Tin Men as she could. Danny silently wished her well.

"Why don't you just kill me?"

The voice rose weakly from below Danny. He glanced down to see Khan staring up at him, teeth bared.

"You killed all of my men and yet you want to keep me alive," Khan said. "Why not kill me, or just leave me to die here?"

"That's going to be the president's decision," Danny replied. "Whatever you know, he'll want to know."

Kate strode over and stared down at Khan. "That's right. You're our gift to the commander-in-chief."

Khan spit on the ground.

"Hey," Torres said, crouching beside him, her ruined eye ghoulish in the late afternoon light. "Don't poke the bear."

"Sergeant Wade," Travaglini called.

Danny and Kate turned to see him standing beside Alexa. The girl's expression seemed carved in stone. Danny thought no seventeen-year-old should ever wear that expression on her face.

They walked over to Trav and the girl.

"Alexa and I have been talking," Trav said.

They glanced at the girl, who met Kate's eyes with a steady gaze.

"I know we need to hurry," Alexa said, unblinking. "But it's not right, dragging my father's body all over the place. Before we go I'd like to bury him here, if you'll help me. I'll come back for him when I can. When the world is better."

Alexa took a deep breath and let it out, and in that moment Danny could see all the little broken pieces of her heart, right there in her eyes.

"Can we do that?" Alexa asked.

Kate nodded slowly. "Yeah, we can do that."

21

Felix knew they were making progress, but in the dark the shadows all looked the same. He felt like screaming. He dared not ask how much farther to Piraeus, afraid the answer might break whatever remained of his spirit. Instead he just shuffled along in the wake of the two presidents, muscles as taut as violin strings. The tunnels were so dark that even with the splashes of light provided by the Tin Men he stumbled again and again over the tracks. Twice he fell and skinned his palms. Others had it worse. People walked in columns, one hand on the person ahead, or they walked side by side in a prison-road-gang shuffle as they tried not to fall. With one robot in front and one in back there wasn't a lot of light to go around, but they made do.

They had passed four underground stations thus far. Each time, the passengers they'd gathered along the way flooded the subway platforms and rushed up the steps in a frantic struggle toward daylight. Each time, Felix had been tempted to go with them. But he stayed in line behind President Matheson and President Rostov, following Chapel's guide light as if it had mesmerized him, and perhaps it had. He thought of Moses leading his people out of Egypt, but he knew the comparison was flawed. Matheson and Rostov might not wish these people harm but neither president showed much interest in their welfare. Leading them to an exit had simply proven to be the most expedient way of dealing with them.

"Platform ahead!" President Matheson called.

Chapel repeated the words, translating into Greek. A cheer went up from the latest congregation of passengers who had marched through the darkness behind them. Felix could hear several people break down in sobs. Others picked up their pace, physically urging the pack onward.

"Don't push!" Chapel shouted. "You'll be there in a minute or two. If you push, people are going to get hurt and I promise, you'll be one of them."

The crowd subsided a bit. The two presidents remained in the lead with Chapel and two Secret Service agents and the Russian president's bodyguard, Grigori. The bodyguard's shoulder wound had been bandaged, but he'd lost a lot of blood. Somehow he kept walking, refusing to give in to the injury.

Ahead, Chapel stopped and turned to face the train platform so that the guide light from his chest plate would illuminate as much of the route to the surface as possible. Grigori and the Secret Service agents moved the presidents out of the way as dozens of passengers hauled themselves off the tracks and began to rush toward the exit stairs.

Felix felt a hand on his arm. In the dark, with only the dimmest peripheral illumination coming from Chapel's light, he turned and saw Maggie. Beyond her, Jun tried to stare through the darkness at his feet, picking each step carefully.

"Hey," Maggie said, linking her arm in his and snuggling up beside him as they walked, almost as if he were taking her on some old-fashioned promenade. "We're leaving."

Felix glanced at Jun, who gave him a nod, eyes alight with urgency.

"You're going to stay in Athens?" Felix asked. "Without the president, you have no way of getting home. It could be weeks or months before the situation normalizes enough for you to find safe passage back to the States."

"You may be right," Maggie said sadly, "but we're focusing on staying alive, not getting home. It's dangerous for anyone in Athens right now, maybe Americans especially, but we think we've got a better chance of being killed with him than on our own."

"You should come," Jun said.

Felix took Maggie's hand. Her skin felt soft and warm, so comforting that it nearly persuaded him.

"Living doesn't matter much to me right now," he said, unsettled by the realization that he meant it. "All I want is to see my daughter again. The only hope I have of doing that is if I can make it to Wiesbaden. But you go, and try to stay safe."

Maggie squeezed his hand, stepped up, and kissed his cheek the same way his daughter had always kissed him good night when she was a little girl. Those days were long gone, but it was nice to remember.

"Good luck, Professor," Jun said.

"And to you, my friend."

Most of the passengers had already made their way onto the platform and through the exit. Only a few stragglers remained as Jun and Maggie walked over to President Matheson to explain their decision. They hadn't gotten more than a couple of sentences into it when the president reached out to take Jun's hand, shook it once, and then offered his hand to Maggie. She hugged him instead.

Felix moved nearer to them. Chapel and Bingham still faced the platform.

"Let's move, Mr. President," Syd said. "The more passengers we return to the surface, the more people there are who have seen your face and know you're alive. Any one of them could point your enemies in the right direction."

"I agree," President Rostov said. "These delays could be fatal to us."

President Matheson ignored them, clasping Maggie's hand. "Thank you," he said. "I hope I'll see you both again one day."

"So do we, sir," Maggie said.

Jun tugged her arm and she went with him. Chapel turned away even as they hurried for the platform, leaving Bingham to light their exit. Chapel's light dispelled some of the darkness ahead, farther along the tunnel. Felix felt a twist in his gut, knowing that they still had miles to hike through the dark. He told himself—again and again—that Kate waited for him at the end.

"Wait," a gruff voice called.

Grigori had spoken, but not to Chapel or to Syd. Felix stared at Rostov's bodyguard, at the blood soaked into the fabric over the left shoulder of his shirt and the hollows around his eyes. Perhaps he was not invincible after all. Grigori took two steps toward the platform. Maggie had already scrambled up onto the concrete ledge but Jun paused with his hand on the painted concrete edge and turned toward Grigori.

"I'm coming with you," the bodyguard said.

He lowered his gaze, but could not hide the shame he felt.

Rostov took two steps toward him, features contorted with anger and a kind of revulsion. "Worm," Rostov said in Russian. "You have a duty to your country."

Grigori hung his head a moment longer, then lifted his gaze. "If I stay with you, even if I live to see the end of this tunnel, I will be of no use to you. Another hour or two of this and you will need to carry me out of the station at Piraeus. Every step I take, I feel the bullet in my shoulder grinding against the bone. It must come out."

Rostov stared at his bodyguard, and after a moment the anger leached from his face.

"Go, then," Rostov said, exhaling loudly. He brushed a hand at the air, ushering his bodyguard away. "Find a doctor. Live, you bastard. I hope you have a long life full of children who break your heart."

Aimee sat on her hard bunk in the Hump's stockade, a sterile concrete corridor that would have reminded her of a hospital ward if not for the steel doors, each with its own mesh grill window. Her cell had a small toilet in the corner and she felt the need to use it. It was clean enough, but part of her believed that by doing so she would be accepting her position as a prisoner.

The cell had no mirror; otherwise, Aimee would have been staring into it, wondering what Zander had seen that he could have mistaken for the kind of person who would betray her country, her battalion, and the whole damn world in the bargain. Her version of events sounded so much more rational, at least to her own mind. How could Zander listen to her and North and not *know* that? Did the guy have some racial or gender prejudice that she hadn't picked up on before or had North been that convincing?

Don't be stupid. North used your access code to get into the system. Zander can't just assume you're not involved because you have an innocent face.

"Hey," a voice called from the corridor. "Hey, Aimee."

She clutched the edges of the bunk, bilious hatred burning up the back of her throat. *North.* She thought for a moment that he'd somehow managed to get out of his cell but realized he wouldn't have been able to do that without her hearing it.

Aimee rose and walked to the door, placing her hands on the cold steel. She stared out through the metal mesh, shifted her head to look up and down the corridor, and saw that it was empty. Diagonally across from her, North had his forehead pressed against the mesh of his own cell door. With his face framed by the small window, his blue eyes were as bright as ever. Images fluttered in her mind like photographs scattered by an errant breeze. Those eyes, when North had first flirted with her. Those eyes, when things ended between them. Those eyes, on a surveillance camera, revealing his true nature.

"I should tell you—" he began.

"There's nothing I want to hear from you," she said. "If you have something to say, tell it to Major Zander when he comes to question us."

"That's not . . ." He pressed his eyes closed for a second and then reopened them, gazing at her across the space between their cells. "I didn't know, you understand? I just wanted to say that to you before things get uglier than they already are."

"Didn't know *what*?" Aimee said.

"What you saw before . . . me mourning those guys . . . that was the real me. I had no idea that they were going to be trapped in the bots. Until you told me, I thought we were remote piloting, just like everyone else. If I'd known—"

"You wouldn't have betrayed your country?"

North hesitated. Even through the mesh, she could see that he looked a little sick. "You haven't seen the things I have. When we're in the tin, we're not human. It's too easy to do ugly shit. You take away the risk and you're not a soldier anymore, you're just a killer."

Is that what this is about? she thought. *Is that what changed you?*

"So who did *you* kill?"

"Her name was Sabeen. Six years old. I don't know what she looked like because I never saw her face," he said, voice a rasp of pain. "Just what was left of her."

Aimee tried to make sense of it. "You know how many soldiers come out of the army haunted by shit they did?" she said. "They get help, if they can. Or they end up topping themselves. But what you've done—you want me to feel bad for you? I don't give a shit who put you up to this or why you went along with it. *After* you found out that your platoon was trapped in their bots, you sabotaged their canisters. You killed some of them with your own damn hands."

North practically snarled at her. "You think those guys are gonna make it back here? Their bodies are just going to rot. They're vegetables now. The ones who died are the lucky ones. I was trying to do them the same favor I'd want them to do for me if I was as completely fucked as they are."

Aimee couldn't reply. She wanted to argue, to tell him that all the Tin Men based out of the Hump would find their way home, but she knew the odds were slim. The world outside would be one of destruction, at least for a time. Chaos would rage; there'd be indiscriminate killing.

"We'll see," she said at last.

"I don't think we will," North replied. "Even if some of my platoon make it back here, they won't find a friendly reception. Not once the people upstairs get in here."

"They can't get in. Not with you in a cell."

"Yeah," North said quietly. "I guess you're right."

Aimee shivered at the hollow chill in his voice.

"I don't get any of this," she said. "How did the anarchists even find you? Or did you go looking for them?"

"It wasn't like that. A lot of people knew what I did . . . how much it fucked me up—"

"I never knew. You never told me, all that time you were rotting inside."

North slammed a hand against his cell door. "I never told anyone. But people knew, get it? There were other people there and someone talked about it, talked about how I'd been *unraveling*. Word got around that maybe I thought the Tin Men were as bad for the world as so many people said we were, that maybe I no longer believed in our cause—"

"Someone offered you a different cause," she said quietly.

His blue eyes stared at her through the mesh. "In a bar. Over a lot of whiskey. That little girl haunted me. This guy told me they had a way to put a stop to the Tin Men, put the world back on an even keel. Make war matter to Americans again. Give them something to lose."

The gate at the end of the hall clanked as it was unlocked and then swung open. Aimee twisted her head to see Major Zander entering the stockade, followed by a pair of MPs.

North spoke so softly she could not be sure of the words, but she thought she understood them. *"I thought they'd all just wake up in their canisters. At least they'd have a chance."*

Aimee felt North's pain, but that didn't make him any less of a traitor.

The tread of the MPs' heavy boots echoed off the walls. Major Zander strode ahead of them and stopped in front of Aimee's cell. He looked in at her.

"I don't have time to be anything but blunt," Zander said. "Most of what you told me checks out. But North had your access codes. I roll this around in my brain and there's a version of it where you were in on this with him and changed your mind when you saw the massacre going on outside, so you shut him down before he could unlock the doors. What happened to Platoon A—you'd have had an easier time getting that done than North."

"Major—"

"The problem for you, Warrant Officer Bell, is this version I've got cooked up in my brain? The one where you and North have been in cahoots the whole time? This version paints a picture that makes a hell of a lot of sense to me. So you're staying right where you are, for now. We'll get to you in a while."

Aimee stared at him, her mouth open, then closed it. How could she argue when she agreed with him? His version seemed more plausible than the truth.

Major Zander turned his back on her and nodded to the MPs.

"Cell Six!" one of the MPs called. "On the gate!"

A loud buzz sounded and North's cell door unlocked.

Aimee watched as Zander and the MPs went in, slamming the door behind them.

North had said things were going to get uglier. It turned out he'd been right.

The wind whistled past Kate's head and the last light of the sun glinted off the robots on board the hydroptere, and on the ship itself. The trimaran sailed above the water so smoothly it felt more like flying, with almost none of the roll and pitch of the sea. As fast as the Tin Men could run, Kate still felt as if they were hurtling out of control across the water and that any second the hydroptere might spin off into the air or tip a wing into the waves and tear itself apart.

She held her scorched and severed arm in her lap and smiled morbidly to herself. If they were going to be torn apart, at least she had a head start.

The smell of the sea pleased her and made her wish she could breathe it in, but of course lungs were part of her original body, not this one. From the first moment she had inhabited a Remote Infantry bot, Kate had known that she had reached a stunning technological horizon—that nothing would ever be the same. After the Pulse, when she finally understood the true genius of the bot's designers, she had found herself even more impressed. In comparison, the hydroptere was elegantly simple, and yet she found herself caught up in the magic of it. She felt like Aladdin on his flying carpet.

Water sprayed her face and she wished she could taste salt on her lips. The trimaran continued to pick up speed, the sail like a knife in the sky, carving the wind into the shape of its own desire, its own needs. Birnbaum had explained it to them all as they were setting sail. The hydroptere had marine wings, foils deployed at forty-five degrees under each of the floats on the trimaran. As soon as they unfurled the sails they began to increase their speed, but the magic truly came once they had reached ten knots. At that speed, the foils generated an upward thrust that lifted the ship from the water in the same way an airplane took off from the ground, increasing speed to forty-five knots in the first twelve seconds or so after rising off the waves.

Now they were slicing through the air fifteen feet above the sea, only the foils actually touching the water itself. The hydroptere was a thing of beauty, and it pleased Kate to feel a kinship between the ship and her own body. Sitting at the stern of the center float, she watched the others at work. Each of the hydroptere's wings was equipped with what looked to her like little more than a steering wheel and a hand crank. The crank reeled in or unspooled lengths of the white rope that made up the ship's rigging, moving the sails. Birnbaum had the wheel on the left wing, with Danny moving the crank at her instruction. She had already trained Hawkins and Trav, who were on the right wing, ready to perform the same job when she gave them the signal. Birnbaum had been modest about her abilities as a sailor. She'd had them under way minutes after boarding and now, an hour and a half into the journey, she had taught the squad the basics.

At the prow of the central float, the two additions to Kate's squad—Zuzu and Broaddus—kept Hanif Khan under guard. Khan's cuffs had been removed to keep him from accidentally slipping over the side of the hydrofoil trimaran. If the murderous bastard decided he wanted to die he could throw himself into the sea and be done with it. From the moment they'd set sail, Kate had been waiting for him to do just that and Khan's apparent decision to keep living surprised her almost as much as her own willingness to let him. She told herself she hadn't killed him because POTUS's people might have better luck getting useful information out of him, but she had started to think the truth might be a bit more convoluted than that. If she killed Khan now and discovered later that her father had been killed in the chaos he and his confederates had wrought, she would have no one left to punish.

According to Birnbaum, they were sailing west-northwest. Chasing the sun, she'd said, and Kate liked that idea. They were skimming along the rim of the world. Due west, she could see the sun sliding toward the sea. In moments it would begin to vanish over the horizon and then it would seem to speed up. She had watched enough sunsets in her life to know to expect that strange bleeding effect, the flashes of different colors before the sun disappeared for the night. Once, when she was ten or eleven years old, she had been sitting with her mother on a beach on the Gulf of Mexico—a place where people applauded the sunset every night as if it had been a show performed exclusively for them—and her mother had said that the sunset reminded her of life. Her own mother, Kate's grandmother, had been dead only a few weeks by then. When Kate asked her about the comparison, her mother said the leisurely progress of the sun across the sky was an illusion, that really the Earth spun with dizzying swiftness, and it was only there at the end, when the sun seemed to dash from the sky, that people could truly appreciate just how scant were the hours in a day, how miserly the God who granted them.

Kate no longer believed in God the way her mother did, but every time she watched a sunset she remembered the meager allocation of hours in a day, or in a life. As the salt air burnished her charred frame and the hydroptere soared beneath her, she thought again of her mother and she understood that she had been given a gift of hours. Inside the robot, the blazing sun of her life had ceased sinking toward its inevitable horizon.

Ahead of her, Alexa Day sat on the hydroptere's left wing, hair flying around her face as she dangled her feet over the edge. Kate had watched Alexa's face while the Tin Men had lowered her father's corpse into a hastily dug grave in a small park overlooking the sea, back in Haifa. Alexa had wept, but the girl had fire in her eyes—the kind of fire that forged steel. Though she grieved for Alexa's loss, Kate had been heartened to see that fire; the girl would need it for the life that awaited her in the coming days and years.

Motion caught Kate's attention and she glanced over to see Birnbaum hurrying along the span that connected the center float with the right and left sides. As she ducked beneath the sail and turned to hurry back to Kate, the sun vanished below the horizon and indigo darkness swept across the sea. Birnbaum turned on her guide light, a shining beacon in the dark. The crescent moon and the stars would provide more than enough illumination by which to sail, but Kate knew the light was not for the squad's sake—it was to comfort Alexa.

Torres lay in the netting that connected the central float to the wings like a spider's web. The netting sagged just a little under the robot's weight, but Torres lay there as if someone had shut her down.

"Get your butt up here," Birnbaum said to her. "I want to have a look at you."

Torres grumbled something that Kate couldn't hear over the raging wind and crawled toward the central float—toward Kate.

"How are you, Sarge?" Birnbaum asked, coming to kneel in front of her.

Kate studied her face. "How fast are we going?"

"The old hydropteres—back when they first started breaking speed records—could do about fifty, maybe fifty-five knots. That's over sixty miles per hour. But that was decades ago. I figure we're nearer ninety mph, which puts us about six hours out from the main port of Athens. I'm estimating based on the charts in our onboard systems. Without a satellite connection, I can't be sure."

Torres clambered up onto the central float just behind Birnbaum. Even in the dim moonlight, her ruined eye socket had a monstrous quality about it.

"You really think you can navigate well enough to get us there?" Torres asked.

Birnbaum turned away. "I do, actually. Now sit there and wait your turn. As soon as I've got Wade's arm reattached, I'll see if there's anything I can do for your eye."

"Don't tell me you have a spare," Torres said.

"No, but I might be able to restore certain basic visual functions without one."

With the tap of a finger, Birnbaum lit up a small screen on her abdomen, displaying rows of symbols, some familiar to Kate but most not, though she had seen the screen before. Tapping in a code, the tech opened a hollow in her carapace just below the guide light.

"There's something weirdly intimate about that whole process," Kate said.

"Tell me about it," Torres muttered.

Birnbaum had begun to withdraw small tools from within her chassis, but now she paused. For several seconds she glanced out to sea, and then she turned and searched Kate's eyes.

"Sarge, I need to ask you something."

Kate nodded.

Birnbaum glanced away again. This time Torres reached out and took her hand, nodding her encouragement. Whatever this was, it seemed Torres already knew.

"I know your father's in Athens—"

Kate bristled. "He's there, yeah. And if he's still alive, I hope to keep him that way. But if you think—"

"No, no," Birnbaum said. "Just listen. If the president was back home or in, like, Australia or something, I wouldn't have sided with you. But he's close enough that there's a chance we can make a difference, and that means it's our duty to do so. I believe you'd have made the same decision even if your father hadn't been traveling with him. I just . . . I need your promise, Kate."

"I don't understand what you're asking."

"We get to Athens, find POTUS—and your father, if we can—and then we head straight to the Hump. No matter what," Birnbaum said.

Kate nodded again, glancing from Birnbaum to Torres. "That's always been the plan. As far as I know there's no safer place for the president than back at the airfield, anyway."

Birnbaum stared at her, wind buffeting them, whistling around them. "What if he has other orders?"

"I hadn't considered that."

"No matter what happens," Birnbaum said, "once we're done in Athens, Torres and I are heading for the Hump."

Kate glanced down at the charred arm in her lap. Her own arm. "What's this about, Naomi?"

Birnbaum didn't respond.

"Look," Kate went on, "if the commander-in-chief gives a direct order—"

"Wade," Torres said curtly, her ruined face unreadable. "She's pregnant."

Kate stared at Birnbaum. "She's—"

"She's got to get back to base," Torres said. "She's carrying—her real body—"

"Her *original* body," Kate said without thinking.

"No!" Birnbaum snapped. "My real body. My baby needs me."

"The process doesn't endanger the baby?" Kate asked. "Who knows what they really pump into us in the canisters."

Birnbaum stared at her. "The doctors promised me."

Kate hesitated a moment and then held out her severed arm to Birnbaum. "Let's just get there," she said.

"Shit, Wade, your bedside manner sucks," Torres said.

Kate focused on Birnbaum. "When the time comes, you do whatever you have to do. Seems like that's the way of the world now."

Danny watched comets streak across the night sky over the Mediterranean and wondered if they were really there. He'd been working the crank on the left wing of the hydroptere until Birnbaum had asked Torres to take a turn. His mind felt exhausted and an unpleasant buzz had begun to infiltrate his head. His thoughts seemed too simple, as though their sharp edges had been sanded away.

Birnbaum had come back to take the wheel after doing whatever repairs she could on Kate and Torres. That had been two hours ago, and now Kate sat alone at the stern of the ship's central float, where she'd been since they had set sail. Danny sat beside Alexa Day on the wing, water splashing up at them from far below.

"Beautiful, aren't they?" Alexa asked.

"The stars?"

Alexa glanced sidelong at him. "The robots. You guys. In the moonlight, with the stars reflecting off the metal, you're beautiful. Not sure how that works in battle—"

"We have a stealth mode," Danny said, triggering it with a thought. His carapace went dull, darker, and non-reflective. At night, he knew, it would almost be as if he'd vanished, except Alexa sat too close for him to have disappeared completely.

"Wow, that's—"

"Cool, right?" Danny said.

"I was going to say 'sad.'"

Danny laughed. "Maybe so," he said, and turned to gaze at Kate again.

"Go talk to her," Alexa said.

"She looks like she wants to be alone," Danny replied.

Alexa bumped him with her shoulder. "I was angry at my dad. Now he's gone and we're all out here in the middle of the sea, and he's almost all I can think about. I don't . . . I feel lost without him."

Danny studied her shimmering eyes. He wanted to tell her it would be all right, but he didn't like to lie.

"You've lost a lot of your friends today. From your platoon," the girl said. "But all of us . . . I don't think we've really even begun to process how *much* we've lost. Birnbaum says we've got another four hours or so before we reach Athens. They're gonna be the longest four hours of my life. So, anyway, I say you go talk to her."

Danny nodded, staring down at the water, and then glanced at her again. "You're pretty damn wise for seventeen."

Alexa did not smile. "Chalk it up to a youth of burning candles and writing emo poetry in my journal. Go."

Rising to a crouch, he made his way carefully across the span to the central float and then worked his way to Kate.

"Hey," he said.

Kate cocked her head at him as if she had only just noticed his arrival. "Pretty out here, isn't it?"

Danny sat down facing her. "Calm before the storm."

"I don't mind whatever fighting we've got ahead of us," Kate said. "I just don't like not knowing. Are they still alive or not, y'know? I'm trying not to think about it."

"How's that going?"

Kate slid her foot out to kick him lightly on the leg. "Lousy, thanks."

"Athens won't be like Haifa or those little villages on the road from Damascus," Danny said. "We get there, it's gonna be full-on madness. Real-deal anarchy. If the G20 summit got hit the way we think, the people in Athens will know none of this is an accident. They're not going to be sitting around waiting for the power to come back on."

Kate nodded. "I've thought about that. We've got to keep the girl safe. Hanif Khan—I don't mind if he catches a bullet, but Alexa . . ."

"So we leave her on the boat, with protection?" Danny asked.

"Maybe Zuzu and Broaddus."

Danny glanced back at Alexa, whose gaze was fixed on the stars. "I don't think she'll go for that. My guess is she'll be begging for her own gun before we even reach shore. Not to mention that we'll need all the soldiers we can get. Zuzu and Broaddus could be really useful if we find the president and need to get him to safety. Someone has to stay with the boat, but only one someone. A sentry."

"So the girl stays with the sentry."

Danny shrugged. "We'll see."

Kate studied him without speaking. Danny shifted, glanced away, and finally met her gaze again.

"Listen," he said, "I know now's not the time. In the middle of all this . . . it's just the worst time imaginable. But there are things . . . things that need to be said."

Her eyes went cold. "Pretty sure you said all you needed to."

"Maybe, but I said it poorly. You mean something to me, Kate. I joined the army because I needed something to believe in, and I believe in *you*."

"Danny—"

"So I'll follow you into battle. I'll follow you to the end—"

"Listen—"

"But I can't *need* you. If you hate me for it—"

Kate kicked him again, harder this time. Sea spray speckled their bodies and the rush of the wind and the roar of the trimaran's foils knifing through the water tried to drown out their words, but they heard each other. They always had.

"Stop talking," Kate told him. She did not look away, but he had the feeling she wanted to. "It's just possible that I love you, Danny. There's *my* confession. But every hour that goes by, I feel more empty inside. Things that used to matter to me are starting to matter less and less."

"What are you saying?"

"I don't want my old body back," she said. "Not ever."

Danny stared at her. "Are you . . . how can you say that?"

"We'd have been dead a dozen times today if we were just flesh and blood."

"Still."

Kate gazed out across the waves.

"You realize what you're saying?" Danny asked. "You'll never feel again. Really feel, I mean. Never feel a human touch or the sun on your face."

Kate laughed. "This from the guy who can't man up and admit when he likes somebody."

Danny threw up a hand. "Hell with that, listen to what you're saying. You'll never taste chocolate or have sex or have a baby or . . . or *anything*."

Kate lowered her eyes, gazing down into the water below them. "You don't get what it means to me to be whole again. I look forward to being in the bot. To being strong. To being able to run. To being more than human."

"*Less than,* Kate. We're less than human."

She glanced out at the sea. "If they put us back in our human bodies, there's no guarantee I'll ever be able to pilot a bot again, and I just can't take that risk. You don't understand."

A chill slithered up Danny's spine. "You're right," he said. "That's one thing I'll never understand."

But it occurred to him that perhaps he understood very well.

22

Snipers waited outside the Metro station in Piraeus. The moment Syd and Bingham stepped into the moonlight, gunshots rang out. A bullet took a piece out of the concrete wall behind Syd's head before she ducked back inside. Bingham stood her ground, taking fire even as she sighted her weapon on the nearest sniper—on a roof across the street—and shot him.

"One down," she called back to the others, who waited inside the Metro station entrance.

Felix tried to breathe. His chest hurt and he told himself it had to be the claustrophobia finally getting a grip on him. His skin felt oily and gritty from their subterranean journey. The idea of a sea voyage made him want to weep with relief, but they still had to survive long enough to reach the marina.

"Two down!" Bingham called from outside the station entrance.

Through the opening at the top of the stairs Felix could see the darkened façades of squat apartment buildings—a row of gray boxes that seemed identical. Piraeus had its share of wealthy residents thanks to the presence of Zea, one of the largest and loveliest marinas in Europe, but the city was also a major port, which meant merchant ships, cruise liners, and cargo vessels docked nearby every day. The whitewashed buildings had a kind of uniformity that made it difficult to gauge the prosperity of the neighborhood. But what did prosperity mean now?

"Chapel," President Matheson said. "You and Bingham clear the snipers."

"Can't leave your side, Mr. President," Chapel replied.

"You don't leave my side, we'll never get out of here," Matheson snapped. He winced with pain, touching the rough stitches where the bullet had grazed his temple. "If we don't act now, we all die right here. You want to do your job, follow orders."

Chapel nodded. "Yes, sir!"

Felix breathed as he watched Chapel step out beside Bingham. All he could think about were rocket launchers and explosives, things that could damage or even destroy Tin Men. Without Chapel and Bingham, they were as good as dead.

"Mr. President," Felix said, stepping up beside Matheson, who seemed to have aged a decade over the course of this day. "You can't afford to risk them both."

Syd put a hand on Felix's chest and shoved him back. "Not now, Professor."

"No, listen," Felix said, grabbing Matheson's arm. "These killers were waiting for us. For *you*. We don't know the extent of the ambush out there. If both Tin Men are destroyed, we'll never—"

President Matheson yanked his arm away, eyes narrowed. "Who the hell do you think you're talking to? The bastards smart enough to plan all this . . . did you honestly think they wouldn't realize some of the world leaders might escape and make their way to the sea? They've likely been planning this for years and you think that didn't occur to them? We don't know how many there are. The ambush is likely on the ground as well, more killers waiting to shoot anyone who doesn't look local. Could be they have photographs of the leaders. If I'd planned this, I'd have made sure they all did. These snipers . . . maybe they know who we are and maybe they don't—"

"Or maybe," President Rostov interrupted, "they weren't here at all. Maybe your aides—the ones who left us in the tunnel—maybe they were captured and revealed our intentions."

Matheson spun on him. Syd and the other Secret Service agent watched warily.

"My people?" Matheson barked. "Why would it have to be my people? It could've been any of the folks we helped down in the tunnels. Hell, your bodyguard pledged to give his life for you, didn't he? Where is he now?"

Rostov sniffed. "Grigori would say nothing. He is a man of honor."

"But he's not here, is he? You want to see a man of honor? Right here in front of you." President Matheson pointed at Felix.

"Mr. President," Felix said, holding his hands up. "You should know—"

"That you've stuck with me because you want to reach your daughter in Germany," Matheson said. "Of course you have. That's honor, Felix. You care more for her than you do for yourself. And I'm putting my country first right now. It's all or nothing for me. The best way I can serve is by surviving, by fighting, by showing my people that we can get through this. The longer we stay in this goddamn doorway, the more time we give the killers out there to round up their friends. That means Chapel and Bingham blow the hell out of however many they can and then we make a break for it."

Matheson fell silent, glancing around at the few who had made it to Piraeus with him. With Chapel and Bingham outside—gunshots echoing off into the night sky—that left only Rostov, Felix, Syd, and Kirkham.

"Well?" Matheson asked after a moment.

"You're asking our opinions, sir?" Syd said, tucking a lock of blond hair behind her ear.

Matheson gave her shoulder a fatherly pat. "Yes, Sydney. Now's the time."

Syd frowned. "All due respect, Mr. President, but it's not my job to have opinions. I go where you go."

Rostov grunted, his craggy features stonier than ever. He stood between Matheson and Syd, and he studied his American counterpart for long seconds, his eyes half-lidded with generations of suspicion and animosity.

"Four snipers down!" Bingham called from beyond the Metro exit.

Chapel shouted her name. "Move your ass!"

"President Rostov," Felix said. "Kazimir." Again he drew Rostov's intense gaze. "The old world has been burned away. The old rules? The old enmities? They don't matter now."

Felix glanced at Matheson, who nodded for him to continue.

"In a moment or two, we're going out that door," Felix said. "With or without you. Peter has a role to play in the world and I just want to live to be a better father than I've been. What we make of this new world is going to be up to us."

Matheson looked hard at Rostov. "Help me, Kazimir. Help me build whatever comes next."

Rostov exhaled loudly, and his whole body seemed to ease. "I have never liked you, Peter. Your arrogance has made you no friends. But you are a man of determination. Yes, my survival will send a message to my people—one that will need to be passed along by the written word or by human voices—but there is a greater message to be conveyed if we survive together."

"Together, with neither of us bargaining?" Matheson said. "No posturing? No exchange of favors, what you need and what I need, to show our people we are the ones in charge?"

"It seems to me," Rostov said in his thick accent, "that right now we both need the same thing. I have been following along in your wake, no different from the train passengers we led to safety. I propose that we change that."

Matheson cocked his head. He winced at the pain in his head but then uttered a small chuckle as he extended his hand.

"Here's a moment I never imagined I'd see," he said.

Rostov shook his hand.

"Allies," Matheson said.

"Not as nations," Rostov replied. "As men."

The gunfire outside subsided for a moment and then picked up again.

Chapel stepped back into the station. "Mr. President, we may not be alone."

"What do you mean?" Matheson asked.

"Of course we're not alone," Rostov said, glancing at Felix. "We are under attack."

Chapel shook his head, taking a step down toward them. "Not the anarchists, sir. Bingham and I . . . we just got a signal."

Matheson pressed the edge of his palm against his right eye. "A signal?"

"An emergency signal, sir. From another Tin Man. Original tech, built in case satcomm went down—though I don't figure anyone thought it would be like this. I'd forgotten all about it. Bingham had to remind me what the hell it was."

"Could be from your other man," Matheson said. "He went down back in Athens. Maybe he's still functional and signaling for help."

"No, sir," Chapel replied. "This signal is coming from due east."

"That's impossible," Syd said. "There are no other Tin Men in Greece, only the ones tasked to the president. It must be some kind of trick."

"Maybe, but a damned obscure one, if so," Matheson replied.

Rostov frowned. "There is nothing to the east but a few blocks leading to the marina, and then the Mediterranean."

"The sea," Matheson said, his eyes widening. "Maybe it's not a distress signal at all. Maybe it's a beacon."

"A rescue?" Felix said. "A ship, do you think?"

The two presidents were staring at each other.

"We go," Rostov said.

"Hell, yes," Matheson replied. "As fast as we can."

Danny had moved to the prow of the hydroptere's central float. There, with only open water ahead, the illusion of flying was complete. They soared more than fifteen feet above the water, speeding toward Athens as fast as the trimaran would carry them. Sea spray spattered his face and chest, coated his entire chassis. A chill had begun to seep inside of him and he could not explain it. Kate wanted to remain inside her bot forever but Danny wanted to scream, needed to escape from this prison. If he could have peeled it off he would have done so. He wondered how long he had to remain inside his bot before he began to forget that he was human.

He put his hands on either side of his head. In his own body, he'd have pushed his fingers through the scruff of his hair, something he did when he was frustrated or trying to sort out a problem. The smoothness of his robot skull revolted him. He could feel himself nearly vibrating with the need to act. Whatever the future held, he wanted to run toward it, to scream his throat ragged as he knocked aside anyone or anything that stood in the way of him putting an end to his purgatorial imprisonment inside this fucking machine.

Danny roared. Wordless and senseless, he unleashed his frustration. The wind carried his shout back to the others on the hydroptere. The scream had broken the wave of his tension, easing it slightly, and he turned to see many faces watching him. Trav and Torres were at the wheel, keeping them flying, under Birnbaum's supervision. Kate remained aft, too far away or perhaps too occupied with her restored arm to have heard him. Hawkins sat with Alexa on the left wing, both of them studying Danny worriedly. Zuzu and Broaddus were guarding Hanif Khan.

Zuzu moved up to join Danny at the prow of the ship, breaking the vitriolic current. "Hey, man. It's Kelso, right?"

"That's right."

"Sorry, man. Still trying to learn everyone's markings. Guess I should remember that target on your chest."

Danny smiled. "Easier for me. Not a lot of Tin Men with painted flowers."

Zuzu shook his head. "I'm just hoping I get a chance for payback." He glanced westward, into the wind. "You all right up here? Sounded like you were freaking out a little."

"Aren't you?"

Zuzu laughed. "Fuck, yeah. But Birnbaum says we should hit this port city, Piraeus, in thirty, maybe forty minutes. Once we make landfall it's four miles to Athens proper. We scout the place, try to find POTUS, and we get the hell out, right?"

"The faster the better," Danny said.

Ping.

Zuzu whipped his head around to stare westward again. "Did you get that?"

Danny nodded. "Sure. Your signal's still broadcasting. Has been since we left Haifa. I thought you knew that. Sergeant Wade wanted to keep the signal going just in case—"

"Dude," Zuzu said, "that wasn't my signal."

Ping.

Zuzu glanced at him. "That one was mine. Much stronger, right?"

Ping. Danny could tell the difference now. The other signal was faint, farther away, but definitely coming from the west.

"Kate!" Danny shouted, turning to see Kate rushing forward along the central float. She ducked under the sail and ran at him.

"Are you getting that?" she asked, shifting her head, trying to see past them. "It's gotta be the president's RIC detail, right?"

She turned to Danny and Zuzu, smiling as fully as her robotic features would allow.

"It could be," Danny said.

"Hell, Kelso, it's gotta be," Kate said. She slapped Zuzu on the back. "Take a bow, Zuzu. Every time a bell rings, a Tin Man gets his wings. If you hadn't started broadcasting that signal we'd never have found you and we'd have had a hell of a time locating the president. If this ping is one of the Tin Men in his protection detail responding to you, I'm gonna kiss you later."

"You're the boss, Sarge."

Danny turned to stare across the water, waiting for the darkened skyline of Piraeus to appear in the moonlight.

Ping.

Felix crouched behind a boxy little car, a dented green thing that had been abandoned at the curb with its doors still open. The presidents were a car ahead, also taking cover. Chapel and Bingham were out in the open, with Syd and Kirkham backing them up from behind a white box truck that sat dead in the road.

"In the bookshop!" President Matheson shouted.

Felix stuck his head up, tracking two people in motion. A pair of anarchists had been hiding in the shadows of an alley and now they came out shooting, ignoring the Tin Men and the Secret Service agents, firing only at the car that Rostov and Matheson were using for cover. Rostov popped his head up, leveled his gun, and fired two quick rounds. One of the anarchists took a bullet in the leg and shouted as he went down. The man had a wild thatch of ginger hair and when he rose, half-bent, clutching the wound in his leg, he looked wilder than ever.

Syd stepped out from behind the white box truck and shot him in the head, then put two in the chest of his companion.

Felix saw Matheson clap Rostov on the back. They had already run a treacherous moonlit gauntlet. He had thought that this far from the G20 summit the only anarchists they would encounter would be those who were pursuing them or lying in wait, and there had been those snipers ready to ambush them. But there were other anarchists as well, there to do a different sort of damage. How many of them had come to Athens to begin with? He thought there must have been hundreds, maybe more. Snipers and bombers and thugs attacking soldiers and cops in the street.

Along blocks where there were no anarchists, they saw people beginning a kind of exodus. Under cover of darkness, those who had realized the enormity of the situation carried backpacks and trundled suitcases along behind them. They led children by the hand or dogs by the leash. Most people moved silently, not wishing to draw attention to themselves. When they saw the Tin Men some quickened their pace, but others stopped to shout at them. A withered old man strode shakily across the street to spit on Chapel.

None of them seemed to notice the presidents.

They did see a handful of police officers out in the street, calling to residents, trying to get people to stay in their homes and to conserve food and water. Gunfire came from distant neighborhoods and if they looked to the north they could see fires burning brightly in central Athens, pillars of black smoke painted against the night sky, defying the moonlight.

"Let's go, Felix," Matheson said.

They hurried along in the shadows of the buildings on the right. Syd and Kirkham took up positions behind and in front of them, while Chapel and Bingham stayed a few yards ahead, out in the street, trying to draw trouble before it could be focused on the presidents.

"What's there?" Syd shouted to Bingham.

Chapel nodded to her and Bingham ran to the end of the block. She looked around the corner and seemed to stare for a second before racing back to them. Chapel joined them all in an alcove in front of a travel agency.

"It's a party," Bingham said.

They all stared at her. Felix wanted to ask if she was serious but they could all hear it now. Guitars and other instruments—several horns, he thought—were being played nearby, but were almost drowned out by the sounds of revelry.

"It's the university," Rostov said, glancing at the surrounding buildings as the realization struck him. "I gave a speech here two years ago. We're not far away."

President Matheson turned toward the source of the music and laughter. "Quickly, then. These kids wouldn't be throwing some kind of end-of-the-world party if the anarchists had been here shooting people. We get through this crowd and we're only a block or so from the marina. Move your butts!"

Matheson and Rostov set off together. The Secret Service agents ran with them and Felix did his best to keep up. His skin prickled and he glanced around as he ran, wondering when the bullet would come.

Up ahead, Bingham had already rounded the corner and the presidents followed suit. As Felix picked up his pace, his right foot came down in a small pothole. He swore as he twisted his ankle and stumbled, sprawling forward onto the sidewalk. He threw his hands out to break his fall. His palms scraped the ground as bits of gravel embedded in his flesh. His left knee banged hard on the sidewalk and he found himself on hands and knees, breathing hard and face flushed.

"Up, Felix," Chapel snapped at him. "I can't wait for you."

Felix didn't have to be told. He scrambled to his feet and hustled toward the corner. His knee stung and he felt a trickle of blood there, but the real pain came from his hands, which he tucked up under his armpits, hugging himself as he ran.

Chapel had paused at the corner. Now he looked back and beckoned to Felix.

"Come on," the bot said. "You're never going to believe this."

Felix reached him, turned the corner, and saw that the presidents had also paused about ten feet away. During Felix's boyhood, the building that housed Piraeus University might have been called futuristic, but it belonged to a future that had never come to pass. Constructed mostly of concrete and glass, it managed a certain elegance due to the windows framed in coppery red and the way the heights of the different wings echoed the plateaus of an elaborate wedding cake. Some of its windows were broken and the only lights within came from candles that burned in several of the rooms, but otherwise the school seemed unscathed.

The anarchists had not attacked the university, but in the streets around it, a different sort of anarchy reigned.

Matheson gestured for them to keep moving. Felix hurried to keep up with Chapel even as Bingham cleared them a path through the revelry. Students danced in the street as they tilted back bottles of alcohol. On the hood of a dead sedan, a young woman wearing only a yellow bra straddled a bearded man whose pants were tangled around his ankles. More than a dozen students cheered them on.

A music circle had sprung up near the university steps, where seven or eight people played guitar and others had brought out violins and various horns. A tall, dangerously thin fellow had even carried a cello into the street and now began to play. Many more students were partially clothed or naked. Some had made torches of items of clothing and set them aflame. A pile of wooden chairs and other items had become a bonfire.

The arrival of the Tin Men caused a ruckus. As Bingham shouted at them, students began to challenge her, standing in the way. When they recognized Rostov and Matheson the voices broke into furious shouts from several men and a young woman who began to weep. Felix saw the desperation in their eyes and wanted to speak, to say something that would comfort them.

"The police haven't even come!" one girl shouted at the presidents, trying to push past Syd. "Why haven't the police come?"

Felix went cold. The students might have begun this wildness as a lark when the power went out and the engines died, but now they were becoming frightened, taking comfort in alcohol and the madness of the crowd.

"Move aside!" Bingham shouted at them, the words coming out in Greek thanks to the bot's translator.

Nobody listened.

Students began to push in toward the presidents. Syd looked at Matheson for instructions, the silent question very clear—*Do I shoot college kids for getting too close?* But the potential for violence spread like an invisible fog in the air, blanketing them all. A bottle sailed overhead and shattered on the ground at Felix's feet and he moved nearer the presidents, turning his back to them as he realized that they were surrounded now and the students were moving closer, demanding answers.

"They're making themselves a target if they don't let us through," Matheson called to Bingham and Chapel.

The Tin Men began to shove back, knocking students into one another. Young men and women sprawled on the ground even as others protested the violence. A scruffy-faced kid with frantic eyes shattered a bottle on the side of Chapel's head and the bot stiff-armed him away with such force that Felix, so close to them, heard ribs crack in the kid's chest.

President Rostov raised the gun he'd stolen from the policeman's corpse and fired into the air. The shot echoed off the faces of buildings and silenced them all. Students stumbled away or ducked their heads or just froze, staring. One guitarist hit a jangling note as the other musicians halted their music.

"You are students!" Rostov shouted at them, spittle flying from his lips. "Even the least intelligent of you is smart enough to have gotten this far with your lives! Most of you have enough sense to see who is standing before you, but do you understand what it means that you're seeing us here, together, with only these few comrades at our sides?

"Idiots!" he shouted. "If there's any hope at all of repairing the damage done to the world today, *we* are that hope. If there is any future in which whatever education you've had so far will mean anything, we are the ones who will build that future. Let us pass, you fools, for if the men who caused today's horrors catch up with us, there will be no hope at all!"

Startled, the students began to fall back, opening a path for them. Bingham moved immediately, while Syd and Kirkham ushered the presidents forward. Chapel nudged Felix into motion and he rushed ahead, catching up so that he found himself striding beside Rostov.

"You believe all of that?" Felix asked in Russian.

Rostov glanced at him, eyes narrowed. "Some," he muttered in his gravelly voice. "People will pull together or they will fall under the boot heels of one oppressor or another. Peter and I . . . we can lead. Create alliances. Rebuild and repair. There's hope in that . . . but not magic."

They passed through the thickest throng of students and moved along the block as small clusters gawked at them. One of the young men shouted drunken words of support that were hard to decipher.

A scream came from behind them, followed by gunfire.

"Here they come!" Syd shouted.

Rostov halted, turning to see how bad a turn the situation had taken. Matheson put a hand on his shoulder and pushed him forward.

Felix ran past them, moving to catch up with Bingham. *The marina!* he wanted to scream. Getting to a boat seemed the only thing left that mattered.

More gunfire drummed the air and the students began to scatter, running for their lives. Felix saw a young woman fall to the pavement and then rise, limping. The two who'd been having sex on top of the dead car in the street slid off the hood and tried to run. The naked girl hurled herself behind a thick tree on the university's tiny lawn while her lover tripped over the pants that were crumpled around his ankles and then tried to rise, only to be shot twice in the back.

"Look there!" Felix shouted, pointing along a narrow side street across from the university.

Armed soldiers in black uniforms ran up the street toward them, carrying assault rifles. Many wore riot helmets, but none of them bore any insignia Felix could see.

"Greek military?" Syd asked.

The soldiers opened fire, giving Syd her answer.

"This way," Chapel shouted, grabbing Felix by the arm.

Felix felt the change in direction but he kept his head down and ran alongside Chapel as bullets flew around them. One dinged off Chapel's back and Felix felt the terrible certainty that he would never leave Athens alive, that his hope of seeing Kate again had been a fantasy.

They reached a row of glass doors. Bullets shattered two of them as Bingham and the presidents approached. The bot crashed right through. Shards of glass rained down around her and then the rest of them were hurtling through the broken doorways, boots crunching on broken glass.

"Move aside!" Felix shouted, certain that bullets would come right into the interior of the university's main lobby and kill them there in the sorrowful darkness that the Pulse had left behind.

"What now?" Rostov asked.

"We work from cover," Matheson said. "Kill as many of them as we can as fast as we can and then we run for it before reinforcements arrive. We're a block and a half from the marina and I'm not giving up when we're this close."

He gestured to Chapel. "You and Bingham go tear them apart."

"Yes, Mr. President," Chapel said. "Gladly."

"Better take another look," Syd announced. She'd slid along the wall inside the main entrance to get a clear view of the outside. Her pale face looked more ghostly than ever. "Those reinforcements are already here."

23

Aimee moaned quietly as she dozed. She had paced her cell for the early hours of her confinement, pausing to try to eavesdrop on the interrogation taking place across the hall. She heard Major Zander's sharp tones but had difficulty making out the words; North's voice never grew above a low rumble as the MPs came and went. Major Zander might have gone out for a time as well, but if so it had been after she had decided to lie down on the concrete-hard cot.

From the cot she could hear even less of what unfolded across the corridor, but she realized that none of it mattered. If they could never confirm that North was guilty, she felt confident that at some point they would at least decide that she herself had not participated in his crimes. She could prove it if they would give her access to a computer. It might take a while, but eventually she would be released.

Aimee rolled that calming mantra around in her mind and tried to make herself believe it was the truth. She had lain there, just breathing and reassuring herself, until she had drifted off to sleep with murmurings and occasional bursts of violence as her lullaby, all coming to her from North's cell.

A shout woke her.

She clung urgently to sleep. There came another shout and then a series of loud thumps from across the hall, the crack of wood, and the muffled snap of a gunshot. Only then did Aimee open her eyes. She lay on the cot and stared at the wall.

They killed him, she thought. *They just executed North.* No matter what kind of traitorous bastard he'd turned out to be, the idea that a man she'd made love to had just died less than twenty-five feet away from her . . . she could scarcely imagine it.

A loud thump echoed across the hall, followed by two more in quick succession. Would they do the same thing to her? Had the world changed so much since this morning that if they did not like her answers they would just kill her?

She heard the hinges squeak on the door to North's cell but no voices. Major Zander and the MPs had finished their work and now they remained silent, as killers often did. Would they try to be surreptitious now, hide what they'd done, or did it not matter? Perhaps this was meant to be a warning to others who would betray their uniforms—*a warning to me.*

She leaped from the bed and rushed to the door of her cell. There might be no such thing as a court-martial in this new world, where the only people they could be sure were safe were those underground with them, but she would argue her case.

"Look," she said, "if you give me a chance, I swear I can prove—"

A shadow ran past her cell. Boots hammered the floor, maybe two dozen steps, and then a second gunshot rang out, this one echoing up and down the corridor. The boots returned and a moment later the shadow slid into view. A man stood just outside her cell, staring in through the small mesh window.

Thomas North.

My God, she thought. Three armed men against one unarmed prisoner. The idea that North had prevailed had not occurred to her.

"If it helps," North said, leaning against the outside of her cell door, "Major Zander never believed you'd been working with me. He couldn't rule it out, but he had faith in you."

Aimee brought a hand up to cover her mouth. "You killed them?"

North stepped aside so that she had a view across the hall. His cell door hung open and she could see one of the MPs in the open doorway, the man's head dented and bloody from where North had bashed it against the wall or the door frame. Beyond him, Major Zander lay crumpled and dull-eyed, a bullet hole just to the left of his nose. Aimee figured the gun had been fired at an upward angle, the bullet tearing through Zander's brain.

"This whole thing was supposed to be an equalizer," North said. "Put the world on a level playing field. I've got family out there, people I love. They're gonna be taken care of, as long as I do what I promised. And I get to live. You think Zander would've made me the same deal? Hell, even if he would have, there'd be no way for him to guarantee it. The old world is over."

He jangled a set of keys in front of the mesh.

Aimee felt sick. "What are you doing?"

"I couldn't work the door release, but these ought to do the trick," he said as he began to try each of the keys in the lock.

Aimee backed away from the door as if it had burned her. "You son of a bitch. Just stay out there, all right? I'm locked up. You'll either finish what you started or they'll shoot you. Killing me won't change that."

The lock tumbled with a clank that made her flinch.

North stared at her through the mesh. "I'm not going to kill you, Aimee. I didn't want to kill those guys—I don't want to kill anyone." He hauled the door open and stood face-to-face with her, stolen gun aimed at her chest. "But I've resigned myself to doing what needs to be done and that means shutting down the Hump's defenses and unlocking the doors. I know where I'm going, how to move around without being seen, but I don't have your skills. The techies will be on guard now, but you're like a fucking virtuoso with this stuff."

Aimee shook her head, her face flushed and her breathing short. "You don't actually think I'm going to *help* you?"

North lifted the gun, aiming it at her heart. "I know you are. Think for a second on the difference between brave and stupid. You opened your heart to me, Aimee. I know you have family, friends . . . people who would be devastated if you died."

"If they're still alive after today," she said, "they'd be ashamed of me for helping you."

"Not if you only did it because some lunatic held a gun to your head," North replied. He nodded to her. "Hurry up and decide. I shut off the cameras on this corridor just now and most everyone's attention is elsewhere, but it won't be long until someone comes to check on the major."

Aimee stared at him. Her throat tightened and her mouth went dry. She told herself that if she lived she could be the base's best hope. Even if he dragged her along with him, she could find a way to thwart him. Dead, she would be of no use to anyone. North took a step nearer and lifted the pistol, aiming between her eyes.

"Don't think I won't kill you if it buys safety for me and the people I love," he said, as if he could read her mind.

In the end it was the anguish in his eyes that convinced her. It tore him up, but he meant it. Safety for the people he loved. Once she had thought she might be one of those people.

He ushered her into the corridor with the barrel of the gun and then followed behind her.

"Into the guard booth," he said. "First thing you're going to do is take down the internal surveillance cams. All of them."

Aimee wanted to tell him to go to Hell. The words were on her lips. But the presence of the gun seemed to burn a small spot at the base of her spine, and she knew that she would do as he'd asked. It would make it harder to locate them, maybe buy North enough time to complete his mission.

Unless she could stop him.

Kate barked orders as the hydroptere skimmed toward Piraeus. The signal had grown louder as they approached Athens and she had intended to sail the ship directly toward that signal, but now it seemed the signal had been coming from Piraeus itself.

"Birnbaum, you've got to slow us down!" she shouted.

Kate still knew next to nothing about sailing the trimaran but Birnbaum had done a credible job of teaching the others the basics.

Sails began to furl and shift and soon they were gliding slowly enough that the angled foils beneath the hydroptere's wings slid into the water. When the floats touched the undulating sea, the ship began to roll with the waves and Kate realized just how much smoother their journey had been on a hydrofoil than it would have been on any other vessel.

"Travaglini!" she called. "I want you and Broaddus in the water on my mark. Each of you take a line and tie us off."

Danny stood on the right wing, staring into the sea spray and the darkness ahead. "You're taking us into the marina?" he asked.

"Why not?" Kate called back.

"Just look!"

The wind had died down with the easing of their speed and she could hear the voices of her squad, mostly Birnbaum snapping commands to Torres and Zuzu. Kate had been so focused on their speed and general direction that she hadn't glanced at the horizon in a minute or two. Now she looked westward and saw the fires burning in Athens. Even from this distance, the orange light of those flames gave a terrible amber aura to the sky above the city. Black smoke drifted in clouds that seemed to swallow moonlight.

Several smaller fires burned in Piraeus, much closer to their position, and as the hydroptere cut its threefold trail across the water Kate realized she could make out the Zea Marina after all. Hundreds of yards wide, it had been constructed as a vast circle with long docks all around its circumference. The only gap in the circle was at the mouth of the marina, between a pair of sea walls. One was stationary but the other looked as if it might be a swinging gate to protect the marina from the sort of storm surge that had been devastating to oceanfront areas around the world. The marina could have held hundreds of yachts and sailboats. At this distance, with the eyesight of a robot and in the light of the moon and stars, she could make out only a handful of masts. The yachts remained, their engines useless, but most of the sailing ships were gone.

"Birnbaum!" she called. "Get us in close to the sea wall but don't enter the marina!"

There would be people looking for any path out of the chaos in

Athens. Most of those who had thought of sailing away were already gone, but Kate wasn't about to take chances. They could not afford any complications.

She bent and then extended the arm Birnbaum had reattached. The hand and elbow joints worked fine but the shoulder had limited range of motion. Kate didn't mind the charred blackness of her carapace or the places where it had warped a bit from the heat of the explosion, but she feared that partially frozen shoulder could cost her in combat. She hoped not to find out.

The hydroptere continued to slow. As they glided toward the marina, Kate glanced back at Hanif Khan. The anarchist had been stitched up and the bullet hadn't hit anything vital, so the wound wouldn't kill him, but he'd lost a lot of blood and they had no way to replenish it. He looked drawn and tired, hunched over to protect himself from the wind and the sea spray. Zuzu kept a gun on him at all times. Once he'd been an Afghani warlord and later a Bot Killer; now he was a wounded prisoner.

Wounded or not, Kate thought, *don't underestimate him.*

Khan couldn't do the bots any harm—not without a high-powered gun and the time to aim—but a man that dangerous would always be dangerous, and they had Alexa to think of.

As if summoned by the thought, the girl began to make her way forward. She had spent the past twenty minutes in Kate's old spot at the rear of the central float but now she stepped carefully along it, ducked under the sails, and hurried up to the prow.

"What's the plan, Kate?" Alexa asked.

"Sergeant Wade," Kate corrected. "And the plan is to rescue the president and whatever remains of his entourage, with POTUS our priority."

"President Matheson and your dad, you mean."

Kate nodded. "That's right."

Alexa held herself differently now than she had when they'd met at the embassy earlier in the day. Seventeen could be a strange age even in the best of times. A kid could go from petulant and whiny to wise and courageous in the space of minutes, and then back again. But most seventeen-year-olds didn't cross that bridge in the midst of combat, and most didn't have to witness the murder of a parent. Alexa had crossed that bridge today and from what Kate could tell, she'd burned the motherfucker down behind her. The girl had a sharp glint in her eyes and a bold tilt to her jaw that bespoke a hardening of the heart.

"I should have a gun," Alexa said.

Kate frowned. "I don't think so. We can handle the fighting. Besides, you won't be going anywhere near combat. You're staying right here on this ship with Birnbaum. She'll be guarding Khan and keeping you safe, just in case anyone decides to try to borrow our boat."

"Not a chance," Alexa said. "No way am I staying behind!"

"Alexa, listen—"

"You're not leaving me!"

The Tin Men who weren't occupied with sailing the trimaran looked up, staring at the furious seventeen-year-old. Khan kept his head down, as if he hadn't even heard Alexa raise her voice.

"You've been in enough firefights for one day, kid—"

"Stop calling me that."

Kate nodded. "Okay. Alexa, then. Do you see the fires burning all over the place? I can hear gunfire from here. It's going to be more chaos, more risk of you being killed. On top of that, if my people have to look out for *you*, that makes *us* less effective. I'll say it one more time. I'm sorry, but you are staying right here."

"And I'll say it again," Alexa replied, the wind whipping her hair across her face. "Birnbaum's going to have to shoot me to keep me on board. What happens when you find the president? Maybe you get cut off and you can't make it back here, what do you do then? I'll tell you what you do—you put the safety of the president of the United States ahead of the safety of some fucking teenager. I am not running the risk of being left here alone!"

Kate flinched at the edge of fear in her voice.

Alexa went on. "You're gonna leave me with Birnbaum and the guy whose buddies murdered my dad? If you don't come back, where do I go then with the three of us as the only possible crew? So I cover

Khan with a gun while Birnbaum tries sailing the hydroptere by herself? I'm coming, Kate. Get it off your conscience. If I die, that's on me, but I'd rather be dead than left alone!"

Kate stared at the girl for a second before glancing at Danny. He gave her a nod and she couldn't argue with it.

"All right . . . Alexa," Kate said. "You're coming along."

"Damn right I am."

As the hydroptere edged toward the marina's sea wall, Kate turned toward the rest of her squad.

"Someone's got to stay here and guard the ship," she said. "Alexa is right. There's always the chance we'll be cut off and need to find another way out of the city, so staying behind is a gamble. But we can't leave this ship unprotected."

Zuzu raised his hand. "I'm your man, Sarge."

Tanya Broaddus shook her head. "Naw, Zuzu. The rest of our squad is dead. I'm not leaving you here."

"Actually, you are," Kate told Broaddus. "We're not voting on it. Zuzu volunteered, and I'm grateful. Zuzu, you're on your own. Don't let anyone take this boat. Broaddus, we're taking Khan with us—"

The Bot Killer lifted his head in surprise. Though pale and drawn, he still had hate burning in his eyes.

Kate pointed toward the hotels and shops on the other side of the marina. "We'll start in one of those hotels. Alexa, you'll stay with Broaddus and Khan while we check out the signal. If we have to move more than a couple of blocks, we'll come back for you and we'll all advance together. That's the way it's going to be."

No one argued the point. This was her squad.

"All right. Trav, over the side and tie us up to that sea wall. The rest of you, check your ammo. Whatever you've got left, now's the time. We run into any rocket-men, I want them dead before they've even had a chance to pull the trigger. Go!"

As the last of the sails furled away, Danny and Trav grabbed lines of rope and dropped off the left-side float and into the water. They vanished instantly, sinking hard to the bottom, and moments later they were clambering from the sea twenty yards away on the sea wall, already dragging the hydroptere toward the rocks.

Kate rotated her arm, testing out her stiff shoulder. It would have to do.

Trav signaled that the hydroptere was moored to the sea wall.

"It's go time," Kate called to them. "Watch one another's backs, eyes open for snipers and rockets. We follow the signal to the source."

"What if POTUS isn't with the bot giving off this signal?" Broaddus asked.

"Signal must be coming from one of the bots on the Secret Service detail. If he's not with the president, the bot's got to know his whereabouts. One way or another, we'll know soon enough. Move out!"

One by one they jumped over the side. Zuzu dropped Hanif Khan into the water, where Broaddus waited to carry him up the sea wall. Soaking wet, the anarchist hung his head as he stood among them, not even looking up as they started to march.

Kate hesitated, wondering if she should just shoot him now and be done with it. Leaving him alive to make trouble felt like keeping a crocodile for a pet. But President Matheson would want answers, and Khan remained the best way for him to get at least some of them.

"Watch him!" she called to Broaddus, who gave her a thumbs-up.

Alexa climbed from the water nearby and Kate went to her.

"Stick by me," she told the girl. "Think bulletproof thoughts."

24

Felix stood just inside the foyer of Piraeus University's main building and tried to hold back a scream. Bullets obliterated the glass doors, spraying shards all over the floor. The broken glass glittered in the moonlight that pooled at the foyer's edge, but Felix stood in darkness, breathing in the shadows and praying they would make him invisible if the anarchists managed to get past Chapel and Bingham.

The two presidents were pressed against the wall nearby. Kirkham stood with them, gun in hand, though compared to the two Tin Men—or to the dozens of anarchists who had pinned them down—the last Secret Service agent seemed almost pitiful.

Not last, Felix told himself. *Syd may still come back.*

He glanced along the pitch-dark corridor where he'd last seen Syd but the shadows remained stagnant. No movement at all.

"We can't stay here!" Felix said, his voice a rasping stage whisper. "We'll die!"

Rostov turned toward him. Hard as the man's features were, the Russian president managed a gentle look.

"It always seemed likely, Professor," Rostov said. "We would have needed better luck than we've ever had to make it out of this."

Felix shook his head. "I can't accept that."

He stepped away from the wall, far enough to get a glimpse through the ruined front doors. Chapel and Bingham were still in front of the university building. The lights on their chests were off—why make themselves even better targets? They were moving from side to side, using decorative stone columns as cover. Felix could hear them shouting to each other even amidst the rain of bullets that fell upon them, ricocheting off the bots or just plunking against their metal skins.

"Police car, three o'clock!" Chapel shouted.

Bingham turned to her right, spotted the abandoned cop car just up the road and the shooters behind it. She took aim and fired twice, killing an anarchist who stood by the trunk and another who crouched at the other end of the car, peering around it. Felix flinched at the sight—head shots, both of them—but in his mind he urged her on, and Chapel as well. They were so badly outnumbered, with more anarchists arriving in the street beyond. The Tin Men were such extraordinary marksmen that he knew they could have killed every anarchist if only they'd had enough time and ammunition, but both were quickly running out. There were too many anarchists—fifty or sixty by now—and soon they would get inside the university from some other entrance.

Anxious, he glanced around for signs of incursion.

Bullets sprayed through the shattered doors, tearing apart the viewscreens and vending machines and the information desk in the foyer. One bullet struck the floor only inches from his feet, embedding itself there. Felix hissed out a breath and took a step back.

As a girl, his daughter had loved to play soccer. For the team to really work well together, she had said, they needed to be like a family, to be able to predict each other's choices on the field. They had to forge a bond, united by a single purpose—winning. Kate had been eleven years old when she gave him that speech and he ought to have known that very moment that she was destined for a military life. But how could he have envisioned that this eleven-year-old, tall-for-her-age girl with the wild hair and those lovely purple eyes would go to war? How could he have imagined that the girl who had so loved to run would lose her legs?

He had missed more soccer games than he would have liked, and he had long felt guilty about that. But he had gone to every one of the father/daughter dances at her school. They had been held in the school gymnasium on the first Friday of December. What had they called the dance?

Yes, he remembered now. *The SnowBall.*

The little girls had never had much use for their fathers at these dances, clustering in groups and giggling or racing around like lunatics. But once during each dance, the DJ would call a time-out to their antics and play a song specifically for the fathers and daughters to dance together. Kate had held him awkwardly, all too conscious of her peers surrounding her, never understanding that they were all holding their fathers in precisely the same way. He had loved that special dance even with its halting discomfort.

As she grew older, Kate had pushed him away. Only later did he realize that he'd chosen not to fight this, had accepted the growing distance between them because it was convenient for him. The less involved he was in her life and the more time he spent away from home, the less effort he made to bridge the gap forming between them. He had told himself that she didn't need him, never realizing how much *he* needed *her.*

"Felix, get back!" Matheson shouted.

A bullet grazed his shoulder. Felix blinked as if coming awake but still he barely moved. Imminent death had become a kind of mirror for him. He stared at his reflection, even if only in his own mind, and he found himself revolted not because he had so rarely been a part of his daughter's life but because much of the time he had been relieved to keep his attention on his work. The angrier she grew, the more alienated she could be made to feel, the fewer demands she'd place on him.

This is it, he thought. *This is where I die.*

"Alone," he whispered to himself, the word lost amidst the gunfire. "You sad old son of a—"

A powerful hand grabbed him by the shoulder and spun him around. He stared into Rostov's stony eyes.

"Idiot," the Russian president said as he shoved Felix back toward the wall where Matheson took cover, with Kirkham protecting him.

Felix stumbled over his own feet and went sprawling across the floor, nearly colliding with Kirkham's legs. Rostov called him an idiot again, a heartbeat before a fresh fusillade of bullets stitched the floor of the foyer. Cursing loudly in his native tongue, Rostov dove into cover, slamming to the ground only feet from Felix, who stared at the grim-faced man, thinking again of how surreal the world had become. The Russian president had just saved his life.

Chapel barreled through the glassless entry doors.

"Incoming!" he roared.

Felix stayed down. Kirkham dragged Matheson to the floor. He heard the scream of the rocket even as Bingham careened through the door behind Chapel, feet crunching glass. The rocket struck the other side of the entrance and exploded, destroying part of the outer wall. The blast blew Bingham off her feet. She tumbled and skidded through the garden of moonlit glass shards.

Felix's ears were ringing and he shook his head to clear them. When he looked up, Chapel was above him.

"Up!" Chapel barked. "Let's go!"

"We've got to move!" Bingham said. "I saw at least four assholes with launchers out there!"

As if on cue, another rocket screamed through the open foyer and struck the far wall. Felix rose as the two Tin Men used their bodies to shield Matheson and Rostov. Kirkham clutched his gun like some kind of talisman, but he looked as if he had never felt more useless in his life.

"We're going!" President Matheson said, pushing against the Tin Men and starting toward the corridor where Syd had gone on recon.

The Tin Men stepped into moonlight and began firing through the door at the anarchists, covering their retreat deeper into the building. Felix hurried to keep up with Matheson and Kirkham, with Rostov right behind him. The darkness slowed them down. Felix reached out and ran his hand along the wall, hoping he didn't run into anything. He imagined that the faculty and many of the students had left school to go find their loved ones earlier in the day, before night had fallen, but where were the rest now? All of them out in the street?

One of the Tin Men clanked up behind them. Only when she turned on the light on her chest plate did Felix see that it was Bingham. She said nothing as she rushed past, guiding them through the darkness. Chapel caught up a second later and they ran along the hall past offices and what might have been a classroom or two, until they came to a spot where corridors branched left and right and stairs led both up and down.

"Which way?" Felix asked.

Matheson did not hesitate. He went left and no one argued. It seemed the option that would take them farthest from the attack on the foyer.

Footfalls came from the stairs they'd just left behind. They all turned, guns raised, and Kirkham fired once. Thankfully the shot went wide, otherwise he'd have killed the only other human member of the president's Secret Service detachment.

Syd had her hands up, gun in her right. Now she stared at him.

"Please try not to shoot at me again," she said. "Your aim might not always suck." She gestured down the stairs. "This way. And running. I found an exit only a few of them are watching, but with no return fire back at the main entrance they'll know we're making a break for it."

"Well done," Matheson said, but nothing more.

They rushed down a flight of steps and then headlong down another corridor, which seemed to run the length of the building, heading south, taking them closer to the marina. Bingham's guide light shone ghostly yellow upon the walls as she ran. Felix felt exhaustion fall upon him, as if the Earth's gravity had suddenly doubled. Weariness dragged at him and his chest ached with the thunder of his heart and the rasp of his breathing. His age dogged him.

Then Bingham's light picked out a narrow set of steps straight ahead. As the bot slowed, Syd raced past her and up the steps, where they found a wide metal fire door with mottled glass sidelights.

"You're on point," Chapel told Bingham. "We'll go out together, try to clear a path. From here we've only got a block or two to the marina. We get clear and we run for it."

Rostov uttered a grave little laugh.

"This is funny?" Felix asked.

"Have you ever seen the end of the American film *Butch Cassidy and the Sundance Kid*?" Rostov asked.

Felix felt nauseated. "I wish I hadn't."

"Go!" Matheson shouted.

Bingham kicked the door. With a screech of tearing metal it flew open and then she and Chapel hurtled into the street outside. Matheson didn't wait. He ran out, with Kirkham and Syd on his tail, trying to get in front to shield him. Rostov and Felix followed, rushing at an angle off to the left, to the corner farthest from the main entrance. The smell of the sea filled the night air and Felix thought they would make it.

Kirkham's head snapped back and the rear of his skull exploded in a spray of blood and gray matter. Syd shouted at Matheson to get back but the president kept running for the opposite corner, knowing as Felix did that retreat meant certain death. Syd, Chapel, Bingham, and Rostov returned fire but Felix had no idea where the bullets were coming from. He focused on the corner of the building across the street, thinking if he could just reach it there would be some cover there.

"You said four!" Chapel shouted.

"There were four!" Bingham replied.

"I count at least eight!"

"Rocket! Rooftop at nine o'clock!"

Felix ran, the world closing in around him. He tried to think himself small, as if by will alone he could make himself a more difficult target. Ahead of him, Syd stumbled, twisted around, and nearly fell. Her momentum carried her forward and then he saw the bloodstain spreading from the bullet wound in her back—left side, just beneath her shoulder. He called her name, thinking of the people out there in the world who loved her. She had her own father; someone needed her to survive.

Please, God, Felix prayed, *don't let her die.*

It had been so long since he had really prayed for anything and he feared that if God existed, He had already turned his attention elsewhere. But as Felix reached the far corner and ducked behind the edge of the building, he nevertheless prayed.

Matheson knelt by Syd, who sat against the building with her eyes shut from the pain. Rostov spotted two anarchists farther south along the street, held his gun in both hands, and fired three times, killing one and wounding the other. He pulled the trigger on an empty clip and tossed the gun aside.

"Weapon!" he shouted, and Syd held hers up to him.

Rostov took it, even as the other anarchist started firing at them.

Bullets strafed the anarchist's chest and he went down. Felix pressed himself to the edge of the building and glanced around the side. Chapel and Bingham were in the middle of the intersection, under fire, trying to kill as many anarchists as they could. Felix counted more than a dozen. A rocket streaked down at Bingham but she dove from its path, the blast making her hit the street and roll before she sprang up again.

"Chapel!" President Matheson shouted. "Trouble!"

Felix whipped around and saw half a dozen anarchists fanning out just to the south, where the other two had been killed. The ones in the intersection had no shot at the two presidents, but these guys had a clear view and they knew it. Arrogant, they marched up the street, weapons ready.

"Shit," Syd groaned.

Rostov aimed her gun at the nearest one and put a bullet in his chest. The man staggered back but did not fall. Unlike the others, he had to be wearing body armor.

Felix glanced around the corner again, scanned the street for open doors or an alley, but he knew it was too late. They had nowhere else to go.

His regrets were so heavy on him that he forgot to breathe.

Gunfire ripped the air and he flinched, steeled himself for death, yet it did not come. Bullets went astray, chipping at the building behind him and shattering windows. Then the guns to the south went silent, replaced by screams and grunts and the sounds of close combat.

Confused, Felix glanced up from his fearful posture to see Tin Men killing anarchists in the street. Five of the six men who'd appeared to the south were on the pavement, broken or dead, blood glistening black in the moonlight. The sixth tried to fight back as a robot soldier stripped him of his weapon, turned it on him, and shot him with his own gun.

"But . . ." Felix managed.

He saw the hopeful expression on President Matheson's face and the bleak smile on Syd's, but still he could not make sense of what he'd seen. There were *three* Tin Men out there, but they had emerged from the Metro station with only two. He stood up, pressed his back to the building, and stole a glance around the corner, where Chapel and Bingham were out of ammunition and had taken to close combat themselves. Bingham's carapace had been splashed with blood.

"Up on the roof!" Rostov said. "Look!"

Felix glanced up just in time to see two more Tin Men rushing along the opposite rooftop, robot frames almost golden in the moonlight.

"Where did they come from?" Rostov asked.

Felix only smiled, not daring to hope.

Farther up the street, past the university building where the student revelers had scattered, a group of the anarchists came around the corner and he knew there would be more—the entire coterie of killers who'd hemmed them in on the other side of the building before they'd made their escape.

An escape still in progress.

"Syd," Felix said, reaching down to grab her arm. "Get up. We're running."

Pale but steady, hand clutching at her shoulder wound, Syd slid her back up the wall until she managed to stand.

"Not sure about the running, but let's give it a shot," she said.

Matheson smiled at her, nodded, and then turned to Rostov. "We go."

With the battle still unfolding around the corner, they left Chapel and Bingham to the fighting and hurried into the street to meet the newly arrived Tin Men. Felix glanced southward. They were so close now that he could see the marina and the dark, moonlight-tipped waves beyond it.

Then they were among the Tin Men and his view was blocked by a robot with a target painted on his abdomen.

"Mr. President," one of the other Tin Men said. "Come with us, sir. We've got a boat waiting."

Felix made a tiny sound. It surprised him, coming from deep within him. He knew that voice. As President Matheson replied, Felix could only stare at her, this robot soldier whose carapace had been charred so black that he could barely make out the devil horns painted on her skull and a tiny pitchfork on her left cheek.

"Is it you?" he asked, his voice very small.

The bot shifted her eyes only slightly, then returned her full attention to the president. The other Tin Men watched her and Felix realized that she was in command.

"Get us all out of here," Matheson said. "President Rostov and I have work to do."

She saluted. "Yes, sir."

A rocket seared the air, shooting into the face of a nearby building. The explosion sent glass and rubble flying. They all turned from the blast, peppered by bits of debris. Glass cut Felix's arm and stone struck him on the back. A chunk of debris hit Rostov in the temple and he swore in Russian, clapping a hand to his face as he went down on one knee. Matheson went to his aid, calling for him to run with them. Rostov glanced up and Felix felt ice trickle along his spine when he saw the bloody ruin where the man's left eye had been.

"Here they come," one of the Tin Men said.

The rocket had been fired from the midst of the battle around the corner. Now the rest of the fight followed. Five robots came racing out of the side street, Chapel and Bingham among them.

"Run for it!" Chapel roared. "We'll cover you!"

Felix caught one glimpse of the dozens of anarchists rounding the corner behind them. Six rocket-men knelt in the street, away from the rest, and shouldered their launchers.

A robot hand closed around his wrist and then Felix found himself running.

"It is you, isn't it?" he asked. "Katie?"

"Run for it, Dad," she said, one hand on his back, hustling him along.

The presidents were ahead of them. One of the other Tin Men had picked up Syd, her blond hair hanging over his arm as he carried her toward the marina, running effortlessly despite the burden. Felix's chest burned as he ran and his legs felt numb and rubbery, but he kept going. All he had wanted was to live to see his daughter again and fate had granted him that wish—though not at all in the way he'd imagined. Now he wanted more than just to see her. He wanted to know this woman she'd become—he had much to atone for.

"I thought I'd never see you again," he said, his voice breaking as he ran toward the marina in the distance. "And I *never* thought I'd see you like this."

"This is who I am," Kate said, and her voice seemed as cold and mechanical as the robot she piloted.

Humphreys Deep Station One was a sprawling complex. Air could be drawn from aboveground but once the anarchists had attacked the airfield overhead, defense protocols had kicked in. For several days—Aimee didn't know how long—the air underground would be filtered and recycled to protect against the possibility of some kind of gas being pumped down into the Hump from above. An air-conducting system that large and that powerful required ducts and vents equal to the task.

"This is stupid," Aimee said, crawling on her hands and knees inside the tunnel of metal ductwork. "You don't think they'll look for us inside the air vents?"

North followed behind her, moving smoothly and quietly. She would have felt his presence even if she couldn't hear his breathing—his urgency and malice gave off a kind of dark energy that made her want to move faster.

"They'll look here," North admitted, "but they won't look here *first*."

The duct was not tall enough for them to stand but not small enough to force them to shimmy or drag themselves through. Still, Aimee felt the metal constricting around her.

"I can't breathe," she said, hating how pitiful her voice sounded. "It's like we're trapped."

"Just keep going," North said. "It won't be long."

"What if I—" she began.

"There's a junction coming up. Turn left," North said. "Meantime, *breathe*. You'll be out of this soon. When the anarchists get in here, I'll make sure you're not hurt. Just play ball, Aimee. I can't save everyone but I can save you, as long as you don't try anything stupid."

She faltered, pausing on her hands and knees.

"Keep moving," North warned.

"No, listen," she said, trying to twist around to see him in the darkened duct. "Just tell someone. Turn yourself in now and—"

"They'll execute me the first chance they get," North said, eyes narrowed.

"Maybe before the Pulse, but now?" Aimee replied. "I don't think they'd be in such a hurry to kill a guy who has intel on the enemy."

North glared at her. "Just crawl, please. I wouldn't *like* to kill you, but don't think I *won't*."

She exhaled, thinking of her mother in her little kitchen at home, worried about how long the food that had been in the refrigerator would last. The milk would already have soured. Meats would go bad quickly. Elena Bell would be feeding the neighborhood, trying to keep herself occupied so she wouldn't dwell too much on her daughter's safety. In the back of her mind, Aimee had an image of her mother that reminded her of Auntie Em in *The Wizard of Oz*, appearing in the witch's crystal ball, so worried for Dorothy.

You're not Dorothy, honey, she thought to herself. *And this isn't Kansas.* Dorothy had killed the witch by happy accident. Aimee knew that when she got her shot at North she would not hesitate, and it would not be an accident.

"Go," North said.

Aimee went, crawling on all fours, and when she came to the junction she turned left, just as North had instructed.

Biding her time.

By now the bodies of Major Zander and the MPs had been found. The hunt would be on for the escaped prisoners. If the techs hadn't gotten the internal cameras working yet, they would manage it soon. Not long after that, she and North would be discovered and whoever had taken command would order them both shot on sight. Her only chance at persuading them otherwise would be to get away from North and lead them to him.

Cool air blew all around her and she shivered.

"Turn right," North instructed.

Aimee did as she was told, though this new duct was smaller and narrower than the others and she had to scramble forward on her belly. Her knees thumped the metal duct and she slowed, afraid that the noise would give them away, afraid to be found with him. After only a minute of this shuffling crawl, she came to a grate that barred her way.

"Roadblock," she said, thinking North must have some kind of tool to remove the grate.

"Knock it out," he said.

"What?" Apparently she was the tool he'd had in mind. "You know how much noise that will make?"

"Better move fast, then."

Aimee cursed under her breath but she didn't hesitate. Lying on her belly she reached out and slammed the grate with both hands, once and then again. Bracing herself against the smooth bottom of the duct with the toes of her boots, she slammed her palms against the grate a third and fourth time, pulling screws out of the wood and plaster around the vent. The grate dangled by a single screw and she hit it one final time, knocking it to the floor with a clatter.

The room ahead was dimly lit. Nothing but goods piled on shelves, with pipes and hanging light fixtures on the ceiling. Aimee peered at the nearest shelf and saw KETCHUP printed clearly on a box. She furrowed her brow in confusion. What did North think he could accomplish from here?

"Go," he said behind her.

Aimee fought the urge to kick him. She crawled forward, pushed her head and shoulders out through the vent, reached up for a pipe overhead, and seared her hand on its hot metal. Swearing, she grabbed the one beside it, this one cool enough to soothe her burn, and hauled herself out of the vent. Dangling, she dropped to the floor and then she took off running.

The first bullet took a chunk out of the concrete floor. The second struck a shelf just ahead of her. So many shelves, and no idea where the exit might be, she darted to the right, into another row of shelving, breath coming fast. She heard North drop down from the vent and land on the floor.

"I told you I would shoot you," he said as he hurried after her.

"Maybe I don't mind," she said. "You put a bullet in me and they'll know I'm not on your side."

"I'm sure that'll be a comfort to your mother when they bury you."

Aimee froze. She took a deep breath full of fresh hatred for him.

"You just sit tight," North went on.

With her back to a shelf full of cereals and other dry goods, she listened as he moved through the stockroom. After a moment she heard a clanking and then the sounds of North grunting as he moved boxes, piling them somewhere. Then came the screech of metal on concrete as he dragged a shelf across the floor.

"Fuck it," she whispered.

With a glance around the corner, she set off in the opposite direction. The storeroom seemed enormous but she soon discovered it was not an endless warehouse floor. Forty feet along the aisle in which she'd hidden, she came to a wall and turned left for the simple reason that she could see a corner to her right. She raced along until she came to an open space with two doors set into the wall. One of them opened into a cubicle with sheaves of paper on a desk, an empty coffee cup, and a computer workstation.

The other turned out to be not one door, but a ten-foot-wide freight elevator.

"You can hack this station."

Aimee spun to face North, who had quietly slipped behind her.

His face looked flushed from effort but his grip on his weapon did not waver. He held the gun aimed at her chest.

"You blocked the door into the kitchen," she said.

"And jammed it," he agreed. "But the first thing you're gonna do when you hack in is reset the coding so none of the kitchen staff's keycards will let them in here. Then you can get to the real work."

"What if I can't hack into the defense protocols from this station?"

"Don't bullshit me, Aimee. Freight elevator goes all the way to the top. There isn't a way out of the Hump that doesn't have defense systems in place, which means the workstation here has got to be wired in. If I had the time, I could hack it. Which means it should be no problem for you. Get into the system—"

"They'll have locked me out by now," she argued, sweat dampening the back of her neck. "My access codes will never work."

"You'll get in."

"I'm telling you—" she began.

North strode over to her and pressed the gun to her forehead, pushed her back until her skull thunked against the elevator doors.

His eyes were full of emotion. More pain than cruelty, she thought, although North seemed to have deep reserves of both.

"You *will* get in," he said.

He was right, of course. She could hack the defense protocols from here. At the very least she could bypass them and unlock this one elevator. The only question would be how long it would take. How long *could* she take, she wondered, before North would realize she was stalling and decide he didn't need her anymore.

A clock on the wall inside the workstation booth ticked loudly. It felt as if the hands of that clock were counting down the last minutes of her life.

How many minutes? she wondered.

How many seconds before the bullet?

25

Alive.

All Kate's thoughts had been pushed from her mind to make room for that one word.

Alive.

Entropy existed at all times. Her high school English teacher, Mr. Herlihy, had assigned her class a report on the great poets of history, choosing one poet at random for each student. She had gotten Yeats and thought she would hate every minute of the task, until she had started reading.

Things fall apart, Yeats had written. *The centre cannot hold.*

The words had stuck with her—so powerfully that she had once shared the poem with her father, hoping to make him understand her—and they had come back to her when she had lost her legs. For her, they were a reminder to appreciate what she had in any moment, because that moment would pass. Entropy eroded everything. Time wore on and the world—and all that existed within it—wound down like an old clock, never to chime again. The Pulse had sped entropy forward toward the disintegration of human society. It might not be too late to slow it down again, but that would depend entirely on people. The future of the human race would be defined by what they did next. What they did *now*.

Sailing across the Mediterranean, she had thought a great deal about entropy and come to the conclusion that her father must be dead. The president had Secret Service agents and Tin Men around him, their sole purpose being to keep him alive, but Felix Wade had only himself. The idea that he might survive a full-scale assault on the G20 summit had begun to seem like a fantasy.

Yet here he was.

"This way," she said, taking his hand and guiding him toward a side street full of hotels that backed up to the marina.

Gunfire ripped the air and she heard a bullet zip past her head. With a single motion she stepped behind her father, shielding him as they hurried onward. She felt bullets strike her back and she moved even closer to him, matching his steps. Then they were in that side street and he was out of danger. Kate guarded him with one protective arm and took a look around. Torres, Hawkins, and Birnbaum were back with the president's two Tin Men, killing anarchists as fast as they could, trying to stem the flow of the attack. Trav had reached the side street before Kate, and he still carried the blond woman with the gunshot wound. Danny had the two presidents up against the wall a few feet away, using his guide light to examine the wreckage of Kazimir Rostov's eye. Rostov would never see out of it again but if he could keep it from getting infected, he would live.

"I can't believe it's you," her father said.

Kate laughed. "*I* can't believe I found *you*."

"Chapel said something about a signal," he said.

Ping, Kate thought. If not for that signal—if Zuzu hadn't used it in Haifa—she'd still have been searching for her father. For the first time, she realized the enormity of the task they'd set for themselves in coming to Athens in the first place. It might've taken them days to find the president if they had found him at all, yet here they were.

President Matheson grimaced, and for the first time Kate noticed the way he'd been clutching at his arm.

"Sir, are you injured?" she asked.

Matheson twisted around to show her the bloodstain on his shirtsleeve.

"I'll be fine," he said. "Just a graze. Now's not the time—"

"Agreed," Kate said. She pointed at the second hotel along the street. "We want that door—the Agamemnon. Let's move!"

Danny covered them, watching the rooftops and the main street from which they'd come, waiting for the battle to reach them. The hotel doors opened and the two presidents ran inside. Kate had her weapon ready, watching for trouble as Felix followed.

"Woman's lost a lot of blood," Trav said as he carried the blonde past her.

Kate shouted for Danny and then went in behind Trav.

"Woman can hear you," said the blonde in Trav's arms. "Woman has a name."

Felix smiled as he went to her, but Kate could see the worry in his father's eyes.

"You're all right, Syd," her father said to the blonde. "You're too mean for one bullet to do you in."

"Damn straight," Syd replied, teeth gritted.

Danny came through the door. Bullets shattered the glass behind him.

"Our guys have thinned them out some, but they're still coming," he said.

"They'll keep coming," Kate said. "Till they're all dead."

"Fine by me," Trav chimed in. "Let's oblige them."

Kate spun around, frowning. Someone had opened the door for them but she hadn't spotted anyone.

"Broaddus?" she called.

Movement in the shadows behind the concierge desk. Alexa Day stepped out into the moonlit gloom of the lobby.

"It's me," the girl said.

"Who the hell is this?" President Matheson asked as he tore off a strip of his shirt for Danny to use as a tourniquet on his arm.

The girl didn't give Kate time to answer. "Alexa Day, Mr. President. My father was your ambassador to Syria."

Matheson's expression darkened. He understood the implication of the past tense. "I'm sorry."

"Enough talk," Rostov said, turning to Kate with his bloody ruined eye still uncovered. "You said you had a boat. Why are we standing here?"

"Broaddus!" Kate shouted, ignoring the Russian.

"Here, Sarge," Broaddus said, coming out of a side corridor with her guide light on.

Broaddus had Hanif Khan by the collar, gun against the anarchist's back. He'd been shot full of morphine to deal with the pain of his wound, but still looked sweaty and pale with pain and trauma.

"Our friend had to piss," Broaddus said. "Ready to go now, on your word."

A rocket exploded nearby and the building shook with the blast. More gunfire punctured the darkness outside and she hoped the rest of her squad would be safe as they tried to destroy the rest of the anarchists.

"Mr. President," Kate said. "Sergeant Kate Wade, sir. This is Hanif Khan. He led the Bot Killers who came after us in Damascus. They were working with the anarchists behind the Pulse. He may know something useful to you."

"Son of a bitch," Matheson said, glaring hatefully at Khan. For a second, he looked like he might be sick.

Rostov smiled. "My cat, Igor, likes to catch birds and bring them to me, drop them at my feet. You remind me of him, Sergeant."

Kate looked at Matheson. "We can just shoot him, sir, but if you want to keep him around, we'll bring him with us."

Matheson strode over to Khan, eye to eye. Kate tensed, thinking Khan might attack him despite the gun at his back, but the anarchist only stared at the president with his crocodile eyes.

"Bring him," Matheson said. "Now let's get out of here."

A fresh torrent of gunfire made them all flinch. *Too close*, Kate thought. She turned and saw a pair of anarchists racing through the moonlight toward the Agamemnon's front doors and then a burst of gunfire stitched into them as they stumbled and flailed through the doors. Dead, they slid and tumbled just a few feet into the lobby. One dropped a handgun that skidded across the floor toward Alexa Day, who scooped it up.

"Alexa," Danny said.

The girl looked up at him. "I know how to shoot."

"As long as you know *who* to shoot," Kate said. They didn't have time to argue about it. "Go! The marina's right outside, Mr. President. Go left. Our boat's at the end, beyond the sea wall."

Trav and Broaddus led the way, making Khan run ahead of them. Trav still carried the blonde, though she protested that she could walk. Kate figured she'd lost too much blood, that she'd slow them down. She hoped the same wasn't true of President Matheson. If Rostov didn't make it, that was no skin off her nose.

"There are gonna be a lot of injuries on board," Danny said as he came up behind her, running with Alexa. "I hope the first aid kit's got what we need."

They reached the glass doors at the rear of the lobby and shoved through. The marina lay before them, its huge circumference dotted with docked pleasure craft, all bobbing dead in the water. A handful of sailboats remained, sleek toys for wealthy owners.

Trav had gotten ahead of them on the circular track that ran alongside the marina. Broaddus had Khan by the back of his shirt and marched him forward like a puppeteer, faster than a wounded man ought to be moving. The wind had picked up and Kate could see the hydroptere bobbing in the water at the far end of the circle, out past the sea wall. *Still there,* she thought. *That's something, at least.*

Alexa appeared beside her. "Come on," the girl said to Kate and her father. "Let's keep up."

They increased their speed, but both presidents were wounded and they had started to lag.

"I've got POTUS," Kate told Danny, her father, and Alexa. "You three catch up with Trav."

Danny took Felix's arm and the two of them raced on. Alexa gave Kate a worried glance and then moved faster.

"You all right, Mr. President?" Kate asked. "I can carry you if—"

Matheson shot her a dark look. "I'm good. But Kazimir. His depth perception—"

"Is fine!" Rostov snarled. "Go!"

Kate wanted to leave Rostov behind. She could pick Matheson up and double her speed. Danny could carry her father *and* Alexa if it came to that, and Rostov could fend for himself. Except POTUS seemed to want the Russian president to live, and she couldn't question the orders of her commander-in-chief.

"Trav, slow down!" Danny shouted. "POTUS is priority one!"

Exactly, Kate thought, wondering if the blonde had brought out Trav's damsel-in-distress syndrome.

They hurtled along beside the water and a kind of glee began to glow warmly in Kate's chest as they ran past dock after dock, the echoes of gunfire chasing them all the way.

Then the gunfire became more than echoes.

"Move it, Sarge!" a voice shouted.

She glanced back and saw Birnbaum appearing from the street where the battle was being waged—a street that ended on the eastern edge of the marina, dovetailing right into the circular drive around it.

The battle followed Birnbaum. She turned and fired and then the fight spilled out into view. Hawkins and Torres and one of the president's Tin Men had run out of bullets and were killing anarchists with their bare hands. With their inhuman strength, they crushed skulls and broke arms and shattered ribs, but still there were twenty or more anarchists flooding around them, all armed and taking aim. For the moment they were shooting at Hawkins and the others, but in a second they would see the presidents—their prey—and realize how close they were to fulfilling their mission.

Kate scooped President Matheson up in a fireman's carry and kept running, leaving Rostov on his own. Both men roared at her to stop but her focus was on Danny and her father and Alexa, straight ahead, and Trav with the blonde in his arms. They had to make it to the boat.

Bullets sprayed wildly, hitting the dead boats and plinking into the water. Kate glanced back and saw that the enemy's numbers were dwindling. She hesitated a second, thinking she should tell POTUS and the others to take cover, that the Tin Men together could easily kill the remaining anarchists . . . that she'd been going about this all wrong.

Then she saw the way Birnbaum had stopped to stare up at a rooftop, followed her line of sight, and saw the three rocket-men perched there at the corner of the roof. Birnbaum tried to take a shot but she was out of ammo.

"Get down, sir," Kate said, setting the president on his feet. "Take cover."

She lifted her weapon, targeting system locking on the nearest rocket-man, and fired. Her bullet struck him dead center and he fell backward, dropping his launcher. The one next to him fired before Kate could sight on him. She shouted and ran forward as the rocket streaked down from the roof, headed for the marina.

Trav turned, wounded blonde in his arms, and then the rocket struck him, blowing him apart and rupturing his power core. The blast also tore at the Secret Service woman he'd been carrying, and hurled Alexa and Kate's father off the path and to the water's edge.

"Goddamn it!" Kate screamed, running to the place where Trav had been.

All that remained to show he'd been standing there were ravaged bits of metal, a burnt bit of pavement, and the splash of the woman's blood. *Syd*, Kate remembered. Her name had been Syd.

"Damn it, Trav," she said, staring down at the blood and the scorch mark. He'd been a good friend and an honorable soldier, a man she'd always trusted to have her back.

"Kate!" Danny called.

"Go!" she said, waving him onward. "Get them to the boat. I'm going to help kill the rest of these fuckers."

Then Danny called her name again and this time she heard something in his voice that drew her attention away from the dwindling battle in the street. She turned and saw the expression on his face. He glanced to the right, toward the water, and she followed the look.

At the water's edge, in the shadow of a rich man's pier, Alexa knelt over Kate's father.

Numb, Kate ran to them, splashing into the water and kneeling there.

Alexa looked at her, bereft. "I'm so sorry."

"Daddy?" Kate said quietly, hating the sound of the word coming from her robot mouth, spoken in a voice that was hers but not hers.

A broad, jagged piece of Trav's chassis jutted from her father's chest. Blood soaked into the ground and spread into the water, diluting, ebbing and flowing with each small wave.

Yet his eyes still had a light in them.

"Katie," Felix Wade rasped.

Still alive.

Her heart darker than it had ever been, she turned toward Danny.

"POTUS is yours. Try to keep Alexa alive," she said, with the girl still staring at her.

Kate lifted her father in her arms, his blood dappling her carapace, and she turned and ran for the sea wall. Ran for the boat, ignoring the dwindling sounds of gunfire.

She had always loved to run.

Until now.

They were going to make it.

Danny ushered the presidents onward. Kate had gotten way ahead of them, no longer waiting for anyone. He saw her sprinting along the arc of the marina's circle and knew she had hope in her heart. But he had seen the size of the shrapnel in Felix's chest and the severity of the wound, and he knew her hope was only delusion. Broaddus had her gun on Hanif Khan, nudging the anarchist forward without getting too far ahead of the wounded presidents.

Alexa ran in front of Danny for a few steps and then paused to look back at him. Felix Wade's blood stained her hands. The dead anarchist's gun looked large and heavy in her grip.

"Go," he said. "Get on board. I'll be along."

"Come with us," the girl said. "They don't need you. It's over."

Danny glanced back across the marina and saw that she was right. Torres, Birnbaum, Hawkins, and one of the president's Tin Men had been brutally effective. Only nine anarchists remained. So many others had been killed that the survivors had given up their objective of killing Matheson and Rostov and instead were attempting to defend themselves with assault rifles and handguns against the robot soldiers. Danny scanned the rooftops and saw no more rocket-men.

Over, just as Alexa had said. Yet he felt as if their struggle had only begun.

He turned to Alexa. "Let's go."

The girl began to run, quickly catching up to the wounded presidents, and Danny kept pace with her. Alarmed by the sound of their approach, Rostov turned, stumbled, and fell. Cursing, he rose shakily, and Danny saw the smear of blood that painted his cheek below his ruined eye.

"Kaz!" President Matheson called, returning to help Rostov to his feet.

Rostov glared at his American counterpart for a moment and Danny thought he would refuse the aid. Then some silent communication passed between the presidents, a grudging respect, perhaps a recognition that they were more powerful together than each was alone. It occurred to Danny that these two men led lonely lives, that each might be the only person in the world who could truly understand the other. Whatever politicking and posturing their jobs usually entailed had become obsolete. Whatever treaties were made from now on, they would take shape due to mutual interests . . . or mutual fear.

As Danny and Alexa strode up to them, and Broaddus shoved Khan back in their direction to make sure POTUS was safe, Rostov allowed Matheson to help him up. The president winced at the pain in his wounded arm.

"We've got a long journey ahead, Peter," Rostov said, and it was clear he was not talking about the trip back to Germany.

Matheson only nodded. For a moment all sounds of gunfire died away, echoing across the waters of the marina. Then the two presidents turned to make their way to the sea wall and Danny nudged Alexa to follow. Ahead of them, Broaddus began to turn, but Hanif Khan stood motionless, hatred and misery in his eyes.

Khan roared and slammed into Broaddus hard enough to stagger even a Tin Man. He lunged forward and struck Rostov in the face, just inches from his injured eye. The Russian reeled in pain and Khan grabbed the gun in his hand, twisted hard, and stripped it from him.

Danny shouted, taking aim, but Rostov was in the way.

The whipcrack of a gunshot echoed across the water.

"No!" Broaddus barked as she brought her own weapon up too late.

They were both too late.

President Matheson staggered back a step, staring down at his chest, but no blood appeared there. It made no sense until Broaddus reached for Khan and the anarchist collapsed, his legs failing him. Khan spilled to the ground with one hand over his heart, blood pumping out between his fingers.

Confused, Danny looked around.

Alexa Day stood off to his right, a dead man's gun clutched in both hands, still aiming at Khan just in case she needed to shoot him again.

"Holy shit, kid," Danny said.

"I'm not a kid," Alexa replied.

"Apparently not," President Matheson said.

Alexa looked at him, her eyes hard. POTUS or not, it was clear she didn't need his approval. She walked over to Khan, gun aimed at his face. The anarchist tried to speak but no words passed his lips, only a froth of blood as he gasped for air.

"It's like you said, asshole," Alexa rasped, her eyes filling with tears but her hands rock steady. "We have to make our own choices about justice now."

Danny went to her and gently placed his hand on her gun. "Why don't you let me have that?"

Alexa shot him a dark look. "I think we've got a long way to go and chances are good that I'm going to need it."

Broaddus and Rostov watched them, but President Matheson only stared down at Hanif Khan as the anarchist died, a last expulsion of bloody foam dribbling from his lips.

"I'm sorry, sir," Danny said. "We really believed he had information that might be vital to figuring out who was behind all of this."

Matheson looked up at him. "Does it matter? It's a level playing field now, soldier. All the power is gone, and the race is on to see who can be first to get it back."

"Kelso," Broaddus said, gesturing inland.

Danny turned to see the rest of the squad jogging toward him. The ruin of Torres's missing eye was an echo of Rostov's wound. Birnbaum stayed with her, Hawkins and the Secret Service bot bringing up the rear. They carried a multitude of weapons—assault rifles they had retrieved from dead anarchists.

"Mr. President," the Secret Service bot said, "if we've got transport, it's time to go. We dealt with the group that attacked us, but there are likely others in the city."

"We're going now, Chapel," Matheson said. "What about Bingham?"

"Rocket launcher," Chapel replied.

"One of ours, too," Danny said, glancing at Hawkins, Torres, and Birnbaum. "Trav."

"Fuck," Hawkins muttered.

Birnbaum took Torres's hand and squeezed.

"We lost a lot of people today," Broaddus said, turning to the president and Rostov.

Cradling his wounded arm, Matheson walked to Alexa.

"We all did," the president said.

After a long moment, Alexa glanced up at him and nodded. Matheson turned to glance at Danny and Chapel.

"I'd like to never see Athens again," he said. "How fast can we get out of here?"

Danny gestured toward the sea wall, beyond which the hydroptere bobbed and rolled upon the sea.

"Faster than you think."

Distant gunfire made him flinch. They all froze a moment, expecting another attack. When it did not materialize they quickened their steps, rushing together to the end of the circle and onto the sea wall.

Zuzu had tied off the trimaran with a pair of lines but Kate hadn't been able to get her father on board by herself. She had set him down on the rocky wall and waited for them, stroking his hair and talking softly to him.

Hawkins and Broaddus took the lines, braced themselves, and began hauling the hydroptere toward the wall. Birnbaum, Chapel, and Torres were there to help Alexa and the presidents over to the boat, but he only half-cared about any of them right now.

"Hey," he said softly, going down on one knee beside Kate and her father.

Felix had gone dreadfully pale, his features slack. His breath hitched in his throat and his eyelids fluttered as if he was attempting to keep himself awake.

Not awake, Danny thought.

Then Felix went still. His eyes ceased their fluttering and his breath its hitching. His body seemed to relax, the peace of death upon him.

Danny saw Felix die, saw the sorrow on Kate's features, and a sudden understanding came upon him, so powerful that he felt helpless in its grip. For so many years he had fought the idea that he might ever need someone. Even before his father's death he had seen love and real compassion as weaknesses that the universe would exploit if he ever indulged in them. His dad's cancer had only cemented that view. Danny had told himself that he had to be a shark, had to keep swimming or he would drown.

Now he saw Kate's pain and he knew that his own fears no longer mattered. He might not have wanted to need anyone, but he hadn't been able to prevent *her* from needing *him.*

"I hate it," Kate rasped, head hanging as she held her father's right hand in both of hers.

"I know," Danny said.

She turned to him, robot eyes gleaming. "I mean the bot. I hate *this!*"

Anguish turned her voice into a wail and she released her father's hand and began to beat at her chest.

"I hate *this!*" she said again, gazing desperately at Danny. "I held him, but not in my own arms. He said he was so happy he got to see me, but it isn't me he saw! Not me, but *this*! I wanted to comfort him but . . . when I touched him . . ."

Danny reached for her and Kate slipped into his arms, metal on metal, emotion trapped inside.

"He cried," she whispered, her voice almost lost in the sound of the wind and the sea. "But I couldn't."

They stayed that way, frozen together like some sculptor's idea of metalwork lovers, until Birnbaum called to them that everyone else was aboard except for Broaddus and Hawkins, who were holding the boat close to the sea wall, waiting for them. Danny told Kate he was sorry. He would have kissed her if he could.

"Let's get back to base," he said.

Kate nodded. She extricated herself from him and knelt to take her father's corpse in her arms.

"Once we're back," she said, standing, "I never want to be in a bot again."

"I'm here," he said, helping her over to the gap between sea wall and boat. He could think of nothing else to say.

Waves slapped the hydroptere's floats and crashed against the wall. On the boat, Zuzu and Torres leaned out, reaching toward them. Carefully, Kate and Danny handed her father's body across the gap and the others carried him on board.

Once everyone had cleared out of the way, Kate jumped onto the boat and Danny followed. Broaddus and Hawkins untied the lines and ran over, making the leap before the hydroptere could drift too far from the sea wall. The starboard float bumped the wall, pushed by the waves, but then they were all on board.

Birnbaum began shouting orders. Danny glanced at President Matheson, who sat with President Rostov at the front of the central float. He might be the commander-in-chief, but he knew to let them do their work. On board this boat, Private Naomi Birnbaum was captain.

The squad began to raise the sails. Kate sat down on that starboard float, the hydroptere's right wing, Felix's body draped across her lap.

Alexa sat behind her, legs dangling over the side, gun stuffed in her waistband. Her eyes were cold and distant.

Danny went to join Kate, walking carefully along the float as the sails began to unfurl overhead and the hydroptere slid away from the sea wall. As he approached them, he could hear Alexa speaking quietly to Kate, words meant to be private, shared between one grieving daughter and another.

26

With Birnbaum snapping orders, the Tin Men had the hydroptere flying all night. They made the journey from Piraeus, through the isthmus into the Gulf of Corinth, and all the way north through the Adriatic Sea in just under eight hours. As the sun rose to the east, they sailed full speed toward the shore and slowed just enough so that when the foils hit the sandy bottom they didn't tear the boat apart.

Zuzu had trained as a medic and he'd cleaned and dressed the wounds of both presidents. In the warm golden light of a new day, Matheson and Rostov slipped down from the trimaran's central float into chest-deep water and slogged to shore, the American president keeping his arm elevated, careful not to soak his bandages.

Danny watched Alexa jump into the sea and swim a couple of yards before her feet could touch bottom. She turned and stared at the hydroptere for a moment, then out across the Adriatic as if she had left her heart behind and could not continue without it. At last her expression hardened and she turned to march up onto the beach, sodden clothes weighing her down.

Birnbaum and Torres weighed anchor while the others dropped

into the water one by one, the contours of their metal bodies gleaming in the morning light. They moved through the sea effortlessly and joined Alexa and the presidents on the sand, taking up defensive positions around them. Rows of blue lounge chairs lined the beach in both directions but from his spot aboard the hydroptere Danny could have told them to stand down. In these moments after dawn, not a single human being wandered the beach within the range of his enhanced vision.

Torres and Birnbaum slipped into the water together, a quiet camaraderie between them as they moved through the surf to join the others, leaving only Danny and Kate on board the trimaran. Danny went to her, still at the rear of the starboard wing, where she had spent the entire journey. Her father's corpse lay across her lap. In the light of the rising sun, Danny could make out the reddish discoloration in his right cheek and in the sides of his arms, where blood had settled as it drained toward the lowest parts of his body. By now Felix's corpse would be gripped by rigor mortis. The idea that Kate had held her father as his body went from the postmortem relaxation of the muscles to the grotesque stiffness of rigor made him shudder.

"Hey, Sarge," he said, kneeling by her.

Kate snapped her head up. "Oh, don't call me that, Danny. Not you."

"You're still in command," he reminded her.

She sat for a while as the hydroptere bobbed and dragged in the water, turning those words over in her head.

"Kate," Danny prodded.

"All right!" she snapped, shooting him a withering glance before her expression softened. "Sorry."

"Don't be." Danny gestured toward her father's body. "Can I help you?"

Kate gazed down into the dead man's pale features. If the body had started to putrefy, Danny couldn't smell it yet. It had been cool out there on the sea at night, so perhaps they'd be spared that for a while longer.

"Take him," Kate said.

Surprised, Danny hesitated a second before he reached out. Kate had made up her mind, though, and slid her father's body into his arms. She slipped over the edge of the hydroptere's wing and sank into the water, vanishing beneath the undulating sea. It took Danny a moment to realize he could still see her through the clear blue water and he tracked her as she walked underwater toward the front of the boat. As she moved into shallower water, her head and shoulders and upper body emerged and she turned expectantly toward him. Danny stood and walked carefully toward the prow, where he handed Felix's corpse down into his daughter's waiting arms.

When Kate turned and waded up onto the beach, Danny stepped off into the sea and followed, salt water sluicing from his carapace. He looked inland, past the beach, at the idyllic Italian seaside village with its rows of colorful shops and buildings and a round tower that might have belonged to a church. A small white train with three trailing cars sat idle in front of a hotel, the sort of thing that would carry sightseers on a tour around town. An aura of calm lay across the village. Nearly twenty-four hours after the Pulse, these people had not succumbed to the chaos that the platoon had encountered elsewhere. He hoped there were other places like this.

By the time Danny reached the sand, the other Tin Men, Alexa, and the two presidents had surrounded Kate.

"Mr. President," she said, nodding toward Matheson. "Unless you have other instructions . . ."

"Go ahead, Sergeant," Matheson replied.

Kate behaved as if she wasn't carrying her father's corpse; no one else acknowledged it.

"Fan out," she said. "Find a car in good shape, standard transmission—"

"Nothing's in good shape," Zuzu said. "Not drivable, anyway."

"We're gonna push," Kate replied. "POTUS and President Rostov and Alexa get in the car. Get it in gear, and Kelso and I will push. Chapel, Torres, and Birnbaum are on protection detail. Broaddus and Zuzu take point, shove any vehicles blocking the road out of the way. Barring trouble, I call it ten hours from here to Wiesbaden. Any questions?"

There weren't.

When they'd found a suitable car, a silver Peugeot, Kate put her father's body in the trunk. The wind and water had acted on her scorched carapace to give the burnt areas the glassy look of black volcanic rock. As she stood there, staring at the corpse in the open trunk, she appeared to have been carved from the stuff.

She slammed the trunk hard, then turned to the wounded presidents, and Alexa Day, who stood a dozen feet away, watching her with eyes slitted against the morning sun.

"All set, Mr. President," Kate said. "We'll be moving fast. Can you handle the wheel or do you want one of us to steer?"

Matheson walked toward the Peugeot's driver's door. "I've got it, Sergeant. Let's go. Quick as we can."

Rostov and Matheson climbed into the car as the Tin Men took up their positions. Danny waited at the trunk for Kate to join him in pushing. Alexa only stared at the car, making no move to get in. It took Danny a second to realize she was staring at the trunk.

"You all right?" he asked her.

Alexa shook her head. "I buried my father in Israel."

"You'll go back for him one day," Danny said.

She said nothing.

Danny frowned. "You mad at Kate because she's not doing the same?"

"I abandoned my father's body to make it easier for myself, for all of us. I don't think I'll ever forgive myself for that."

Danny wanted to argue with her, to give her all the reasons that what she had done made sense. But he knew she wouldn't hear him—not now.

"Give it time," he said.

"Yeah," the girl said numbly, and then she went over and climbed into the Peugeot's backseat. Studying her through the window, Danny thought he had never seen anyone so alone.

"Move out!" Kate called as she came around to the trunk.

Matheson put the Peugeot into gear and Danny and Kate began to push. Zuzu and Broaddus ran ahead to clear the road.

Ten more hours and they'd be back at the Hump. Not home, but close enough.

Danny only wished he knew what they would find waiting for them when they got there.

North felt the stockroom closing in around him. His sweaty hands made it hard to keep a firm grip on the gun. He had known it was a risk, locking them in, but he had gambled that they would have a couple of hours—more if he got lucky. Humphreys Deep Station One was massive. Whoever was next in command after the late Major Zander would know what he had been attempting before and the whole base would be searching for him and Aimee, but North had figured they would focus on the hundreds of workstations in the complex. He'd gambled that their focus would be away from the kitchen and that nobody would think to check for them back here.

The variable, of course, was that he'd jammed the door locks from the inside. They couldn't be opened by anyone unless someone could override the hack Aimee had used on the locking mechanism.

Now, less than an hour later, he could hear the pounding and shouting at the door, all the way across the stockroom. The muffled crump of gunshots followed, and then nothing. He could picture them all standing there—MPs and techs and other soldiers—trying to figure out how to get past the door. If they had an acetylene torch, they might be able to burn through, but that would take a while. Their fastest option would be explosives, but the way the Hump had been built it would take a lot more than a grenade or two to blast that metal door open. First, they would try hacking the controls.

"Keep them out of here, Aimee!" North said, gun leveled at her.

Aimee sat inside the little control booth, typing away on a flat keyboard and occasionally stopping to tap the screen or to slide one image aside to make room for another. North wished there was room in that cubicle for both of them—he didn't trust her—but he had to rely on the gun in his hand to get him what he wanted.

One way or another, his life was over. Even if he succeeded in getting the anarchists inside, the guilt would carve out his heart eventually. But at least his mother would be looked after. His sister and her kids would be protected under the new world order.

He felt a darkness at the edges of his mind. When he closed his eyes, he still saw the ruin of flesh and bone that had been a six-year-old girl. A roadside bomb had gone off that morning and an informant had pointed to a crumbling gray apartment house and told Sergeant Morello that the bomber lived there. The little girl had been hiding in a closet, just as her mother—afraid of the robots—had taught her. She'd shifted her weight, bumped the wall, and North had strafed the closet door with bullets.

The door swung open, latch blown out of it. The little girl spilled out, blood and brain and skull fragments where her face had been. Pretty, pristine, hand-sewn doll clutched in her left hand. It had been reflex. Inside the tin, North had programmed himself to shoot anything that seemed like a threat, get the message across to the populace. Sabeen hadn't been the first civilian he'd killed, but this time . . .

They'd never found the bomber.

"Listen—" Aimee began.

He rounded on her. "Just keep them out!"

"That's what I'm doing!" she shouted, hands shaking, her nerves clearly frayed. "They think I'm in this with you. Do you seriously think I want them barging in here just in time to see me hacking the system for you?"

North closed his mouth.

This isn't what I wanted, he thought. *I never asked for—*

A static hiss came from the other side of the stockroom. He snapped around, sweeping his gun back and forth in search of the source. It took him a few seconds to realize that the sound came all the way down the aisle from the kitchen door and that it wasn't a hiss at all—it was the sound of liquid fire cutting metal.

An acetylene torch.

He swore and hung his head. Of course, they didn't have to cut their way through the door—they could just use the torch to cut away the locking mechanism.

"Damn it," he snarled, and he stormed over to Aimee and thrust the gun against her skull. "We're out of time! You're going to do this or they'll kill us both."

She brushed a finger against the screen and he glanced up too late to see the image that had been there. He wished she would look up at him. The first time they'd been together all he could think about were her eyes and the gentle curve of her jaw, her lovely dark skin. He knew she would have hate in her eyes if she looked at him now, but it would make her no less beautiful.

"Aimee, I'm serious!"

"You think I don't know that?" she asked, her jaw clenched.

She did not turn to look at him. Instead, she kept at the keyboard, tapped in half a dozen consecutive commands. At the end of the sequence, she hit Return.

A series of metal clanks made North turn and stare in surprise at the elevator. The noises had come from within and above, and a moment later they were followed by a low hum and a whir of moving cables.

He stared at her, a wary smile on his face. "This . . . it's done?"

Aimee buried her face in her hands, shoulders shaking, grief-stricken over her complicity. North wetted his lips with this tongue, heart still racing, and stood a few feet away. He glanced back and forth between the elevator and the kitchen far down the aisle. Even at this distance he could see the bright orange blade of flame cutting through the metal door.

"Come on, come on," he said as he stared at the green UP arrow above the elevator. Aimee had actually figured it out. It would have taken him hours more, if he could have done it at all.

The UP arrow went dark.

His heart stopped.

Seconds passed and then the red DOWN arrow lit up. He could hear the cables moving inside the elevator shaft, could hear the whir and grind as it descended from high above. Hope ignited a spark within him.

Again he glanced down the aisle at the burning blade of the torch carving out a rectangle of metal around the lock. They were almost in. A minute or two, no more.

"Come on!" he shouted at the elevator.

This time he glanced at Aimee, still tucked inside the booth. One hand still covered her face but not completely, and North saw something that didn't belong. Something that didn't fit the picture.

Aimee's hand partially hid a wide grin.

He thrust the gun toward her. "What have you done?"

Her smile faded. "Only what you asked, Tom. I brought the goddamn elevator down."

Ding!

North swung his gun toward the elevator and felt a vast chasm open inside him. He only wished he could fall in.

"What did you do?" he whispered.

The only reply was the hiss of the torch way on the other end of the stockroom.

Aimee knew what she'd see when the elevator opened. The first thing she had hacked when she had slipped into that little cubicle workstation had been the three still-functioning exterior cameras. All the while, as she had been working to cancel defense protocols—or at least unlock the one door and one elevator—she had watched events unfolding aboveground. With the sunrise, she had seen the anarchist forces camped around the airfield, awaiting a chance to infiltrate the Hump. With the Wiesbaden personnel defeated, she'd gauged that more than a hundred anarchists remained.

But morning had not arrived alone. As the sun rose, she had seen a new battle begin, all the while hiding the hope that blazed in her heart.

"It's over for you, Tom," she said.

North swung his gun back toward her, wearing a desperate look. "But my family—"

"It's out of your hands now," she said.

The elevator doors slid open. He clutched his weapon in both hands and took aim. North shook his head, eyes wild. "No no no."

The Tin Men stepped off the elevator. Aimee spotted the bird in flight painted on Birnbaum's chest plate and the smile-and-crossbones on Hawkins's forehead. Behind them came others, among them a charred, blackened robot and several human faces whose presence made Aimee catch her breath.

Hawkins saw the gun in North's grip, the desperation in his eyes.

"Hold up, soldier," he said, raising his hands in mock surrender. "Just the prodigals returning. And we cleaned up your mess upstairs while we were—"

North pulled the trigger. Bullets pinged off Birnbaum and Hawkins and Torres. There were shouts as other bots threw themselves back into the elevator, covering the humans with their bodies.

Hawkins roared and hurled himself at North, batted the gun from his hand, and grabbed him by the throat to slam him against a massive shelving unit.

Choking, North clawed at Hawkins's metal fingers.

"He's a traitor," Aimee said, surprised to find that she could barely speak above a whisper. The whole of her ached and she wanted to weep with exhaustion and sorrow. "He faked sick so he wouldn't be with you all when the Pulse hit and he's been trying to override defense protocols to let the anarchists in—"

"The *dead* anarchists," Torres sneered.

"Oh, you son of a bitch," Hawkins said, and Aimee flinched, sure that he was about to break North's neck.

The burnt robot lunged from the elevator and grabbed Hawkins by the arm. Only then did Aimee notice the pitchfork still barely visible on Kate Wade's cheek.

"Stop!" Kate snapped, pulling at Hawkins's arm. "Let him go!"

Kate stepped between Hawkins and North, pushing at their chests, and separated them. Hawkins scowled. North looked relieved until Kate pressed him back against the shelf and turned toward the elevator.

"Mr. President," she said. "I have a present for you."

Aimee stared openmouthed as President Matheson stepped off the elevator, with the Russian president and a young woman behind them.

"You think he's got answers?" President Matheson asked.

Kate stared at North. "Probably not many. But it's like a kitten with a ball of string, sir. You bat it around enough, start tugging, and sooner or later it starts to unravel."

The others came off the elevator then. Aimee counted eight Tin Men in all, three of whose markings she didn't recognize. She had watched them on the monitor but hadn't been sure if there were others. Now she thought not, and wondered what had become of the rest of Platoon A, if they were still out there in the world somewhere or if the worst had happened. She took a closer look at the three she didn't recognize, hoping somehow their markings had been worn away and she would see traces of the familiar WWII–era blonde riding a rocket.

Hopeful heart aching, she looked at Danny. "Travaglini?"

Danny shook his head.

Fists began hammering at the door into the kitchen, on the far side of the stockroom. The hiss of the cutting torch grew louder, drawing Kate's attention.

"Private Torres," she said. "Go and open that door. Save them having to finish cutting through. The president's going to want a word with Private North, and I think it's high time the rest of us got our bodies back."

They all froze and then turned to stare expectantly at Aimee.

"You can do that, right?" Kate asked. "Tell me you can do that."

Aimee exhaled. "I think so."

Later, Danny would remember them as having woken up together, but his canister hissed open a minute or two before Kate's. The lid rose and he found himself looking up into the face of Aimee Bell. His thoughts were like cobwebs, all strung together and quivering as he tried to make his way from one to another. His eyelashes stuck together a bit until he blinked them free and his legs and neck ached until he began to stretch and groan.

"Everything in working order?" Aimee asked.

Danny twisted his head to crack his neck. "Ugh. I think so. I figured I'd feel rested, but this is like the world's worst hangover."

Aimee helped him remove his headgear and the leads on his chest. "How can you feel rested when your brain's been active for more than thirty hours?" she said. "You need sleep. Real rest."

Danny sighed. "Sounds good."

Although he knew they wouldn't be getting much rest for the fore-seeable future. The handful of members of his platoon who'd made it back to the Hump were getting their human bodies back but the rest of the world was still falling apart. There was no way to tell how many anarchist cells were operating around the globe, never mind terror-ists and would-be warlords. Other Tin Men would be working their way back to the Hump, but whether any of them would make it was still in question . . . and the world needed them more than ever.

Technology was dead. Every community would have to circle the wagons and try to rebuild and the people making decisions would have to step carefully into the future. So much weighed upon their every move, but fortunately that was their problem. He was just a soldier. A Tin Man. He would go where he was needed.

Danny got himself into a sitting position and immediately felt dizzy. Exhaling, he held on to the sides of the canister and waited for the dizziness to subside. Blinking, he remembered the way his imag-ination had begun leaking into his perception. In one particular mo-ment he had thought he had seen his dead father. Now that his mind had been returned to his flesh, he couldn't help but think about ghosts and visions. If there were such things as ghosts, would they be very different from the consciousness of a soldier torn from his body and trapped inside circuits and metal?

Maybe you're still out there somewhere. Huh, Dad?

Or maybe that was just bullshit, more cobwebs in his brain.

Beside him, Kate's canister hissed and the lid climbed upward. Aimee bent over the open canister a moment before returning to the control panel at its feet.

Grunting, Kate sat up. She huffed out a long breath and then pulled off her own headgear.

"God," she rasped, "I need to brush my teeth maybe a dozen times."

Danny gave a soft laugh. "This is you in the morning, huh?"

Kate glanced at him with the mischievous eyes he had so missed, and her smile held all the sadness that Danny knew must be in his own. Around them, other canisters began to hiss as their lids rose. Aimee and several other techs were monitoring vital signs, but a single glance reminded Danny just how few of Platoon A's canisters would be opening. Trang, Reilly, and Guzzo were still back in Damascus, as far as anyone knew, along with a handful of other soldiers from the platoon. Rawlins had stayed with Trang, too, but nobody knew what would happen if Rawlins made it back to the Hump.

Danny stared across Staging Area 12 at Rawlins's canister. It stood open, no lights on the control panel readout. Rawlins had no body to come back to. Looking at that empty canister, Danny wished Hawkins had snapped North's neck after all, no matter what Peter Matheson wanted.

He studied the green lights on nearby canisters. Hartschorn. Prosky. Corcoran. Their hearts were still beating, their lungs drawing breath, but for all intents and purposes, they were dead. Their minds were simply gone, souls departed. Had Rawlins made it back, could Aimee and the other techs have found a way to slip Rawlins's mind into Hartschorn's body? He didn't know.

"Hey," he said.

Kate didn't reply.

Danny glanced at her and found her staring at him.

"Don't even suggest it," she said, and he understood that her thoughts had strayed into the same dark and impossible waters.

"You sure?" he asked. "I don't . . . I mean, it's crazy, I know. But none of them are coming back."

"Danny, look at me," she said.

He studied those purple eyes again. He had wondered many times what it would be like to kiss her, but this time there was something more in that curiosity than there had been before. Something urgent and protective.

Danny climbed out of his canister and moved to hers, his hands on the smooth metal. Torres and Birnbaum were awake and sitting up, which meant good things for Birnbaum's baby, he hoped. Hawkins hadn't gotten up yet, but his lid stood open and his control panel was green.

Danny lowered his voice to just above a whisper, so only Kate could hear him.

"You're not interested in living in someone else's body," he said, gaze fixed on her. "I get it. Crazy idea. Stupid, even. I have a lot of those."

"I don't want to wake to see someone else looking back from the mirror," she said quietly.

"I just thought you might want to . . . I mean . . ."

"My legs."

". . . run."

"I'm never going back into a bot," Kate told him. "I need to be human. My face in the mirror has to be mine. And if something's going to happen between us, I want my own hands and my own arms. Even my own legs. I want to be the Kate you know."

Danny was silent.

"That is, if you *want* something to happen," she added, her eyes narrowed with hurt. "I know you've got this wandering samurai thing in your brain where you feel like you can't—"

Danny reached into her canister and twined his fingers in hers.

"Stop," he said, and squeezed her hand.

For a moment, neither of them spoke a word.

"Well, you two aren't wasting any time," a voice said.

He flinched and turned to see Aimee leaning against another canister, watching them with a smile.

Danny looked past her, up toward the catwalk at the far end of the staging area. Alexa Day sat there on the latticed steel, watching them, her arms draped over the railing.

"Has she been there the whole time?" he asked.

Aimee and Kate both glanced over at the girl.

"Never left," Aimee replied.

"She doesn't have anywhere else to go," Kate added.

As if summoned, Alexa climbed to her feet and hurried down the metal stairs, weaving through canisters as she came toward them.

"Okay," Alexa said, pushing a lock of hair behind her left ear. "They're all awake, safe and sound. Now how long is it going to take for you to format Kate's bot for me."

"Alexa—" Kate began.

"You don't want it anymore. You said so yourself. Aimee told me the bots have these synthetic gangli-whatevers. They can insert one that hasn't been imprinted yet and map almost anyone's brain onto it, so the consciousness moves from one to the other and it's no different from an impulse sending emotion or pain from one part of your brain to another. Like adding an external drive to your mind."

Danny held up a hand. "Whoa, kid—"

"I'm not a kid, Kelso," Alexa snapped, and the flint in her eyes showed the truth of it. "I'm a year or so younger than that asshole Mavrides. That's it. Kate doesn't want her bot and I do!"

"Just slow down," Aimee warned. "I said it was possible. I can't snap my fingers and make it happen. This is a military operation. You want to sign up, you're going to need training, and you're going to have to get authorization from whoever ends up in official command of the base now that Major Zander's dead."

Alexa glanced at the floor, frustration and grief almost steaming out of her. She took a deep breath and then looked up.

"I'll be patient for now, but I'm going out there. The Tin Men can go wherever they want, can do the things that human beings can't do, and protect the people who don't have anyone else looking out for them. Right now that's most of the world. So whatever's gonna happen, it better be quick."

Torres, Birnbaum, and Hawkins had come over to join them while Alexa spoke. Not one of them said a word, waiting for Kate. Whether she wanted to be or not, Danny realized, she really had become queen of the Tin Men.

But Kate wasn't looking at Alexa anymore.

"Who's this now?" she asked.

The man coming down the metal steps stood at least six and a half feet tall and had arms like redwoods. His hair was shaved down to stubble and he wore a beard the same length.

"I know him," Aimee said. "Fourth Battalion."

"Which one of you is Sergeant Wade?" the giant asked.

"That'd be me, soldier. And you are?"

"Corporal Sedensky."

Danny frowned. "I know that voice."

Sedensky nodded. "It's Zuzu, Sarge."

"Wow," Alexa said.

"POTUS is asking for you, Sarge," Zuzu said. "Time to put our heads together, he said. Figure out the next step."

"Why does he want us in there? We're a bunch of grunts," Hawkins growled.

"We're survivors," Zuzu replied.

Danny looked at Kate, wondering. She didn't want to be in a bot ever again, but did that mean she had stopped being a soldier? She glanced at him, and he knew the answer.

"Warrant Officer Bell," she said, turning to Aimee. "Bring my chair."

Zuzu blinked in surprise. "Wait, you're Bell?"

Aimee hesitated. "Yes?"

"Got a message for you, too," Zuzu said. "Chief Schuler says to tell you it's a good thing you're not a traitor. You were trying to get one of the old satcomm lines working, right? And you got a signal?"

They all turned to stare at her.

"I thought I did. An underground research base in Vancouver."

Zuzu grinned. "Well, apparently you got through. One of the other techs was at your station and heard voices. They lost the signal, and Schuler wants you to get it back."

"I have no idea if I can do that," she said.

"Well, *he* thinks you can."

Danny turned to her. "Go, Aimee. Fast as you can."

"What's the hurry?" Hawkins asked.

"Vancouver's a hell of a lot closer to home than Germany," Danny said. "Maybe they can get messages out, spread the word. And not just to the people we're worried about. America needs to know their president is alive, just like Russia needs to know that Rostov is alive.

There are going to be a lot of people who think this is the end, that society is shattered—"

"It *is* shattered," Torres said.

Danny wanted to argue, but he couldn't deny the truth. With a grim nod, Aimee turned and headed off and everyone watched her go—except for Kate, who turned to Danny. He took her hand, saw the determination in her eyes, and knew she shared his reaction to Torres's words.

The world had fallen apart.

Time to start putting it back together.

ACKNOWLEDGMENTS

My deepest gratitude to Howard Morhaim, Pete Donaldson, and Mark Tavani—agent, manager, and editor respectively—for their faith in me and in *Tin Men*. Thanks are also due to Danny Baror, Caspian Dennis, Adam Rosen, John Wordsworth, and Daniel H. Wilson. I'm fortunate to have a stalwart group of friends who see me through the stressful days and who always make me feel like I'm not alone in the trenches. There are many, and they know who they are, but special thanks to Tom Sniegoski, Tim Lebbon, Amber Benson, John McIlveen, Jim Moore, Mike Mignola, Rio Youers, Nate Kenyon, Weston Ochse, and Ashleigh Bergh. Thanks to Allie Costa, Lynne Hansen, and Laura Marshall, for all of their efforts on my behalf and for keeping me focused when my brain strays. Finally, thanks and all my love to my magnificent wife, Connie, and our most excellent brood, Nicholas, Daniel, and Lily Grace.

© TT Zuma

CHRISTOPHER GOLDEN is the award-winning, *New York Times* bestselling author of such novels as *Wildwood Road, The Boys Are Back in Town, The Ferryman,* and *Of Saints and Shadows.* He has collaborated on books, comics, videogames and scripts with other writers, including Mike Mignola, Amber Benson, and Charlaine Harris. He has also written novels for teens and young adults, and, as an editor, he has worked on several short-story anthologies. Golden was born and raised in Massachusetts, where he still lives with his family.

www.christophergolden.com
Facebook.com/christophergoldenauthor
@ChristophGolden

It was the deadliest winter in living memory. Until now.

SNOWBLIND

Twelve years ago the small town of Coventry, Massachusetts was in the grasp of a particularly brutal winter. And then came the Great Storm.

It hit hard. Not everyone saw the spring. Today the families, friends and lovers of the victims are still haunted by the ghosts of those they lost so suddenly. If only they could see them one more time, hold them close, tell them they love them.

When a new storm strikes, it doesn't just bring snow and ice, it brings the people of Coventry exactly what they've been wishing for. And the realisation their nightmare is only beginning.

headline

**Evil is lurking in the Harrison House . . .
and it wears your face.**

DEAD RINGERS

When Tess Devlin bumps into her ex-husband, she's furious
that he seems not to know her.

And then Frank Lindbergh is attacked by an intruder in his
home . . . an intruder who wears Frank's face.

In the heart of the city, a mansion stands on a hill and
behind its wrought-iron fence an evil force is at work,
leaving everyone who comes near it hysterical with fear.

But the real terror lies inside the house. Tess and Frank
have no choice but to confront a mistake made years ago. A
mistake that summoned an ancient evil . . . and means even
their own reflections could kill them.

headline